CHOKE POINT

Also by Brad Thor

The Lions of Lucerne
Path of the Assassin
State of the Union
Blowback
Takedown
The First Commandment
The Last Patriot
The Apostle
Foreign Influence
The Athena Project
Full Black
Black List
Hidden Order
Act of War
Code of Conduct
Foreign Agent
Use of Force
Spymaster
Backlash
Near Dark
Black Ice
Rising Tiger
Dead Fall
Shadow of Doubt
Edge of Honor

Cowritten

Cold Zero (with Ward Larsen)

CHOKE POINT

A THRILLER

Brad Thor

EMILY BESTLER BOOKS

ATRIA

New York Amsterdam/Antwerp London
Toronto Sydney/Melbourne New Delhi

ATRIA

An Imprint of Simon & Schuster, LLC
1230 Avenue of the Americas
New York, NY 10020

First Emily Bestler Books/Atria Books hardcover edition June 2026

EMILY BESTLER BOOKS/ATRIA BOOKS
and colophon are registered trademarks of Simon & Schuster, LLC

Map designed by Peter Sucheski

Manufactured in the United States of America

1 3 5 7 9 10 8 6 4 2

Library of Congress Cataloging-in-Publication Data has been applied for.

ISBN 978-1-6680-6592-1
ISBN 978-1-6680-6594-5 (ebook)

For my brother, Scot Thor.
A devoted son, husband, father, and brother.
A great American for whom Scot Harvath was proudly named.

The man who does ill, must suffer ill.

—Aeschylus

CHINA
TAIWAN STRAIT
TAIPEI
TAIWAN
HONG KONG
YANMAR
HANOI
ITBAYAT IS.
LUZON STRAIT
GULF OF TONKIN
LAOS
THAILAND
MANILA
SOUTH CHINA SEA
BANGKOK
CAMBODIA
PHNOM PENH
VIETNAM
PHILIPPINES
KRA
HMUS
GULF OF THAILAND
SULU SEA
HUKET
PATTANI
BRUNEI
MALAYSIA
CELEBES SEA
RAIT OF MALACCA
KUALA LUMPUR
MALAYSIA
SINGAPORE
KARIMATA STRAIT
INDONESIA
JAVA SEA
JAKARTA
FLORES SEA
N
SAVU SEA

PROLOGUE

BANGKOK, THAILAND
FRIDAY

Kevin Koebler was an exceptional bombmaker. He never built the same bomb twice. His signature was that he had no signature—at least not one that could be traced back to him—which was what his client was paying for.

The bombs for tonight were works of art—big, loud, and packed with devastating shrapnel. The body count, if everything went according to plan, would be off the charts. The only thing outstripping it would be the political fallout.

His targets, or more appropriately the neighborhoods where the bombs were to be placed, had been selected for him in advance. How he got them there and where, specifically, they would be detonated was up to him. His client had only one demand—that the explosions cause maximum damage. And as luck would have it, "maximum damage" was Kevin Koebler's forte.

From the beginning of his career as an elite United States Navy explosive ordnance disposal (EOD) technician, Koebler had been different. He was more aggressive, more fearless, and more dominant than his colleagues or any of his superiors. If he wasn't poring over technical manuals, he could be found either in the gym or on the firing range.

Standing six feet tall, with a muscular two-hundred-pound frame, blond hair, a Van Dyke–style beard, and sleeves of tattoos, he looked more like a Navy SEAL than a Navy EOD tech.

His intensity was also more in keeping with the Navy's elite tactical operators and it didn't take long for the SEALs to recognize his potential. Putting a skilled EOD tech through Navy SEAL training was something the brass had been toying with for a while.

With the assorted bombs and explosives SEAL teams were encountering around the world in response to kinetic action against Islamic terrorists, it made sense to add personnel who were experienced and adept with anything that went *boom*, but only if those personnel could complete the highly selective BUD/S and SEAL Qualification Training. Koebler did—with distinction, setting several new records in the process.

He and the other EOD techs who made it through the process were distributed among the East and West Coast SEAL teams, with Koebler being assigned to SEAL Team Two in Little Creek, Virginia.

As a member of the EOD-to-SEAL pilot program, he did very well, racking up numerous awards and commendations for his performance. And then, on an op like so many they had conducted before—the takedown of a midlevel terrorism target in Anbar Province—the unthinkable happened. His unit was ambushed, and three of his teammates were killed.

Whether it was his sense of justice, his loyalty to his fallen comrades, or pure bloodlust, Koebler planned, equipped, and carried out his own campaign of revenge.

When it was over, six buildings had been destroyed, multiple alleged noncombatants were dead, as well as the terrorist believed to have been the mastermind of the ambush, who was found flex-cuffed with his hands behind his back and his head blown off. Initial reports suggested that the man had either had a grenade placed in his mouth or an explosive detonating cord wrapped around his neck.

Everyone in the unit knew Koebler had been behind it. Those who didn't like him—those who resented his bullying, his corner-cutting, rule-breaking, and over-aggressiveness—turned on him. Others, who were either afraid of him or supported what he did, remained quiet. The ensuing investigation was like a ruptured appendix, which spread toxicity throughout the unit, the platoon, and SEAL Team Two overall.

In the end, there was neither enough physical evidence nor eyewitness testimony to tie Koebler to the most serious of the crimes he was alleged to have committed. There were, however, a series of lesser offenses, and the Navy stacked them one on top of the other to use against him in court. He was stripped of his SEAL Trident, drummed out of the service, and dumped back into society with a poisonous grudge against his country and only the skills he'd learned in the military.

It didn't take him long to figure out where he was wanted and how to make a decent living for himself.

He began in a small Mexican beach town, where a cartel operative spotted him in a shitty dive bar drinking dollar beers chased by fifty-cent shots. Even at a distance, it was obvious that Koebler was a man with a past and absolutely no future. The operative watched him for the rest of the afternoon, studying him closely, before making his move.

Like a top-tier intelligence officer, which he had been in a previous life, the man struck up a conversation with Koebler, slowly building rapport with the disagreeable and largely standoffish ex-SEAL. By the end of the week, he had created enough trust to begin reeling the American in. Twenty-four hours after that, he had made Koebler an offer that would change the course of his life.

His days of cartel work now seemed like a lifetime ago. He had tired of the incessant, brute-force violence. Whether he was crafting bombs or honing the skills of the cartel's top hitters—many of them Mexican ex–Special Forces soldiers—there was no art to it, no pride taken.

Matías, the former intelligence operative who had found him in that surfside bar, had sensed the discontent in him as well. Something had shifted. Koebler was growing bored. He craved excitement. And as good as the cartel was paying him, he was looking to get out. That was when Matías had made him a new proposition, one even more promising than the first. He would take Koebler's skill set global.

The ex–intel officer would act as his handler, sourcing and vetting assignments, handling the payments, passports, travel, and all logistics. Koebler would function as a one-man SEAL team. All he had to do was successfully complete the jobs, which he did—over and over again, until eventually arriving in Bangkok.

He had long since grown numb to the death and misery he caused. Losing the SEAL Trident, his identity had collapsed. Violence, coupled with Matías, who validated his worldview, had restored his sense of self and purpose.

Anything that harmed the United States or one of its allies, like Thailand, was justified in his twisted mind. To not take advantage of such an opportunity was a form of moral weakness, or, more simply put, cowardice. It would be an admission that America had been right in going after him and that he had been wrong. There was no way he would ever admit that.

And he would never have to. His mind didn't work like that. He was devoid of emotions like guilt or shame. He was also blessed with a luxury few killers were able to enjoy.

As a bombmaker, he didn't have to look into his victims' faces. He wasn't made to witness the lives of the men, women, and children he tore apart. He could feast upon whatever macabre justifications he fed himself.

What wasn't up for debate, however, was that this would be the biggest bombing of Koebler's career. Bangkok's most touristed neighborhoods—Banglamphu and the backpacker-clogged Khaosan Road; Rattanakosin, with the Grand Palace and the Temple of the Reclining Buddha; Thonglor, with its trendy nightclubs and restaurants; and Bangkok's very own bustling Chinatown, were all on the target list.

For his part, Koebler had chosen a perch high above the city where he could sit, enjoy a cocktail, and watch the mayhem unfold. Sixty-four stories in the air, the luxurious Sky Bar atop the lebua Bangkok hotel was the perfect spot, and he was sparing no expense.

Dressed in a black Brunello Cucinelli suit with a matching black shirt and black Tom Ford boots, he ordered a bottle of Perrier-Jouët Champagne and a two-hundred-gram tin of beluga caviar.

Sweeping his eyes across the terrace, there was no end to the sea of attractive women—several of whom could be purchased for the evening or even just an hour. Koebler, however, was here for a different kind of fireworks.

Once his Champagne had been poured and the caviar service set up on his table, he took a moment to breathe everything in. This was the first time he would get to enjoy one of his own bombings in such luxury.

Though it felt somewhat odd, he couldn't help but feel that he had "made" it—that he was at the very pinnacle of his game.

And while no one would ever know his name, they would forever remember this night. It would be his legacy—an everlasting scar he would leave upon the world.

As he prepared another spoonful of caviar, he looked out across the sparkling city. Even at this height, he could hear the thrum of traffic below and feel the pulse and throb of all the unsuspecting people as they went about their evening. Lives were about to change. *History* was about to change.

Placing the caviar in his mouth, he chased it with a long swig of Champagne and removed a phone from his inside pocket. It was time to begin.

The app he wanted was buried beneath several layers of advanced 256-bit encryption. With each digital portal he passed through, there were electronic tiger traps and devious self-destruct features that would be triggered if anyone attempted to hack his system or force him to open his device against his will.

When he finally arrived at the program he wanted, he was greeted by a bright yellow laughing emoji.

Pausing, he raised his glass and silently toasted himself. Then he pushed the button.

Seconds later, five and a half klicks north of the lebua Bangkok, the first bomb exploded along the Khaosan Road.

CHAPTER 1

Itbayat Island
Batanes Province
Northernmost Philippines
Saturday

There was a *click* somewhere up ahead, and Scot Harvath, who was on point, gave the silent command for his team to freeze.

The sound had been so faint that he couldn't distinguish what it was. Had a twig been snapped? Had someone, somewhere out in the darkness, flipped off a weapon's safety?

Ever since they had moved into the forest, he had wondered if they were stepping into a trap.

Half of his discomfort was because of the men they were hunting. The other half was because operating in Itbayat's subtropical forest reminded him of jungle warfare. He hated jungle warfare. He had hated it as a SEAL and he hated it even more now. It was hot, humid, and entirely too close for comfort. There were too many bugs, particularly mosquitoes, and the dense shrubs, vines, and ferns were a colossal pain in the ass to move through.

There was something ironic about having quit his job at a private intelligence agency that specialized in taking on the CIA's most dangerous overflow assignments, only to return and be handed a jungle-style operation on Day One. He couldn't tell if the powers that be at the Carlton Group were happy to see him back or trying to convince him he should have stayed away.

In all fairness, no one had truly wanted to see him go. What had pissed off his colleagues was his constant one foot in, one foot out, Hokey Pokey dance wherein he refused to even consider ceding the plum assignments to any of the just-as-qualified, younger operatives. He was scraping all the cream off the top for himself. But to his credit, Harvath was very good at what he did.

And while the other operatives may have been equally "qualified," none of them came close to having the wealth of experience that he did—not in the Special Operations community, or in the espionage world. He was a freakish mashup of both, trained by the best, and he sat atop a very deadly food chain with few who could match him.

In his mind, failure was never an option. Neither were rules. If the bad guys weren't going to play nice, then he wouldn't either.

From the Geneva and Hague Conventions to the Marquess of Queensberry, if the other guy's gloves came off, he was happy to follow suit. But once Harvath's gloves were off, there was no "de-escalation," no slow ride up the use-of-force curve. Things would get ugly, fast. As his friends liked to say—Harvath didn't get PTSD, he *gave* it.

But now, out here in this subtropical coastal forest—less than 150 klicks across the Bashi Channel from Taiwan—his Spidey-senses were tingling and his cortisol levels were starting to spike. That *click* had put him even further on edge. He didn't want to move until he had a better understanding of where that noise had come from.

Via a series of hand gestures, he let the team's designated marksman, Mike Haney—an ex–Force Recon Marine—know where he wanted him to set up with his Heckler & Koch HK241 battle rifle and where former Delta Force operative Tyler Staelin should position himself with his SIG Sauer M250 light machine gun. If Harvath and his team were headed into an ambush, he was going to make the people who had prepared it sorry they had ever done so.

The next thing he needed to do was get some sort of visual on what was in front of them. Unfortunately, the canopy was too heavy to get one of their drones in the air. They would have to do it the old-fashioned way. Someone was going to have to quietly creep forward.

Normally, Harvath wouldn't ask anyone on the team to do anything he wouldn't do, but crawling along the jungle floor was a younger person's game, and so he chose the youngest member of the team, a man in his early thirties, who was also an ex–Delta Force operative, named Palmer.

Palmer lived for getting dirty. Having recently rained, there was plenty of mud to keep him happy. Turning toward him, Harvath signaled what he wanted done.

Pulling his boot out of the heavy mud, Palmer looked down and then, looking back at Harvath, gave him the finger.

The good-natured insult notwithstanding, Palmer knew his place on the totem pole. Dropping his pack, he readied his weapon, and disappeared into the understory.

Besides Haney and Staelin, everyone else on the team was carrying suppressed, 10.5-inch short-barreled rifles in 300BLK from a company called Noveske in Grants Pass, Oregon. Considering the variety of environments within which the Carlton Group was called upon to carry out its assignments—urban, maritime, and even underground—the Noveske "Shorty" SBR was hard to beat.

In addition to their encrypted, satellite-connected radios with bone-conducting microphones, they were also sporting ENVG-B night vision goggles with overlaid thermal imaging fusion. When it came to the safety and performance of its operatives, the Carlton Group spared no expense.

Despite all that money and technology, however, Harvath and his team hadn't been able to locate four Chinese nationals who had vanished into the woods as they'd pulled up to their safe house. It was almost as if the men had known they were coming and already had an escape plan in place.

Affixed to Harvath's chest rig was a hinged, hard-plastic case containing his cell phone. Flipping it down, he let his eyes adjust and studied the imagery from the NSA satellite passing overhead in low earth orbit. If the Chinese were in the woods, there was absolutely no sign of them. Wherever they were hiding, they were doing a damn good job of it. Too good of a job.

The fact that their trail had gone cold almost the moment they were in the forest, the fact that no trace of them could be seen via the team's night vision devices or the satellite, told Harvath that he was hunting the right men. These guys were pros. And that confirmation only elevated his stress levels. *What the hell was he walking into?*

The four Chinese were believed to be military intelligence agents working for the PLA. Their job was to covertly surveil joint U.S.-Philippines military exercises, specifically how the United States and the Philippines would deny Chinese naval vessels the ability to transit the Bashi Channel—a vital maritime corridor between the Philippines and Taiwan linking the South China Sea to the broader Pacific Ocean.

U.S. Intelligence also had information that the four-man team was additionally responsible for sabotaging American ground-based anti-ship missiles on Itbayat if hostilities broke out.

Harvath's assignment had been to capture and interrogate the men. Should that prove too difficult, he was authorized to kill them, but in such a way that it sent a strong message back to Beijing as to what would happen if it sent any more spies.

Of course, Washington didn't want their fingerprints on the job and neither did Manila. Neither country was itching to directly antagonize the Chinese. Hence, Harvath and his team had been dispatched to handle the situation while providing plausible deniability to both America and the Philippines.

But none of that was going to matter if he couldn't track down his target.

Activating his radio, he was about to hail Palmer when the forest erupted with the sound of automatic weapons fire and Palmer's voice came over all his teammates' earpieces.

"Contact left!" he exclaimed. "Contact left!"

CHAPTER 2

With the trackers they all wore, Harvath could see on his screen exactly where Palmer was located. Re-engaging with his night vision goggles, he could also clearly make out enemy muzzle flashes and instructed Haney and Staelin where to fire.

The Chinese were on the move, firing as they retreated farther into the forest. Harvath's team took turns laying down cover fire as they moved up to Palmer's position.

Once they got to him, they adjusted their assault and pressed their biggest advantage—they now knew where the enemy was.

Bullets cracked and sizzled through the air around them, shaving the leaves and sometimes even whole branches off trees. Harvath and his team returned fire and pressed forward.

The fact that the Chinese had pre-deployed weapons in the forest not only confirmed Harvath's previous suspicions about their readiness, but it also brought something else to mind—the possibility that they had laid booby traps.

"Watch for tripwires!" he cautioned, as the firefight continued to rage.

He had been on assignment in a similar, wooded environment recently and had seen men sawed in half and otherwise obliterated by cleverly placed mines. It was a series of mental pictures he would never be able to shake.

As if on cue, the lone female operator on his team, ex-Army soldier Sloane Ashby—who was now running point—gave the command to stop and indicated that she had indeed found a tripwire. The Chinese were doing all they could to lure them to their deaths.

Confident that her teammates were aware of the wire and where it had been strung, she stepped over it and continued to give chase. The rest of the team followed.

The gun battle continued its fevered pitch. If Harvath and his people weren't shooting or reloading, they were moving.

First to take out one of the enemies was Haney, hitting a man with one of his heavy 7.62 rounds and knocking him down to the forest floor, dead.

Staelin, the team's machine gunner, was next. With a muzzle velocity of three thousand feet per second, when his 135-grain .277 Fury rounds found their mark, he tore right through the next Chinese operative—shattering the man's hips and pelvis, while simultaneously severing his spine and ripping massive holes through his bowels. If he wasn't dead when he hit the ground, he would be soon enough.

That left just two more.

This time it was Palmer who, exposing himself from behind cover, made an incredibly difficult shot. His bullet, fired at a complicated, upward angle against a fleeing target, found its mark, entered the base of the third Chinese man's skull and traveled up into his brain, killing him instantly.

The fourth and final target was Harvath's and, if possible, he wanted to take him alive. Even if the man only had limited intelligence value, it would be better than nothing.

Harvath radioed the rest of the team to start pulling their shots. If they could wing him or knock him down, great. If not, they were to keep the pressure up on him. At some point, the man was going to run out of energy or ammunition. Either way, when that moment came, he'd be theirs for the taking. What Harvath hadn't realized was that there was a third option.

Itbayat was the largest of the Batanes Islands, but also the most remote and windswept. The Philippines' last inhabited outpost before the Taiwan Strait, it rose steeply out of the sea, formed entirely from uplifted coral reefs and limestone cliffs—sheer walls that plunged right down into the ocean. It was on one of those cliffs where the final Chinese operative now found himself.

Scrambling the last several yards, the man turned to fire at his pursuers but only managed to get off two more shots before his weapon ran dry. He was now out of runway and out of ammunition.

Casting the rifle aside, it clattered onto the hard, stony ground. Harvath instructed his team to cease fire. As they covered him, he moved forward.

The Chinese man appeared to be somewhere around Harvath's age, mid to late forties. He was lean and sinewy. He had dark circles around his eyes, which made his face look gaunt and hollowed out. Harvath had no idea how long the men had been on the island, but he figured they didn't make lots of runs into town for supplies, out of fear of drawing attention to themselves. Very likely, they had been stretching whatever rations they had. No matter how bad Harvath had thought his assignment was, this guy's had likely been much worse.

Not only that, but the price for mission failure in China wasn't simply a bad performance review and the possibility of getting passed over for a promotion. This man was facing nothing but bad options. Harvath hoped that might make him pliable, open to a deal.

And if it didn't, there was always the enhanced interrogation route. Either way, the man was going to share everything he knew—whether he liked it or not.

Harvath watched as the Chinese operative took a couple of steps backward, right up to the edge of the cliff, and looked tentatively over his shoulder. It had to have been over a thousand feet down, and even in the cloudy moonlight, the view must have been vertigo-inducing.

Lowering his weapon, Harvath beckoned the man forward, away from the edge. "Let's talk," he said, not knowing if the man spoke any English.

The Chinese operative didn't budge.

"If I wanted you dead," Harvath continued, "you'd be dead. We can make a deal. The two of us. No one is going to hurt you."

Weighing his options, the man glanced once more over his shoulder.

"Eyes here," instructed Harvath, slinging his SBR and pointing at his own eyes.

The operative seemed to understand. Turning his head, he looked at Harvath's face.

Harvath felt himself relax.

Then, without warning, the man took one giant step backward and dropped from the cliff.

CHAPTER 3

WASHINGTON, D.C.

Connor Jameson had served two tours in Iraq and one in Afghanistan. As the saying went—there was no such thing as a *former* Marine. Once a Marine, *always* a Marine. Which was why, even though not fully awake, he already had his hand wrapped around the butt of his 1911. Call it his training or call it his instincts, his brain was already springing into action.

Rolling away from the door, he kicked out from under his comforter and scrambled off his bed, landing on the floor with a muffled thud.

Even though he always left his pistol hot, he retracted the slide and glanced down to confirm that a round was seated in the chamber. With the hammer already cocked, he released the safety, and was good to go.

But good to go for what?

Maybe the noise had come from one of the neighbors' units.

It was possible, Jameson thought, but he knew better than to dwell in the realm of "possibilities." He had either heard someone enter his apartment or he hadn't. It was black or white. There was no gray.

If someone had broken in, his mattress and box spring were lousy concealment and even worse cover. He needed to find a better place to be.

Getting into a crouch, with his 1911 ready to fire, he elevated his position just enough to peer over the tangle of bedclothes and pillows he'd left atop his bed.

He leaned toward the door, straining his ears for even a hint of sound. There was nothing.

Could he have dreamed it?

He was no stranger to lucid and quite often disturbing dreams, but this wasn't that. He'd heard what he had heard. And it hadn't come from a neighbor's unit. Someone was in his apartment.

Chastising himself for not having grabbed his compact tactical flashlight from the opposite nightstand, he kept his eyes on the door and quickly moved away from the bed.

He only had the bathroom or the closet, which while they might have provided better concealment, were not going to provide much improved cover. Then he realized he had a third option.

"Look high or die" was a phrase his CQB instructors had used repeatedly in low-light training. Invariably, when entering darkened rooms, most human beings failed to look up. With all of the threats that had lurked in trees, it was amazing that human beings had tuned out threats from above. They expected everything to be at their level or below.

Keeping his pistol trained on the entrance to his room, he used his left hand to grab the stack of books off his old-world wooden dresser and place them quietly on the floor.

While only one drawer wide, the marble-topped dresser was six drawers high, clocking in at a little over five feet tall. He had no idea if it would support his weight, but considering how heavy it was and what a pain in the ass it had been to lug up to his apartment, he sure hoped so.

He set his gun on top and then, placing the palms of his hands on the marble, leapt up like a forty-two-year-old gymnast mounting a pommel horse. The piece of furniture groaned in protest beneath him, but it held.

Without missing a beat, he snatched up his 1911, pointed it toward the door, and began applying pressure to the trigger.

In addition to leaving his flashlight in the nightstand drawer, he'd also left his spare magazines. With one round in the chamber, he had eight more in the gun. If those weren't enough to stop the threat, he'd do what any good Marine would do and bludgeon the intruder to death with his empty weapon, tear off the man's head, and then use his skull as a drinking vessel. *Ooh-rah*.

He was wondering how long he was going to have to wait when he saw the doorknob begin to rotate. Half a second later, the door began to slowly and quietly open.

Whoever was in his apartment was about to show himself, and Connor Jameson was going to fill him with .45-caliber holes.

But the intruder didn't show himself. Instead, the tip of a pistol suppressor materialized and fired four times in rapid succession.

The target was the tangled-up comforter and pillows on his bed, which in the half-light spilling through the window could have been mistaken for a human form.

This wasn't a robbery. It was an assassination attempt.

Jameson didn't wait for the intruder to realize his error. Guesstimating where the man was standing, he pressed his trigger.

The *boom* that erupted from his 1911 was deafening, and the room was illuminated by its massive muzzle flash. Like the good Marine he was, Jameson followed up with not one, but three additional shots, adjusting his fire each time, hoping to finish the would-be killer on the other side of his door before the intruder could adjust his aim and kill him.

At least one of his shots appeared to have found its mark because he heard the shooter stagger backward and fall to the living room floor.

Leaping off of the dresser, he shifted quickly to the other side of the bedroom—just in case the man had pinpointed his location and was about to return fire. But no fire came.

He waited several more seconds. When no sound came from the living room, he prepared to investigate.

Creeping toward the bedroom door, the first thing he saw was the shooter's boots, followed by the rest of the man's body splayed across his living room floor. Two rounds from the 1911 had hit the man center mass, square in the chest.

The intruder didn't fit Jameson's mental picture of a D.C. home invader. He didn't look like a junkie or a gangbanger. He actually looked like him—white guy, late thirties to early forties, short hair, fit. Then there was his weapon.

In his years of living in the nation's capital, Jameson didn't think he'd ever heard of a suppressor being used in a burglary.

Just then, his thoughts were interrupted by movement from the kitchen. *There was a second intruder.*

As soon as he had clocked the additional threat, he saw the barrel of another suppressed pistol and a wave of subsonic rounds was sent in his direction.

Jameson dove back into the bedroom for cover.

Bringing his 1911 to bear, he fired three rounds at the kitchen, straight through the drywall.

He had two bullets left—at least until he could get to the four fully loaded magazines in his nightstand drawer. But to get to them, he would have to risk exposing himself in front of his open bedroom door.

As another wave of rounds rained down on the bedroom, he scanned for anything he might be able to use to swing the door shut.

There was nothing. He was going to have to risk exposure.

Getting to his feet, he moved as close as he could to the door. Then, sticking his 1911 into the opening and aiming for where he imagined the threat was, he fired twice as he lunged for his nightstand.

In the instant he was exposed, he saw how far off his last two rounds had been. The second intruder was no longer in the kitchen. He was at the front door.

With his slide locked back, Jameson dropped the spent magazine, slammed home a fresh one from the drawer and, snatching up a second mag in his left hand, depressed the slide release. He was not only ready to get back in the fight, but to end it.

Positioning himself near the bedroom entrance, he exhaled, applied pressure to his trigger, and stole a peek into the living room just in time.

The front door was wide open and the other shooter was about to flee. Jameson lit him up, dumping almost his entire magazine into him. The man fell dead, half in the former Marine's apartment, and half outside in the hallway.

After checking to make sure the man in the living room was actually dead, Jameson did the same with the second intruder, dragged him back inside the apartment, and then closed and locked the front door. The police would already be on their way. He needed to act fast.

Quickly patting each of the men down, he looked for something, anything, that would tell him why they had come to his apartment and why they wanted him dead. This was no run-of-the-mill burglary.

Neither of the men had wallets. They didn't have phones either. They were completely sterile, which cemented one very chilling fact for Jameson—the men were professionals.

But who the hell would send professional killers after him? Was it possible that they had made a mistake? Maybe they had hit the wrong apartment.

Somehow, he knew this wasn't a mistake. He also knew that he was allowing himself to slide back into the realm of possibilities again. Guys who were professional enough not to carry a single piece of pocket litter were likely professional enough not to hit the wrong apartment.

Until he had evidence to the contrary, everything he did from this moment forward was going to be based upon the assumption that *he* was the intended target. Right now the *why* of it didn't matter. Neither did the *who*—as in who were these guys and who were they working for?

There was no time to process what had happened. That would come later. Right now, he needed to move. He needed to be gone before the police arrived.

After taking pictures of the would-be killers, he air-dropped them to his personal cloud and pulled the hard drives from his network attached storage device, which he threw in his go-bag, along with his laptop. He set the backpack as close as he could to the front door without getting any blood on it and got dressed in record time.

He dressed in jeans, boots, a sweatshirt, and a ball cap, hid the 1911 in a holster at the small of his back, and shrugged on a waxed Barbour jacket, the pockets of which were stuffed with two boxes of ammo, his tactical flashlight, and his spare magazines. Thirty seconds later, he was descending the fire stairs two at a time.

Out on the street, he kept his head down and moved with purpose, but not so much purpose that it would draw attention.

Near a nightclub at Dupont Circle, he found a hammered bachelorette party tending to their bride-to-be, who was throwing up on the sidewalk, and planted his cell phone on one of the young women. If anyone was trying to track him, it wouldn't throw them off for long, but it would buy him a little added time, and that was all he cared about right now.

With that bait and switch complete, he needed some place safe to hole up—some place no one would ever expect him to go.

There was only one location that fit the bill. It was a long shot, but it was the only shot he had.

CHAPTER 4

MANILA
PHILIPPINES
SUNDAY

After the Itbayat operation, Harvath and his team went through the safe house of the spies-cum-saboteurs, gathered anything of intelligence value, cleaned themselves up, and headed for the tiny local airport.

The runways on both Itbayat and nearby Batan Island were too short for their Gulfstream G800, so they had to utilize a smaller, slower plane to get back to the Philippines' capital city.

A CIA team met them on the tarmac at Ninoy Aquino International Airport, where the midmorning sun was already baking the concrete. The air was thick with the scent of jet fuel, but was mercifully less humid than it had been up north.

Once they had transferred their gear from the charter plane to the fleet of black Chevy Suburbans, they rolled out of the airport. Harvath, riding in the lead vehicle, was heading to the embassy. The rest of the team was heading to their hotel. He had promised them the night off and would catch up with them later.

The U.S. Embassy, Manila, was one of the State Department's largest diplomatic missions. At one point, it catered to over eighteen thousand American and Filipino veterans, as well as their widows, and still housed the only U.S. Department of Veterans Affairs office on foreign soil. It was staffed by three hundred Americans in addition to one thousand foreign service nationals, across two compounds, which occupied a combined total of forty-two acres. The size and scope were a testament to the deep connection between the Philippines and the United States.

As they drove toward the Ermita district, it was hard to believe that Manila had been the second-most-destroyed city of World War II. It was now one of the most densely populated cities on the planet. It was also one of Southeast Asia's most rapidly developing.

All in less than a hundred years—and all of it thanks to the United States, which had ushered in a post–World War II rules-based order, particularly upon the high seas.

Without the U.S. Navy, much of Asia—especially the Southeast—would have been mired in piracy and constant warfare, and denied the economic advancements and opportunities that it had enjoyed.

After passing through the security checkpoint, they arrived at the Chancery building, where the CIA's chief of station, Todd Gilbert, was already outside waiting.

Gilbert was an unremarkable man in his late fifties with crew-cut gray hair, a large nose, and very dark circles under his eyes. He was dressed in a gray Brooks Brothers suit with a thin gray tie and a perfectly folded, and probably pressed, pocket square in his breast pocket.

He looked like a CIA operative who had been cryogenically frozen decades ago and recently brought back to life. Glancing at the man's left wrist, Harvath wasn't at all surprised to see him wearing a Timex, which in all fairness to Gilbert had become fashionable again, but he doubted that was why the station chief was wearing it.

"Thanks for coming in person," said Gilbert, extending his hand.

"That was the agreement," Harvath replied, grasping the man's hand. "Is your Filipino counterpart here yet?"

The station chief shook his head. "It's just going to be us for the debrief."

Harvath thought that was a bit odd, but he got paid the same either way. "Any chance we can grab a coffee first? The only thing they had on the flight was salabat," he stated, referring to a popular ginger tea.

"No problem. I've got a machine in my office."

Carrying a hard-sided case with the evidence his team had collected from the safe house, Harvath followed the man inside the building. They passed through two more checkpoints before finally arriving at the CIA's part of the embassy.

After checking in, they left their cell phones in individual, locked cubbies and then Gilbert led the way to his office.

The station was alive with activity. Flat-panel monitors displayed myriad international news channels. Almost all of which were focused on the Bangkok bombings.

"Any updates?" Harvath asked.

"The death count is now three hundred fourteen and more than two hundred twenty-two injured."

"How many Americans?"

"At last count, eighty-three dead," said Gilbert, "and fifty-six wounded. U.S. Embassy, Bangkok, is still trying to get their arms around it."

"Has anyone claimed credit?" asked Harvath, angry at the loss of life, especially the loss of *American* lives. He envied the team that would eventually be dispatched to wreak vengeance upon the perpetrators.

"Not yet, but as this bears some hallmarks of the Bali bombings of 2002, Islamic terrorism is definitely on the table."

Harvath remembered that attack. The death toll was also horrific. It was made even worse by the fact that the bombings had been staggered across multiple devices, just like Bangkok appeared to be, in order to maximize the carnage and the terror.

Entering the station chief's office, Gilbert pointed out his coffee machine, and Harvath availed himself of a mug that read *Spooks are* ***C****lever,* ***I****ntuitive, and* ***A****wesome*. He brewed himself a tall black coffee with two shots of espresso, and moments later one of the CIA's tech people arrived to collect the case.

After inventorying the contents, the young operative had Harvath sign a release, snapped the case shut, and carried it out of the room.

"Let's head to the SCIF," said Gilbert, referring to the sensitive compartmented information facility—a sound- and signal-proof room where anything they discussed couldn't be overheard or intercepted.

Harvath nodded and the station chief led the way.

As soon as the pneumatic locks and door seals had hissed closed behind them, Gilbert directed Harvath to a chair near the head of the conference table and then sat down across from him.

"Four targets, zero interrogations," the man stated. "Is that correct?"

"Four targets, two hundred–plus rounds of ammunition fired, and zero American casualties," Harvath replied, taking a sip of coffee and clarifying what had happened.

"What about the bodies?"

"One of them jumped off a cliff and was dragged out to sea by the tide. We took the other three and dumped them back at their safe house."

"Dumped them how?" asked Gilbert. "I believe your instructions, should you not have been able to capture and interrogate the suspects, were to send a clear message to Beijing."

"It's in my preliminary report. Did you look at the attachments?"

The CIA man had not. Accessing Harvath's after-action report via the SCIF's secure system, he scrolled to the end where multiple photos had been appended.

"Jesus," the station chief replied, when he got to the attachment in question. "Are those railroad spikes?"

The three Chinese corpses had been arranged to mimic the three wise monkeys of *See no evil*, *Hear no evil*, *Speak no evil* fame.

"They're called spike nails," said Harvath. "They weigh a lot less, but other than that, they're fairly similar."

"What kind of unit travels with shit like that?"

Harvath hadn't traveled with them. They'd found them at the safe house, but Gilbert didn't need to know that. "I think Beijing will get the message," he stated, returning to the subject. "Anything else you need from me?"

Gilbert, who was not an easy man to shock, paused for an additional moment before closing out of the file. "No, we're done."

"Good," said Harvath, standing. "Can one of your guys run me back to the hotel?"

"Actually, your boss wants a word," said the station chief, as he cued up the SCIF's secure video conferencing software. "I'll wait outside."

Harvath had no idea what couldn't wait until he got back to the States, but something told him the conversation wasn't going to be good.

CHAPTER 5

Like Harvath, former CIA director Robert "Bob" McGee had also come to the conclusion that he missed being in the game. Out on Maryland's Eastern Shore, there were only so many seascapes he'd be able to paint before he lost his mind. When the board of the Carlton Group presented their lucrative offer to head the organization, which only required that he be in-office three days a week, he realized he really wasn't cut out for retirement and grabbed the opportunity with both hands.

Harvath's experience was similar, except for the fact that he didn't have any hobbies—not even golf. He had been in the same field ever since he had graduated college.

He had gone from SEAL Team Two to the storied SEAL Team Six, then been recruited into the Secret Service to help protect the first family, before moving into a host of covert assignments, and ultimately winding up at the Carlton Group.

Falling in love with a Norwegian intelligence officer, as well as falling into a massive pile of money, had changed everything. Or so he and Sølvi had thought.

They got married, he quit the Carlton Group, and she took an open-ended leave of absence from her position as a deputy director at the Norwegian Intelligence Service.

For six months, they traveled the world and celebrated their honeymoon. But the moment they landed back in D.C., they found themselves dead center in the middle of a terrorist attack and were sucked right back into their old lives.

What they didn't realize, until after the dust had settled, was how much they had missed those old lives. Sølvi enjoyed her focus on countering Russian aggression toward Norway. It gave her a sense of accomplishment and fulfillment. She had worked hard to become a deputy director and wasn't ready to hang it up. Not just yet.

And for the first time ever, Harvath had more money than he knew what to do with. It was fun to travel first class and not worry about the bills. The hotels they had stayed in and the houses they had rented during their honeymoon were beyond incredible. But once they got home, reality had set in.

As insane as it might have sounded to most people, the money was not enough—at least not enough to make Scot happy. Like Sølvi, his sense of accomplishment came from what he did, not what he owned.

So when she had floated the idea of returning to work, he had encouraged her, while also opening his own line of dialogue with the Carlton Group.

He and McGee had a long-standing friendship and an exceptional working relationship. Though McGee was older, the two men were cut from the same cloth. They were old-school, more concerned with the ends than the means. The line about not being able to make an omelet without breaking a few eggs applied to both of them. They were each willing to do whatever it took to keep America, its citizens, and its interests safe.

Once Gilbert had exited the SCIF and the door had sealed shut behind him, Harvath activated the secure video call back to the U.S. and Bob McGee.

"How'd the debrief go?" McGee asked. No hello. No preamble. Straight to the point. He was a tall, no-bullshit guy in his sixties with gray hair and a thick, Wyatt Earp–style mustache.

"One would think that four dead Chinese spies and a pillowcase full of electronics would have been a good haul, but there's no satisfying some people."

"They'll get over it," McGee replied and then abruptly changed the subject. "How much do you know about the bombings in Bangkok?"

"I know a lot of Americans are dead and that's not good."

"No, it's not."

"Other than that," said Harvath, "all I know is what I've seen on my phone."

McGee picked up a handwritten list and read from it. "Those bombings hit prime tourist areas. The Brits, the Aussies, the Kiwis, and the Canadians—all the Five Eyes members—lost people. Three other U.S. allies—India, Japan, and South Korea—also saw significant numbers of their citizens killed.

"No one thinks the Thai government has the expertise or manpower to handle something this big. And they're probably right. So everyone is sending in their own specialists. Quantico already has FBI evidence response teams, as well as explosives experts and agents from the Counterterrorism Division, on the ground in Bangkok."

Harvath nodded. "They're the best. If anyone can get to the bottom of this, it's the Bureau."

"Agreed," McGee stated. "But the FBI guys can only do so much. The White House wants a second option in place. Just in case."

The man let his words hang in the air for a moment.

Finally, Harvath asked, "In case of what?"

"There may be certain rocks the FBI either doesn't want to or can't kick over."

His boss didn't need to say anything further. Harvath understood the assignment he was being handed. "Do you have a contact person for us in Bangkok?"

"I will by the time you land."

Checking his watch, he asked, "When do we leave?"

"As soon as you and your team can get to the airport. You'll get a full briefing in-flight. The plane is already being refueled."

CHAPTER 6

BANGKOK

Kevin Koebler didn't like surprises. Taking a meeting with the people who had hired him was highly unusual. It was also incredibly dangerous.

The plan was for him to lay low after the bombings. Airports, trains, bus and ferry stations were all out of the question, as was any travel out of the city by car, truck, or motorcycle. There was no telling what checkpoints the police and military had already established. The best way to stay off someone's radar was to stay under it.

His handler, Matías, however, was of a different opinion.

The client had made it clear that money wasn't a problem. They were willing to pay for a face-to-face and to do so in advance.

While usually just as cautious as Koebler, Matías believed it was too lucrative an opportunity to pass up. The client wanted to discuss extending his contract.

Against his better judgment, Koebler agreed to the meeting, which took place just off Yaowarat Road, on the edge of the crowded Samphanthawong district—also known as Bangkok's historic Chinatown neighborhood.

It was behind two thick wooden doors, in the back room of a seedy gin bar with an even seedier name—*Teens of Thailand*.

Teens, as it was referred to by locals, had no connection to underage patrons, but the name lent the place a deliberately illicit aura, which drew throngs of Thai hipsters lured by its taboo air and rakish swagger.

As was common in his line of work, Koebler knew next to nothing about the client. It was Matías's responsibility to vet the job, make sure it was legitimate, and do everything he possibly could to be certain he wasn't being led into a trap.

Anonymity had always been his greatest protection. Only Matías knew who he was and what he looked like.

Once a client knew you and you them, it complicated things—in a *big* way. That's what had happened with the cartel boss in Mexico. He liked having a Navy SEAL around. Thought it made him look tough. Invincible.

He got way too chummy for Koebler's taste and started wanting him around all the time. Koebler couldn't stand the guy. He was tasteless, crude, and dumb as a bag of hammers. Even worse, the guy loved to stay up late drinking and expected Koebler to do the same.

While all of that was a pain in the ass, Koebler could put up with it as long as the money was good. Which it was. Until it wasn't.

As the old saying goes, *familiarity breeds contempt*, and eventually the cartel boss began to take Koebler for granted. He greatly expanded his duties, demanding that he accompany him to all his meetings, including his doctor appointments, of which there were many because the man was so overweight and in such poor health. Never once, however, was there a commensurate bump in pay.

Not that it would have mattered. The more ridiculous his boss's demands became, the more ridiculous the work seemed. The Mexican and South American cartels were worse than the Muslim fundamentalists, in his opinion. He stopped caring who they were at war with, and once the bloom was off that rose, there was no putting it back.

Like his operation to avenge his fallen SEAL comrades, he had put together a plan to take out not just his cartel boss, but also his sons and the top players in his organization—anyone that he might have to spend the rest of his life looking over his shoulder for. Luckily for the cartel, however, Matías figured it out and channeled Koebler in a different direction. Which all brought him to where he was now.

In all fairness, Koebler had done repeat work in the past. But he always charged more because repeat clients meant that authorities would have, at least in theory, a common thread connecting him to previous attacks.

He referred to it as an insurance premium, and none of the clients ever complained. They were all satisfied customers and they all paid on time. Just like this client had.

Once the cryptocurrency had hit his digital wallet, Matías notified Koebler that the funds had been received and that the meeting was a go.

Having shaved his beard and dyed his hair, the ex–Navy SEAL wore sunglasses and a ball cap, as well as dark jeans and a shirt with long sleeves to cover up his tattoos.

In his backpack he carried multiple changes of clothes to further alter his appearance, if need be. He also carried a collapsible rifle with six magazines, as well as two smoke and two fragmentation grenades, along with a Vietnam-era Claymore mine.

On his person, he had secreted a jet-black, razor-sharp knife made from polymer, while a 9mm Glock pistol was tucked into a neoprene holster and wedged inside his waistband, just in front of his appendix. If the SEALs had taught him anything, it was to be prepared for everything.

That lesson was no less relevant now than it had been then. In fact, his SEAL training—though he was loath to admit it—was what continued to keep him alive.

Another lesson was to do your homework, which, in advance of a rendezvous like this, meant to do your own reconnaissance.

The client, however, also knew what they were doing and hadn't released the meeting location until the last minute. That put Koebler at a distinct disadvantage and didn't give him much time to get the lay of the land.

Cycling through his different disguises, he made as many passes as he dared, both along the sidewalk in front of Teens, which wasn't open for business for another four hours, as well as the narrow warren of pedestrian alleyways behind it.

In his pockets, he carried over a dozen miniature video cameras. They were smaller than Ping-Pong balls, with magnetic backing, and were all synced to his phone.

Each time he found a metal surface that afforded an optimal view, he stuck one in place.

While he might not be able to field his own countersurveillance team, the network of cameras and the live feed they would provide were the next best thing.

As soon as he was done, he found a café up the road, ordered a Thai iced tea, also known as *Cha Yen*, took out his phone, and monitored who was coming and going.

For the fifteen minutes he was monitoring the foot traffic, he didn't see anyone enter or leave Teens. Whoever he was supposed to meet, he had a feeling they were already inside.

Finishing his drink, he exited the café and snuck back into the labyrinth of passageways behind the gin bar. It was still morning, and there wasn't a lot of activity yet.

One of the adjacent buildings was under construction, and he had picked out the perfect spot to hide his backpack. The construction crew hadn't turned up yet, and he had no problem, after tucking his phone inside, putting it exactly where he wanted.

With that task complete, he retraced his steps back to the sidewalk, walked down to Teens, the façade of which was plastered with stickers, and knocked on the wooden front doors as he had been instructed.

The doors were opened by a tiny old man in traditional peasant clothing. With bright, crinkled eyes and a toothless grin, he looked to be at least eighty if he was a day.

A broom was set against the wall behind him, and obviously having been told to expect a guest, he beckoned Koebler inside and pointed him toward a door in the back, just beyond the bar.

To be honest, Koebler didn't know what he had been expecting. It was a gin bar, so maybe a group of Al Capone–style mafiosos arrayed in a line, waiting for him to step in off the street? Maybe a more Wild West feel, with a row of black hats knocking back whiskeys, one boot each upon a brass footrail? The poster child for brushing at least twice a day with his two-dollar broom was definitely not it.

At the door by the bar, he looked up and noticed a cleverly, but not perfectly, hidden camera and realized he was being watched. The client knew he had arrived. If they were going to take a shot at him, they would have already done it. One man, hidden behind the bar with a shotgun, would have easily beaten him to the draw.

He took it as a positive sign that the client didn't see him as a loose end that needed tying up and actually did want to extend his contract.

Taking a deep breath, he turned the knob, opened the door, and stepped into the back room.

CHAPTER 7

Upon entering, he came face-to-face with four very large Asian men in plain clothes, all of whom were carrying PP-2000s—Russian personal defense weapons, or PDWs for short.

Seated at a nicked-up wooden table, with a glass of brown liquor and a lit cigarette, was the person who appeared to be their boss. He was also Asian, dressed in a cream jacket, a dark linen shirt, blue jeans, and brown loafers with no socks.

Not saying a word, the man took a drag on his cigarette and watched as one of his security detail approached Koebler and motioned for him to raise his arms. The American did as he was instructed.

Patting him down, the security man found the Glock, withdrew it from Koebler's waistband, and handed it off to one of his colleagues. He then produced a handheld metal detector and wanded Koebler from top to bottom. Finding nothing, he turned to his boss and nodded.

The man at the table motioned for Koebler to join him. "Bourbon?" he asked as the American sat down.

"Sure," Koebler replied, as he tried to place the man's country of origin. Maybe Singapore? Maybe China? Perhaps even Macanese? It was hard to tell, as he was so nondescript. What's more, the size of the security men also cut against the typical Chinese stereotype.

In the end, none of it mattered to Koebler. They'd paid him a fortune for the Bangkok bombing and an additional fortune for this meeting. As long as their crypto kept flowing in his direction, they could be from Mars for all he cared.

"Ice?" the man seated across from him asked as he produced a bottle of Blanton's. "Water?"

"Neat. Thank you."

The man poured two fingers of liquor and handed the glass to his guest. "To a job well done," he said in perfect English, as he raised his own glass in salute.

Koebler raised his in response, and without clinking, they both drank.

Eyes half-closed, the man savored his bourbon as the security team scanned the room.

Several moments passed. The murky room, which was predominantly lit by two dirty skylights overhead, smelled like old beer and damp cardboard.

Koebler said nothing. It was his host's dime. The man would get to the point eventually. Or he wouldn't. Koebler didn't care. He had already been paid.

Finally, the man opened his eyes fully and said, "We'd like to hire you for another job."

Koebler noted that the man had said "we" and not "I." Evidently there was someone further up the food chain who he reported to. "What kind of job?"

"Something similar to what you just did for us, but on a smaller scale. We'll double your fee."

"Smaller job, double the fee," Koebler remarked. "What's the catch?"

"No catch," the man replied.

Koebler took another sip of his bourbon and smiled. "You just said you would double my fee. No one offers something like that unless the job is considerably more difficult."

The man in the linen jacket smiled back. "I said the job was *smaller*. I didn't say it was easier. We'd need you to do it in the next twenty-four hours."

Koebler was taken aback. "You want another attack? By tomorrow?"

"Yes."

"That's not possible."

The man looked at him. "It's not possible? Or *you* can't do it?"

"I absolutely can," Koebler said. "But not the way you want it done."

"Meaning?"

"Meaning clean. No signature. Without anything the authorities can trace."

"On the contrary," the man replied, a smile forming. "We very much want the authorities to trace it. Just not back to us. Nor to you."

So they want to frame someone, Koebler thought to himself. In theory, that wasn't difficult. In practice, however, it took time and a lot of precise planning. At least if you wanted to make it believable.

"That's still a complicated assignment," the American stated. "For starters, I'd need to know who you wanted it to trace back to. Then I would have to study up on them and select what our 'giveaway' would be. It couldn't be anything too obvious. The harder it is for the authorities to discover, the more likely they'll believe it. Then there's the matter of choosing the target. And we haven't even begun to discuss securing the materials, much less pre-attack surveillance on the site, which—"

The man held up his hand, cutting Koebler off. Reaching into his pocket, he withdrew an envelope and pushed it across the table. "Everything you need is in here."

Koebler doubted that, but he took the envelope anyway, folded it in half, and slipped it into the front pocket of his jeans. But as he did, a change in the room's lighting caught his attention.

No sooner had he noticed it, than he realized it had come from movement at the skylights above. Immediately, his instincts kicked in.

He dove to his left and scrambled for cover as broken glass showered down from the ceiling and the storeroom door burst open.

Four armed men charged in, guns blazing, as two more rappelled down through the shattered skylights.

The man in the linen jacket pulled his own PDW as he and his team returned fire. Lead, along with hot shell casings, flew in every direction as eleven different weapons were being fired—some in three-round bursts, others on full auto.

The bullets tore through flesh and bone, as well as everything else in the storeroom—beer bottles, liquor bottles, kegs, and jugs of cleaning solution.

Three of the attackers were already down, as was one of the security detail for the man in the linen jacket. Despite being taken by surprise, the men Koebler had been meeting with seemed to be the superior fighters. They were much more disciplined and accurate.

Nevertheless, Koebler watched another member of the security detail go down, and a fraction of a second later the man in the linen jacket was struck. It appeared the tide might be turning against them.

Either way, Koebler had no desire to stick around. If he didn't catch a fatal bullet himself, the cacophony of gunfire was sure to draw a rapid police presence. It was time to move.

From his earlier surveillance, he knew that there was a back door that led into the maze of pedestrian alleyways behind Teens. And while he couldn't see it from where he was crouched, he figured the door was somewhere at the rear of the storeroom. He just had to get there. But, like framing someone for a bombing, it was a lot easier said than done.

He needed a path that provided cover, but with all the crates and boxes stacked against the walls, there was only a zigzag around the storeroom's tall shelving units. If he tried to make a mad dash of it, he'd be a goner for sure. The only answer was to create his own cover.

There was just enough room for him to edge toward the front right-hand corner of the storeroom. It wasn't much of an advantage, but it was the only advantage he was going to get, and he'd have to make the most of it.

As the bullets continued to fly, he stayed low and attempted to remain concealed as he moved closer to the nearest attacker.

Pulling the polymer knife that the security team had missed, he waited until he was less than a meter away and sprang, driving the blade through the man's left eye and twisting it upward into his brain.

At the same time, he spun the man toward the next attacker, using him as a shield.

Pulling the attacker's sidearm, he fired at the man's other teammates, forcing them to retreat.

Without missing a beat, he dragged the dying attacker backward, through the storeroom shelves, continuing to use the man as a bullet sponge.

The moment he could see the rear exit, he pulled his knife out of the man's eye, let him drop to the ground, and charged behind a stack of boxes. From there, it was only a few meters to the door.

Ejecting the magazine from the attacker's pistol, he confirmed how many rounds remained, reloaded, and then, giving himself a three-count, began firing backward into the storeroom—not caring who or what he hit—and charged for the exit.

The door crashed open, banging into the wall behind it, and Koebler exploded into the passageway behind Teens. He needed to get as far away as fast as possible. But first, he needed to reclaim his backpack from the construction site where he had hidden it.

The attacker's pistol was red-hot from all the rounds that had been fired through it, which meant tucking it into his waistband, where his Glock would have been, was out of the question. As he moved quickly, but calmly, down the alleyway, he saw some laundry on a line and snatched a small towel, wrapping the weapon in that. This way, witnesses wouldn't be describing to police a man fitting his description, leaving the scene with a gun.

Along the way, he retrieved as many of his tiny surveillance cameras as he could. The rest would have to be abandoned. They weren't worth risking being apprehended over.

At the construction site, he fished out his backpack, tucked the pistol inside and, making sure that he wasn't being followed, began a very circuitous route out of the Samphanthawong district.

He had no idea who the attackers had been at Teens, nor did he know who their ultimate target was. The only safe bet was to believe that he had been blown.

It was time to go to his Plan B, which meant plunging even deeper into Bangkok's deadly underground.

CHAPTER 8

WEST PHILIPPINE SEA

A commercial flight from Manila to Bangkok normally took three hours and fifteen minutes. At Mach 0.935, the Carlton Group's new Gulfstream G800—the world's longest-range business jet—could do the trip in two hours and twenty minutes.

As soon as they were out over the ocean and the aircraft had a secure satellite uplink, Harvath let the office know the team was ready for the briefing. Moments later, the screens in the main cabin came to life.

Over a spinning logo, they could hear the voice of the Carlton Group's "brain" before they could see his face. Nicholas, or *Moonracer* as he was code-named for security purposes during operations, stood less than three feet tall due to primordial dwarfism.

"All good on your end?" he asked, having patched his feed in, followed by McGee's. "Audio and video?"

"Five by five," Harvath responded, flashing a thumbs-up at the nearest monitor, all of which came complete with built-in cameras and microphones.

Gathered around Harvath in the cabin were Haney, Staelin, Ashby, and Palmer—all handpicked for the Itbayat operation, now along for the ride to Bangkok and whatever their new assignment might entail.

"Let's go over what we know about the bombings thus far," Nicholas said, as he cycled through a series of video clips captured immediately before, during, and after the explosions.

They were followed by a tally of dead and wounded, broken down by nationality. A percentage of the deceased were so badly disfigured, they had yet to be identified. Similar to the aftermath of the 9/11 attacks, it was going to take an army of DNA technicians to fully complete the task.

And in relation to the 9/11 attacks, Nicholas explained, the international media was now calling this Thailand's very own 9/11.

"Has any group claimed credit yet?" Harvath asked, repeating the same question he had asked the CIA's Manila station chief.

McGee shook his head and chimed in. "There are multiple online rumors that have taken off and spread like wildfire, but so far, nothing credible."

"Don't terrorist organizations like to jump out fast and grab the limelight?" Ashby asked.

"Not always," said Nicholas. "After 9/11, it was U.S. Intelligence—based on intercepted communications and prior intel—that announced the attacks had been carried out by al-Qaeda. Bin Laden denied it for years before finally admitting responsibility."

"Do we even know if what happened in Bangkok is Muslim terrorism?" said Haney.

Once again, McGee shook his head. "Thailand has had its share of terrorism from Muslim separatists in the south, but so far there's no evidence connecting them to what happened in Bangkok. And if they did it, this would mark a massive escalation."

"If not Islamist terrorists, who else would want to carry out a bombing like this?"

"Thai intelligence and the Thai military are looking very closely at their neighbor, Cambodia," Nicholas responded.

"Why?" Palmer interjected. "Are they trying to start a war?"

"Depending on who you talk to, it's already started. Last July, fighting broke out in multiple locations along their disputed border. Heavy weapons were involved."

"How heavy?" Staelin asked.

"Howitzers, multiple launch rocket systems, tanks and armored vehicles, combat aircraft," said McGee. "They've also been using cluster munitions and land mines. Nasty, nasty stuff."

"This is state-on-state conventional warfare," Nicholas added. "Not merely border skirmishes. It has been the most intense fighting in over a decade. Forty-eight people have been killed and over three hundred thousand civilians have been displaced."

"All over a disputed line on a map?" Ashby wondered aloud.

Nicholas pulled up another set of slides and explained, "It's more complicated than that. There's a lot of history that goes back to the ninth century and the rise of the Khmer Empire, which ruled most of Southeast Asia for six hundred years. But then the Siamese kingdom became the big kid on the block and pushed the Khmer—or the Cambodians if you like—out.

"From the fifteenth to the nineteenth centuries, Cambodia got pushed around and squeezed by its neighbors until it became a French protectorate and ultimately part of French Indochina. Cambodia wouldn't be fully independent until the early 1950s. Thailand, however, maintained its independence during the colonial era and developed much faster, especially economically, than Cambodia."

"So Cambodia has a chip on its shoulder when it comes to Thailand," said Palmer.

"A big one," McGee agreed.

"But the border itself," Nicholas interjected, "is the real bone of contention. In 1907, the French forced Thailand, then Siam, to cede a bunch of territory, culminating in the Franco-Siamese Treaty. Included in all the land that Siam was forced to give up was the ancient Hindu temple of Preah Vihear. When Thailand allied with Japan in World War II, they took a huge chunk of the territory back, including Preah Vihear.

"In 1962, the International Court of Justice forced Thailand to give the temple back. What the ICJ failed to do was to definitively rule on the land around it. That led to lots more fighting until 2013, when the ICJ finally said the land around Preah Vihear also belonged to Cambodia, which should have put an end to everything.

"Last spring, however, there was a skirmish near the temple and a Cambodian soldier was killed. Each country blamed the other and a bunch of border and economic sanctions were enacted. There was a huge political scandal in Thailand where their PM was seen to be too sympathetic to the Cambodians, and it ended up destabilizing the Thai government. There were massive protests and the PM was ousted.

"Then, a couple of months later, in July, a Thai border patrol stumbled across a land mine, accidentally triggered it, and five Thai soldiers were injured. Bangkok accused Phnom Penh of cutting barbed-wire fences, sneaking into Thai territory, and laying new land mines. Thailand curtailed diplomatic relations, which ended up with both countries recalling their ambassadors and eventually the aforementioned fighting with heavy weapons breaking out.

"Thailand declared martial law in several border districts. Civilian areas in both countries were alleged to have been hit by rocket and artillery fire, with Bangkok alleging hospitals had been struck and Phnom Penh claiming one of their schools had been hit. It went back and forth like this until a very tenuous ceasefire was put in place."

Palmer looked at Nicholas via his monitor. "How well has it held?"

"Very touch and go. Forbidden from exchanging gun, rocket, or artillery fire, the Cambodians have been finding other ways to antagonize Thailand. One of their favorites is finding anything significant in Thai culture and, where justified, accusing them of cultural appropriation. Thailand replies that there wasn't ever much culture in Cambodia to begin with and what the Siamese took was taken hundreds of years ago. They claim that the Cambodians are only angry because they have to live in such a crappy backwater that no one in the world cares about. The rhetoric, on both sides, only serves to piss people off.

"Both countries are now wrestling with tsunamis of angry nationalists who are agitating for all-out war. With every passing day, the political clout of the populist factions is growing and the Thai/Cambodian confrontation clock is ticking closer to midnight."

"So in other words," said Harvath, "it's a total powder keg."

Nicholas nodded. "It's beyond volatile. Someone could sneeze in the wrong direction and that'd become the spark."

"So, all of this over a temple *and* a disputed line on a map," Staelin stated, uninterested in getting involved in a border war between Thailand and Cambodia.

"Obviously, it's deeper than that," McGee interjected. "But if you're looking for a thirty-thousand-foot explanation, that's as good as any other."

"You said that the Thai government was looking into it, but do they have any evidence that Cambodia was behind the bombings?" asked Harvath.

"As far as we know, nothing yet," said Nicholas, cuing up a new deck. "But when we look at the bombs themselves, that's where things start to get interesting."

CHAPTER 9

Preliminary reports from the FBI agents on the ground indicate that the devices in Bangkok used white phosphorus," said Nicholas, moving through his slides.

"To what end?" Palmer inquired. "Increased lethality?"

"Increased terror," Haney argued. "White phosphorus projectiles were used in the second battle of Fallujah. They create a kind of fire that can't be extinguished with water. Absolutely horrific stuff. Melts the skin and muscle right off your body."

"True," Nicholas agreed. "White phosphorus spontaneously combusts when it comes in contact with oxygen, and can burn anywhere from thirteen hundred to fifteen hundred degrees. There's no question that it does incredible damage. And yes, it could have been included to increase casualties, but we would have expected to see a lot more of it. We think it was used for another reason."

Staelin leaned toward his screen. "Such as?"

"It's the perfect delete button. White phosphorus burns so hot and so fast that almost any forensic signature the bomber might have left behind is completely erased."

"Insurgents did the same thing in Iraq and Afghanistan," Palmer said. "IED makers would add white phosphorus so we couldn't trace any of their stuff."

Nicholas nodded. "Yes, some cells did it to burn away the bomb's internals, but its use wasn't that common. White phosphorus is incredibly dangerous to handle. You have to know what you're doing."

"So our bomber isn't an amateur," stated Harvath.

"Definitely not," Nicholas replied. "They've done this before."

"Outside of Iraq and Afghanistan, where else has white phosphorus been used in improvised explosive devices?"

"It's predominantly been seen in the Middle East. In addition to Iraq and Afghanistan, it's been seen in Syria, Lebanon, Pakistan, Libya, Gaza, and the West Bank."

Harvath thought about those locations for a moment. "So, we could be looking at an Islamic militant, from Thailand, who trained or operated in the Middle East and then brought their skills back home to Bangkok."

"Absolutely," Nicholas replied.

"And if you were a Thailand-based Islamic militant looking for white phosphorus, where would you go looking for it?"

The man studied one of his computer screens, just off camera, as he walked Harvath through a few possibilities. "One of the places worth considering is Clark Air Base."

"The old U.S. air base northwest of Manila?"

Nicholas nodded. "Plenty of U.S. munitions have leaked from old Philippine military stockpiles there. The corruption inside the Philippine army and police force is a widespread problem. Clark has long been a hub for ex–military contractors, arms traffickers, and shady logistics groups. White phosphorus from old M825A1 rounds has shown up on the black market there. Considering how cheap and easy travel between the Philippines and Thailand is, that'd be high on my list."

Harvath made a mental note and said, "What else?"

"The Thai army is notoriously lax with its weapons inventories. Like the Philippines, corruption is widespread. White phosphorus rounds from the 1960s through the '80s could easily be sitting inside some forgotten depot. All it would take to shake a few loose would be one corrupt Thai military officer. Such a person could easily arrange to 'lose' a few without raising any alarms."

"That seems like a big risk," Harvath replied. "If one single bomb fragment traced back to the Thai military, the heat that would come down from that would make the temperature of white phosphorus pale in comparison."

"I don't disagree," Nicholas responded. "Which leaves me one other contender—Sihanoukville. It's a Wild West coastal city on the Gulf of Thailand in southwestern Cambodia. Completely controlled by the Chinese. Casinos, organized crime syndicates, prostitution . . . you name it, they've got it."

"How about illegal arms trafficking?"

"They've got that too. In spades. White phosphorus munitions have been known to show up there through illicit global arms shipments, often sourced from African conflicts and even corrupt Chinese PLA stockpiles. The city is like that lawless spaceport from *Star Wars* that Han Solo operated out of."

"Mos Eisley?" Harvath asked.

"That's the one," said Nicholas, imitating Obi-Wan Kenobi. "You will never find a more wretched hive of scum and villainy."

Harvath hadn't heard of Sihanoukville, but he didn't doubt it—especially if the Chinese were involved. "How would you transport the cargo in question to Bangkok? I would imagine, considering the current state of relations between the two countries, that overland border crossings are quite contentious."

"Most of the illegal shipments move via fishing trawlers across the gulf to Trat Province, a quiet, underpopulated Thai coastal area. There, contraband is hidden beneath fresh seafood, loaded onto refrigerated trucks, and driven to Bangkok for distribution. If the white phosphorus came from Sihanoukville, it would have taken that route, or one very similar to it."

It was a lot to consider. None of the possible white phosphorus sources, however, brought them any closer to figuring out who was behind the bombings.

After turning it over in his head for a few more moments, Harvath looked at Nicholas and said, "When I asked you where else white phosphorus had been used for IEDs, you replied *predominantly* in the Middle East. Where else has it been used, even on a non-predominant basis?"

Nicholas turned again to his off-camera monitor and typed a series of commands into his computer. It took him several minutes to sift through the search results.

Finally, he shared his screen and went through a series of one-off bombings that had taken place around the world.

"Could these be the work of the same bomber?" Harvath asked.

"Possibly," Nicholas replied. "They all used white phosphorus and they all went unsolved." He stopped sharing his screen and went quiet for several beats. After scrolling some additional intelligence networks he had access to, he stated, "This is interesting."

"What is it?"

"A classified report that doesn't look like it has been accessed in years. Are you familiar with the Drug Enforcement Administration's Sensitive Investigation Unit?"

"The SIU?" said Harvath. "They were supposed to be the DEA's elite strike force in Mexico. All top-tier Mexican cops, vetted and trained in the U.S."

"And apparently, all corrupt as hell," stated Nicholas. "The unit leaked like a sieve, normally to the cartels, who, in turn, crafted disinformation for them to feed into their reporting streams. Essentially, a ton of SIU agents—people the DEA was supposed to be able to trust implicitly in Mexico—were double agents. After more than twenty-five years in operation, the program was shut down."

"Jesus," Harvath remarked. "I'd heard it had been shelved, but I didn't know why. What did SIU have to do with white phosphorus?"

"From what I can see, at the height of the cartel violence, the DEA brought the ATF down to Mexico to investigate a series of bombings. Many of the areas where the attacks took place were designated 'denied access,' meaning too dangerous to enter and collect evidence.

"But when the ATF *was* able to access other blast sites and conduct forensic investigations, all those bombings had one thing in common—the use of white phosphorus in such a manner that it appeared the bombmaker was attempting to erase any and all potential signatures."

CHAPTER 10

WASHINGTON, D.C.

Erin Delaney was exhausted. Stumbling into her Georgetown townhouse, she kicked off her shoes and dropped her travel bag just inside the front door.

She was looking forward to a stiff, predawn drink, a hot bath, and a few solid hours of sleep before having to get up and head back to work.

If only her friends in Wisconsin could see her now—*especially* the ones envious of her "jet-setting, international lifestyle."

A senior staffer for Indo-Pacific Strategy at the National Security Council sounded a lot more glamorous than it was. She shared a tiny White House office with three other "experts" who helped shape the administration's region-wide strategy. Signature minilateral partnerships were their specialty. They included the Quad—a foreign policy dialogue among the United States, Australia, India, and Japan focused on promoting a free and open Indo-Pacific region while countering China's growing influence—as well as the American-Japanese-Korean trilateral pact, which aimed to strengthen deterrence against North Korea and counter regional threats from China and Russia. Her department pushed for lots of initiatives. Chief among them were joint military exercises, intelligence sharing, and high-level consultations.

It was a largely thankless position that the majority of Americans didn't even know existed. You were on call 24/7 and the only thing worse than the hours was the pay. Nevertheless, Delaney loved it. She was not just a good fit, she was perfect for the job.

The higher the stakes, the harder she dug in. While others folded under stress, unable to make decisions, she came alive. She was smart, sharp, and ambitious, with an instinct for spotting angles others missed. She had a master's in Asian studies, but she wasn't an academic. She was a hands-on practitioner who understood how power actually moved. The National Security Council, and the nation, were lucky to have her—particularly at this moment. The situation with the Chinese had gotten worse.

Because of her value to the Indo-Pacific team, not to mention her reputation as the "fixer" for urgent briefs and crisis memos, she had been flown up to Camp David with her boss and other key NSC members for the weekend. The President was urgently trying to craft a strategy and wanted his most important hands on deck.

The People's Liberation Army was moving substantial assets within striking distance of Taiwan. It had all been done under the cover of a pre-announced military training exercise.

This one, however, felt different. Too much was being moved. And too openly. Specific pieces of hardware and tech, which the Chinese had previously gone to great lengths to keep under wraps, were now showing up on U.S. satellite passes.

It had the same feel as Russia's "joint exercises" with Belarus just before the Ukraine invasion. Some on the NSC were even making comparisons to the Nazis and their 1939 "border protection exercises" before invading Poland.

What Delaney knew for certain was that despite past Chinese saber-rattling, this was unprecedented. The United States was seriously concerned. And with good reason. So was she.

But the world's problems would have to wait. Right now, all she wanted was that drink and that bath. Maybe a book, though she doubted she'd stay awake long enough to get through a single page. The latest Clémence Michallon thriller would unfortunately remain in her bag, untouched, for at least one more night.

She pulled out her hair tie and let her long red hair fall loose. *Amazing*, she thought, *how kicking off your shoes and freeing your hair can make you feel human again*.

She walked into the kitchen without turning on a single light. Rocks glass from the cupboard. Bourbon from the bar cart. Ice from the freezer. Muscle memory. She could have done it all blindfolded.

Which was why the ice being in the wrong place sent a chill down her spine. *Someone had moved it. Someone had been in her house.*

Her heart began to pound in her chest as she fumbled for the switch.

Then she heard it—a *man's* voice—low, strained, coming from the pitch-black dining room.

"Erin . . . don't turn on the lights."

CHAPTER 11

"Connor?" she replied, startled. Her hand was frozen, inches from the switch. "What are you doing here? How'd you get into my house?"

There was a scrape of a chair leg in the darkness. Not aggressive; just the sound of someone shifting their weight after sitting too long in the same position. His breathing was uneven. Weary.

"Don't turn the lights on," he said again. Softer this time. "Please."

Erin's pulse spiked as her anger flared, hot and immediate. At the same time, there was a tension in his voice that was unmistakable.

"Connor," she said, lowering her hand, but not relaxing. "I'm serious. What the hell are you doing in my house?"

He waited a beat before responding. "I didn't know where else to go."

"That's not an answer," she sighed, exhaling. "And breaking into my place sure as hell isn't a solution."

"I didn't break in," he responded. "The lock on your back door hasn't worked right since . . . well, since the last time I fixed it."

The memory was annoying. Personal. Too familiar. As was his entering her house without permission. "That still doesn't explain why you're here," she snapped, the anger seeping back in.

Finally, he stood and stepped toward her. As he picked up his glass from the table, she could hear the rattle of ice. *He'd been drinking.* She had half a mind to throw him right out. But then he got close enough that she could finally see him. The once handsome Marine with his neatly kept brown hair and crisp green eyes looked terrible. Broken.

"Are you okay?" she asked, the harshness in her voice receding. "Did something happen to you?"

She was slipping into caregiver mode—something she had sworn she would never allow to happen again.

Connor Jameson wasn't her fiancé anymore. It wasn't her job to fix him. She had already been down that road. *Repeatedly*.

She had loved him deeply, but had come to realize that you couldn't fix someone who actively chose not to get better. His PTSD was something she could handle. His choosing *not* to deal with it, however, had spelled the end of their relationship.

"Two men broke into my apartment last night," he said, answering her question. "Two professionals."

"*Professional* what?"

"Hitters."

Her pale blue eyes narrowed. "Assassins?"

Jameson nodded. "Pistol suppressors, the works."

Was she hearing him correctly? Was he even hearing himself? Or was this all happening in his head? Maybe this was nothing more than a worsening of his condition.

"I can prove it," he replied, sensing her disbelief. He grabbed his laptop from his backpack and put it on the dining table, along with the key hard drive from his network attached storage device that acted as his personal cloud.

After attaching a series of cables, he powered everything up. As soon as he found the images of his assailants, he spun the laptop so that Erin could see for herself.

Right away, she recognized Connor's apartment, but not the bloody corpses of the men on the floor. They looked real. That didn't mean they were. Anyone could manipulate images these days.

She hated to think that of him, but he had grown more unstable over the last six months. Their engagement had not only come to an end, but he'd been forced to resign from the Sentinel Foundation for National Security. It was a hawkish, Washington, D.C.–based defense/foreign-policy think tank focused largely on China.

Sentinel had been happy to snap up the bright, combat-tested, U.S. Marine intelligence officer. His insights into China, Indo-Pacific military postures, PLA developments, U.S. readiness, and Taiwan contingencies had been top-notch. But after a while, his work began to suffer.

Connor had begun to exhibit erratic behavior. He had difficulty collaborating. There was friction with his supervisors and concerns about his judgment. They had tried to get him help, but he had refused, claiming he didn't need any.

Eventually, he was encouraged to resign for mental health/performance issues. When he refused that as well, they quietly pushed him out, terminating his employment and banning him from the building.

It was a dramatic move for a business that was proudly pro-military and pro-vets, but such was the extent of the difficulties surrounding Connor's issues.

Unable to sit still and believing he had a national security voice that needed to be heard, he reinvented himself as a military blogger. Via a thin network of contacts he managed to maintain, he gathered and analyzed mostly "open source" intelligence and published it on his website. It was a weekly deluge of hot takes, speculative analyses, China/Taiwan assessments, and criticisms of the current administration.

Jameson absolutely despised America's new, young president and railed at him every chance he got. There were many evenings, especially when alcohol was involved, that he had even turned that vitriol against Erin. He had repeatedly called President Mitchell naive, isolationist, intellectually impaired, historically and economically ignorant, and a puppet of America's enemies.

The worst of these alcohol-fueled rants were the ones where he went after Erin for working in the administration, calling into question not only her judgment, but also her patriotism. Despite his apologies, these accusations always cut the deepest and were the hardest for Erin to forgive.

But again and again, forgive them she did. At least she had tried—until Connor's demons became too big and too dark for her to handle.

Like Hemingway had said about bankruptcy, the dissolution of their engagement had happened slowly at first, then all at once. Connor had strip-mined every ounce of empathy from her, only to continue swinging at the barren walls of her soul with his rusty pickaxe. It had been sad, exhausting, and incredibly painful. She'd had no choice but to put an end to it.

Now here he was, standing in her dining room, claiming something that—despite D.C.'s crime stats—still sounded insane.

"Why would someone want you dead?" she asked.

"Jesus," he muttered. "Even after those photos. You still don't believe me."

"It's not that I—"

He held up his hand. "Don't. I know you well enough to know that look."

She wanted to deny it, but the words wouldn't come. At least not fast enough.

He saw it.

Rubbing the back of his neck, he let out a humorless laugh. "I probably wouldn't believe me either. I mean, who shows up at their ex's house on a Saturday night—"

"You've been here since last night?" Erin interjected.

"I needed some place safe. This is safe. *You're* safe."

"Connor, you can't just—"

"By the way," he plowed on, "where have you been?"

"Camp David," she stated. "Not that I owe you any sort of an explanation."

"You were up there because of Taiwan, weren't you?"

"A, that's none of your business. And B, it's classified."

"The White House isn't reading the PLA buildup as a training exercise, are they? You all actually think this is a precursor to an invasion—that China is about to cross the Strait, don't you?"

"No comment," she replied.

He shook his head. "You're wrong. All of you. It's a feint. A deception. The Soviets used to call these types of psyops *maskirovka*. Have you not gotten a single email or voicemail I've sent you?"

She had gotten them. *All* of them. But his conspiracy theories were not something she wanted to get into right now. "Things at the National Security Council have been a little busy."

"That's precisely my point. You're all looking at Taiwan, but the

Chinese movements don't match a Taiwan strike window. Something else is happening under the noise."

Erin tried to steer him back on course. "You were going to tell me why someone would want you dead."

"Obviously, I figured out something I shouldn't have," he replied. "Or . . . ," he continued, his voice trailing off.

She was afraid to ask what the other possibility was, but her curiosity got the better of her. "*Or* what?" she asked.

"Or Mitchell has decided to start silencing his critics."

It was such a ridiculous assertion that she couldn't help but scoff. "You think President Jim Mitchell is dispatching hit teams to take out his critics?"

"The White House doesn't like being contradicted. Especially not by someone who used to be in the system."

"Connor, nobody in the administration is sending assassins after a blogger."

"Why not?" Jameson protested. "Is it any less believable than a coup, launched by government insiders, to push him from power?"

As unstable and unpredictable as his PTSD had made him, there were still parts of his brilliant brain that operated logically. And when he could access those parts, he was able to make perfectly good, even winning arguments.

Over the summer, Mitchell's administration had suffered an attempted coup. It had been launched by members of his own party who felt that he wasn't living up to his campaign promises; that upon taking the oath of office, he had moderated too many of his positions.

Feeling that the political window was closing and that America would miss a once-in-a-generation chance at true structural reform, the plotters had launched a deadly, but in the end failed, campaign to push Mitchell from office.

The idea, however, that the President was now quarterbacking his own reverse Night of the Long Knives, was beyond nuts. She needed to tether her ex back to terra firma.

"I think you're safe from Jim Mitchell," she stated. "An extrajudicial hit list, much less one targeting his political detractors, isn't his style."

"Then it has to be the Chinese. They don't like me calling their bluff on my blog and pointing out the holes in their alleged Taiwan buildup."

Erin suppressed the urge to roll her eyes. Either the President of the United States wanted to take him out *or* it was the Chinese government? He really did have a high opinion of himself. She'd have to check to see if delusions of grandeur were a known symptom associated with PTSD.

"I don't think it's the Chinese either."

"You think I'm crazy," he whispered, the fatigue evident in his voice. "But someone put two professionals in my apartment last night, Erin. *Two*. And they didn't come to talk."

She looked back at the photos of the dead men on his laptop. "I see their suppressed weapons. What were you shooting with?"

"My forty-five."

"Jesus, Con," Erin exclaimed. "The forty-five you're not allowed to have? That gun's supposed to be at your buddy's farm in Virginia. You had an involuntary psychiatric admission last year—"

"Which was a misunderstanding—"

"Which," she interrupted him right back, "makes you legally ineligible to possess a firearm in D.C. What the hell were you thinking?"

"I was *thinking* that I might need it someday. And guess what?"

Erin was done guessing. If what he claimed to have happened did happen, it would be all over the news. But if it wasn't, if this was another delusion, she needed to get him help. Retreating to the entry hall, she fished her phone out of her bag and powered it up.

Part of the NSC's security protocol had been no personal phones at Camp David over the weekend. They didn't want any digital signatures that could tip off the Chinese or the press as to what was going on.

It didn't take her long to find the story. "**Double Shooting in Adams Morgan Area—Person of Interest at Large**" the headline read. She recognized Connor's building immediately. He hadn't been named—at least not yet. Metropolitan Police were referring simply to a "tenant" whom they wanted to speak with in the hopes that they could gather more information.

There was no mention of pistol suppressors or professional assassins.

But why would there be? The police normally held back important details from the public as they worked their leads.

Neighbors, however, had no such reason to exhibit restraint and plenty of Connor's had spoken to the press. The one thing they were all in agreement on was that there had been a lot of shots fired.

Erin looked at a couple more sites, her jaw tight, then set her phone aside.

"Now do you believe me?" Connor asked.

But before she could answer, a knock sounded at her front door. Subdued, but deliberate. *Not a cop. Not a neighbor.*

Erin froze. Connor's eyes shifted past her, narrowing on the entry hall and the glass panel beside the door.

She turned, peering through the darkened kitchen, and saw it—the silhouette of a large man standing outside.

Connor's voice dropped to a whisper.

"Erin, don't move."

CHAPTER 12

BANGKOK, THAILAND

The Carlton Group Gulfstream landed at Don Mueang International Airport and taxied to a stop. Waiting for them on the tarmac were a fleet of black U.S. Embassy Toyota Land Cruisers.

Once the private jet's forward door was open and the airstairs had been extended, the team exited the aircraft.

It was hotter than Manila, but the early evening Bangkok air was less humid. Beneath the usual notes of airplane exhaust and jet fuel, the breeze carried with it something exotic.

Harvath had been to Thailand as part of his honeymoon. He had loved the culture, as well as all of the sights. It was an incredible country.

As long as the on-the-ground contact the embassy had sent was solid, the mission would already be off to a good start.

It was at that moment that the rear door of the lead Land Cruiser opened and their contact stepped out.

Harvath couldn't believe his eyes. "You have got to be fucking kidding me," he said, the roar from the engines of a departing plane drowning him out.

Though none of his teammates had heard what he had said, they could read him like a book. Whoever that man was who had just climbed out of the SUV, he and Harvath had history. And by all appearances, it wasn't good.

The man was tall, muscular, and close in age to Harvath. He had an angular face with a cleft chin and close-cropped, obviously dyed, jet-black hair.

Unlike the other representatives from the embassy, the man wasn't wearing a suit. He was dressed in street clothes, sported a pair of mirrored aviator sunglasses, and carried himself with a palpable arrogance.

"Scot Harvath," the man exclaimed, walking over to the bottom of the airstairs. "If ever there was a better argument for a retirement home being welded shut and covered in concrete, I haven't seen it."

"And if it isn't Rick 'The Prick' Morrell," Harvath replied, tilting his head at the setting sun and adding, "Aren't you contractually required to remain in your coffin until nightfall?"

He smiled. "And miss welcoming America's biggest mistake to Bangkok? Not on your life."

Off to the side, Staelin muttered, "Who's this asshole?"

"Ground Branch guy," stated Haney, as he waited to help offload the team's gear from the jet.

"You know him?"

"Not really. He landed at CIA several years before I got there."

"Ever deploy with him?"

"Thank fuck, no. He had a rep as a real dickhead."

Staelin grinned. "Doesn't look like much has changed. Where was he before Ground Branch?"

"Some SEAL Team," said Haney. "I think he was asked to leave. I'm not sure."

"That tracks."

Haney shot him a return grin and the pair aided the crew with the bags. In the meantime, Harvath and Morrell came together and shook hands.

"It's been a minute," Morrell observed.

Harvath nodded. "It has."

"Heard you got married."

"I did."

Morrell cocked an eyebrow. "To a woman?"

Harvath nodded again. "Yup. Your mom didn't want people to think I was only with her for the sex."

"Jesus," the man replied, shaking his head. "Fuck you, Harvath."

"Speaking of which," Harvath continued, "it'll probably take some getting used to, so don't worry about not calling me Dad right away."

Morrell gave him the finger and Harvath smiled.

The two men had started out as bitter antagonists, but over time had developed a grudging respect for each other. That respect had eventually evolved into a lukewarm friendship.

"What the hell are you doing in Bangkok?" Harvath asked, genuinely surprised.

"Bangkok's where they park you when you're useful, but inconvenient," Morrell responded, taking in the rest of the team. "You going to introduce me, or am I supposed to guess who does what?"

Typical Morrell, he kept his mirrored aviators on as the introductions were made.

After one of the embassy people collected their passports and sped them through the private customs-and-immigration process at the MJet FOB building, they piled into the Land Cruisers and got moving.

The private aviation area was already heavily secured, but as soon as they drove past the commercial side, they could see masses of soldiers and cops, as well as checkpoints augmented by columns of military and police vehicles. In the aftermath of the bombings, the Thai government was leaving nothing to chance. The country's most vulnerable targets were seeing triple, and in some cases quadruple, the security.

As they made their way into the city, Morrell—who was riding shotgun while one of his guys drove—gave Harvath and his team the lay of the land.

"Bangkok is crowded and busy as fuck. It's got about eleven and a half million residents, shit urban planning, and lousy infrastructure. The traffic is a nightmare and is only made worse by the fact that for the last two years running, Bangkok has been the most visited city in the world with over thirty million arrivals each year. All of those factors played into making the bombings even more devastating.

"As for who's handling things, the Royal Thai Police are doing most of the grunt work. Their Special Branch Bureau is directing their efforts with special emphasis from their intelligence, counterintelligence, and counterterrorism divisions. The Thai Armed Forces have spun up both their Counterterrorism Operations Center and their domestic security apparatus known as the Internal Security Operations Command.

"Hovering over the top of all this and pushing down hard is Thailand's

National Intelligence Agency. They're the ones getting the most heat from the politicians. Two schools of thought are already taking shape. Either the bombings were the work of Islamist terrorists from the deep south of Thailand who as part of their ethnonationalist insurgency are looking to break away and form their own state, or it was a black op by the Cambodians in hopes of getting Thailand to abandon its territorial ambitions along the disputed border region."

"What does the CIA's Bangkok Station think?" Harvath asked.

Morrell turned around in his seat to look at him. "Bangkok Station thinks the bomber came from outside the country."

"Because?" Staelin inquired from the back row of the vehicle.

"Because the bombs were practically perfect. Whoever built them knew what they were doing. In more than twenty years, none of the bombings that Thailand has experienced come anywhere close."

"The Muslim insurgents could have imported a bomber," stated Palmer. "Correct?"

"It's possible," the CIA man agreed. "But they don't have a lot of transnational connections. And besides, when they strike, they focus on Thai security forces in their own backyard—the Narathiwat, Pattani, Songkhla, and Yala areas. Their fight is with Thailand, not foreign tourists. What happened in Bangkok would signal a *major* escalation."

"So that's a clue," said Haney. "By being too good, the bomber exposed himself as an outsider."

"That's what we believe. The FBI has been helping scour all of the bomb sites for evidence, but beyond shrapnel, there's not much."

"How about CCTV and other cameras?" asked Ashby. "With all of the tourists taking photos and videos in those areas, there's got to be mountains of footage."

Morrell nodded. "That's the problem. The Thai government created a social media hashtag and a website where people could direct anything they think might be helpful. The response has been overwhelming. It's like drinking from a firehose. And on top of that, there has been a lot of bullshit AI content that takes a while to debunk."

"Who makes a terrorist attack worse by submitting fake AI content to investigators?" Ashby remarked.

"Could be the aforementioned insurgents in the south. Could be the Cambodians. Thailand's relationship with its northern neighbor Myanmar hasn't been too cozy either. Could be random internet trolls. No one knows at this point, and nobody has the bandwidth to get to the bottom of it."

Harvath shook his head. "What about the placement of the bombs? Any further intel there?"

"The first wave appears to have been all car bombs—or more appropriately, based on CCTV footage, van bombs. The second wave of explosive devices were hidden in food delivery boxes strapped to scooters and motorcycles. All of them, it appears, had been strategically parked to maximize casualties."

"What about the drivers? We were told these were not suicide bombers. They placed the vehicles and left the scenes. Is there any CCTV footage of them?"

"There is," Morrell replied. "But they were all disguised. The motorbike and scooter operators wore inconspicuous clothing, including gloves and helmets with darkened visors. The van drivers also wore unremarkable clothing, as well as hoodies, ball caps, sunglasses, gloves, and neck gaiters pulled up over their noses."

Harvath was reminded of the footage several years ago of the D.C. bomber who placed pipe bombs outside of the DNC and RNC headquarters. He had gone to similar lengths to disguise his appearance and it had taken the FBI forever to track him down. "Have the Thai police run the footage of the drivers through gait analysis?"

"They did, which revealed another problem. All of the drivers appeared to have some sort of a limp."

"Which means they were expecting to be seen and probably put something in their shoes to make them limp."

Morrell nodded again. "They also knew where the blind spots in the camera coverage were. Slipping into those, where they couldn't be seen, it appears they ditched their disguises, lost their limps, and then blended in with the rest of the public and disappeared."

"Have they retrieved any of the helmets or other clothing? There'd probably be DNA and other trace evidence on them."

"Nope. Nothing was left behind. We think another team covertly picked everything up."

"So we're dealing with some sort of a cell that's both thorough and well organized," said Harvath.

"Agreed," Morrell replied. "Right down to the license plates they used—all of which were stolen from vehicles on the outskirts of Bangkok where there's less camera coverage."

"And the vehicles themselves? Any luck identifying those yet?"

"That'll take even longer. The explosions were massive. Finding a VIN somewhere in the rubble, if not blocks away from the blasts, is going to take a while. Our guess is that the vehicles were probably stolen down in Phuket and smuggled up here for the attack."

The man had a point. "Pretty intense operation," Harvath stated. "Is this something insurgents could have pulled off?"

Morrell shrugged. "Who knows? I wouldn't have thought a bunch of assholes living in caves in Afghanistan could have pulled off 9/11, but they did."

Another good point. "What about CCTV footage or tips coming in via social media? Are the Thais being cooperative? I've got to think CIA and NSA could really help speed the process."

"Don't get me going on Thai cooperation. They want to be in complete and total control of everything. They're okay with foreign boots on the ground, helping sift through the wreckage, but handing over digital evidence has been a nonstarter."

"Why?" asked Harvath. "Are they afraid something is going to happen to it?"

"I think they realize they've got the eyes of the world on them and want to look like they can handle this situation. They don't want to appear to need help from anyone—especially America. Between the border clashes with the Cambodians and the ongoing insurgency problems down south, the current government in Bangkok was already balancing on a knife's edge. If they botch the response to these bombings, they could end up with another coup on their hands."

Harvath was familiar with that part of Thailand's history. There'd been a dozen successful coups since 1932, with the last one only twelve years ago. Despite its natural beauty and tourist appeal, just beneath the surface, the country remained a powder keg.

At the same time, Harvath knew how much Thailand mattered to the United States. It sat within reach of the Malacca and Singapore Straits, as well as the Indonesian passages beyond—strategic, maritime choke points that carried traffic between the Indian Ocean and the Pacific. In any war with China, controlling those narrow stretches of water would be central to cutting off Beijing from energy, trade, and reinforcements.

Thailand was also one of America's oldest security partners in Asia. It allowed access to its bases for transit, refueling, and training, and—most important—provided the U.S. military with an invaluable foothold in the region. If hostilities ever broke out, the alliance—much like America's relationship with the Philippines and other aligned Indo-Pacific nations—would be a game changer.

As complicated as some of those relationships could be, to Harvath's mind Winston Churchill had summed it up best when he said, "There is only one thing worse than fighting with allies, and that is fighting without them."

"So where does that leave us?" he asked.

"In need of a break. A *big* one," Morrell replied. "We're coming up on forty-eight hours since the bombings and we've got next to nothing. Everybody can sense that the trail is going cold."

Harvath drew a breath to comment, then stopped.

A tiny electronic chime cut through the vehicle. Two quick notes, high and sharp, like a digital cricket buried somewhere in the SUV.

Morrell swore under his breath, dug into a pocket, and came up with a scratched, no-name handset. One glance at the screen wiped the sarcasm off his face.

"What is it?" Harvath asked.

Morrell looked back at him, eyes suddenly razor sharp. "We may have just caught our break."

CHAPTER 13

Talat Noi was a gritty Chinese-Thai neighborhood on the edge of Chinatown. It was permeated with the constant smell of oil, river water, and hot metal. Above an old warehouse jammed between a machine shop and an auto parts yard was the loft belonging to Tommy Sombat.

Sombat was an oleaginous underworld figure who made his living as one of Bangkok's more ruthless black-market fixers. He wasn't big-time, but he also wasn't small-time. He occupied the juicy middle where most of the crime in the city happened. Almost anything you wanted, within reason, he could get for you. And anything you wanted to get rid of, including bodies, he could do that for you too. All you had to do was meet his price.

What had landed him on Morrell's radar and eventually his payroll, however, was his information gathering capability. Whether it was his call girl connections, the drug dealers he knew, or the crooked Thai police, Sombat seemed to have eyes and ears everywhere. That made him exceedingly valuable to Morrell—who was under no illusions as to how many other payrolls he might be on.

After a slow pass in front of the building, Morrell turned at the next corner and nosed his Land Cruiser into a spot about half a block down.

Turning off the ignition, he looked at Harvath, who was now riding shotgun. Everyone else had been dropped off at a CIA safe house in Suan Phlu. "Like I said, Tommy's no altar boy, but he's not going to give us any trouble."

"And the fact that you haven't been able to get ahold of him since the bombings, and only knew he was back because you paid a local shopkeeper to keep an eye on his place? That doesn't bother you?" asked Harvath.

"I didn't say it didn't bother me," Morrell replied. "I just said he wasn't going to be any trouble."

Shaking his head, Harvath removed his SIG Sauer, did a quick press check to confirm a round was chambered. He may have developed a grudging respect for Morrell, but that didn't mean he trusted him—not fully. After all, the last time they had operated together, Morrell had left him for dead. Tucking the pistol back beneath his shirt, Harvath exited the vehicle.

"How do you want to do this?" he asked, once the CIA man came around and joined him on the sidewalk. "You take the front and I'll take the back?"

"He's not going to run. Don't worry."

Shaking his head again, Harvath gestured for Morrell to lead the way.

With all of its neon light, Bangkok—particularly at night—resembled a noir graphic novel. It reminded Harvath of the movie *Blade Runner*, minus the flying cars and bioengineered replicants.

At the corner, they paused and looked down the street toward Tommy Sombat's darkened loft.

"Either your shopkeeper lied to you," said Harvath, "or your guy doesn't want anybody knowing he's home."

"I'm going with option two," Morrell responded, heading toward the building like it was just another day and he had been here a thousand times before.

Harvath was more cautious. His head on a swivel, he kept his eyes peeled.

At the entrance to the building, they slipped under a metal roll-up gate that was halfway down, and headed toward a narrow staircase. Whatever the warehouse had once been used for, it reeked of rust and old fish.

As this was Morrell's "trusted" guy, when they arrived at the steps, Harvath didn't fight to be the first one up. He continued to let the CIA man lead. If anything went down, Morrell would make a much better bullet catcher.

Climbing the crumbling stairs, they began to hear something. A muffled pleading, interspersed with wet coughs. Even as they neared the landing, Harvath had no idea what was being said.

Someone was asking cold, short questions, which were met with more pleading and more wet coughs.

Pausing at the last stair, Morrell leaned forward and strained his ears. "They're not speaking Thai," he whispered over his shoulder. "It sounds like Mandarin."

Suddenly, the questioner raised his voice and shouted in anger. It was followed by a high-pitch, mechanical whine and unmistakable screams of absolute agony.

Neither Harvath nor Morrell needed to hear anything else. In unison, both men drew their pistols. With a rapid series of hand gestures, the CIA operative laid out his plan.

When Harvath nodded, Morrell counted down from three and kicked the door in. That was when all hell broke loose.

A horrifically beaten, half-naked Tommy Sombat had been tied to an old drafting table at the far end of the dingy loft. He looked like a medieval torture victim splayed out on the rack. His face was covered in lacerations. His lips were split open. Both of his eyes were nearly swollen shut. And there was blood. Lots of blood. *Everywhere*.

Standing above him were two large men with jet-black hair who didn't look Thai to Harvath. If anything—they looked Chinese.

The major tell, however, wasn't their features, it was their look: tight, military-style haircuts, no jewelry, latex gloves. It spoke to a level of uniformity and professionalism. These guys didn't read like underworld figures. They looked like pros. And whatever was going on, they'd done this before.

One held a small sledgehammer and the other an electric concrete cutoff saw, which was biting halfway into Sombat's thigh, just above his left knee. This wasn't a beating, it was a deadly serious interrogation.

Beyond that, Harvath had no idea who these guys were and he didn't care. Bringing his pistol to bear, he pressed his trigger and fired off two rounds in lightning-quick succession. The first round hit the man right between his eyebrows, killing him, while the second went directly through the bridge of his nose.

Before Harvath could refocus on the other assailant, Morrell had already fired four rounds. Two hit dead center mass, tearing through his heart, with the other two ripping through the suprasternal notch at the base of his neck, between his clavicles.

Just like Harvath's shot placement, the first round had been fatal. Everything thereafter was simply icing.

The bodies of the assailants dropped to the floor as Morrell rushed toward Sombat. He was only halfway across the loft when Harvath noticed movement at the rear of the apartment and yelled, "Gun!"

Before the third assailant could get a shot off, Harvath fired multiple rounds in his direction, forcing him to retreat from view.

He then took cover behind a concrete pillar, inserted a fresh magazine into his SIG, and glanced backward at Tommy Sombat. The blood was gushing from his leg.

Morrell had received the same combat-medicine training Harvath had. He knew that if he didn't get some sort of tourniquet on Tommy's leg, the man was going to bleed out.

But before they could give the man any medical attention, they needed to make sure that the threat had been neutralized. Where there was a third assailant, there could easily be a fourth, or even more.

This time, as Harvath had a better fix on where their target was, he gave the hand signals, instructing Morrell on how he wanted to attack.

He was about to conduct his own rapid countdown, when there was the sound of breaking glass, like a window had been shattered. The third assailant was trying to escape.

"I've got Tommy!" Morrell shouted. "Get that asshole."

The idea of chasing an unknown number of attackers through a darkened apartment didn't exactly fill Harvath with joy.

These weren't street thugs. They felt like operatives—either intelligence or military. They'd shown up at exactly the same time looking for exactly the same thing: answers from Tommy Sombat. Harvath didn't believe in coincidence. If these men were connected to the bombings, he needed to know how and why.

Readying his pistol, he took a deep breath, peeked around the edge of the pillar, and then charged after his quarry.

CHAPTER 14

Harvath chased the assailant into a back bedroom, where the man had thrown a chair through the window, climbed outside onto the roof, and taken off. Harvath took off right after him.

The rooftops of Bangkok were the city's armor against the elements—a sea of corrugated metal and aging water tanks punctuated by satellite dishes, vent pipes, and endless laundry lines strung at shoulder height.

The pungent air had that Bangkok mix of diesel and old cooking oil that drifted up from the kitchens. Underneath it all was the odor of the river that never seemed to fully disappear—regardless of the tides.

With every step, the metal roof flexed and popped under Harvath's weight. If he hit a weak enough spot and fell through, he had no doubt he'd be severely injured, maybe even dismembered, but he'd been left with no choice. Not if he wanted to catch this guy.

Twenty meters ahead and picking up speed, the man was widening the gap. Only occasionally did he glance over his shoulder to gauge the position of his pursuer.

Like his colleagues, the man was tall and fit, had a military haircut, and also appeared to be Chinese.

There was one other thing Harvath noticed about him—despite the slick surfaces, the crenelated parapets, and even the gaps between buildings, this guy was familiar with the route. *This team had an escape plan.* Which once again spoke to the assailants' professionalism.

Harvath, however, hadn't been on these rooftops before. Each one he crossed seemed to have been repaired by laying new panels over the old, which created raised lips, practically impossible to see in the dark. More than once, he caught the toe of his boot and almost went down.

But as close as he came to wiping out, he managed to retain his balance and repeatedly used the momentum to propel himself forward. He couldn't let the man out of his sight.

Whipping through laundry line after laundry line, he used his forearm to slash through the sheets, towels, and random articles of clothing. He could feel his lungs burning, his chest heaving for air. It was not exactly a great moment to figure out that as much jogging as he had been doing, he hadn't been doing enough sprints.

If he had to guess, the man he was chasing was at least ten, maybe fifteen years younger than him—and it showed. Willing himself to move even faster, Harvath increased his pace.

But increasing his speed meant increasing his risk, and that meant there was much less room for error. If he caught the toe of his boot again, or garroted himself on an unseen length of wire, the damage had the potential to be quite serious—potentially unrecoverable.

And if the assailant managed to escape, there was no telling what the fallout might be. Regrouping with his colleagues might be the least of their worries. The more Harvath had seen of these guys, the more his Spidey-senses were tingling and the more he wanted to know who they were *and* what the hell they were up to.

As that thought formed in his mind, he saw the man up ahead launch himself off the building and disappear from sight.

It wasn't until Harvath got to the edge of the roof that he realized what had happened.

They were at the end of the block. The man had leapt over the narrow street below to the next, lower, set of rooftops. *Big mistake*. He had just handed Harvath a huge opportunity.

Tired of chasing this guy, Harvath pulled out his pistol and, using the higher elevation to his advantage, fired.

With the third shot, which appeared to strike the man somewhere in his lower back, Harvath watched him fall face-first onto the roof.

The gunshots had caught the attention of the people down below, who, already unnerved by the bombings, screamed as they stampeded in a variety of directions.

After watching the man for a few more moments and not seeing any movement, Harvath judged the distance of the leap, backed up until he felt he had given himself enough runway, and then sprinted like he was being chased by a pack of rabid dogs.

At the edge of the roof, he launched himself into the air and sailed over the street below, before landing hard on the opposite roof, where he rolled in an effort to dissipate the force.

Somewhere in his clumsy ballet, he had caught something sharp, which tore through his shirt and opened a gash on his left side. There was no time, however, for a proper damage assessment.

Drawing his pistol and leaping to his feet, he spun to target the assailant, but the man had vanished.

In his place, all that was left was a faint trail of blood that led off toward a stairwell enclosure, beyond which were two large solar panels attached to a pair of hot water tanks.

Both locations provided concealment, as well as perfect spots to launch an ambush. But without better lighting, there was no telling where the man was hiding.

Creeping forward, his pistol up and at the ready, Harvath strained his ears for any sound of the assailant.

He followed the trail of blood as best he could until it disappeared behind the stairwell enclosure. The structure was nothing more than a flimsy box made from thin pieces of sheet metal. If the man was indeed hiding on the other side and if he decided to pull his own weapon and begin firing, Harvath was a sitting duck.

Glancing to the side, he saw a pile of discarded roofing tiles. Using his left hand, he reached down and picked one up. It wasn't terribly heavy, but it was going to be tough chucking it with the wound he had sustained to his left side. At this point, however, he didn't have much choice.

Twisting at the waist and drawing his left arm back as far as he could, he let the tile fly.

In the next moment, with his finger applying pressure to his trigger, he swung around the stairwell enclosure, prepared to engage the third assailant. But as the tile landed on the other side of the roof and shattered into a million pieces, he realized his would-be distraction was a waste. The man wasn't there.

Moving quickly to the hot water tanks, Harvath spun around them, ready to neutralize his target, but the man wasn't there either.

Before he could reacquire the blood trail and figure out what had happened, he heard a sound from the other side of the roof.

Turning, Harvath raised his pistol to fire just as he saw the man drop off the edge of the roof toward the sidewalk below. *Fuck.*

Charging after him, Harvath arrived at the parapet, which was covered in blood, and prepared to leap over it and give chase. But before he did, he risked a look over the edge to assess what would be breaking his fall. The moment he did, two bullets screamed right past his head.

The man he'd been chasing hadn't dropped all the way down to the street level. Just beneath the parapet was a narrow ledge where he now lay in a pool of blood. From somewhere in the distance, the sound of approaching police cars could be heard. Harvath was running out of time. He needed to make up his mind.

If he stuck his head above the parapet again, he could get it blown off. That said, the man had lost a ton of blood and the two shots he had taken, regardless of how well aimed, might have been the last thing he was capable of.

Harvath was weighing his odds when a barrage of gunfire erupted, tearing up the roof around him. For a moment, he thought another shooter—perhaps a fourth assailant—had entered the fray. But soon enough, he realized that the bullets were coming from underneath him. The man on the ledge was still very much alive.

Rolling away from the danger, Harvath returned fire. He emptied his magazine, inserted a fresh one, and fired five more rounds before pausing and trying to assess the situation. The only thing he was certain of was that the police were getting closer.

He waited as long as he dared. When no further gunfire was directed up at him, he changed position and risked another look over the parapet.

This time, he was not met with a hail of bullets. The man on the ledge, eyes open and unblinking, was definitely dead.

Keeping his pistol trained on him, Harvath climbed over the parapet and dropped down to search his pockets.

The man had no wallet, wasn't carrying a phone, and didn't have any pocket litter. Even the labels had been removed from his clothes. Aside from his Russian-made Grach pistol, there wasn't anything on his person that could be used to help identify him. At least that was what Harvath was thinking until he took a closer look at the man's watch.

Like the other two attackers back at Tommy Sombat's loft, this guy wasn't wearing any jewelry. No rings. No gold chains. None of the flashy stuff one might associate with underworld operatives. The watch, however, was something different.

The other assailants had been wearing similar watches—black and chunky, with thick bands made of rubber. And now that he saw this one up close, Harvath knew exactly what it was.

Crafted out of titanium and selling for over $20,000, the ruggedized Breitling "Emergency" watch was one of the most expensive adventure chronographs in the world.

But its price tag wasn't its most eye-popping feature. What made the watch so unique was its integrated antenna, miniaturized transmitter, and dual-frequency distress beacon.

After taking a picture of the man's face with his phone, he removed the watch, tucked it into his front pocket, and climbed back up to the roof.

He needed to get back to Morrell and Tommy Sombat before the cops flooded the neighborhood. But if history was any guide, Morrell had already taken off and Harvath had been left to fend for himself.

CHAPTER 15

Kevin Koebler had entered Thailand on a Dutch passport under the name of Frederik Rijneveld. The Rijneveld identity had been approved for an extended-stay "kickboxing" visa. The visa had been sponsored by a threadbare, down-on-its-luck gym in south central Bangkok called Khlong Kiat Muay Thai.

Classes were twice a day, six days a week, and included accommodations in decrepit, single or double dormitory-style rooms. If you paid up front and in cash, the owner didn't care what you did. Attendance wasn't taken and there were no "bed checks." Students were free to come and go as they pleased.

Even more to Koebler's liking, there were no security cameras. KKMT was the perfect bolt-hole.

Despite the loose rules, he had drifted in and out, showing up for the occasional class and spending enough time in his room to make his presence look believable.

When he wasn't in the ring or his rack, he was exploring the surrounding slums, dive bars, drug dens, and whorehouses of Khlong Toei.

It didn't take him long to pick up on the area's anti-establishment and particularly anti-cop sentiment. Pinned between the motorway and the river, he couldn't swing a bamboo cocktail umbrella without hitting someone who was either bent or on the make. Like his gym, if you paid in cash, you could get just about anything you wanted. And what Koebler wanted was invisibility.

He found it in a local landlord nicknamed "Mr. Baht," after the Thai currency. Mr. Baht specialized in go-go bars and nudie clubs. He also dabbled in some of the neighborhood's commercial real estate, such as tattoo parlors, storefronts, a handful of warehouses, and a little office space here and there.

The best thing Baht had going for him, at least as far as Koebler was concerned, was that the man was discreet. That, and the fact that he didn't care about background checks, credit worthiness, or formal lease agreements. Baht understood his customer base and had no illusions about what kind of service he was providing. As long as tenants paid on time, nothing else—within reason—mattered.

Without giving his name, Koebler explained what kind of space he was looking for. He would be creating "adult content" and needed an open floor plan and a private bathroom. The building also needed to be quiet, and he wanted his own private entrance; one that didn't have to be shared with other tenants.

Baht had a spot, not far from the docks. It was above a shuttered storefront. The "*farang*," as Westerners were referred to in Thailand, would be the building's only occupant. They agreed to a price and Koebler paid him for two months in advance.

"What should I call you?" Mr. Baht asked as he pocketed the money and handed over a set of keys.

"You can call me Ben," Koebler replied, peeling off five more U.S. hundred-dollar bills and handing them over, along with a list of items he wanted the landlord to source and have delivered.

Checking the list, Baht nodded. "What about models?"

"*Models?*"

"Yeah, you know—girls? Only the most beautiful. Very good price. Boys too. Maybe ladyboys? More expensive, especially for the beautiful ones. But still good price."

Koebler thanked the man and told him he already had everything taken care of. All he needed were the items on the list.

When he returned to the space two days later, everything that he had asked for was there. The mattress and sheets were in the middle of the front office; a small refrigerator, coffee maker, and microwave had been set up in the break room; towels and toiletries had been placed in the bathroom.

After installing a couple of his small Wi-Fi cameras to monitor for any intruders, Koebler changed the locks on the door and reinforced the windows. He had been clear with Baht that during his tenancy, he didn't want to be disturbed. At the price he was paying, he expected the landlord to honor his wishes. From what he could tell, no one had been anywhere near the space.

It was here, at his tertiary bolt-hole, that he had ultimately headed after the ambush at Teens. After making certain that he wasn't being followed, he wiped the data off his phone, disassembled it, and scattered the pieces. He then made his way to an internet gaming café on the other side of the river, where he traded a series of coded messages with his handler.

Matías was disturbed by what had happened. He told him to go to ground and he would reach back out once he'd worked his contacts and had more intel.

By the time the encrypted app on Koebler's new burner phone rang, three hours had passed. Matías had news. None of it was good.

Seated in his Bosques de las Lomas penthouse in western Mexico City, Matías cut to the chase. "One of my sources says Thai police recovered three of your wireless cameras near Teens."

"And?"

"They don't think it's a coincidence. Everything has been kicked upstairs to the Special Branch Bureau. ISOC has also stepped in."

While Special Branch was the intelligence division of the Royal Thai Police, Internal Security Operations Command, or ISOC for short, was part of the Royal Thai Armed Forces responsible for counterintelligence and counterinsurgency. Despite a PR makeover that aimed to make it appear more akin to the United States Department of Homeland Security, it had a fearsome reputation for ruthlessness.

"Why is ISOC involved?"

"Four of the bodies at Teens are suspected Cambodian nationals," Matías replied, texting him photographs of the corpses. "Recognize any of them?"

"I do," Koebler stated. "They were part of the team that attacked our meeting. Who are they?"

"We don't know yet."

"What happened to the rest of the attackers?"

"At the moment, that's not our problem," Matías replied, trying to focus the conversation.

"The hell it isn't. I need to know if I've been burned—and if so, how badly and by whom."

"You haven't been burned, but the temperature is definitely rising."

Koebler gripped his phone tighter. "Meaning?"

"*Meaning* hundreds of rounds fired at Teens, four dead Cambodians, and some very expensive hardware which, by the way, was still transmitting when the cops showed up. That's unlike you."

"Things deteriorated quickly. I had to improvise. How bad is it?"

"Special Branch and ISOC have already begun pulling CCTV and gathering witness statements. They're convinced the cameras are connected to the shooting. They're also investigating if what happened at Teens is in any way linked to the bombings."

"Not good!" Koebler exclaimed.

"Not good at all," Matías agreed. "And we should assume it's going to get worse."

"How much worse?"

"Every piece of security video from a four-block radius over the last twenty-four hours is being uploaded into one of the government's massive cloud servers. They'll compare it against all the footage they've gathered from the days leading up to and including the bombings. If they're able to put you in two or more places you shouldn't have been, that's it. Game over."

Knowing that the Thais had sophisticated surveillance systems, Koebler hadn't relied only on disguising his appearance. He'd also used crutches, a wheelchair, a knee walker, an electric scooter, a bike, and a motorcycle to defeat gait analysis. Even today—pain in the ass that it was—he'd alternated stones in one shoe, then the other. Unless there was some sort of new tech that no one had ever heard of, he was certain that he was in the clear.

But that brought up another issue.

"There was a camera inside Teens," he said. "Near the bar, by the storeroom door. It was hidden, but not well."

"I know," Matías replied.

"Tell me it wasn't recording."

"According to police, the DVR had been turned off. The clients wouldn't have wanted to be recorded any more than you did. Our problem remains what the Thai authorities can pull from outside CCTV."

"Don't worry," Koebler said. "They won't find any video that ties back to me."

"What about prints? On your cameras?"

He shook his head. "No. They're weatherproof. Nano-coated. They don't pick up fingerprints."

"Well unless you dropped your wallet at the scene," Matías responded, "you're bulletproof."

Koebler hadn't dropped his wallet.

But *bulletproof* knocked loose a thought that had been floating at the edge of his mind.

"You said *four* were Cambodians. How many other bodies were there?"

"Two more," Matías replied. "On the client's side."

Koebler's brain raced back to the operative at the door who had taken his pistol and had handed it off to a colleague. An unremarkable act—practically standard operating procedure considering the nature of the meeting. Now, however, everything had changed.

"Fuck," Koebler mumbled.

"What is it?"

"They patted me down when I walked in. Took my Glock."

Matías texted him a pair of additional crime scene photos. "Was it one of these guys?"

Koebler looked and felt the bottom drop out.

The second photo was the man who had accepted custody of his pistol. He was splayed on the floor, mouth slack, and jammed in his waistband was the Glock.

Thai authorities now had multiple pieces of evidence tying him to the scene.

CHAPTER 16

Harvath crossed another two blocks of rooftops, found a blind spot behind a water tank to climb down, and then circled back on street level toward Tommy Sombat's loft.

In the process, he stripped off his shirt, twisted it into a makeshift pressure bandage, and put on another shirt he had stolen along the way. It wasn't perfect, but it was enough to contain the bleeding and not draw attention.

By the time he got within sight of the building, the street was clogged with police cars and ambulances. If Morrell was still upstairs, he was screwed.

Harvath pulled out his phone and dialed Morrell's number. It went straight to voicemail. He hung up and tried again. Same result.

Changing direction, he walked back to where they'd parked the Land Cruiser. The spot was empty. *So much for Morrell.*

Harvath stepped off the curb and scanned the street, trying to orient himself. He needed distance from Tommy's building—and a clean route back to the safe house in Suan Phlu.

An earsplitting *chirp-chirp* exploded behind him.

Two motorcycle cops came hard through the knot of traffic, klaxons blaring, emergency lights flashing as they threaded between cars. Harvath sprang back onto the curb as the first bike knifed past, close enough for him to feel its wake. The second cop snapped his head to the side, eyes scanning Harvath, then gunned it to stay on his partner's tail.

They ripped up the street toward Sombat's and the thickening crowd. A few more minutes and all these cops were going to morph into a cordon—one that would be very hard to slip through.

He picked the darker side of the road and began moving. He needed to get out of this neighborhood as quickly as possible.

He had only made it about fifty meters when an engine growled somewhere to his left. Not a tuk-tuk. Not a taxi. Deeper. Throaty.

Whatever it was, it had its high beams on. Harvath raised his hand to shield his eyes but couldn't make out what kind of vehicle it was.

The heavy beast surged out of a dark side street—known as a *soi*—like it had been kicked loose. Its big tires hopped the broken edge of the pavement and a tornado of grit and pieces of gravel followed right behind as it came straight at him.

Harvath shifted, squaring his shoulders, ready to launch out of the way . . .

The SUV braked hard, its nose dipping. The driver's window was already down.

Morrell, who had blood on his clothes, leaned across the wheel and said, "Get in. *Now*."

Harvath came around the other side of the Land Cruiser, yanked open the door, and hauled himself inside.

Before he could even pull the door shut, Morrell was accelerating. "If your phone's on, kill it," he instructed. "There's a Faraday bag in the center console. Toss it in there with mine."

It was smart tradecraft and Harvath did it without argument. Just to be safe, he put the Breitling watch in there as well. They'd already spread enough digital breadcrumbs around. There was no reason to leave a trail heading back to the safe house.

"Are you hit?" he asked, looking at the blood.

Morrell shook his head as he turned hard at the next corner. "I tried to put a tourniquet on Tommy. He didn't make it. What about you? Are you hit?"

"No," Harvath replied. "Just a scratch. I'll live."

"What about the guy you were chasing?"

"He's dead."

"Get any information from him?"

Harvath shook his head. "No, just a photograph. I also grabbed his watch."

"His watch? What the hell for?"

"Because, given the circumstances, I thought a twenty-thousand-dollar timepiece was a little out of place on him."

"Twenty k? What was it? A Rolex?"

"No, a Breitling. And a super unique one at that. Comes equipped with an emergency locator beacon. I think the other two operators at Tommy's had them as well."

"*Operators?*" Morrell repeated. "You think these guys are state-sponsored?"

"I suppose they could've been private contractors, but that's not how the Chinese do business. I'm guessing they're Special Forces or on the intel side."

"Maybe."

"Speaking of Tommy," said Harvath, "I'm sorry he didn't make it."

Morrell paused a moment before responding. "He plied a rough trade. Not much of a margin for error in his business."

"How about you? Did Tommy give you anything?"

Seeing a pair of oncoming police vehicles, Morrell turned another corner—executing the move slowly so as not to appear suspicious. After checking to make sure they weren't being followed, he replied, "I didn't get much, but he did give me some information."

Harvath winced as he adjusted his makeshift pressure bandage. "Did he say who was responsible for the bombings?"

"No."

"Meaning he didn't know anything or he didn't want to tell you?"

"There was no reason for Tommy to lie to me," said Morrell.

"Why'd he disappear then?"

"The Thai cops were rounding up all the usual suspects—and they weren't being gentle about it either. Tommy went to ground hoping they'd nail the real culprits and it'd be safe for him to surface."

"But yet he did surface," Harvath replied. "Why?"

"Going dark and staying off the radar isn't cheap—especially in the aftermath of something like this. He needed cash and kept a lot of it hidden in his loft. If the cops showed up and took the place apart, he was worried that they might find it. So, he rolled the dice."

"And instead of cops, he came home to Mandarin and a concrete saw. If they were questioning him in Mandarin, somebody already knew he could answer. This was not a group of strangers."

Morrell nodded. "Tommy spoke a few languages. And you're right, they weren't strangers. According to him, they were clients."

"Apparently, clients who weren't too happy with his performance. Who the hell brings a saw to a meeting? That's Saudi-level brutality. Did he say what happened?"

Morrell's eyes flicked to his mirrors and then back to the road. "He didn't have much left. He was in and out, and the sirens were getting closer. I asked, but I only got one word."

Harvath looked at him. "What was it?"

"*Teens*."

CHAPTER 17

WASHINGTON, D.C.

The large silhouette on the other side of the front door had a disturbingly deep voice. "Ms. Delaney?" the man asked, pressing his credentials against the glass panel. "I'm Special Agent Mark Scofield from the Department of Homeland Security. I need to ask you a few questions, please."

Erin shot Connor a concerned look.

"Ignore him," Connor whispered.

"I can't ignore him," she replied. "If he saw me come home and I don't answer, he's going to suspect something is going on."

As if he could hear the conversation, the man knocked on the door once more and announced, "Ms. Delaney, I know you're home. Please open the door."

Even if she had wanted to sneak upstairs and pretend that she was asleep, or taking that bath she had been envisioning, she'd have to pass the front door to get to the stairs. If he was peering through the glass panel, he'd see her. There was nothing she could do. She had to comply.

"Stay here and be quiet," she said. This time, she was the one giving the orders. "I'll get rid of him."

Nodding, Connor removed his equipment from the dining room table and returned it all to his backpack.

Once everything was cleared, Erin pressed her finger to her lips one last time and exited the dining room.

In the vestibule, she turned to confirm that Connor wasn't visible.

Then, taking a breath to steady herself, she flipped on the overhead light and answered the door.

"Ms. Delaney?" the man asked, holding out his credentials for her to see. "I'm Special Agent—"

"Mark Scofield," she stated, reading the name on his ID, cutting him off. "What do you need?"

He looked past her, deeper into her house. "Do you mind if I come inside?"

"Agent Scofield, I haven't slept all night and am due at work in a few hours. So, if you don't mind, how can I help you?"

Returning his ID to his pocket, he removed a notepad and flipped it open. "Do you know a man named Connor Jameson?"

"Knew."

"Excuse me?" he replied.

Erin kept her right foot firmly planted behind the door, which she had only opened partway. "I *knew* a man named Connor Jameson," she answered. "Past tense. He was my fiancé. Why? What happened to him?"

"I really think we should discuss this inside."

"Agent Scofield, I am going to ask you one more time, politely, to please get to the point."

"Have you seen or heard from Mr. Jameson in the last twelve hours?"

"No. In fact, I haven't spoken to him in months."

"He hasn't called you? Texted? Nothing at all?"

"No, he hasn't. And whatever he's done," said Erin, preparing to close the door, "I don't care. Now, if you'll excuse me, I'm going to get some sleep."

"I don't think so," said the agent, putting his arm out and preventing her from closing the door.

"What the fuck are you doing?" she demanded, more pissed off than frightened. "I'm a member of the National Security staff."

The man smiled. "I know exactly who you are."

"Good. Because I'm going to have your ass. Now get the fuck away from my house."

"Not until I come inside and have a look around."

“No way in hell that’s going to—” she began, but before she could finish her sentence, he had burst into the foyer and snatched a fistful of her hair.

“Listen closely,” he warned. “If Jameson’s not here, you’ve got nothing to worry about.”

She knew it was a lie. She’d seen his face. He had no intention of letting her live. “Get the fuck off me,” she yelled, struggling to get away from him and to alert Connor at the same time.

As soon as she started to pull away, the man drew his pistol and placed the muzzle against her temple. Her nostrils flared at the pungent smell of gun oil.

“Move,” he commanded.

She shook her head, refusing to comply.

He twisted his hand, gripping her hair tighter, and forced her forward—toward the kitchen and just beyond it—to the dining room.

There was nothing she could do to slow him down. He was incredibly strong and was almost lifting her off the ground. If she had tried to break out of his grasp, she had no doubt it would have meant ripping out a piece of her scalp.

He searched the coat closet, the living room, and then the powder room. Entering the kitchen, he removed the gun just long enough to turn on a light and then put it back against her head—this time at the base of her skull.

Shifting her fully in front of him, he shoved her toward the last place on the ground floor he had left to check—right where Connor was hiding—the dining room.

They entered the space, but like everywhere else, it was empty. There was no sign of Connor. *Where the hell was he?*

Retracing their steps into the kitchen, Erin noticed something at the same time Scofield did—the back door was barely, almost imperceptibly, ajar. *Is that where Connor had gone? Had he fled? And if so, when? Before or after it was obvious the man was a threat and intended to harm her?*

She found it hard to believe that he would abandon her, but it made no difference now. Connor was gone, and whoever the man with the DHS credentials was, he was going to kill her.

Whether or not he'd make it quick and painless was little consolation. This was how her life was going to end.

She couldn't let it happen this way. Not without a fight. Even if he took her entire scalp, Erin Delaney was going to make this the most difficult murder the man had ever committed. But in order to do so, she needed a weapon.

As the man shoved her toward the back door, Erin was within inches of the bar cart. Hanging on a small display stand on top were a set of cocktail tools, including a garnish knife. Though she would have preferred an ice pick, she didn't have one. The oddly shaped knife would have to do, and she would have to make the absolute best of it. She was only going to get one chance.

Opening the door seemed like it would be that chance. He only had two hands, and in her mind, that meant he only had two options. Either he could let go of her hair or he could holster his weapon.

It was obvious that he suspected Connor was close, which seemed to mean that he would let go of her hair and use that hand to pull the door the rest of the way open. That's when she would make her move. But instead, he surprised her.

"Open it," he said, pushing her toward the door.

She felt so stupid. *Of course he would force her to do it. Why hadn't she seen that coming?*

Without him loosening his grip, there was no way she could grab the knife. And without the knife, there was no way she'd be able to escape.

There was, however, one thing she absolutely could do. When she opened the back door and they stepped into her tiny backyard, she could scream bloody murder.

Some of her neighbors would hear her. And all those who did would call the police. It might not save her life, but it would draw tons of attention. It would also throw one hell of a wrench into whatever else her captor had planned. Before that happened, though, there was one other thing she could do.

If Connor had indeed fled, she could buy him a little more time. Even if it was only a second or two, she felt she owed him that for having doubted him—for having used his PTSD as a reason not to believe him.

So, when Scofield punctuated his command by pushing her toward the door, she literally dug her heels in.

The beast of a man responded by shoving her forward so hard she thought her spine would snap if she continued to resist. That was when she kicked her left leg out in front of her and drove her foot into the partially open door, slamming it shut.

"You stupid bitch," he growled, cocking his right arm as if he intended to strike her across the back of her head with the weapon.

But right before he could bring the pistol crashing down, there was a voice from behind them in the kitchen.

Psssst.

Erin didn't need to see what was going on, nor did she need to be told what to do.

The moment Scofield let go of her hair, she dropped to the floor. That was when the shooting started.

With his pistol raised above his head, Scofield was already a dead man. Before he could spin fully around, identify the threat, and bring his weapon to bear, Connor had shot him five times.

The kitchen was rank with gun smoke, its back wall splattered with the man's blood, as Scofield's lifeless body fell to the floor.

With her ears ringing, Erin scrambled to get away from him.

"Are you okay?" Connor asked, loud enough for her to hear.

She nodded. "I thought you were in the dining room. Where the hell were you?"

"We can't talk now," he replied, helping her to her feet. "The cops will be here soon. We've got to move."

"I'm sorry I didn't believe you."

She had blood across her face and in her hair. Grabbing a towel near the sink, he moistened it and wiped away as much as he could.

"That'll have to do. Where are your shoes?"

"At the front door."

Bending down, Connor fished Scofield's credentials from his jacket. Pocketing the photo ID, he tossed the badge and wallet aside.

"Let's go," he said, taking her hand and leading her toward the foyer.

"My phone," she responded. "It's in the dining room."

"Leave it. We can't afford to take it with us. Whoever these people are, we can't give them any advantage."

"Where are we going?"

Slinging his backpack, he stated, "I know a place. It's a long shot, but if we can get there without anyone seeing us, we might be safe. We need to move, though, now."

CHAPTER 18

BANGKOK

When's the last time you had a tetanus shot?" Staelin asked, stripping open a dressing and going to work on Harvath's wound.

They were sitting at the banged-up kitchen table of their CIA safe house, just off Sathorn Soi in the Suan Phlu area. They were tucked away on a quiet street, three klicks from the U.S. Embassy, with Lumphini Park in between.

"Got all my shots before my honeymoon," he replied.

"For Sølvi's sake," Haney interjected, pulling a Singha beer from the fridge, "I hope it included penicillin."

With his left hand behind his head so Staelin could access his injury, Harvath raised his other hand and flipped him off.

His eyes then shifted to Morrell, who was fingering the seam on the Faraday bag.

"You're not going to open that thing here, are you?"

The CIA man shook his head. "We've got an RF-shielded cage at the embassy. I think one of our tech people should take it apart. That way, if the beacon gets triggered, the signal won't go anywhere. In the meantime, do you have a burner phone you can use?"

"Mike?" Harvath inquired.

"On it," said Haney, setting his beer down and retreating to the bedroom where their gear was stored.

"So who the hell were those guys at Tommy Sombat's?" he continued.

"Based on everything we saw, plus the Mandarin? Could be some sort of PLA unit, but the more I think about it, the more I'm leaning toward Chinese intelligence."

"What would Chinese intelligence want with a guy like Tommy?"

"Probably the same stuff the CIA does," Morrell admitted.

"Enough to cut him into pieces?"

"The Chinese don't fuck around. If Tommy screwed them badly enough, who knows how they might respond."

Harvath thought about that for a moment. "What about the word he gave you? Any idea what it means?"

"There's a bar near Chinatown called Teens."

"Did Tommy hang out there?"

Morrell shrugged. "Tommy was like mold. He was all over Bangkok."

"Is there anything else he might have been referring to? Prostitution? Sex trafficking?"

"I suppose. But why would you use your dying breath to cough up some nonsense word?"

Harvath knew people lied all the time, even with their dying breath. Tommy Sombat didn't seem like the type of guy that merited much benefit of the doubt.

He also knew that Morrell had been around the block enough times to have a similar opinion. "What's your gut tell you?"

The CIA man didn't take long formulating his response. "If a couple of guys had just tortured me with a ball-peen hammer and a concrete saw, I'd want to fuck them in the ass as hard as I could. No mercy. And absolutely zero lube. But that's me."

It definitely was him, all right, and Harvath was once again reminded of Morrell's penchant for colorful scene setting. He wasn't wrong, however.

Tommy Sombat had no obvious reason to take his killers' identities to the grave. If he could out them as a final *fuck you* and get some modicum of justice, even posthumously, why not?

As far as Harvath was concerned, this was a textbook situation where Occam's razor should be applied. Unless and until they could come up with a better explanation, they'd take the most obvious route. What's more, any chance to screw with the Chinese, and possibly disrupt an ongoing operation, was always good by him.

"Is Teens a locals-only spot?" he asked. "Or do they have enough Western patrons that we'd blend in?"

"They get plenty of *farangs* in there. We'd be okay."

Harvath looked at his watch. "In that case, let's get our act together. I want to be wheels-up in fifteen."

CHAPTER 19

After having his wound closed with Dermabond, though Haney had been egging Staelin on to use staples, Harvath changed clothes, made sure his new phone was fully charged, and gathered up the rest of his gear.

By the time they arrived at Morrell's apartment, a CIA team from the embassy was already there to pick up the Faraday bag. Once the handoff had occurred, it took him less than five minutes to clean up and change before they were back on the road.

From Morrell's, it was about four and a half kilometers to Teens. As they drove, Haney used his laptop to pull up satellite imagery of the neighborhood. Harvath had no idea what they were walking into. If things went south, as they had at Tommy's, he wanted to know what all their options were.

The Land Cruiser made for a shitty mobile command post. Unless you were sitting right behind or right next to Haney, he had to pass the laptop around so everyone could see the different spots he was calling out. The team members then had to verify the locations on their own mobile phones, confirming they were all on the same page.

Three blocks up from Teens, Morrell pulled over and dropped off Ashby and Palmer. They'd be coming the rest of the way on foot.

With a block left to go, the CIA man found a parking space and pulled over. He left the key fob in the driver's cupholder and hopped out to join Harvath on the sidewalk. Staelin and Haney would stay with the vehicle and act as a quick reaction force if needed.

Harvath and Morrell crossed to the opposite side of the cracked street and started walking toward Teens. But the closer they got, the more police and technical services vehicles they saw.

"What's going on?" Harvath asked.

"No clue," Morrell responded.

Soon enough, they could see that a cordon, complete with crime scene tape, had been established outside the bar's entrance. It was being enforced by a quartet of uniformed Thai police officers toting automatic weapons. Whatever this was, it was serious.

Up ahead was a passageway that led deeper into the buildings behind Teens. Morrell gave Harvath a signal and they veered off into it. At multiple points, it was so narrow that either man could have touched the walls on both sides without ever fully extending his arms.

Harvath hated spaces like this. They were death traps. If anyone started shooting at them, the walls would funnel the bullets right at them. The sooner they were out of there, the better.

The passageway snaked along and branched off into other passageways, maze-like. Morrell, to his credit, kept them advancing toward the back side of Teens.

They knew they had arrived at the right spot when they turned a corner and came upon an army of crime scene technicians, bright work lights mounted upon telescoping stands, and even more cops than there had been in front.

Mixed among them were a bunch of plainclothes, who Harvath figured were detectives. One of them was a fit, very attractive, dark-haired woman in her late thirties. As soon as she noticed them, however, the expression on her face hardened.

Harvath was about to ask what her problem was when she began walking in their direction and Morrell uttered, "Oh shit."

"Friend of yours?"

"*Was*," the CIA man replied. "We should get out of here."

"We just got here."

"Trust me. You do not want to—"

"Richard Morrell," the woman said, quickly closing the distance. "Why am I not surprised?"

Harvath suppressed a grin and kept his voice low. "She is definitely not a fan of yours."

"I'm a bit of an acquired taste."

"So is horse meat. What'd you do to piss her off?"

"It's a long story."

"It always is with you."

"Just keep your mouth shut," he said. "And let me do the talking."

"This'll be fun," Harvath replied, taking a step away from his colleague. Whoever this woman was, she was coming in hot.

As she walked up to him, Morrell took a stab at being charming. "Hello, Davi," he said, attempting a smile. "You look good."

"Don't start with me," she replied. "What are you doing here?"

"My friend was in the mood for a gin and tonic, so I thought we'd—"

She cut him off. "Under the internal security act, I could have you taken in for questioning right now. It could be weeks, if not months, before you were brought in front of a magistrate. So, when I say don't start with me, *don't* start with me. Now, one more time, what are you doing here?"

"We heard that something went down at Teens, and so we came to check it out."

"Heard from who?"

"Come on," he said. "Look at all these cops. The word's all over the street."

"Things happen every day in Chinatown," she responded. "Yet I don't recall anyone from your embassy ever showing up to check them out. That tells me something."

Morrell held her gaze. "A lot of Americans died in those bombings. What it should tell you, is that we're paying attention. To *everything*."

It was an excellent response. Even Harvath had to hand it to him. It not only summed up the current situation in Bangkok, but also suggested the U.S. had its finger on the pulse and was aware of a lot more than it was letting on.

"Now," Morrell continued, "ISOC wouldn't be involved in an investigation in Chinatown unless it was in the national interest. And right now, the most pressing interest for Thailand is figuring out who was behind the attacks. So, what do you have?"

"Fair enough," the woman responded, before pointing at Harvath. "But first, who's he? Besides being someone who likes gin and tonic."

"I'm more of a bourbon man, to be honest."

Morrell shot him a look and then answered the woman's question. "His name is Harvath. He's a liaison."

The woman cocked an eyebrow. "What kind of *liaison*?"

"The kind who doesn't like to talk about his job in front of people he's never met."

Extending her hand to Harvath, she stated, "Davika Rattanprasert. Internal Security Operations Command."

"Scot Harvath," he replied, shaking her hand.

Rattanprasert raised her eyebrow again and waited. When Harvath didn't extend any further explanation as to who he was, she turned back to Morrell. "I'm not going to find him on a list of embassy personnel, am I?"

"I think a couple of guys have him in their fantasy football league," the CIA man responded.

"So, he's a NOC?" she asked, referring to intelligence officers that operated with official embassy cover.

"What I can tell you is that he's here to help, and he's good at his job. He was sent because Washington wanted its best people assisting Bangkok."

"Mr. Harvath," she began.

"Scot," Harvath offered, trying to warm her up.

"Mr. Harvath," she continued, "because of your proximity to Richard, I can only imagine what line of work you're in. To that end, let me make something very clear to you. You're not in the United States. You're in Thailand. And this isn't Dodge City or Tombstone. This is Bangkok. You respect our laws, or you will suffer the consequences. Is that clear?"

"Crystal," Harvath responded.

"Good," the woman said, tilting her head toward Teens. "They're almost finished processing the crime scene. Once they're packed up, I can walk you through and give you a briefing myself."

CHAPTER 20

It's obviously bad," Harvath said to Morrell once Rattanprasert was out of earshot, "but what's your history with her?"

"We dated."

Harvath had figured as much. "Does the chief of station know?"

Morrell nodded. "His wife introduced us."

"You've got to be kidding me."

"Wish I was."

Harvath looked at him. "So why does she hate your guts?"

"It didn't end well."

"I bet that happens to you a lot."

Discreetly flipping him the bird, the CIA man suggested, "Why don't you text the team and have them stand down? We may be here for a bit."

It was a good idea. Sliding his phone from his pocket, he sent a message to their encrypted chat and let everybody know he'd text them again once they were on their way out.

Once they'd all confirmed, he turned back to Morrell. "Why'd you two break up?"

"I don't want to talk about it."

"You're the one who chose to go fishing off the diplomatic pier. I just want to know if she can be trusted."

"You can trust her," the CIA man replied.

"Really?" Harvath responded. "I don't even trust *you.*"

Morrell chuckled. "Jesus, you really can hold a grudge."

"They keep me warm. They've also done a good job keeping me alive.

You know what's also helped keep me alive? Working with people who tell me the truth. Why'd you end it with her?"

"What are we, in therapy now?"

"Joke around all you want, Rick, but I'm not dropping this. You were sleeping with a foreign national—from your host country, no less. On top of that, you did something to piss her off. I need to know, so I can balance whatever intel we get from her."

"*If* we get any intel from her," Morrell clarified.

"I'm not kidding around here. And believe me, learning about your private life is even more painful for me than it is for you."

"I doubt that."

Harvath shook his head. "Would you man up already?"

"Fine," Morrell confessed. "You want to know why it ended? It ended because I OD'd."

"You what?"

"You heard me. Don't make me repeat it."

"Wow. I knew you could be a heavy drinker, but I had no idea you were into drugs. You really went *full* Bangkok, didn't you? What was it? Meth? Heroin? Opium?"

"Shut the fuck up, Harvath," said Morrell, lowering his voice. "I didn't OD on street drugs. I OD'd on Viagra."

Harvath's eyes went wide. "You can OD on Viagra?"

The CIA man nodded. "It's rare, but I had a heart attack."

"How much did you take?"

"None of your damn business."

"Touchy. Okay. I was just asking."

"Well, you're now done asking," said Morrell. "Understand?"

"Not quite," Harvath replied. "Where'd you get it? Some black-market source? Was it Tommy Sombat? Did he sell you knockoff Viagra?"

"No, it wasn't from Tommy. It was legit Viagra that I got via prescription from a legit doctor."

"Do the doctors here not put dosing instructions on the label?"

"Everything's on the label," Morrell admitted. "It's even in English. I just took too many."

"You'd have to have taken *a lot* too many," said Harvath, his voice trailing off as he looked over at Davi, who was talking with the crime scene technicians. Suddenly, everything fell into place and he smiled. "We're going to have to give you a new nickname."

"What are you talking about?"

"Rick 'The Prick' *hardly* seems appropriate anymore."

"Fuck you, Harvath."

"Kind of an empty threat, all things considered, don't you think?"

"I swear to God, I will kill you."

"Relax, I'm just busting your balls."

"One more dick joke," Morrell warned, "and I'll shoot you right here in front of everyone. I don't care if I have to spend the rest of my life in a Thai prison."

"You should care. I don't think the term 'hard ass' means the same thing to them that it does to us."

"That's it," Morrell growled, his patience all but gone.

"A, that wasn't a dick joke, and B, I'm done."

"You think this is funny, but just you wait. I know about the age gap between you and your wife. We'll see how many jokes you're making in a few years."

Harvath shook his head. "My God, you are touchy. So that's it? You had a heart attack and broke it off?"

"Can you blame me? It was embarrassing. I couldn't keep up with her. Guys think it'd be so cool to date a younger woman, but they have no idea how much work it is."

Harvath felt no sympathy for the man. He'd always been a shallow asshole, and it didn't surprise him at all that Morrell's relationship had revolved solely around sex. "Did you even tell her?" he asked.

"What? About the heart attack? Hell no."

"Didn't she wonder what had happened to you?"

Morrell shrugged. "I told her I had to head out of the country for a while and I just laid low."

"Told her or *texted* her?"

"Texted."

"And then what?"

"Six weeks later, when I was fully back on my feet, we met for a drink, and I told her I couldn't see her anymore."

"That's it?" Harvath asked.

"That's it," Morrell replied.

"What about Langley? They just rubber-stamped you for fieldwork again. That's not normally how these things shake out."

"My station chief took care of everything. As far as the CIA is concerned, I had my ACL repaired. They left it up to him to clear me to go back into the field."

"And he dummied up your medical records just because you're a great guy?"

Morrell paused, waiting for Harvath to figure out this one as well. He didn't have to wait long.

"Your station chief never fed it up the chain? Never reported that you and Davi were dating?"

"Nope."

Harvath had worked with some CIA stations that had played fast and loose with the rules, but Bangkok Station appeared to be operating in some rarefied air. Nevertheless, this wasn't his circus and therefore Morrell and his colleagues weren't his monkeys. He wasn't a big believer in process either, and so, he decided to let it go.

"By the way," the CIA man continued, "I'd appreciate it if you kept this chat between us. Don't say anything to Davi. Okay?"

Harvath wasn't quite sure if Morrell was trying to protect his ego or Davi's feelings. If he were charitable, he'd suspect it was the latter. That said, there was a tinge of something in the CIA man's voice that he hadn't heard before. It sounded a lot like *humanity*.

Harvath was a gentleman and never would have said anything to upset Davi or to make her feel uncomfortable. He also appreciated that it couldn't have been easy for Morrell to make that admission. Taking a breath, he nodded, acknowledging that Morrell's secret was safe with him.

Just then, the last of the forensic specialists walked out of Teens, and Davi waved Harvath and Morrell over. They were about to learn what Tommy Sombat had spent his last breath trying to say.

CHAPTER 21

Over the course of his career, Harvath had been to his share of crime scenes. This one looked no different.

Yellow plastic evidence markers, each with its own number, indicated where shell casings had fallen. The bodies of the dead had been outlined in chalk before being carted off to Bangkok's "City Morgue," which was used for foreign nationals and cases involving the Royal Thai Police.

"Feel free to take a look around before we start," said Davi, as she sat down at a wooden table in the center of the storeroom and opened her laptop.

Harvath and Morrell did just that. The damage to the space was substantial. It was amazing how many bullet holes there were.

Bending down, Harvath examined the variety of shell casings littered across the floor.

"What do you see?" Morrell asked as he picked at a bullet lodged in the wall.

"Nine-millimeter, 5.56, and 7.62," said Harvath.

"Pretty standard stuff."

"True, but this is like a drive-by shooting on crack. There were hundreds of rounds fired in here."

"Correct," said Davi. "Based on the witness statements we've gathered and the pockmarking on the walls, there were semi and full auto bursts."

"How hard are weapons like that to find in Bangkok?" Harvath asked.

"It's difficult, but not impossible," said Davi. "You just need to know the right person to ask."

"Tell me about the bodies," said Morrell, as he walked over to the table, his examination of the room complete.

Harvath joined him.

The ISOC operative pulled up a series of photos. "We have identified these four here as Cambodians. We believe the other two are Chinese."

Harvath and Morrell shot each other a knowing glance.

"How do you know those four are Cambodian?" Harvath asked.

Davi pulled up a second set of photographs. "Each of them was carrying one of these."

Harvath peered at the monitor. On it were pieces of what looked like knotted cord. "What is that?" he asked.

"*Ksae sin*," she replied. "Also known as 'blessed cord.' It's a type of good luck charm. Like the Thai, Cambodians are very superstitious. They believe the cords will protect them from harm and misfortune while delivering health and good luck."

"Even in a gunfight?"

She nodded. "Especially in a gunfight."

"If Thai people carry them too, how can you be sure those four were Cambodian?"

"Because of the colors and types of knots," Morrell interjected, familiar with the custom. "They represent different temples or monasteries."

"Like some kind of Buddhist GPS?"

"In a way."

Harvath turned back to Davi. "Is that all you got on them? No phones? No wallets? No IDs whatsoever?"

"None. Just the cords."

"So, they were comfortable enough self-identifying as Cambodian, just not anything beyond that. Why?"

"If I had to guess," said Morrell, "it's because they were pros. And they knew that if their employer was revealed, it would stir up a shitstorm."

Having tentatively concluded that the men at Tommy's were Chinese Intelligence operatives, Harvath couldn't help but wonder if maybe the dead Cambodians were also intel operatives. Why they would be mixing it up, in Thailand of all places, was beyond him. "Can you go back and focus on the two you believe were Chinese?" he asked.

Davi nodded and pulled up the photos. "What are we looking for?"

Harvath had to be careful. If the men were in fact Chinese and they were somehow connected to the dead men at Tommy's, he didn't want to blow up the one lead he and Morrell had.

"I don't know," he said. "Any cell phones on these guys? Wallets? ID?"

The ISOC operative shook her head.

"Nothing?" Harvath pressed. "No tattoos? Nothing? How about blessed cords or any other kind of jewelry?"

He didn't want to ask what kind of watches they may or may not have been wearing. If the men at Tommy's had the same Breitling as the man Harvath had killed on the roof, and if that information made it back to Davi, she might get suspicious and tie Harvath and Morrell to what had happened. It wasn't worth the risk. They didn't need that kind of hassle right now.

Changing the subject, he asked Davi to slowly run him through each photo, pausing to zoom in at different spots.

Finally, he said, "So no personal effects beyond the weapons they were found with and the clothes they had on."

"Correct," she replied. "Each man carried a few thousand baht, but that was it. Nothing else."

"Like I said," Morrell added, "professional hitters."

Harvath nodded. "Both groups. But what were they doing here and what kicked off the bullet stampede?"

"Based on the ropes and the shattered skylights, not to mention the battered door leading in from the bar, I'd say somebody crashed somebody else's party."

Harvath agreed. Turning back to Davi, he asked, "What do you and your colleagues think happened? Is this somehow connected to the bombings?"

"We agree that there's a high degree of professionalism here. In several strategic locations outside, we found three high-end remote cameras that we think were being used for some sort of surveillance of the building."

"Have you been able to gather any information from them?"

"They're locked down with very sophisticated software. It's going to take our tech people a while. We're not holding out a lot of hope. But back to your question, based on this happening so soon after the bombings, we're staying open to the possibility that the events are connected. There's no evidence at the moment, however, linking them."

"What about staff from Teens?" Harvath asked. "Somebody had to know people were using the building."

"There was an uncle," Davi began. "That's what we call an older person who does odd jobs, cleans up, that sort of stuff. Police found him in the bar area when they arrived. He had multiple gunshot wounds, likely from all the rounds flying through the walls. He was unresponsive and died before the first ambulance arrived."

"Anyone else?"

"Police have spoken with the bar owner and his staff. No one has any idea who was here, nor why anyone would be here outside of business hours."

"This uncle," Harvath said. "Was he married? Did he have any family?"

Davi shook her head. "Dead end. No next of kin."

Harvath was running out of ideas and asked to see photos of the weapons that had been recovered.

There was a little bit of everything—Russian, Chinese, American, and even Indonesian firearms. What was most striking, however, was that there was only one Glock—the most popular and most common handgun in the world.

"The dead Chinese guy there," said Harvath, pointing at the man's picture on the screen. "He has a Glock in his waistband."

Davi enlarged the image and then created a split screen, pulling up an additional evidence photo of the pistol itself.

"Correct," she replied. "Glock 19."

"He and his partner, the other dead Chinese guy, they were both carrying the same kind of PDW, right?"

"Yes, they were. Russian-made KBP PP-2000s."

"And on top of that," Harvath continued, "each of them had the same sidearm. Russian-made Grachs."

It wasn't lost on him that the man he had chased across the rooftops had also been carrying a Grach. And even though he hadn't bothered to ask Morrell if the two guys torturing Tommy Sombat had been carrying weapons, if they had, he was willing to bet they'd also been Grachs.

"Again, correct," said Davi. "Grach MP-443s in nine-millimeter."

"So why does this guy here also have a Glock 19? And why does he have it carelessly tucked in the front of his pants like an idiot, while he and his partner carried their Grachs in holsters on their belts?"

"Excellent questions."

"How about spare magazines? Was he carrying any specifically for the Glock? Did the evidence techs find any on scene?"

After clicking through several reports, she looked back up and said, "No, he wasn't carrying any spare Glock magazines. Also, the weapon was fully loaded when they pulled it from his waistband. It had recently been cleaned and didn't appear to have been fired."

"Has it been processed for prints yet?"

"Let me check," said Davi, as she pulled out her phone and dialed a number.

As she did, Morrell looked at him and asked, "What are you thinking?"

"I think I'd like to know who that Glock belongs to."

CHAPTER 22

At the top of the list of rules Koebler operated by was to never know who the client was. That was his handler's job. Matías was his firewall.

By not knowing the client's identity, he was spared any speculation over their politics, motivation, or ultimate endgame.

There was also a degree of mutual security. He didn't know who the client was and the client didn't know him. If ever placed under duress, he couldn't be forced to give up a name he didn't have. Conversely, without a name, there was no reason for a client to see him as a loose end.

He had bent that rule and had almost gotten himself killed. That was not a mistake he planned to make again.

Per Matías, the attackers at Teens had been Cambodian and, from what he had observed, his clients appeared to be Chinese. Both sides were professional and well trained. They were disciplined and, while not at the level of American Special Forces, they knew what to do in a firefight. They weren't muscle from rival organized crime groups.

These were state actors, which meant current military, or former military who were now on the intelligence side.

The most overwhelming fact was that the Cambodians had come in hard. They weren't there to capture his Chinese clients. They had been there to kill them—and had appeared perfectly fine with killing him too. Only the Cambodians had been meant to walk out of Teens alive.

That kind of speed and overwhelming violence of action suggested an exceedingly short timeline. Whatever the Cambodians were up to, they needed it done fast. Which, considering that Cambodia was China's closest regional ally, didn't make much sense at all. If these guys were military or intel operatives, why would they be going head-to-head, and why in Thailand of all places?

Then Koebler had opened the envelope the client had given him. After a quick internet search of the target, everything began to make sense. He not only had a better picture of what his clients were trying to do, but he also understood why the Cambodians were prepared to go to any length to stop them.

This, however, was all background noise. He neither cared nor wanted to know what his clients and their adversaries hoped to achieve. The only thing he cared about was his fee. And the fee for this next assignment was significant—double what the last job paid.

But once it was complete, he was done. All the crypto in the world was worthless if you weren't alive and free to spend it. No matter what the client offered, he was leaving Thailand. In fact, he was starting to think about taking a long-overdue vacation. Someplace safe, where he could live quietly and let the heat die down.

He was about to have enough money to disappear. In fact, depending on where he decided to put down stakes, he could live very well for the rest of his life. But he understood that the road between here and there was potentially deadly and fraught with an incredible amount of peril.

Complicating matters was the fact that in addition to the Thai authorities having his Glock and three of his cameras, the Cambodians—at least the ones who had survived the attack at Teens—had seen his face.

He doubted that either group could put two and two together and track him down before he fled the country, but he was experienced enough not to take anything for granted. He needed to act both quickly and carefully.

The "quickly" part was what bothered him the most. When you moved too fast, that was when mistakes happened. They also happened when there were too many elements outside your control.

For the original round of bombs, Matías had sourced the ingredients. This time, however, the client claimed to have assembled "everything you will need" and left it in a storage unit. Koebler was to build the bomb on-site and then transport it to the target, where he would hand it off to an intermediary.

With each step, there were over a thousand things that could go wrong—not the least of which being that the client might be setting him up. But to what end?

It was a logical question, but one that he couldn't answer. Had the client truly considered him a liability, they could have already done away with him. There was no reason to keep paying him and stringing things out. The bottom line was that they wanted a very specific type of bomb, they wanted it within twenty-four hours, and they were willing to pay double. As the saying went—*Good, fast, or cheap. Pick any two.*

He doubted they could have found anyone else who could deliver what they needed on the clock they'd set. He was their only option.

Being their only option, however, didn't mean he was going to let his guard down. Not for a moment.

After running a long surveillance detection route, he seeded the area with several of his wireless surveillance cameras, parked himself at a plastic patio table of a late-night noodle shop, and monitored the storage facility.

Across the street, under the lights of an illuminated tuk-tuk stand, a group of drivers smoked and played cards. From the distance came the hum of traffic on the elevated expressway.

Koebler studied everyone and everything that came and went. He was looking for anything that seemed out of place, but this was Bangkok. There was no "normal" here. Everything was loud and frenetic, bright and slightly unusual—a constant assault on the senses. Finding what didn't fit meant filtering out almost everything. It was hard to get a baseline.

Finally, after enough time had passed and nothing repeated or converged, he decided it was as clean as it was going to get. Having paid his bill, he stood up and walked slowly to the storage facility, collecting his cameras as he went.

In the envelope the client had given him, there had been an electronic key card. He pulled on a pair of latex gloves, pressed the card against the reader, and opened a service gate. The unit he was looking for was in the back—one with direct exterior access.

Even though he was once again disguised, he took pains to avoid letting the storage facility's CCTV cameras get a good look at him. Whenever he found a dead spot without coverage, he placed one of his own cameras.

Upon locating the unit, he entered the code he'd been given, removed the padlock, and lifted the steel roll-up door.

After slipping underneath, he lowered the door back down, locked it from inside, and removed a flashlight from his pocket.

It was hot and muggy inside the unit—not exactly the perfect working environment. Activating his light, he looked around.

There was a workbench complete with task lighting and a magnifying lens on an articulating arm. Alongside it were multiple cardboard boxes and hard-sided cases filled with tools, bombmaking components, and other specialized equipment. His clients had indeed thought of—and provided—everything he needed.

The most interesting piece of gear, however, was underneath a grease-stained canvas tarp. Peeling it back, he stared at what had been left for him. Immediately, Koebler understood how they expected him to get so close.

And why no one in the world was going to stop him.

CHAPTER 23

When Davi completed her phone call and let Harvath and Morrell know that the Glock was still being processed, there wasn't much else the two men could do at Teens.

Recalling the team, they met up with Staelin and Haney down the block and all drove back to the safe house. As they pulled up, Morrell's cell phone chimed.

The CIA man read the text message and then looked at Harvath. "Our tech guys think they have something on the watch you recovered. Want to swing by the embassy with me?"

Harvath nodded, and after dropping off their colleagues, they headed back out.

Looping around Lumphini Park, they made a left onto Wireless Road, so named for having been home to the country's first wireless telegraph and radio station. The irony wasn't lost on Harvath as they were on their way to learn more about a Breitling with an emergency radio beacon.

The U.S. Embassy sat upon eleven acres at number 95, Wireless Road. It was the fourth largest U.S. diplomatic mission in the world—and for good reason.

Thailand was a major non-NATO ally. Its geography made it ideal for monitoring China, Myanmar, Laos, Cambodia, and Vietnam, as well as the Gulf of Thailand and the Andaman Sea. Historically, it had been a fallback and transit hub during the Vietnam War and had subsequently never lost that role.

Because of its importance, the CIA, DIA, NSA, and other critical U.S. agencies operated regional desks out of the embassy. In addition to coordinating military cooperation, training, and arms sales, they also handled intelligence sharing and joint planning across the Indo-Pacific.

Simply put, the U.S. Embassy Bangkok was enormous because it functioned less like a normal embassy and more like a headquarters for U.S. power in mainland Southeast Asia. It was big because the job was big.

After clearing security and parking the Land Cruiser, they proceeded to a highly secure area within the newly completed New Office Annex building, or as embassy staff referred to it—the NOX.

Despite being after 9 p.m., the CIA's science and technology department was still buzzing with activity. Ever since the bombings, they had been operating around the clock, aiding the FBI teams who were bagging and tagging evidence from the attack sites.

Morrell led Harvath to a small lab crammed with electronics equipment, the centerpiece of which was the aforementioned RF (radio frequency) cage.

Inside were two men in their mid-twenties. One was wearing jeans, a Randy Watson tee, and canvas Converse. The other had on cargo pants, vintage Air Jordans, and a denim shirt with the sleeves rolled up. Along with their messy haircuts, patchy beards, and slim builds, they looked more like a pair of Silicon Valley coders than CIA tech specialists.

Knocking on the outer glass window, Morrell opened the door, not waiting to be invited in. Harvath followed behind him.

Looking up from the table where they were working, the man in the T-shirt said, "Sorry, Morrell. The exploding vibrator you ordered won't be ready until next week."

"Very funny," Morrell replied. "Scot Harvath, meet KitKat and Mo."

"If you're here to intimidate us," the other man said to Harvath, "we already told him we're not selling any urine to help him pass his next drug test."

Harvath chuckled. "Wow. You can't kick over a single rock in Thailand without coming across your fans."

Morrell rolled his eyes. "Yeah. I only attract the best people."

"KitKat and Mo?" Harvath continued, nodding at the techs. "Are those call signs?"

"No. I call this one KitKat," Morrell replied, pointing at the man in the T-shirt, "because he's always on break. And this one," he said, pointing at the man with the Air Jordans, "Mo, which is short for Motion Light, because he only works when someone walks by."

Harvath shook his head and laughed once again. Morrell was definitely not going to be named coworker of the month anytime soon.

Looking at the two men, Morrell said, "You texted me something about a breakthrough on the watch?"

The man named KitKat opened a folder on his table and pretended to read from a list. "Exploding vibrator. Switchblade nipple clamps. Fifty-caliber butt plug. I don't see anything about a watch. What about you, Mo?"

Opening his own folder, the other man looked down and stated, "Bulletproof biker vest with matching chaps, spiked leather dog collar with integrated digital camera, flashbang ball gag . . ." His voice trailed off. Then, after flipping the page over, he said, "Yes. Hold on. Here it is. We did receive a Breitling chronograph watch. Emergency edition. Rush analysis for one Richard 'Blister' Morrell."

"*Blister?*" Harvath repeated.

"That's what we call him," said KitKat. "Because he only shows up after the hard work is done."

"Again, very funny," the CIA man replied. "Are you finished?"

"For the record, I voted for calling you G-spot," said Mo, "since nobody can ever find you."

Harvath liked these guys. It was good to see that they weren't afraid to give it to an older operative with both barrels.

"*Now* are we done?"

Laughing, KitKat and Mo stood up and waved their visitors into the RF cage. Harvath and Morrell followed. On a workbench inside was the watch. Next to it was a detailed schematic that the tech team had downloaded from Breitling.

After closing the cage door behind them, KitKat walked over to the workbench, picked up the watch, and said, "Professional-grade, emergency locator beacon watch. Fifty-one-millimeter case. Standard replaceable battery for the watch movement lasting two to three years, rechargeable lithium-ion battery for the distress beacon, lasting anywhere from eighteen to twenty-four hours depending on ambient air temperature.

"Beneath the crown is an additional larger crown, which is attached to a coiled piece of wire that can be extended out and which functions as an antenna. Once it is removed, another antenna pops out of the other side, and the emergency locator beacon activates.

"Per its design, the signal broadcasts on the 121.5-megahertz International Air Distress frequency, as well as the more powerful 406-megahertz frequency, which is monitored by the Cospas-Sarsat system of low earth orbit and geostationary orbit satellites."

Handing the watch to his colleague, KitKat finished his presentation. "That's it," he said. "Binary system. Antenna comes out, beacon turns on. No menu. No software tricks. It's designed to be idiot-proof."

"At least that's how it's supposed to work," Mo stated, taking over. "This watch, however, goes a step further."

"Further how?" Harvath asked.

"As soon as we began probing it inside the cage, we noticed a blip of RF activity that shouldn't have been there. We're talking milliseconds. Not any sort of sustained transmission.

"We thought it was just noise at first, so we began cycling everything that might interact with the transmitter—crown, bezel, antenna housing. One variable at a time.

"What we found was that when the bezel was rotated to a specific index and the lower crown was depressed before unscrewing it, we got a series of short, deliberate bursts. And they weren't on the 121.5 or 406 frequencies."

"Someone had modified the beacon," Morrell replied.

Mo nodded. "Exactly. It piggybacks on the existing transmitter and broadcasts via an undedicated, midrange frequency. So, unless you're looking for it—"

"You're never going to notice it," said Harvath, finishing the tech's sentence for him.

Mo nodded again. "This isn't a replacement for the original beacon.

It's a parallel one. A covert emergency channel. One that doesn't trigger international search and rescue protocols."

"Any indication who modified the watch?" Morrell asked. "Could it be the Chinese?"

KitKat shook his head. "For all we know, it could be the Pennsylvania Dutch. We took it completely apart and even after comparing it to the Breitling schematic, there's nothing—not the workmanship or the additional components—that tells us who did this."

"If the Thai authorities had access to a similar watch," said Harvath, concerned about the two dead men at Tommy Sombat's, "what kind of a conclusion do you think they'd come to?"

"That depends," Mo replied. "With all the evidence they're poring over from the bombings, unless they believe the watch is connected, it's not going to be their highest priority. If anything, maybe an evidence tech who doesn't know what he's doing activates the default beacon. Beyond that, the odds are probably pretty low that they'll discover what we did."

Harvath agreed and glancing at Morrell saw that he felt the same way. That just left him with one other question. "Since the alternate beacon is on such an uncommon frequency, is it possible to scan for who's monitoring it?"

Jumping back in, KitKat shook his head again. "Not with our resources. Unless and until that secondary signal starts broadcasting, you're not going to know who's on the other side of it."

This time, Harvath didn't need to look at Morrell to confirm that they were both on the same page. There was only one option available to them. They were going to have to trigger that beacon, and when they did, they'd have to have set a trap so strong that no matter who showed up, they were guaranteed to be captured.

CHAPTER 24

Morrell had wanted a big, open space with plenty of opportunity for a sniper to conduct overwatch and to be able to see who was coming. Harvath had wanted to minimize as much collateral damage as possible. In the end, they had agreed to compromise.

From top to bottom, proper tradecraft dictated every move they made. It started with putting themselves in the shoes of the dead operative from whom Harvath had taken the watch. If the man was truly in peril and needed to activate his distress beacon, where would he do it from?

If he had to call in the cavalry, it would mean that he was unable to return to his base of operations, which normally only happened in one of two circumstances. Either local authorities were actively seeking him, and the dragnet was too tight to escape, or he was injured and unable to make it to any fallback locations.

After retrieving his cell phone and Harvath's from the Faraday bag, Morrell thanked the two techs and then led Harvath to a secure conference room where they could talk.

"How wide should we draw the perimeter from Tommy's?" the CIA man asked, booting up the encrypted laptop he had grabbed on his way in.

"Four klicks I would think. Maximum," Harvath replied. "Any place you can find that might have medical supplies—a family doctor, a pharmacy, even an outpatient cosmetic surgery center. All that matters is that they're closed for the night."

"How about a vet's office?"

"Only if they don't board pets. If there's animals on-site, they're going to have overnight staff."

Morrell nodded and kept looking. "How about a periodontist?" he eventually said, turning the laptop so Harvath could see the location on the map.

"That would work. Sutures. Bandages. Antibiotics and pain meds. They'd have all of it. What do the satellite and street views look like?"

Morrell spun the laptop back around, pulled up what Harvath was looking for, and then showed him.

The address corresponded to a drab four-story building on an equally drab commercial block. Scrolling up and down the street, there were no bars, nightclubs, or other late-night businesses visible.

Zooming back in on the building, Harvath pointed at the rooftop and said, "This is the place. We'll do it here."

If Tommy Sombat and the shootout at Teens were in fact connected to the bombings, then the beacon was a direct line into the network that had slaughtered Americans.

"What are we going to need?"

It was a question Harvath couldn't fully answer. They had no idea who or what they were up against. His gut told him to bring everything. His brain went a step further.

If he had an injured operative calling for exfiltration, he'd want to gather intel and that would start with getting a drone overhead as soon as possible. Before putting any personnel near the target, he'd want confirmation—or as close to it as he could get—that his operative was indeed the one requesting the exfil and was in legitimate distress.

Failing that, things began to get very complicated, which was exactly where Harvath found himself now.

If they were dealing with a Chinese intelligence unit, lulling them into a false sense of security was key. The easier the job appeared, the smaller the footprint they'd likely employ. Whereas a quick pickup of an injured teammate might only require a few men, the murkier the job, the more manpower they would dispatch.

Harvath wanted his adversary to send in the smallest number of people possible. That was part of why he was focusing on the roof. He also knew that for the emergency locator beacon to have the greatest chance of success, it needed to be deployed outside.

In real-life situations, a downed pilot or stranded adventurer would lash the watch to a pole of some sort that had been shoved into the ground. Then, after removing the antennas and extending them in separate directions, the beacon would be activated, and they would simply cross their fingers and wait.

While not the best idea he had ever come up with, that was Harvath's plan too. He was not only going to use the watch as bait, but he was also going to use himself. And that was where his hastily crafted plan began to fray at the seams.

If the Chinese did send a drone, which they'd be fools not to, he had to give them just enough bait to draw them the rest of the way in. They had to not just pick up the distress beacon, they'd need to see their man, alone, on the roof.

But while he'd passed for a handful of nationalities over his career, Chinese had never been one of them. Shy of lying face down in a wig or wrapping his head in bandages, both of which would be unusually suspicious, he had yet to come up with a ruse strong enough to convince a potential rescue team that he was their missing operative.

He and Morrell were in the middle of brainstorming options when the CIA man's cell phone vibrated.

Looking down at it, he recognized the caller ID and held up his index finger, asking Harvath to pause while he took the call.

"Hey, Davi. What do you have?"

He listened to his ex for several moments. Then, after a pause, as if he was considering something, he replied, "I can probably do you that favor. I'm going to need one in return though."

Placing the phone against his chest, he looked at Harvath and said, "The Chinese guy you shot on the roof. You said you took a picture of him, right?"

Harvath unlocked his phone, pulled up the image, and held it out so Morrell could see it.

"I need you to find someone for me," the CIA man said, returning to his call. "And I'm going to need you to do it with no questions asked."

CHAPTER 25

Because of the bombings, Bangkok's morgues were overflowing with bodies. The excess corpses were in body bags, lining the basement hallways of every hospital in the city.

It had taken Davi about an hour to locate the body Morrell had asked for. It had also created a firestorm of questions. She had wanted to know everything, starting with why Morrell wanted the body, how he had come to possess a photo of the deceased, and what his involvement had been in the man's death.

To his credit, Morrell had tried to remind her that their exchange of favors had been based on no questions being asked. To her credit, Davi reminded him that she had agreed to the deal before she knew it involved a murder.

What's more, it didn't take her long to hear about the additional bodies discovered at Tommy Sombat's and to suspect that all of it was connected somehow to Morrell and his new American visitor, Scot Harvath.

Her ask had paled in comparison to what Morrell wanted her to do. All she wanted was for the United States to quietly run a partial fingerprint they had pulled from the mysterious Glock at Teens. Thai authorities had run it against all the dead bodies on the scene, as well as through all of their own databases, but had come up empty.

Knowing that U.S. intelligence services could access almost any database on the planet, she had hoped Morrell could help her ID who the pistol belonged to. Thailand was pulling on any and every string, trying to get to the bottom of who perpetrated the bombings.

Time was slipping away from them, and the country needed a win. If Davi could deliver that win, it would be very good for Thailand, and her career.

Which was why, even though it went against every rule in the book, she had agreed to help Morrell.

After the orderlies had placed the man's corpse in the back of the van Morrell had borrowed from the embassy, she waited for them to head back inside before addressing her ex.

"I want that body back before sunrise," she stated. "Understand me?"

"You have my word."

"I don't want your word. And I don't want any of your bullshit either," she replied. "You text me the minute you're back and then you and I are going to have a chat."

"About?"

The ISOC officer glared at him. "Everything."

"We'll be back with the body by sunrise," Harvath interjected, closing the van's rear doors, eager to get things moving. "And I'll make sure he texts you. Thanks for your help."

Morrell stood there for a moment, seemingly unsure of how to close out the conversation. Awkwardly, he stuck out his hand and parroted Harvath, "Thank you for your help."

Exhaling a disgusted breath of air, Davi shook her head, turned on her heel, and headed back to her car. "Before sunrise," she ordered, as she walked away without looking back.

"It's not a put-on," Harvath said, watching her go. "She really doesn't like you."

"Fuck you," Morrell responded, following her with his eyes.

Harvath gave the man a moment longer and then, slapping the side of the van, stated, "We're burning darkness. Time to move."

Morrell slid behind the wheel, and drove while Harvath traded messages back and forth with the team, who were already at the periodontist's office.

While Ashby and Palmer had circumvented the locks and rudimentary alarm system, Haney had kept watch downstairs as Staelin went up to check out the roof.

By the time Harvath and Morrell arrived on scene, all the advance work had been done. The only things they needed to do were to conduct a quick reconnaissance and then to bring the body inside.

Thankfully, they found a spot in front of the building, and the body bag had straps, making the corpse easier to transport.

Deadweight was still deadweight, however, and Morrell bitched all the way from the van to the elevator, nicknaming their dead body Wei Too Phat. It made no difference that the man was just as fit as his colleagues.

Palmer met them on the roof with the medical supplies he had "liberated" from the periodontist's office.

"Where are we propping up Mr. Phat?" Morrell asked, unceremoniously dropping his side of the body bag.

"Over there," Harvath replied, nodding at an AC condenser unit.

Reaching down, Morrell picked up his end again, and they walked the bag across the roof.

When they got to the unit and set it down, Harvath could already tell they had a problem. Unzipping it, his fear was confirmed. Rigor mortis had set in.

It usually happened within two to six hours after death. Warm weather, and it was plenty warm in Bangkok, only helped to speed up the process.

The jaw and face were where the stiffness began. From there, it spread, and the rest of the body followed. Individuals with less body fat experienced rigor mortis faster, as did those who had been involved in strenuous physical activity right before death. Not only was their corpse trim, but he'd also been involved in a serious footrace in advance of his ticket being punched.

One of the telltale signs of rigor mortis was when the smaller muscles of the face tightened, creating the appearance of a grimace as the jaw and eyes locked into position. This guy had one of the worst grimaces Harvath had ever seen.

At some point in his career, Harvath had learned about Nysten's Rule, which dictated the sequence of facial effects. First the eyelids stiffened, then the jaw and mouth, then the overall face and neck.

People used to believe that a corpse's facial expression somehow reflected their emotions or state of mind at the time of death. In reality, as Harvath knew, the entire rigor mortis process was a chemical reaction that "froze" muscles in whatever place they were in when their ATP, or energy reserves, were depleted.

Facial stiffness, along with stiffness in the rest of the body, reached its peak anywhere between six and twelve hours. Normally, rigidity disappeared in about twenty-four to forty-eight hours, with the facial features being the first to relax. Harvath, however, didn't have that kind of time.

Unzipping the bag the rest of the way, he said to Palmer, "I'm going to need a good-sized bowl of warm, soapy water. The warmer the better. But not scalding. I'll need some towels or rags too."

Flashing him the thumbs-up, the young operative headed back downstairs to get him what he needed.

"Okay," Harvath continued, motioning Morrell over. "Let's see if we can sit him up against the condenser."

On the count of three, they lifted the corpse out of the bag—Harvath handling the torso and Morrell the legs. The body was rigid and difficult to position.

"We need to put something on his left or right side, so he doesn't tilt over."

As Harvath donned a pair of latex gloves and began massaging and stretching the man's muscles to break up the rigor and make him more pliable, Morrell disappeared to the rear of the roof. He returned with two pallets, followed by a stack of cinder blocks—typical, and more importantly, believable Bangkok roof garbage.

"What now?" the CIA man asked.

Harvath tossed him a pair of gloves. "Roll up his left sleeve. That's where we'll put the IV."

Exposing the man's forearm, Morrell retrieved the bag of saline from the pile of medical supplies and began to probe the corpse's arm for a vein.

"You don't need to stick him," Harvath instructed, as he worked the body into position. "Just tape the IV to his arm. Make it look good."

"Good. Because I am not a fan of needles."

Harvath was about to jab him for having a needle phobia, when he saw Palmer reappear, carrying a large, stainless-steel bowl and a stack of hand towels.

While firm, steady pressure could break the chemical bonds of rigor, you had to be extra careful when it came to the face. Washing it first made it safer to massage the deep tissue, helping to avoid surface damage and tearing. It also helped to reduce the appearance of gooseflesh—another symptom of rigor mortis.

They moved as quickly and as carefully as possible. The corpse didn't need to be perfect. It just needed to be passable.

Once the dead man's eyelids had relaxed enough to be closed, Harvath glued them shut. His corneas had already become opaque due to the rigor and lack of moisture. But the literal "dead" giveaway would have been that his eyes weren't blinking. Better to make it look as if he had patched himself up, started an IV, and activated his emergency beacon before passing out.

After placing a bandage along the man's right cheek and at his left temple, Harvath stood back and took in the totality of his work.

The corpse's clothes were covered in blood. Without an actual, physical inspection, however, there was no way to know what had happened to him or the extent of his injuries.

This was as good as it was going to get. There was nothing else Harvath could think to do. So, with the scene set, all that was left was to invite the audience.

Taking out the Breitling Emergency watch, he used the same piece of rebar Morrell had wedged between the cinder blocks to hang the IV from and cinched the watch to it with a piece of surgical tubing.

"Everybody in place?" he asked over his radio.

There was a chorus of "Roger that," "Good to go," and "Standing by." Morrell flashed him the thumbs-up.

Adjusting the bezel, Harvath made ready to depress the lower crown and began to count down, "Activating the locator beacon in three, two, one."

CHAPTER 26

Harvath and Morrell left the few remaining medical supplies scattered around the corpse. A mess, particularly in a situation like this, wouldn't raise any eyebrows.

What they did clean up, however, were the paper packages the latex gloves had come in, the stainless-steel bowl, and the hand towels—all of which came back inside with them.

Before exiting the roof, they camouflaged one of their portable drones under a stack of roof debris and hid the other in the lobby. Both would function as CCTV cameras.

At the periodontist's office, Haney parceled out their gear—tactical vests with spare magazines, the Noveske Shorty SBRs, night vision goggles, and some of the fragmentation and smoke grenades they had brought with them for the operation on Itbayat. The HK241 battle rifle and M250 light machine gun had been left back at the safe house. Those didn't make much sense for a close-quarters, urban environment.

Morrell had brought his own gear from the embassy—a compact HK MP5 MLI submachine gun, body armor, and a bunch of extra thirty-round magazines, which he carried in his vest, as well as a drop holster strapped to his left thigh.

While Harvath had never been in a firefight where he'd lamented bringing too much ammo, it both looked and felt a bit over the top. The idea wasn't to slaughter whoever showed up, but rather to take as many prisoners as possible. You couldn't interrogate dead men.

As they double-checked their weapons, Harvath went over the plan one last time. Then, when there were no questions, they divided into their two-person teams and took up their positions. All they could do now was wait.

Harvath was tempted to circle back to his question about how Morrell had ended up in Bangkok. He figured it couldn't be worse than his Viagra story.

But before he got the chance, the CIA man said, "You've got to be the dumbest person I've ever met. You've got a hot young wife and, if the rumors are true, you just fell into a shit ton of money. What the hell is wrong with you? You hit the jackpot. Why are you doing this?"

There were about a dozen reasons he could give, the majority of which dealt with patriotism and purpose. He chose the one he thought would resonate most with Morrell.

"I missed the job," he replied.

"What part? The shitty hours? The shitty conditions? Or the shitty pay?"

Harvath smiled. "The shitty people."

Morrell chuckled. They were sitting together on the fourth floor, near the stairwell.

"What about you?" Harvath asked, shifting focus. "You said Bangkok's where they park you when you're useful, but inconvenient. I get the inconvenient part, but who in their right mind ever labeled you useful?"

The CIA man laughed again. "Even after we pulled out of Iraq and Afghanistan, the Agency was still making omelets. Not as many as before, but enough that they still needed experienced people out there breaking eggs."

"So that's why you're in Thailand? To break eggs?"

The man nodded. "Terrorism, drugs, weapons smuggling, human trafficking . . . there's a lot going on in this part of the world. More than enough to keep me busy."

"And your station chief? What kind of dirt do you have on him that he buries your medical records, and his wife plays matchmaker for you with local intel operatives?"

"John and Emily? Ten years ago, in Burkina Faso, they were operating under non-official cover, posing as a husband-and-wife team. They zigged when they should have zagged and got jammed up. I grabbed a couple of Marines from the embassy and—against orders from Langley, as well as the Ambo—pulled them out.

"Bangkok is John's last ride. He's retiring after this. Emily is already ex-Agency. She parachuted out after they got married for real and had their first child. They thought I'd enjoy it here and John still had a few favors he could call in back at headquarters. I suspect Langley was more than happy to have me posted all the way on the other side of the world."

"If Emily had been a NOC," said Harvath, "what was the deal with hooking you up with Davi?"

"Bangkok is full of social clubs," Morrell replied. "They met playing tennis. Emily is no dummy and figured it probably wasn't a coincidence."

"Meaning Thai intelligence was trying to recruit her."

"Exactly. So, she leaned into the relationship and introduced me to Davi at a party."

"Intending for you to run the same game back on her."

"Which I did," the CIA man said, a wistful smile on his face. "With pleasure."

"Obviously. So, what happened?"

"Professionally speaking? In the end, nothing. Davi didn't turn Emily and I was unable to turn Davi. But while it lasted, I had the time of my life. She's an amazing woman."

"Did you ever consider that, in the end, maybe Davi was trying to turn you?"

Morrell scoffed at the idea. "Have you not seen how pissed she still is at me?"

"Not so pissed that she wouldn't let you borrow a corpse from a Bangkok morgue," Harvath replied.

"I know I sound like every other asshole who fell into a honeypot, but we had something. It was special."

This time it was Harvath's turn to scoff. "So, you're not only useful, but you're also irresistible. Got it. I'll make sure to write that down."

Morrell gave him the finger.

Harvath was about to rib his friend again about calling him "Dad," when Haney, who was monitoring the drone cameras, radioed. "Look alive," he stated. "We've got a visitor up on the roof."

CHAPTER 27

Just as Harvath expected, someone had sent in a drone. It was unlike anything he'd ever seen before.

Instead of being shaped like a typical quadcopter with four foldable arms, this one appeared more compact and much denser. Its arms were short and thick. And rather than one rotor at the end of each arm, there were two—twin counter-rotating blades stacked one above the other.

Even in the semidarkness, its skin appeared to be some sort of matte graphite, likely meant to devour light, not reflect it. There were no blinking navigation lights. No manufacturer markings.

The sensor package beneath it was what really caught his attention. Instead of a simple camera dome, there was a multi-lens gimbal cluster. In addition to regular high-definition video, it was probably also gathering infrared and thermal. If he had to guess, the other components of the gimbal included a LiDAR emitter for 3D mapping, as well as a laser range finder for establishing focus and target points. In short, the device was a compact, self-contained intelligence, surveillance, and reconnaissance system that any military would have loved to have at their disposal.

Everything about it screamed both sophisticated and expensive—neither of which surprised him. Any organization capable of outfitting its operatives with tricked-out twenty-thousand-dollar watches probably had plenty left over for pricey, next-level high-tech gear.

Harvath watched the drone hover over the corpse. It was tilted slightly forward, as if hunting. Every few seconds, it would move and re-examine the body from another angle.

"C'mon," he coaxed, quietly urging whoever was on the other end to take the bait.

Minutes passed.

Finally, the drone lifted back into the night sky and disappeared.

"Do you think they bought it?" Morrell asked.

"We'll see," Harvath replied, as he hailed Haney over the radio. He wanted to see if his colleague recognized the type of drone that had been used.

Haney was already one step ahead of him. Using a still image, he tried to reverse search it on the internet. When that failed, he uploaded a picture to Nicholas back at the Carlton Group, but nothing in their database was a match either. With nothing further to go on, they were back to playing a waiting game.

Harvath's teammates knew him well enough to trust his plan. Morrell, however, had his doubts. Yes, Harvath had more experience dealing with the Chinese, but the idea that they'd be so painstakingly methodical when it came to an injured colleague just didn't sit well with him. He also thought Harvath's plan was a little bit nuts.

When sufficient time had elapsed and they were confident the drone wasn't coming back, they returned to the roof.

Unfurling the body bag, the pair placed the corpse inside and zipped it up, along with the IV. They left the watch where it was, its silent emergency locator beacon still transmitting. Then, each taking an end, they picked up the bag and returned inside, carrying the body down to the third floor.

As the periodontist's had already been broken into, there was no need to disturb any of the other offices. They would deposit the dead man there, inside a small, easily locked bathroom.

With the trap baited, Harvath and Morrell returned to their position. They made small talk until a figure materialized downstairs and Haney's voice came back over the radio.

"Here we go," he announced. "Someone's at the lobby door."

It was a small woman who appeared to be pushing a janitorial cart filled with cleaning supplies. Opening the door, she let herself in—the fact that she found it unlocked seemed to neither surprise nor disturb her.

She paused at the building directory and looked to be studying the list of tenants. Once she had finished, she headed for the elevator.

"Look sharp," said Haney. "She's on her way up."

Harvath and Morrell retreated into the stairwell and made ready. They could hear the old elevator as it descended to the lobby, followed by a chime as its doors opened. Moments later, the doors closed and a loud, metallic grumble reverberated throughout the building as the elevator made its cranky ascent to the fourth floor.

If this was the first probe by the Chinese, which Harvath suspected it was, the woman would have been tasked with locating the "injured" operative and reporting back on his condition. The people who had sent her would want to know—was the man alive, how bad were his injuries, and was he ambulatory?

What she wouldn't have been told was that her mission would also have a secondary purpose—to smoke out any potential ambush.

Knowing the Chinese, the odds were pretty good that they would have co-opted someone from the local diaspora; someone with family back in China who could be threatened if they didn't cooperate.

It was a tactic Harvath had watched them use for years. The Chinese Communist Party ruled by fear. With over a billion people subject to an autocratic system built on control, power was the only principle. Human lives were currency and the exchange rate was brutal. The Party did whatever was necessary to stay in power, even employing the most abhorrent forms of coercion and extortion. Harvath despised them.

Slamming shut his dislike of the CCP, he pushed those thoughts to the back of his mind and focused on the issue at hand.

"Everyone remain in position," he radioed. "We're going to zero comms. No one moves and no one speaks unless I say so."

Ever the professionals, the team members affirmed Harvath's orders, not with their voices, but rather with a series of squelch clicks over their radios.

When the woman walked into the lobby, one of the first things—

besides the janitor's cart—that Harvath had noticed about her was that she was wearing glasses. The frames were dark, thick, and seemed out of place.

If he had to guess, they were some sort of smart glasses, which provided a live feed of everything she was seeing and hearing. They probably also included a feature similar to a bone-conducting headset, that allowed her to receive instructions, or she had been outfitted with a well-hidden earpiece. Either way, he figured somebody—a handler of some sort—was giving her instructions.

That meant that she was likely a walking, talking relay station and it was critical that everyone stick to the plan.

"How'd you know she'd be wearing glasses?" Morrell whispered.

"Lucky guess," Harvath replied.

In reality, it was the option that made the most sense—especially if the woman was a civilian. Throwing on a pair of glasses was easier than wiring her up with a bunch of hidden surveillance equipment. What's more, if at any point she felt her cover had been blown, she could easily pull them off and toss them.

Morrell was about to ask a follow-up question, when the elevator chimed. He and Harvath both fell silent.

They heard the doors open, followed by several seconds of silence, as if the woman was awaiting instructions or trying to decide where to go.

Then there was the sound of the janitor's cart being pushed out of the elevator and into the hallway.

As they strained to listen, they heard it rumble away from them, toward the door out onto the roof.

Leaving the cart behind, the woman stepped outside. The moment she did, Harvath could see her via the feed on his phone.

The woman paused and did a slow visual scan of the roof before heading right to the air-conditioning unit where the body had been.

All that remained was the watch—the only evidence to prove the man had ever been there.

Removing it from the pole, she gathered up the antenna wires and placed everything in her pocket. Then she did a quick but methodical search of the roof.

"We should take her," Morrell stated, second-guessing Harvath's plan. "This could be the only chance we get."

"We're not taking her," Harvath replied.

"What if she knows more than you think? What if KitKat and Mo can pull evidence off those glasses? We can't just let her walk."

"Yes, we can," said Harvath, his eyes never leaving the screen. "That's the plan."

Morrell shook his head. "I'm starting to think this is a bad plan."

Harvath smiled. "The only thing you need to worry about is getting that body back to your girlfriend on time."

"*Ex*-girlfriend."

As the woman completed her search of the roof, Harvath radioed for Ashby and Palmer to stand by. While he and Morrell had been covering the fourth floor and Haney and Staelin were covering the lobby, they were responsible for covering the third floor.

Harvath doubted the woman would go office to office looking for the missing Chinese operative, but he had two reasons to think she might peek inside the periodontist's office.

The first was that it was the only medical business in the building. It wasn't a coincidence that she had stopped and looked at the directory on her way in. Any intelligence outfit worth its salt would have determined that that was where the operative had sourced his IV and bandages and that he might have returned there.

The second reason was that Harvath had made sure that the office's front door had been left ajar.

Much like her search of the roof, he figured she would conduct a quick in and out. If the operative wasn't visible, she would leave the property, and her handlers would be forced to make a decision. That was when things would get interesting.

Not knowing if the woman would get back on the elevator, or ditch the cart and take the stairs, Harvath and Morrell descended two stories and held their position. Within moments, they heard the elevator again.

It stopped on the third floor and Ashby quietly relayed what she and Palmer could see from where they had hidden themselves. The woman had entered the periodontist's office.

In less than sixty seconds, however, she was out again. Getting back on the elevator, she headed down to the lobby and, pushing the cart in front of her, exited the building and disappeared from view.

The moment she had gotten back on the elevator, Ashby and Palmer had stepped from their hiding place and reentered the periodontist's office. Their job was to make sure that the operative's body hadn't been found. It hadn't, and they sent a quiet confirmation over the radio.

For the moment, everyone could exhale. Harvath's plan had worked. The most complicated and dangerous part, however, was yet to come.

CHAPTER 28

McLean, Virginia

By 2:15 in the afternoon, Erin and Connor were finally someplace safe. Shawna Vaughn had been the only person Erin could think to turn to.

The rustic, one-room structure, modeled after a Japanese teahouse, sat on a half acre of land inside the Scott's Run Nature Preserve. It had been listed for sale at just under a million dollars. The agent was Vaughn's old college roommate and had generously provided the code for the key box.

Vaughn had intimated that it was "work-related," which was technically true as she and Erin were White House colleagues, but she knew her former roommate understood that to mean that it had something to do with the Secret Service. A white lie to be sure, but for the moment completely necessary.

Connor had been reluctant to trust anyone in "the system." It didn't take much, however, to convince him that he didn't have a long list of options. If his pursuers had tracked him to Erin's, they'd probably be able to track him to any of his friends, family, or the people he had served with. Running through her personal network, she hoped, would prove more difficult.

Shawna Vaughn was one of a handful of female Secret Service agents assigned to the president's protective detail. She and Erin had become friendly over several international junkets, as well as always seeming to be in the White House Mess at the same time. They respected and liked each other but didn't socialize outside of work. For Erin, that made Vaughn the perfect choice to reach out to.

Having left her phone at home, and with Connor putting a ton of restrictions on how she could contact her, it had taken a while to track her down.

After they finally connected, Vaughn had needed time to put a plan together. When the Secret Service agent next made contact, she provided a place to meet and explicit instructions on how to get there, including how and where she wanted them to run surveillance detection routes.

Two miles out, she had fallen in behind them, covertly making sure they weren't being followed. Finally, they had all ended up at the teahouse.

The structure was musty, dank, and felt like it hadn't been occupied in a very long time. In addition to a small kitchen and a bathroom, there was a large, freestanding metal fireplace suspended by chains hanging from the ceiling. It was topped with a wide, soot-stained hood attached to a conical flue that ran up through the roof. The mesh-screened firebox hovered above a pad of slate and smooth river stones. It was a definite mid-century touch, probably installed at the same time the structure was built, somewhere in the 1940s or '50s.

In the kitchen, a faded runner covered most of the floor, though one corner refused to lie flat. Beneath it, Connor noticed an old iron ring set into a wooden hatch.

"Crawl space access," Vaughn said when she saw him looking. "Plumbing, I think. Watch your step. It doesn't sit quite flush."

Vaughn, who had gotten to the house before them, had stacked some camping gear near the front door and had loaded a few supplies into the fridge.

"There's no Wi-Fi and cell service is hit-or-miss," she explained, "but the electricity works, there's a couple cords of wood stacked outside, and the house isn't officially on the market until next week."

She was a tall, tough woman in her late thirties, with long, dirty-blond hair, deep-set eyes, and a prominent Roman nose, and she radiated a confident don't-fuck-with-me aura. A distinct plus in her line of work.

After powering up a tablet and showing them how to access the short-range Bluetooth trail cams she had placed around the property, she produced a bottle of Johnnie Walker Black, took three glasses from a cabinet, and carried everything to the table.

"You both look like you could use this," she said, pouring two fingers of the smoky, golden liquid into each glass.

For the first time since this morning, Erin felt the tension begin to drain from her body. "Thank you," she said, touching her glass lightly to Vaughn's. "I don't know what we would have done without you."

Connor didn't lift his. "Did you tell anyone else about us? About this place?"

Erin glared at him. "How about you start with *thank you*?"

"It's fine," Vaughn said evenly. "He's right to ask."

"No he's not," she replied, glaring at Connor once more.

A moment passed.

"Thank you," he relented.

"You're welcome."

He held her gaze. "Did you tell anyone?"

"No," Vaughn responded. "No one knows you're here."

Connor studied her a moment longer. "What did you do before the Secret Service?"

"Air Force. Seven years. Base law enforcement. Then detainee ops."

"Why'd you leave?"

"Better mission, broader impact," she said, taking a sip. "I wanted something beyond a perimeter fence. They were recruiting more women at the time. I figured I'd try for the counterassault team. Protective work wasn't even on my radar."

Connor watched her for another second. Then he gave a small nod.

"Did I pass?"

"For now," he replied, lifting his glass and taking a drink.

Vaughn set hers down. "Okay. My turn."

Erin felt her shoulders tighten.

"The shootings," Vaughn said. "Walk me through all of it. Starting at the beginning."

Connor did—starting with the two men who broke into his apartment.

Suppressed pistols. Completely sterile. No phones. No ID. Then Scofield at Erin's. Forced entry. Same objective.

Erin filled the gaps where she had to.

When they finished, Vaughn asked, "Did you get any photos?"

Nodding, Connor handed her Scofield's DHS credential, then reached into his backpack and removed his laptop and one of the portable drives.

While she examined the ID, he booted up the computer, connected the drive, and opened the folder.

He turned the screen toward her. Two dead would-be assassins stared back.

Vaughn moved closer and studied the first image. Then the second. Her hand came up, dragging the cursor, and enlarged the picture of the second man's face.

Her expression didn't change, but Erin sensed something. A shift. "What?" she asked.

Vaughn didn't answer.

"You know him," Connor said.

A long moment passed.

"Yes."

"From where?"

Vaughn sat back, eyes still on the screen. "He's not a contract killer."

"What was he then?"

"A federal agent."

CHAPTER 29

BANGKOK

Haney's voice came over the radio. "Black Toyota 4Runner just pulled up."

Harvath was already moving. "How many?" he asked.

"Four," Haney replied. "All males. Late twenties to forties. Wearing suits. No visible long guns."

Suits? That was unusual. None of the men at Tommy Sombat's had been wearing suits.

He and Morrell held on the stairwell's fourth-floor landing. The building was quiet. Down in the lobby, the overnight lights cast a muted glow onto the street as the 4Runner's doors opened in sequence. In position, Harvath watched all of it unfold via the feed on his phone.

As the men stepped out, they gave the surrounding rooftops only a quick scan and then adjusted their jackets as if arriving late for a meeting. There was a controlled urgency to their movements.

"One of them appears to be carrying some sort of medical bag," Haney added.

"Good copy," Harvath acknowledged.

Seconds later, Haney reported, "Okay, front two appear headed into the lobby. Back two are hanging back a couple of steps. Still no weapons visible."

Not a hard entry, Harvath mused. *Not an assault team—at least not overtly.*

He felt his pulse settle into a familiar, controlled rhythm. Whoever these men were, they didn't seem to be expecting trouble.

"Everyone stay frosty," Harvath ordered. "Let them commit."

Two floors below him the lobby door swung inward. One of the men tried the handle, found it unlocked, and pushed the door open. All four then stepped inside as if they belonged there.

Crossing the lobby, one pair headed for the elevator while the other headed for the stairs.

Harvath glanced at Morrell. The CIA man gave the slightest shake of his head. They were thinking the same thing. These guys were definitely not an assault team. Or, at the very least, not a very well-trained one. Elevators were a death trap. Whenever possible, you always took the stairs.

"They're splitting," Haney confirmed. "Two are taking the stairs and the other two are waiting for the elevator."

All of it tracked. If they believed the man they were looking for was injured and had moved under his own power, speed mattered. So did splitting up. One pair to confirm the roof. The other pair to check the periodontist's office.

This was one of the contingencies they had planned for. All of the assignments were clear. Haney and Staelin were responsible for the lobby. Ashby and Palmer would handle the third floor, including the periodontist's office. Harvath and Morrell had the fourth floor and the roof.

The elevator indicator chime rose like a signal flare. "Go time," Harvath said quietly over the radio. "Zero comms."

Putting his phone away, he readied his weapon as he and Morrell took up their positions.

They were experienced enough operators to know that anything could happen. The elevator and stairwell teams might both head to the roof together. They might all go to the third floor and check out the medical office together. If either of those scenarios rolled out, either Ashby and Palmer or Harvath and Morrell would be facing a two-on-four fight. That would be a less-than-optimal situation as they needed to take at least one of the intruders alive. The key was to get the drop on all of them before any of them knew what was happening.

Harvath's money remained on the two teams' number one goal being to get in, find their missing man, and get out as quickly as possible, which meant a rapid divide-and-conquer strategy.

They had no reason to expect any resistance. The cleaning lady had come and gone with zero issues. As far as the two teams now headed upstairs were concerned, this was a recovery operation. Nothing more. Nothing less.

The heavy fire door on the ground floor opened with a groan that echoed up the stairwell. Footsteps climbed quickly, punctuated by the occasional whisper of Mandarin. Leather soles slapped concrete, growing louder.

Harvath applied pressure to his trigger just as the first man came into view. It was at the turn between the third and fourth floors. The man's colleague was only two steps behind. Neither of them was holding a weapon.

The first man came around the corner. He was breathing hard. His eyes were down—neither alert nor searching. Harvath waited until he had both men in his sights.

"Freeze," he ordered. "Don't move."

Whether by instinct or training, the first man didn't hesitate. He swept the right side of his jacket back and went for the pistol holstered at his hip. It was the last mistake he would ever make.

The two suppressed shots from Harvath's SBR clapped in the confined space—muffled, flat, and hopefully swallowed by the noise of the elevator machinery. Both rounds struck high, center mass.

The man's expression flickered from confusion to shock as he fell backward and crashed into his partner. The second man never even got his pistol clear.

Leaping down the stairs, Harvath drove into him, smashing him against the wall. The man's hand clawed for his weapon, but Harvath trapped his wrist and slammed his forearm across the man's throat.

"Don't," he said quietly.

The captive froze.

Looking up, Harvath saw Morrell at the top of the stairs, weapon steady, covering the landing. That had been the plan.

If both elements had pushed to the fourth floor together, Morrell would have been able to exit the fire door and deal with whoever stepped out of the elevator. Harvath's job had been the stair team. No matter how it broke, they would control the choke point.

Beneath him, the man he had pinned tried to twist free.

Harvath tightened his forearm against the man's throat and drove him harder into the concrete, cutting off his air and his voice at the same time. "Not a sound," he warned.

The oxygen being cut off to his brain, the man stopped struggling.

From somewhere, Harvath couldn't tell exactly which floor, the elevator chimed. For a split second, everything hung in the balance. Then, over the radio, three squelch clicks.

Ashby. Third floor. *Good.* Harvath exhaled slowly but maintained pressure on his captive's throat.

His eyes were beginning to bulge, and he clawed at Harvath's sleeve.

"Easy," Harvath murmured. "You breathe when I tell you to."

Morrell broke from the fourth-floor landing and moved down the steps to Harvath. With his eyes glued to the stairwell below, he disarmed both the captive and his fallen accomplice. He removed their radios as well.

Morrell produced a pair of flex cuffs and secured the captive's hands behind his back. The man sagged against the wall, coughing as air returned to his lungs.

Harvath conducted a rapid search. Jacket pockets first. Inside the breast pocket, he found a wallet.

He flipped it open and saw a red-and-gold crest. *People's Republic of China. Embassy of the PRC—Bangkok.*

Harvath's eyes narrowed.

He checked the dead man next. Same crest. Same credentials. These weren't intelligence officers from some clandestine unit. They were diplomatic security.

Morrell unwound a long piece of duct tape from one of his magazines and wrapped it around the man's head, gagging him.

"Chinese Embassy?" he asked, looking at the credentials.

Harvath nodded. "Not at all who I thought they'd send."

"Smart, though. They've got functional immunity and, if they need to, can liaise with local law enforcement."

"Perfect errand boys. I should have seen this coming."

Morrell was about to tell him there was no way of knowing who the

Chinese would send, when three additional squelch clicks came over the radio. Palmer.

"Go down to three and back the team up," said the CIA man. "I'll keep an eye on this guy and hold the stairs."

Flashing him the thumbs-up, Harvath turned and crept down to the third floor. He knew Ashby and Palmer could hold their own, but having another friendly gun in the fight was always a good idea.

Cracking the stairwell door, he peered into the hallway and quietly radioed Ashby and Palmer to let them know where he was and that he was headed to them. Each operative squelch clicked back.

Stepping into the hall, he hugged the wall and made his way forward. Up ahead, he watched as the other two Chinese Embassy security men were about to enter the periodontist's office.

One of the men was carrying the medical bag. The other had his suit jacket open and his hand near his holstered weapon.

Pushing open the door with his foot, man number two called out in Mandarin. When he didn't get a response, he called out again. *Nothing.*

That made sense, but why was his hand hovering near his pistol? Had he heard the two suppressed shots from the stairwell as he was riding up in the elevator?

Harvath, however, immediately discounted that as a possibility. If the man had heard anything resembling gunfire, he would have radioed his colleagues. It had to be something else. Maybe the silence. Maybe the hour. Maybe he was just jumpy.

Whatever it was, the man was alert. Too alert. He stood at the threshold, sweeping the darkened reception area with his eyes.

As he had with the drone, Harvath once again found himself quietly urging his adversaries to take the bait.

Instead, the man used his opposite hand to slowly pull his walkie-talkie from his belt.

Harvath knew exactly where this was going and it wasn't good. The man was going to attempt to hail his teammates and get nothing in response. That silence would be an answer in and of itself.

Over his own radio, Harvath ordered, "Take them. Now."

"Don't move!" he heard Palmer yell from inside the medical office.

"Hands!" Ashby yelled, flanking the two men. "Let me see your hands!"

Harvath was about to close the distance to the door, when a rapid thunder of gunfire erupted.

It was a mixture of suppressed and unsuppressed rounds. One or both of the Chinese had drawn his weapon and had gotten off several shots, as had Ashby and Palmer.

As quickly as the gunfire had started, it stopped.

Moments later, Harvath heard Ashby's voice over his radio. "Targets neutralized," she stated. "Office clear."

"Friendly!" Harvath shouted, announcing himself as he approached the doorway.

Stepping inside the periodontist's waiting room, he saw two dead Chinese. Ashby had kicked their pistols away from them. Palmer was going through their pockets.

Holding up the first man's credentials, he said, "Chinese Embassy security."

"Same as the guys in the stairwell," Harvath replied. "Are you two okay? Anyone injured?"

"We're fine," said Ashby, "but it looks like you're bleeding."

Harvath looked down and sure enough, he was. It was from the wound he had incurred chasing the operative from Tommy Sombat's across the rooftops. Wrestling with the man in the stairwell, he had opened it back up.

"Just my scratch from earlier," he responded. "I'll get Dr. Staelin to squeeze some more Krazy Glue on it. In the meantime, let's grab our dead guy from the bathroom and get out of here."

While Harvath and Palmer retrieved Mr. Phat, Ashby headed for the roof to grab their drone. Morrell was already headed down the stairs with their captive.

They all knew they needed to move quickly. If anyone had heard the gunfight, Thai authorities could already be on their way. There was also no telling if the Chinese Embassy security team had backup nearby, or if any of the shooting had been picked up over the radio.

"Elevator," Harvath said.

Palmer nodded and grabbed the front end of the body bag. Harvath grabbed the rear. Together they carried it out of the office and down the hallway. When they reached the elevator, Harvath hit the call button.

It was still there and the doors opened immediately.

Maneuvering the body inside, they set it on the floor, and Harvath pressed the button for the lobby.

As the doors began to close, Haney's voice cut back in over the radio. "We've got company. Two more vehicles just rolled up hot."

Harvath jammed his hand between the doors and they bounced back open.

"Say again?" he replied.

"Black SUVs. Lights off. Six men. Weapons already visible."

"Embassy?"

"I don't think so," Haney answered. "No suits. But very switched on. Definitely pros."

Having pulled out his phone to check the feed, Harvath could see them now. They *were* pros. Their weapons up before their boots even hit the pavement. Half scanned windows and rooftops, while the other half swept for more proximate threats.

"What's our plan?" Haney asked.

Harvath paused a beat, as a plan began to take shape in his mind.

Using his boot to keep the elevator doors open, he signaled to Palmer to help unzip the bag and take the body back out.

"Everyone out of the lobby. Stairwell. Now," he ordered, pulling two of his grenades. "I'm sending something down."

CHAPTER 30

The second wave stacked outside. Then, guns up, the tight column flowed through the lobby doors as one. The instant the last man cleared the threshold, Harvath sent the elevator down.

They were dressed in dark street clothes and carried Russian-made PP-2000s. The triangular-shaped handguards were unmistakable. It was the same type of personal defense weapon that had been recovered at Teens.

These were definitely the guys Harvath and Morrell had been looking for, but they were coming in on high alert.

He watched the way they moved as a unit—disciplined, precise. These men were highly trained pros. Peeling off even one wasn't happening. Not on such a hot entry and not with Thai police likely minutes away.

Harvath and his team needed to get out of the building as quickly as possible. There was only one way out—through the attackers in the lobby.

As the elevator began its descent, Harvath joined Palmer and Ashby in the stairwell and took the stairs fast but controlled. At the ground-floor landing, the rest of the team was waiting for them.

Outside the heavy fire door, they could hear the muted thud of boots crossing marble as the attackers spread out. Via the feed, it was obvious from the cover positions they took that they knew the elevator was on its way down. What or who was inside, however, was a mystery to them.

No one on Harvath's team spoke. No one needed to. They all knew the plan. It would all come down to speed, surprise, and overwhelming force.

The elevator's motor changed pitch as it began to slow. Harvath signaled them to get ready. It felt like an eternity. Finally, the chime sounded.

At first, none of the attackers moved. Then, a figure could be seen issuing orders. Seconds later, two men emerged from behind cover and moved cautiously toward the elevator. The corpse Davi had let Morrell borrow from the morgue was lying face down inside.

As soon as the two attackers entered the carriage and rolled him over, two violent explosions detonated—venting outward in a brutal flash of debris and fire.

Shards of steel, bone, and shrapnel blasted into the lobby. The two men inside the elevator were obliterated.

Sprinkler heads erupted and alarms screamed as Harvath drove the stairwell door open and the team charged, weapons up.

Heat and dust rolled across the lobby, thick with the metallic tang of explosives. The steel elevator doors had buckled and been blown off their tracks.

One attacker near the elevator bank had been thrown hard against a column. Bloody but still moving, he fought to shoulder his weapon. Harvath double-tapped him in the head.

Palmer shifted left and finished a wounded operator crawling toward his PP-2000.

That left two. Both had fallen back near the entrance.

The first man stepped forward and fired controlled bursts through the haze, chipping the wall above Harvath's head.

Ashby pressed her trigger once. The man went down.

The last attacker moved fast and low, using the lobby's reception desk as partial cover, firing as he advanced.

The marble floor was already slick with sprinkler runoff. Harvath closed the distance carefully.

But when the attacker leaned out to fire again, it was Staelin who ended him. Two shots to the face. Two shots to the chest. He dropped dead where he stood.

Above the alarms and spray from the sprinklers, Harvath caught the distant wail of approaching sirens. He scanned the lobby. Six men in. Six men dead.

While Haney retrieved the other drone, Ashby and Palmer took up a security position at the front door. Morrell kept an eye on their captive as Harvath and Staelin conducted rapid pat-downs.

No embassy credentials. No diplomatic badges. No phones. No wallets. Nothing. These men were even cleaner than the men from Tommy Sombat's. Harvath checked their wrists.

No Breitling Emergency watches. No emergency beacons. Only cheap, matte-black digital watches.

They weren't embassy security. They were the cavalry. And if they got into trouble, nobody was coming for them.

Harvath straightened and looked across the wrecked lobby. Embassy security had been used as a cutout. Then a tactical team had been sent in.

Two tiers, back-to-back—all because one operative had activated a beacon. Obviously, the man on the roof hadn't been expendable. He'd been important.

But why? That was the key question.

The sirens were getting closer.

"Let's move," Harvath ordered.

CHAPTER 31

MONDAY

The storage unit was stifling. The heat, the humidity, and the lack of properly circulating air were all conspiring to exhaust Kevin Koebler. He was dripping with sweat and his eyes stung—not a good situation for a bombmaker, particularly one under a particularly tight deadline.

In a job where precision and attention to detail were critical, a ticking clock was not something anyone would have voluntarily undertaken. Not unless the money was right. Which in his case, it was.

He reminded himself of that as he knocked back another large bottle of water and set it aside to urinate into later. Everything now was about discipline.

He had been inside the storage unit for hours. The worst of the work, however, was behind him. And as uncomfortable as his current circumstances were, he'd built bombs under worse conditions—in deserts with twice the heat and jungles just as hot, plagued by mosquitoes, venomous snakes, and fevers that swept through entire camps, leaving men delirious and too weak to even stand.

Rolling his shoulders, he stepped back from the bench. The sharp scent of burnt soldering flux and heated wire insulation pooled beneath the low ceiling.

He used his shirt to mop his brow and then assessed what he had built. It certainly wasn't subtle.

The earlier bombs had been built for spectacle—fire, panic, shrapnel scything through crowds. This bomb was something else entirely.

It wasn't designed to scatter bloody bodies across pavement. It was designed to move stone and steel. To hit hard enough to fracture reinforced concrete and tear through everything behind it. This was about brute force.

He walked the perimeter of his work, rechecking and finalizing each element. His clients had asked for an echo of the previous attacks—but flawed. Imperfect. A survivable signature that would suggest haste. A mistake that investigators could seize upon and would then chase.

He had given them exactly that—a narrow, deliberate trail pointing precisely where it needed to.

And while the earlier bombs had shaken Bangkok, this one would shake the balance of power.

Satisfied with the "brain" he had built for his bomb, he turned toward the far end of the unit. Beneath the grease-stained tarp loomed the real weight of the operation.

He crossed the concrete floor, gripped the edge of the canvas, and pulled it back. Underneath was a white Toyota Fortuner, its dark glass swallowing the glare from the work lights. The bulk of the device was already seated inside.

He moved to the rear hatch and lifted it. The fabricated cargo deck concealed the charge. Beneath it and forward under the seats, the weight was dispersed across the chassis. There was no visible distortion, no sag in the suspension.

Returning to the bench, he retrieved the control assembly and carried it carefully back to the vehicle. Inside the cargo space, beneath the fabricated deck, he attached the final connection.

He held it in place for a moment, confirming the lock. Then he lowered the deck into position and pressed it flush. A black duffel and a folded tarp went on top. Ordinary clutter—nothing that would raise suspicion. With the bomb complete, he closed the hatch.

Sweat ran into his eyes and he wiped it away again with his shirt. The Fortuner's air-conditioning would be a relief.

But before he could leave, there was one final precaution. When it ignited, the unit would not survive. By the time authorities arrived, there'd be nothing left worth collecting.

He gave the space one final scan. Everything personal had remained in his backpack. Any DNA evidence like hair, skin, or the urine and saliva tied to the water bottles would be incinerated.

Picking up his pack, he was about to toss it in the Fortuner's front passenger seat when a distinct alarm tone chimed on his phone. One of his wireless cameras had been tripped. He froze.

Pulling it out, he opened the app and brought up the feed. Two men had entered the storage compound. They didn't look like cops. And they didn't appear to be renters.

As they passed the facility's CCTV cameras, they angled their bodies away. Faces turned. Chins tucked. Professional.

His next camera caught them turning down his row.

The lead man slowed just enough to study the numbers illuminated above the doors. They moved past one. Then another.

They were getting closer.

On his last camera, they stopped at his door. The lead man looked up at the number and gave a small nod. The men, who resembled the attackers at Teens, had found what they were looking for.

The lead man reached for the handle. The roll-up door didn't move.

The lead man glanced down at the latch. There was no padlock. Stepping back, he drew his pistol. His partner removed a pry bar from his bag and went to work on the latch.

In that instant, Koebler knew this wasn't random. These men were here for him. Without making a sound, he unzipped his pack.

The metal door shuddered as the bar bit into its seam.

Removing the claymore mine, he placed it facing the entrance, killed the lights, and retreated behind the Fortuner. As he did, the door shrieked louder and the latch began to give way.

The wrenching of metal culminated in a sharp *crack* as the door's internal lock snapped off. A thin line of light appeared at the base.

Outside, the lead man used his free hand to roll the door upward. The slats rattled as it climbed and ambient light spilled into the unit.

When the door was all the way up and both men stepped forward, Koebler squeezed the claymore's clacker.

The blast was deafening and sent a tsunami of seven hundred steel balls through the entryway of the storage unit at over thirty-nine hundred feet per second. The men standing outside never had a chance.

Koebler was already moving. He yanked open the driver's door, tossed his pack on the passenger seat, and slid behind the wheel. The Fortuner roared to life. Throwing it into gear, he punched the accelerator and the vehicle surged forward.

He grabbed a cap from his bag and kept his head down as he steered toward the compound gate. Though the SUV's windows were tinted, he knew better than to rely on that feature alone. Adjusting his seat back, he pulled the brim low, and let the A-pillar shield his face from the cameras mounted overhead.

The gate arm hesitated, and for a split second he considered ramming it. Then it began to rise. He passed through and rolled onto the street.

Fifty yards later, he removed the remote from his pocket and depressed its switch. Behind him, the storage unit erupted.

The explosion punched outward, swallowing the row in fire and debris. A rolling concussion wave chased him down the street. In his rearview mirror, he saw the flash and a rising column of flame.

Everything inside was now gone.

But twice now he had been where his clients had told him to be and twice he had come under attack.

He didn't intend to let it happen a third time.

CHAPTER 32

They hadn't gone back to the safe house. Instead, Morrell had directed them to a different location—an abandoned, half-finished condominium development on the outskirts of the city.

It was little more than a shell. Raw concrete floors. Rebar bristling from the ceiling like broken bones.

The best part was what it didn't have: cameras, neighbors, or any reason for anyone to be there.

The embassy security guard sat on a plastic chair several feet in front of one of the team's vehicles, its high beams drowning him in harsh white light. His hood had been removed and his hands were zip-tied behind his back. He was in his early forties, fit but not particularly menacing. He looked like what he was—someone who followed orders and didn't ask many questions.

It was his answers, however, that Harvath cared about, and he had made the stakes crystal clear. If the man cooperated, he would be allowed to live.

Thankfully, there wasn't a language barrier. The man spoke good-enough English and, having seen at least one of his colleagues killed, had made it clear he didn't want to suffer the same fate.

He had attempted a lame version of *name, rank, and serial number* at first, but Morrell had put an end to that. A threat to tie an anchor around the man's neck and drop him in one of the city canals had done the trick.

Standing just outside the wash of the headlights, Harvath took the security officer back earlier in his story. Before being sent to the periodontist's building, he and his team had been given another unusual task.

"You said there was a medical emergency and you were told to drive the embassy physician somewhere."

"Yes," the man replied. "We were told there was a medical emergency. Ban Phan Thom neighborhood. A Chinese businessman had been shot."

Harvath studied him for any flicker of deception. So far, he hadn't seen any. "Who told you that?"

"Our chief of security. He didn't have many details. Just said to be on guard."

"Why not send the businessman to a hospital?"

The security officer swallowed. "The order came directly from the ambassador. We were to drive the physician to an address, bring him back, and forget everything. Including the address."

"Did you go inside?"

"No. The doctor told us to wait in the car."

"How long?"

"About forty minutes."

"What about once he came out?" Harvath asked. "Did he say anything?"

"He said that the bullet had gone through and through," the officer answered. "That the man would live."

"Was there anyone else inside?"

"I saw a couple of men when the door opened. Both armed."

"Embassy people?"

"No."

"How were they armed?" Harvath asked.

"Submachine guns," the security agent responded. "Like the men in the lobby. PP-2000s."

Harvath glanced at Morrell, who gave him a knowing nod.

Turning back to their captive, Harvath said, "Give me the address."

* * *

Within thirty-five minutes of the man rattling it off, Harvath, Morrell, Haney, and Staelin were in Ban Phan Thom. Ashby and Palmer had remained behind with their captive.

The neighborhood was quiet—the narrow, early-morning streets still awash in sodium-vapor light.

They didn't risk a drive-by. Whoever was in that safe house would be on high alert. There would be cameras and men would be standing guard in shifts. They would be expecting trouble and fully prepared to respond.

Parking several streets over, Harvath and his team went in slowly on foot, carrying only what they could each fit in a backpack. Staelin had reglued Harvath's wound, but he could feel the strap of his pack rubbing uncomfortably against it. Ignoring the irritation, he pushed on.

They moved in staggered formation, keeping to the shadows, checking rooftops and balconies as they advanced. At the corner, Haney paused and studied the building through a handheld thermal device. *Nothing.* There were no heat signatures in the windows. No movement on the roof.

"Either these guys are very good," Morrell murmured over the radio, "or they're not here."

Harvath didn't answer. He was too busy scanning the target. It was exactly the kind of structure he had expected—discreet, gated, and surrounded by a high wall. The kind of place that was easily defensible and afforded plenty of privacy.

What he hadn't expected was for the place to be so quiet. Dangerously so. That bothered him more than anything else.

Backing up around the corner, they launched the smaller of their two drones and sent it up and over the rooftops for a detailed view of the building and the property.

Neither its night vision nor its thermal vision registered anything. There were no detectable humans outside or inside. There were also, thankfully, no dogs anywhere near the target building. Strangely enough, there were no vehicles—no cars, no motorbikes, nothing. For all intents and purposes, the building appeared to be completely empty.

Harvath had Haney put the drone in "follow" mode, and they proceeded cautiously down the street toward the target. None of this felt right.

At the gate, Haney picked the lock in under twenty seconds and they all crept inside. The hum of air conditioners could be heard. Harvath's instincts were on edge.

Avoiding the front door, they moved to the back of the two-story house, alert for motion sensors and ducking under each window they passed.

When they reached the rear, they tasked the drone with one more sweep, searching for interior movement, a heat signature, anything that would suggest someone was home, but it didn't find anything.

Finally, they approached the back door. Morrell reached out and tried the handle. *Unlocked*.

They all exchanged a look. These were not the kind of people that left their door unlocked. Every instinct Harvath had was telling him that something was wrong. He was beginning to think that maybe the shoe was on the other foot and that *they* were now walking into a cleverly laid trap. Holding the door open, he had Haney fly the drone into the house.

The device moved from room to room, downstairs and up. It gave them a sizable advantage. About the only thing the drone couldn't do was open doors. They would have to clear the bathrooms and closets themselves.

Where a trained canine would have been able to go in and hunt people via scent, the drone was able to do something similar with heat. It could read hotspots that humans had left behind—palm prints, the warm outline of where a person had been lying in bed, even urine that a sleepy or careless person had failed to get into the bowl of a toilet. Its sensors were incredibly accurate.

When it had completed its search, Haney sent the drone to hover over the property, the team lined up in a stack, and with their night vision goggles illuminating their way, they swept into the darkened house and cleared it from top to bottom.

There wasn't a single soul to be found—not in the closets, not in the bathrooms, nowhere. It was completely empty. But it hadn't been that way for long. Whoever had been there had made a rather hasty exit.

Dresser drawers stood open, wet towels had been left on floors, and in one of the sinks upstairs, there was ash from papers that had recently been burned.

In a trash can in the master bedroom, beneath a layer of used gauze and torn antiseptic packets, Harvath found a linen jacket. Dark blood had stiffened the fabric. A clean hole in front marked the likely entry. A ragged tear in back marked the exit. Dropping it back in the wastebasket, he continued his search before returning downstairs.

At the kitchen table, Morrell was sorting through a bag of trash he had found. "Take a look at this," he said.

Among take-out containers and crushed water bottles were two empty blister packs.

Harvath pulled out his phone and scanned the writing. The script was Khmer. A reverse image search of the branding brought up a Cambodian telecom provider. Each pack had contained a SIM card.

He turned the screen toward Morrell, who said, "Cambodian."

Harvath nodded and neither of them spoke for a moment. Upstairs, the air conditioners continued to hum. The house felt recently vacated—cool, but abruptly abandoned.

Morrell spoke again, breaking the silence. "They moved fast."

Harvath didn't answer. He was tumbling all of the pieces in his head, trying to figure out how they fit together—the embassy physician, the ambassador's direct order, the armed men with PP-2000s, papers sensitive enough that they needed to be burned, the bloodstained jacket, and now Cambodian SIM cards in a Chinese safe house. *What the hell were the Chinese up to?* he wondered. *And what did it have to do with Cambodia?* He didn't like it.

He joined the team, and they swept the house one final time before stepping back into the humid, predawn air.

Outside, they were in the middle of stashing their gear in their backpacks and about to exit through the gate, when Morrell's phone vibrated. Sliding it from his pocket, he looked at the message and stopped.

Harvath noticed immediately. "What?"

Morrell didn't speak, he simply handed him the phone. The partial fingerprint—the one Davi had given him from the Glock found at Teens—had been identified. The match came from a Department of Defense database.

Kevin Koebler. Former member: SEAL Team Two.

Harvath didn't look up from the screen.

"You were at Team Two about the same time," said Morrell, watching him. "You recognize him, don't you?"

"Yeah," he replied. "I do."

He handed the phone back and pulled out his own. "I think we may have just found our bomber."

CHAPTER 33

McLean, Virginia

Connor had grown disenchanted with D.C. and it was evident in his tone. Staring right at her, he replied, "Which agency?"

"State," Vaughn answered. "Diplomatic Security Service."

Erin felt her stomach tighten. "DSS protects foreign dignitaries."

"And the secretary of state when he's overseas," Vaughn added. "High-risk movements. Advance work. Protective intelligence."

Connor's eyes flicked back to the photo. "Was he active?"

"He was when I worked with him," said Vaughn. "We participated in a joint detail. Large footprint. Multiple agencies."

"Here in the U.S.?"

The Secret Service agent nodded.

"And now he's doing hits on American citizens in the middle of the night. How is that even possible? Better yet, why me?"

"That's what I was about to ask," said Vaughn. "What reason would anyone have to kill you?"

Leaning back, Connor thought about it for a moment. When he replied, however, he kept his eyes fixed on Erin. "Because I've been saying something nobody wants to hear."

Taking a sip of her whiskey, the Secret Service agent said, "I don't know what's going on between you two, but would you mind filling me in?"

"He doesn't believe the Taiwan buildup is real," said Erin.

"Define real," Vaughn responded.

"China's not posturing for an invasion," said Connor. "They're posturing for a reaction."

Erin folded her arms. "In other words, the intel community, the National Security Council, the Pentagon, all the experts, are wrong, but somehow Connor has it all figured out."

Vaughn could feel the tension between these two. She sensed it wasn't the first time they'd had this conversation about China and Taiwan. But who was right and who was wrong wasn't the most important consideration at the moment. What mattered right now was who was trying to kill them.

Looking at Connor, she said, "Explain it to me."

"Ever heard of Operation Fortitude?" he asked.

She shook her head.

"It was a deception campaign the Allies launched in 1944 to fool the Germans regarding D-Day. Fake armor divisions. Inflatable tanks. Phantom radio traffic. They convinced Hitler that the invasion was going to come at Pas-de-Calais instead of Normandy."

"*Maskirovka*," Vaughn said.

Connor nodded approvingly. "Exactly."

"And you think China's doing the same thing?"

"Yes."

"Why?"

"For starters, they're the world's largest energy and food importer," Connor stated. "They know that if we went to war, one of the first things we'd do, after sinking their navy, is to impose a crippling embargo."

"So?"

"So, where's the stockpiling? Crude oil, natural gas, grain, soybeans. If they really believed we were going to lock horns, they'd be buying everything they could get their hands on. From Shenzhen to Chengdu, warehouses and fuel depots would be overflowing. Rail transport and trucking would spike. None of that is happening."

"I can see your point," Vaughn agreed. "But the PLA buildup across the Taiwan Strait is real. Those tanks and landing craft aren't inflatables. We're also seeing weapons systems they've never allowed to be photographed before. What would be the endgame?"

“They want to provoke us—to see how we’ll respond. It’s a probe. How do we reposition our assets? What’s our reaction time? How about alliance cohesion? What are our domestic political fracture points? There’s only so much you can learn from satellites. The other stuff you learn by triggering a crisis.”

The Secret Service agent looked at him. “The largest PLA mobilization in history is nothing but theater?”

“There’s another possibility,” Connor said.

“Which is?” Erin pressed.

“That Taiwan is Pas-de-Calais,” he replied. “And China has the world staring at the wrong beach.”

CHAPTER 34

Bangkok

By the time Harvath stepped through the safe house door, the sky was beginning to pale, the night draining away in thin bands of gray. Ashby and Palmer arrived minutes later, having handed custody of their captive to a CIA team Morrell dispatched. The Chinese security agent was already en route to a remote location where he'd be held until it was safe to cut him loose.

Maps of Bangkok lay spread across the table beside open laptops, spare magazines, and a half-empty first aid kit. Gear was set down. Weapons were cleaned. The air smelled of gun oil and strong coffee.

When Harvath's phone chimed with a text, he had the team gather around for a briefing. Firing up his computer, he waited for Nicholas's face to appear on the screen.

Once it did, Harvath asked, "What have you been able to find out?"

"I've built a working picture," Nicholas replied. "It's not complete, but it's enough to move."

"Give us the thirty-thousand-foot view," Harvath said.

Popping up the man's service photo, Nicholas did just that. "Kevin Koebler. Age forty-four. United States Navy explosive ordnance disposal technician. Selected for the EOD-to-SEAL pilot program. Assigned to SEAL Team Two. Strong operator. Technically advanced. Aggressive."

Everyone knew that Harvath had been a Team Two guy, but no one spoke. For a moment, all eyes drifted toward him, but Harvath's expression didn't change.

"Sixteen years ago," Nicholas continued, "there was an ambush in Anbar Province. Three of Koebler's teammates were killed. Shortly after, there was what appeared to be an unofficial retaliatory action. Six structures were destroyed. Multiple casualties.

"There was nothing direct tying him to it, but there was enough circumstantial evidence that the Navy decided to stack a bunch of lesser violations, strip him of his Trident, and hand him an Other Than Honorable discharge.

"Within sixty days of his discharge, he boarded a commercial flight for Mexico and was never heard from again. No tax filings. No credit card usage. Even a small bank account he has never touched. Three months after his departure, an eviction judgment was filed against him. He had just up and walked away from his life."

Morrell looked across the table at Harvath. "How well did you know him?"

"Not well," Harvath replied. "Different platoon. But everybody knew Koebler."

"Meaning he had a reputation."

"He was scary smart," said Harvath. "If something tricky needed to go boom—or not to go boom—he was the guy."

"And?" Morrell pressed.

"He liked pushing the envelope. More than once, the instructors had to pull him back from experimenting. He wasn't reckless, but rules didn't mean much to him if he thought the mission justified it."

Harvath paused, before adding, "For Koebler, results mattered more than the method."

Nicholas switched slides. On the screen, Koebler was still staring back at them, but this time it was from a passport photo. He had grown a beard, his hair was longer, and his face was fuller than in his service photo.

"Here's the identity he used to enter Thailand three weeks before the bombings," Nicholas said. "Meet Dutch national Frederik Rijneveld. He came in on an extended-stay visa to study Muay Thai. Had a sponsor and everything."

"Any record of him leaving the country?" Harvath asked.

Nicholas shook his head. "No recorded departure. No outbound booking that I can find. No land crossing either. Unless he swam to Malaysia, he's still in Thailand and may still even be using that identity."

"Then why go to Teens?"

No one answered.

"If I'm Koebler, the only place I'm going after those bombings is to ground," Harvath continued. "I lay low, wait for the heat to die down, then I leave the country."

Morrell pulled out a small notebook and flipped it open. "Who was the sponsor for his visa?"

"A Bangkok kickboxing gym called Khlong Kiat Muay Thai in the Khlong Toei neighborhood."

Morrell wrote the name down.

"And we're certain this is our guy?" Palmer asked.

"It's an eighty-eight percent facial similarity against Koebler's DoD file. The ears and orbital structure align. A beard can only change contour, not bone structure."

"That's him," Harvath said confidently.

Nicholas didn't disagree. "Now for the bombs," he continued, as he brought up a new slide showing images from the Friday blast sites. "As we previously discussed, white phosphorus was used in the devices, not to enhance the lethality, but rather to eradicate any signature."

Sitting next to Harvath, Haney—who had seen his share of roadside bombs and Marines getting blown up—leaned forward, studying the blast photos.

"I did a global search across every unsolved, high-grade IED event over the last fifteen years," Nicholas said. "I was looking for similar yields, similar burn profile, and similar absence of claimed responsibility. Then, for each country, I ran their surrounding immigration data, any available imagery, and whatever border CCTV footage could be pulled from online archives, through facial recognition. Within weeks of Koebler showing up under one of his aliases, a bomb matching his style goes off."

"And the same goes for Mexico?" Staelin asked.

Nicholas nodded. "That's where the 'Kevin Koebler' identity falls off the grid. It also appears to be where he perfected his craft. Before he showed up, bombings there were quite crude—pipe bombs, fertilizer charges, that sort of thing. But as soon as Koebler arrives, the sophistication ramps straight up—anti-tamper circuits, shape-charges, and of course the aforementioned white phosphorus."

Ashby took a sip of her coffee. "So he was working for the cartels?"

"Based on the victims—prosecutors, judges, and rival cartel figures—that's the most likely explanation."

"And then what?" Palmer asked.

Nicholas switched slides again. "Then the pattern stops."

"Why?" Morrell said.

"Years ago, when I was still doing work in the darkest corners of the internet, there were occasional whispers about a freelance bombmaker. Not ideological. Just expensive. He supposedly worked through an intermediary—a handler of sorts."

Looking back at them through the camera, he added, "I think those whispers were about Koebler."

For a moment, no one spoke.

It was Harvath who finally broke the silence. "So Koebler leaves the cartels and starts selling his services."

"That's what it looks like," Nicholas replied.

"To who?" Staelin asked.

"Whoever can afford him. Someone with lots of money and a reason to want sophisticated explosive devices that leave no forensic trail."

Harvath looked back at the images from the Bangkok blasts. "Who would want him to hit Bangkok?"

"Anyone who benefits from destabilizing Thailand," said Nicholas.

"Which brings us back to Teens."

Around the table, everyone knew what he meant.

"The Cambodians," Ashby said.

"Possibly," Harvath replied. "But they weren't the only ones present."

"And the Chinese," Haney added.

Morrell tapped the table with his pen. "And Koebler's Glock was found in the waistband of one of the dead Chinese operatives."

"Which tells us what?" Harvath asked. "Koebler was there to meet someone. Someone he didn't trust. That's why he planted the cameras outside and went in armed."

"And the people he was meeting with didn't trust him either," Morrell replied. "That's why they searched him and took his gun."

"So if there's a dead Chinese guy with Koebler's Glock, it's a good bet that's who he was meeting."

"Okay," Palmer agreed, playing along. "Let's say it starts with Koebler meeting with the Chinese. Then the Cambodians show up. Why? Were they there for him? Or the Chinese team?"

Morrell ran his hand across his stubbled chin. "Whatever the reason, it's obvious they didn't come to play mahjong. Crashing through skylights. Slinging all that lead. They came to wipe the room."

"Agreed," said Harvath. "If these guys are Chinese intelligence, working with an American bombmaker, to attack Thailand—that's nightmare fuel. But to have it also draw in Cambodia—a Chinese client state—and to have Phnom Penh risk going kinetic against Beijing? That's a nightmare wrapped in a horror movie."

"What could the Chinese have done to piss off the Cambodians so bad?" Ashby asked, circling back to Palmer's question.

"Maybe they haven't done anything yet," said Harvath. "Maybe the Cambodians showed up to short-circuit something."

He let that hang in the air for a moment before turning his attention back to the screen and the most pressing matter at hand. "So when the bullets start flying and Koebler bolts, where does he go?"

"If he's still using the Rijneveld identity," Nicholas replied, "there's only one place tied to it."

"The visa sponsor," Morrell said, glancing down at his notebook.

Nicholas brought up another image. "Khlong Kiat Muay Thai. The kickboxing gym in the Khlong Toei district."

"Doesn't mean he's staying there," Morrell clarified. "But it's connected to his alias."

"And aliases," said Harvath, "sometimes leave a trail."

"If he's maintaining that cover," Nicholas offered, "someone there may have seen him."

"Then we start with the gym."

“We’re going to have to loop Davi in,” Morrell stated. “The question is when.”

“After,” Harvath replied. “The minute we give her his name, every cop in the city starts looking for him.”

“And the minute that happens,” Morrell continued, “Koebler disappears.”

Harvath nodded. “And nobody gets a shot at him.”

CHAPTER 35

A smog-washed light spread across the city as metal shutters rattled upward and morning commuters pushed their way through the streets. Orange-robed monks moved along the sidewalks collecting alms as vendors arranged stools outside their noodle stalls already filling with customers. Bangkok was waking up.

For Harvath and his team, the day had never ended. They had been at it since the operation on Itbayat, grabbing only brief snatches of sleep along the way. The adrenaline from last night's work had burned off, leaving behind the fatigue that came from too much caffeine and too little rest. No one, however, complained. They were professionals and they kept moving.

Their Land Cruisers rolled southeast toward the port district of Khlong Toei, where the city's skyscrapers gradually gave way to warehouses, shipyard cranes, and long strips of aging concrete buildings.

Harvath rode shotgun next to Morrell in the lead vehicle. Ashby, Palmer, Staelin, and Haney were in the SUV behind them.

As the morning traffic thickened, Harvath kept his eyes peeled and his head on a swivel. Bicycles, delivery scooters, battered taxis, and pickups filled with crates bound for the docks were everywhere. Not since Delhi could he remember being in a city this crowded.

"There it is," said Morrell, double-checking his GPS. "Up there on the right."

A weathered sign hung above a largely open-air structure with a corrugated metal roof. *Khlong Kiat Muay Thai*.

Harvath radioed the team to look sharp, adding, "Ashby and Haney, I want you watching the alley. Staelin and Palmer, stay with the vehicles and keep an eye out front."

Grabbing the first spot they found, Harvath and Morrell got out and walked toward the gym.

The rhythmic slap of elbows, knees, and shins against Muay Thai pads echoed into the street. Morning conditioning was already underway.

Inside the gym, two fighters worked in the ring while another jumped rope near the entrance. A trainer barked instructions in rapid Thai. Each command was followed by the sharp cracks of strikes hitting leather pads.

The place had seen better days. Rust streaked down the metal roof supports. Faded fight posters curled away from the wooden posts holding up the structure.

Outside, painted across one of the gym's exterior walls, was a large mural of a Muay Thai fighter driving a knee into his opponent's side. Years of heat and monsoon rain had bleached the colors and cracked the paint, but the power of the image was still unmistakable.

Harvath took everything in. There were no cameras mounted on the building and no security lights above the entrances. A narrow alley ran along the left side of the gym, vanishing between two concrete shop houses.

Morrell noticed it too. "Good place to disappear."

Harvath nodded. "Let's see if our Dutchman's actually been here."

They stepped beneath the roof and into the gym. The odors of canvas, sweat, and stale liniment hung in the air. A handful of fighters glanced at them, but it was only a passing curiosity, and they quickly went back to work.

At the far end of the gym, an old Thai man—clearly the one running the place—sat at a nicked-up desk reading a newspaper while the morning class trained around him. He had a wispy beard and his hair pulled back in a bun. A half-smoked cigarette rested beside a small glass of dark coffee. He didn't look up as the two *farang* approached.

Only when the men stopped in front of the desk did he lower his paper and look at them over the top. His eyes moved from Harvath to Morrell and back again.

"Beginner class Wednesday, Friday morning. Six hundred baht a week. Shower and towel fifty baht extra."

Harvath held up his hands. "I'm more a lover than a fighter."

The old man jerked his chin toward Morrell, though his eyes stayed on Harvath. "How about your boyfriend? He here to fight?"

Morrell didn't miss a beat. "Only if you're volunteering."

The old man snorted.

"We're not here to train," said Harvath.

"Then what you want?"

Harvath pulled out his phone and brought up the photo Nicholas had sent. "We're looking for one of your students. Dutch guy."

The old man bent forward slightly and gave the screen a quick glance. "Many Dutch students. Good fighters."

Harvath didn't smile. "You signed off on his visa."

"So?" the old man replied, setting his newspaper down and reaching for his cigarette.

"So the last place this man was seen, a lot of people died."

The cigarette stopped halfway to the old man's mouth. The bombings had been on every television in Bangkok for the last three days.

Harvath let the silence stretch as Morrell leaned casually against the desk, blocking the old man's view of the gym.

"You've got a very serious problem," Harvath continued. "Either you talk to us, or you talk to police and Immigration Bureau. Your choice."

The old man took a drag and studied them again. Longer this time. Smoke drifted slowly from his nostrils as he considered the situation.

Finally, he reached down, opened one of the desk's drawers, and withdrew a weathered ledger.

Flipping it open, he ran his nicotine-stained finger down one of the dog-eared pages and stopped. "Rijneveld," he muttered, as he studied a column of names. "Yes. Dutch."

"Is he here now?" Harvath asked.

The old man shook his head. "No."

"When did you last see him?"

"Maybe week," he replied, taking another drag.

Harvath returned his phone to his pocket. "Does he have a room here?"

The old man studied them again and then closed the ledger. "Yes. Upstairs."

"Show us."

"Six hundred baht a week," the old man repeated, exhaling a cloud of smoke. "Fifty for shower and towel."

Harvath looked at Morrell. "Pay him."

The CIA man didn't like being extorted, but he also understood this was how the world, especially the Bangkok underworld, worked.

Pulling out a roll of Thai currency, he peeled off the appropriate amount of notes and placed them on the desk.

"Each," the old man stated.

Morrell rolled his eyes at Harvath before peeling off the same amount again and dropping the bills beside the first stack.

The old man scooped up the money, gave it a quick count, and then tucked it into his shirt pocket.

Crushing out his cigarette in a tin tray, he stood and gestured toward a wooden stairway at the back of the gym. "Come," he said.

He was smaller than he had appeared behind the desk, but despite his age, there was nothing frail about him.

At the stairs, he climbed toward the second floor without looking back. Harvath and Morrell followed, keeping their eyes peeled for any signs of covert surveillance, particularly the tiny Wi-Fi cameras Koebler was suspected of having planted around Teens.

They arrived at a long hallway with eight doors. The old man led them to the very last one, where he produced a set of keys from his pocket.

"Rijneveld," he said, unlocking it and standing back so Harvath and Morrell could enter.

The room was barely bigger than a storage closet. A thin mattress sat on a wooden platform against the wall, the sheets rumpled. An old metal fan turned lazily in the corner. There was a small sink, a cracked mirror, and a blue plastic chair beneath a dirty window. The Ritz Carlton this was not.

On the sink sat a cheap toothbrush, a travel-sized toothpaste, and a disposable razor. Harvath picked each item up and turned it in his hand, studying it. Then he set them all back where they had been.

Only a few pieces of clothing hung in the wardrobe, a couple pairs of socks and underwear in the lone drawer. In the trash can was a single, empty water bottle.

Harvath stood there for a moment, taking it all in.

Morrell had been watching him. "What do you think?"

Harvath gave the room one last slow scan before responding. "The toothbrush and razor are brand-new. The sink doesn't have a single hair in it. There's no luggage. And there's only one item in the trash." Nodding toward the mattress, he added, "Someone staged the bed."

Looking back at Morrell, he concluded, "He doesn't live here. This place is a prop."

CHAPTER 36

In the short time they'd been inside the gym, the heat and the humidity had climbed even higher. Stepping back outside was brutal.

Horns blared as motorbikes threaded between buses and dock trucks pushing through the thick morning traffic. Thai pop music blasted from open storefronts while vendors called out to the crush of pedestrians moving along the crowded sidewalks. Above them, neighbors leaned over railings and across adjoining rooftops, calling to one another as they pulled in laundry and started their day. Bangkok was fully awake.

Aside from showing them Koebler's room, the old man at Khlong Kiat Muay Thai hadn't been much help. He had no idea where the man had been spending his days—much less his nights—when he wasn't at the gym. If the man known as Rijneveld returned, the old man now had Morrell's number and promised to send a text.

Harvath didn't expect that to happen. For all practical purposes, the lead had turned out to be a dry hole.

What Harvath needed now was a shower and a solid eight hours of sleep. He also needed something to eat. So when Morrell mentioned that the best breakfast in Bangkok was only three blocks away, Harvath agreed to join him.

The rest of the team opted for take-out and climbed back into their Land Cruiser for the return to the safe house.

Harvath and Morrell decided to walk. They left their vehicle where it was parked, turned right at the corner, and headed toward the port.

It was a sea of people as far as the eye could see. Harvath couldn't imagine grinding through a commute like this every day. As dangerous as his job could be, it came with its perks—setting his own hours among them. The corporate jet didn't suck either. He reminded himself to be grateful.

Exactly three blocks later, they slowed in front of an unassuming bar tucked into a row of shuttered nightclubs. Neon beer signs glowed in the windows. From inside came the muffled thump of a funked-up yacht rock track.

"Here we are," said Morrell.

Harvath had a feeling he was going to like it and followed his friend through the front door and into a much-welcome blast of air-conditioning.

The bar was called the Lucky Monkey. The night shift was still in full swing. Morrell spotted an open booth in the corner and steered them toward it.

They slid into the cracked vinyl seats just as a waitress appeared with two laminated menus.

"Coffee?" she asked.

Morrell nodded and waved off the menus. "Two coffees. And we'll each have the chicken and waffles."

The waitress gave a quick nod and headed back toward the kitchen.

Harvath looked at him. "Chicken and waffles? In Bangkok?"

"And a remix of 'Ride Like the Wind,'" Morrell replied. "I told you this place was the best."

They listened as the Christopher Cross tune transitioned into a just as funky version of the song "Brandy" by Looking Glass.

Harvath took in the room. In a small booth a DJ worked the turntables, while a bunch of club workers, still dressed for the night, clustered around the bar. At tables in back, office-bound young professionals enjoyed a hearty breakfast, drawn in by the food, the music, and the easygoing vibe.

A moment later, the waitress returned with two heavy mugs of coffee and set them on the table, along with tall glasses of ice water, beaded with condensation.

"Food coming," she said, before heading back to the kitchen.

Harvath wrapped his hands around the mug and took a sip. It was strong and hot—exactly what he needed.

Across the room, the DJ blended another track into the mix—"What a Fool Believes" by the Doobie Brothers.

Morrell took a swallow of his coffee and motioned toward the DJ. "Guy knows what he's doing."

Harvath nodded. "Not a bad way to start the morning."

The CIA man was about to agree when his cell phone vibrated. He pulled it from his pocket and checked the caller ID.

"Fuck," he muttered, showing it to Harvath. "Davi."

He hesitated, weighing whether to answer, then slid the phone back into his pocket. "I'll call her back."

The waitress returned with their plates and set them down in front of them. "Chicken and waffles." Sliding a bottle of syrup between them, she lingered a moment, looking them over.

"No wedding ring," she said with a smile, gesturing at their hands. "You want girlfriend?"

Harvath chuckled. "Tempting, but I still live with my parents."

The waitress laughed. "You too old for that."

"I know. I keep telling them to move out, but they don't listen."

She shrugged. "Then you get own place."

"Can't afford it," Harvath teased. "Bangkok is too expensive."

"Khlong Toei cheap. You want own place? You talk to Mr. Baht. I introduce you. He make you good price. Best price in Khlong Toei."

She leaned a little closer and added, "And he no tell your parents."

Harvath smiled. "Good to know. I'd hate for them to find out."

"Trust me," she said, waving her hand. "Many *farang* rent from Mr. Baht. One week, one year. You pay cash. No lease. No problem."

"We'll think about it," said Morrell.

The waitress gave them a quick smile and moved off to another table.

Harvath reached for the syrup. "She's sweet. I almost don't have the heart to tell her I'm your dad."

Morrell laughed. "Or that I'm your boyfriend."

After drizzling syrup over his chicken and waffles, Harvath took a bite. It was superb.

"You were right," he said after a moment. "Best breakfast in Bangkok."

Morrell glanced around the bar. "Told you."

They enjoyed their food as the DJ seamlessly wove yet another pumped-up yacht rock track into the mix.

Morrell nodded toward the front where the waitress was working another table. "She's a hustler. People like her know everything that goes on in a neighborhood like this."

Harvath followed his gaze. "Bartenders. Waitresses. Doormen."

"Taxi drivers," the CIA man said.

"Yep. They notice who passes through. Who stays."

"They help make the underworld go round."

Harvath took a sip of his coffee. "Sometimes it's drugs. Sometimes it's women. Maybe even weapons."

"Or sometimes," Morrell said, "it's something quieter."

Harvath set down his mug. "Like a place to hide."

Morrell's fork hovered over his plate. "Cash. No lease."

"Foreigners."

"Mr. Baht," the CIA man repeated.

"If he's renting places for cash without a lease, maybe he knows our Dutchman."

Morrell tilted his head toward their waitress. "And lucky monkeys that we are, we've already got an introduction lined up."

Harvath reached for more syrup. "Let's finish breakfast. Then we go meet Mr. Baht."

CHAPTER 37

As Koebler left the storage facility, the blast behind him had rolled through the neighborhood like thunder, shattering windows and setting off car alarms. Every dog for blocks had been barking.

He had only looked back once—just long enough to see the roiling column of fire spiraling up into the night sky. After that, there'd been nothing left worth watching. The storage unit and anything that could implicate him had been destroyed.

The rest of the city was still asleep, the roads quiet. Even so, he hadn't driven any farther than was necessary.

Soon enough, he had come to a service road that ran along the rear of a long-haul bus depot. Rows of idle coaches sat nose to tail beneath dim lighting, their dark windows reflecting the faint glow of Bangkok's skyline.

He eased the Fortuner toward the far end of the lot where several buses were parked close together. Like circled wagons, their bulk created a pocket of shadow that enveloped his SUV and made it nearly impossible to be seen from the street.

There, he killed the engine and listened. No voices. No footsteps. No approaching vehicles. For the first time since leaving the storage facility, he had been able to feel himself exhale. After taking a moment to allow some of the knotted tension to leave his neck and shoulders, he stepped out of the Fortuner and opened the rear hatch.

The night air had continued to be thick with humidity. His shirt clung to his back, soaked from the hours he had spent working inside the storage unit. From his pack, he removed a package of wipes and methodically cleaned his hands, forearms, and face, removing the last traces of solder debris and bombmaking residue.

Next, he stripped off his clothes and replaced them with the uniform his client had provided. First, the tactical fatigues. Then the plate carrier. He left the helmet and balaclava inside the Fortuner for the time being, turning his attention to the vehicle itself.

Donning a pair of latex gloves and armed with nothing more than a utility knife, he got to work.

Sliding the blade under the edge of the vehicle's vinyl wrap, he lifted the material and pulled. Having been pre-scored, the outer skin pulled away in long strips, revealing Thai lettering along the doors, followed by the insignia of the Internal Security Operations Command. ISOC.

Panel by panel, the SUV's civilian disguise vanished. Within minutes, it became something entirely different.

From the cargo area, he removed a light bar and mounted it to the roof, the magnets snapping it into place with a sharp, metallic click. Seconds later, he connected it to a thin cable that fed beneath the weather stripping and disappeared into the cabin.

Next, he attached the laminated placard behind the windshield, positioned so anyone approaching the vehicle would immediately see the ISOC unit identification.

By the time he finished, the Fortuner looked exactly like what it was supposed to be—a Thai internal security vehicle. A vehicle that, in Bangkok, was rarely ever stopped, much less questioned. Once more, his client had indeed thought of everything.

Koebler removed the gloves and tossed them into the cargo area before climbing back into the driver's seat. For a moment, he just sat there, examining the vehicle through the windshield.

Under the dim depot lights, the Fortuner looked indistinguishable from any of the ever-present security vehicles pulsing through Bangkok's streets in the aftermath of Friday's bombings. Everything about it was correct.

Satisfied, he reached back into his pack, pulled out his burner phone, and activated the encrypted communications app he used with his handler.

Matías answered on the second ring. "Go ahead."

"The storage unit was compromised."

There was a brief pause. "Police?"

"No. Two men. Same type that hit the meeting at Teens. They came straight to the door. It wasn't an accident. They knew exactly what they were looking for," Koebler said.

"Did they make entry?"

"Yes."

"And?"

"They're dead."

"Are you damaged?" Matías asked.

"Negative."

Silence settled briefly over the line. "What about the unit?"

"Destroyed," Koebler replied. "Along with everything left inside."

"And the device?"

"Fully assembled. In my possession."

Another pause.

"That's twice now," Koebler continued. "Two locations. Both compromised."

"Operations sometimes encounter friction," Matías replied.

"Both locations were provided by the client."

More silence.

"I don't want the third time to be the charm," Koebler said.

Matías drew deep breath and let it out slowly. "Your window remains unchanged."

"And after the mission?"

"After," Matías replied, "we will no longer be working with this client."

"Understood," said Koebler, pausing. "What about my pistol?"

"Still in Thai custody. Neither Special Branch nor ISOC have been able to make a positive ID on the fingerprints."

"Good."

"Do not miss the window," Matías instructed.

Then the line went dead.

Koebler powered down the phone and returned it to his pack. Around him, the depot remained still. The buses sat motionless, their engines cold, their drivers hours away from returning.

Pulling the balaclava over his head in case anyone happened upon him, he set the alarm on his watch and tilted his seat back. He cracked the window slightly, then reached up and nudged the rearview mirror so it framed the narrow lane between the buses.

Nothing moved.

Satisfied, he placed his pistol under his thigh and closed his eyes. He knew how important sleep was, especially in his line of work. He couldn't afford to be one millimeter off his game. Professionals slept whenever the opportunity presented itself.

When he opened his eyes again, the sky over Bangkok had begun to lighten.

For a moment he remained still, letting his bearings settle. The faint gray light filtering between the buses told him it was just after dawn. He checked his watch: 6:17 a.m. Right on schedule.

The depot was no longer as quiet as it had been during the night. Somewhere near the front gate, the low rumble of a diesel engine could be heard coming to life, followed by the sharp hiss of air brakes releasing. Soon after, another engine turned over as a driver's voice carried across the lot, calling to someone Koebler couldn't see.

Sitting up, he rolled his shoulders beneath his plate carrier, holstered his pistol, and reached for the helmet resting on the passenger seat. He put it on, adjusted the chin strap, and started the engine.

Easing the Fortuner between the parked buses, he rolled out toward the service road.

Within minutes, he had merged with morning traffic and was heading toward the city center.

He flicked on the light bar, and its blue strobes, along with the vehicle's ISOC markings, did exactly what they were intended to do. Instantly, the cars in front of him cleared a path.

His next test, however, would be the real one. Up ahead, the first checkpoint was coming into view.

CHAPTER 38

The waitress had texted Mr. Baht while they were settling the check. Ten minutes later, Harvath and Morrell were headed deeper into Khlong Toei.

The bars and neon of the nightlife strip faded quickly behind them, replaced by the sights and sounds of the port.

Men in rubber boots hauled coils of rope across the pavement while others stacked wooden pallets near a warehouse. A mechanic sat on a low stool rebuilding an outboard motor, its parts arranged in careful rows on a sheet of cardboard. Nearby, chains clattered, and a forklift's warning alarm chirped as it backed out of a loading bay. Out on the river, a vessel's horn sounded long and low, followed by the sharper blast of another.

Morrell checked the address on his phone and gestured toward a lane between a freight broker's office and a welder's shop. The lane felt quieter, closed off from the noise of the port.

They turned off the main road and the foot traffic thinned almost immediately. Halfway down the block sat a small office, its open doorway shaded by a faded awning.

"That's it," said Morrell, slowing.

Inside, a heavyset Thai man in his sixties sat behind a metal desk with two cell phones and several rings of keys spread across the blotter. His thinning hair was poorly combed over a widening bald spot, and his short-sleeved shirt stretched tight across his paunch. A thick gold chain hung beneath his double chin. Behind him, a small spirit shrine sat on a shelf, its base crowded with incense sticks and half-melted candles.

He looked up as Harvath and Morrell entered, his eyes moving over them with the steady calculation of someone used to sizing up strangers.

"Mr. Baht?" the CIA man asked.

The man studied them for another moment before nodding. "You from Lucky Monkey?"

"That's us."

"How long you need room? Short stay? Long stay? Cash only."

Harvath pulled out his phone and brought up Koebler's Dutch passport photo. "Actually, we're looking for someone."

Baht's eyes dropped to the screen, but only for a second. When he looked back up, his face had gone flat. "Never see him."

Harvath could tell the man was lying. "Take another look."

Baht didn't. Instead, he reached back and adjusted one of the incense sticks in the spirit shrine, brushing a little ash from the base, before settling again in his chair.

"Never see him," he repeated.

"You rent to a lot of foreigners."

The man shrugged. "I rent to everybody." Then, after pausing a beat and fingering one of his key rings, Baht asked, "What he do?"

"Private matter."

Baht watched him for a moment. "He owe you money?"

"Something like that."

"*Farang* always owe somebody money."

Harvath met his eyes. "Let's not waste time. You recognized him."

Baht didn't answer.

"I saw it when you looked at the picture."

"Maybe," the older man said. "I see many people."

Harvath slipped the phone back into his pocket. "The man in that photo is bad for business. He brings problems with him. Bad ones. We can make sure none of them touch you."

"And we'll pay you," Morrell added. "For your trouble."

Baht looked at him. "How much?"

Morrell reached for his wallet.

* * *

The space that Baht had rented to Koebler was above a shuttered storefront near the docks.

Harvath took his time, carefully surveilling the building. He knew that the Glock wasn't the only dangerous item that Koebler had left behind at Teens.

All of a sudden, he stopped. "Camera," he said quietly.

Morrell shifted a step to the side, his eyes following where Harvath was pointing, until he saw it too—no bigger than a golf ball, tucked behind a downspout.

Harvath didn't say anything, he was already scanning the rest of the building. A moment later, he nodded toward a different spot. "And there's another."

"Only two cameras?" said Morrell.

"That we can see. He's probably got more inside."

"So, what's our play?"

"Right now? Nothing. I guarantee you that if we so much as breathe on one of those, Koebler's going to know."

Morrell studied the cameras. "Maybe not."

Harvath glanced at him.

"I've got an idea," the CIA man said, taking out his phone.

Thirty minutes later, a battered white panel van rolled down the block and pulled in along the curb.

Harvath and Morrell crossed the street, slipped around to the rear doors, and Morrell knocked twice. When the left door popped open, they climbed inside.

The cramped cargo area had been converted into a mobile workspace. Two laptops glowed on a makeshift table surrounded by cables, signal scanners, and battery packs.

KitKat barely looked up. "Please tell me you didn't start poking those cameras."

"We didn't touch anything," Morrell replied.

Mo turned one of the screens toward them. A live view of the building appeared with each camera angle boxed in digital overlays.

"Five cameras total," he said. "Three outside, two inside."

"And if we get near any of them?" Harvath asked, looking at the screen.

"The person who placed them gets an alert," KitKat replied.

Morrell nodded at the gear spread out across the table. "So what's our workaround?"

The young operative reached into his backpack and pulled out a small, matte-black device with a rubberized antenna that folded out from the side. "Gentlemen, meet the Gremlin."

Even tech people weren't immune to trends, Harvath noticed. At least not when it came to naming their devices. Over the summer, Nicholas had helped him take down a security network with a small electromagnetic pulse device called a Goblin.

"What's it do?" he asked.

"It allows us to hijack the Wi-Fi system the cameras are using," said Mo. "The feeds will remain live, but the Gremlin's AI software erases you in real time from the footage."

"What about the motion alerts?"

"The Gremlin overrides those as well. Once we set it loose on the network, every scrap of data belongs to us."

Harvath looked at him. "How long to get it up and running?"

KitKat extended the Gremlin's antenna. "Thirty seconds from the moment you tell us to go live."

After inserting earpieces, testing their radios, and double-checking their pistols, Morrell looked at Mo and said, "Do it."

Once they had confirmed that the Gremlin was up, running, and had control over Koebler's Wi-Fi, KitKat and Mo flashed the thumbs-up and Harvath and Morrell exited out the back of the van.

At the front of the building, they stepped into view of the camera behind the downspout and paused.

"You're ghosts," Mo radioed, confirming the device was doing its job. "Good luck in there."

Harvath stood guard, his hand wrapped around the butt of his weapon beneath his shirt, as Morrell took out the key from Baht and slipped it into the lock. But when he went to turn it, nothing happened.

"Koebler changed the locks."

"Smart," Harvath replied, scanning the street as Morrell removed a set of lockpicks KitKat had provided and went back to work on the door.

Seconds later, the CIA man had it open, but he waited for Harvath to help him scan for booby traps, before they both agreed it was safe and slipped inside.

Halfway up the stairs, weapons drawn, they noticed the first interior camera. Harvath had no idea how much the CIA had paid for the Gremlin, but as far as he was concerned, it was worth its weight in gold. Without it, there was no way that they'd have been able to get this close. The only thing it couldn't do was tell them if Koebler was actually inside the building.

KitKat and Mo had run a passive scan, and as far as they could tell, there were no devices, other than the cameras, actively on the Wi-Fi network. That didn't mean Koebler wasn't using a cellular or satellite network for things like his phone or laptop.

Hitting the second-story landing, they discovered the final camera. It was positioned to provide a perfect view of anyone standing outside the door. If Koebler was on the other side with a shotgun, he'd have known exactly where to aim. For all intents and purposes, however, Harvath and Morrell were invisible.

They stood and listened for any sign of life—a TV playing, a floorboard creaking, a drawer opening, or a toilet flushing. There was nothing.

Morrell produced the key Baht had given him and tried it one more time, just in case. He quietly slipped it into the lock and attempted to turn it, but it wouldn't budge. Returning the key to his pocket, he pulled his picks back out.

When he had the door unlocked, he signaled to Harvath, who once again helped him scan for booby traps. They wouldn't have put it past Koebler to have rigged some sort of improvised explosive device meant to take out anyone unfortunate enough to stumble upon his lair.

Morrell was just about to give the all clear, when Harvath whispered, "Stop! Don't move."

The CIA man froze. "What is it?" he whispered back, afraid to even breathe. "What do you see?"

Through the crack where the door was hinged to the frame, Harvath could see inside. Just below waist-height, attached to the wall, was a Coke can with its top sawed off. Inside the empty can was a very nasty surprise.

"Hand grenade," Harvath replied, pulling out his flashlight. "I think it's attached to the door. Give me a second to figure it out."

It was a simple, yet deadly booby trap Harvath himself had used. Playing the light along the frame, he looked for the wire.

With the pin removed, the grenade had been set inside the Coke can, the spoon held in place by the rim. A piece of wire had been wrapped around the neck and attached to the door. When the door opened, the grenade would lift free, releasing the spoon and igniting the fuse.

Within seconds, the grenade would detonate. Though not as inspired as hiding two grenades on a Chinese corpse and sending it down in an elevator, it was still a highly effective means of taking an opponent completely by surprise.

What Harvath was looking for now was its "off" switch.

It was a set-it-and-forget-it trap—one that Koebler could make hot when he left the building and then render safe when he returned home. That meant it had to all be controlled manually at the threshold.

Running his fingers along the inside of the jamb, he finally found what he was looking for. Unspooling the wire, he carefully put slack in the line, allowing the grenade, which had already begun to rise from the can, to come back to rest.

"Okay," he told Morrell. "Very slowly, you can begin to open the door."

Once it was open wide enough, Harvath slid in sideways, found the pin atop the doorframe, and put it back in the grenade.

"One hell of a doorbell," said Morrell, as he entered and took a look at the trap. "I'm glad you knew what you were looking for."

"We got lucky," said Harvath, sweeping his flashlight around the space. The windows had all been reinforced and papered over.

Morrell reached for the light switch, and as he did Harvath snapped the bright white beam of his light directly into his colleague's eyes. "Don't!"

"What the fuck, Harvath?" he demanded, dropping his hand, temporarily blinded.

When his vision returned, Harvath gestured to the overhead light fixture.

"And?" Morrell asked, still seeing spots.

Illuminating the bulb with his flashlight, it looked like it had been filled with sand and short screws. "Booby trap number two."

"Jesus," the CIA man exclaimed. "You think that's gunpowder?"

Harvath nodded. "Plus shrapnel."

"Death from above. This guy is one sick bastard."

Harvath didn't disagree. "I'm going to look around. You coming?"

"No thanks. I'm going to watch the door. I've seen enough."

"Don't move and don't touch anything."

"Don't worry," Morrell responded. "I don't plan to."

Harvath left him where he was and walked farther into the space. It appeared to have been offices at some point, and unlike the Muay Thai gym, this wasn't a prop. This was definitely where Kevin Koebler had been laying his head.

The sink, toilet, and shower had all been used. The bed, though covered in wrinkled linens, had been made perfectly, just like they had been taught in the Navy. You started the day by making your bunk—one successfully completed task built upon the next.

A cell phone charger was plugged into the wall outlet. There were stacks of recent newspapers, all with big, front-page stories about the bombings. One of the closets was full of neatly hung clothes and had two pieces of luggage.

The biggest discovery, however, came when Harvath entered the kitchen area. It had been stocked with cases of water and weeks' worth of food. Canned fruits, canned vegetables, eggs, cookies, crackers, and all sorts of soups, stews, and broths. There were medical supplies, soaps, shampoo, razors, and even hair-coloring kits.

Either Kevin Koebler was expecting the Zombie Apocalypse to kick off within days, or he was planning to go to ground and stay hidden for weeks.

As far as Harvath knew, there'd been no reports of the dead walking the earth, which could mean only one thing. Koebler was out, moving around, and taking meetings because he wasn't done yet. He had another attack planned.

CHAPTER 39

In addition to his helmet and balaclava, Koebler had added a pair of Oakley sunglasses—popular with Thai tactical units—to his disguise. His nine-millimeter pistol was out of its holster again and back under his left thigh as he approached the checkpoint.

There was a glowing river of brake lights as cars slowed up ahead. Thai soldiers in helmets and body armor moved between vehicles, their rifles slung across their chests. A pair of police trucks sat angled across the far lane, while several motorbikes had been waved off to the shoulder for inspection. Bangkok remained on edge from Friday's bombings.

Koebler approached with his blue strobes already flashing, and within seconds a narrow corridor opened through the traffic.

Two of the soldiers at the checkpoint looked up, their eyes going straight to the paint scheme and markings on the Fortuner. ISOC.

Since the bombings, ISOC units had become a common sight across the city. The soldiers didn't signal him to stop. Instead, they waved the vehicles ahead of Koebler aside, clearing the way and allowing him to pass straight through. The deception had worked.

The checkpoint eventually disappeared in his rearview mirror as Koebler guided the Fortuner farther into the city center. Morning traffic had only continued to build, but the flashing ISOC lights kept working their magic, creating a navigable path before him.

Within minutes, crowded commercial blocks gave way to a quieter stretch of road lined with tall rain trees and high hedges, which shielded some of Bangkok's most exclusive properties.

Up ahead, set back behind wrought-iron gates and impeccably manicured grounds, stood the gleaming white façade of Koebler's next target—the Royal Bangkok Sports Club.

Founded back in the days when European diplomats and trading houses had dominated much of the city's business life, the club had remained one of the city's most exclusive institutions.

Its membership roster read like a directory of the Thai elite—senior military officers, cabinet ministers, industrialists, and old-money families whose influence spread across politics, finance, and the armed forces. A handful of foreign ambassadors belonged as well, along with several Western executives whose companies had deep roots in Southeast Asia.

On weekday mornings Bangkok's powerful came here to talk. Deals were made over coffee on the terrace, and quiet conversations shaped decisions that would ripple through ministries, boardrooms, and military headquarters by the afternoon.

Koebler turned onto the entrance drive and approached the main gate. Security had been upgraded since Friday, and a pair of guards checked arriving vehicles as a police van idled nearby with its lights flashing. Under the shade of an adjacent banyan tree, a quartet of soldiers kept an eye on the road.

His flashing blue strobes caught everyone's attention immediately. He didn't slow. He kept the ISOC-marked Fortuner moving at a controlled pace, one hand resting lightly on the steering wheel as if he had driven through a dozen gates like this already that morning.

One of the guards signaled his colleague, who swung the barrier open, and once again, Koebler drove straight through.

Inside, the perfectly planted flower beds gave way to a wide sweep of emerald lawn. Golf carts hummed along the paved paths and several early players were making their way to the first tee.

The circular drive in front of the clubhouse was already buzzing with activity. Multiple luxury sedans sat near the entrance, their chauffeurs leaning against them smoking cigarettes and checking their phones. Waiters in white jackets moved from table to table along the terrace carrying coffee and breakfast trays.

After it passed through the front gates, no one paid attention to the

ISOC vehicle and Koebler killed the light bar. Having guided the SUV toward the valet area, he selected a space near the entrance.

From there, the blast would reach both the terrace and the lobby.

He shut off the engine and sat for a moment, watching the morning routine unfold. A contingent of businessmen laughed over something at their table. Two Royal Thai Army officers stood near the rail discussing something as a waiter refilled their coffee cups. While outside the club life may have changed, inside it was business as usual. Predictable. Just what his client had counted on.

Koebler stepped out of the Fortuner and walked to the rear, where he opened the hatch. Beneath the false panel, the bomb sat bolted into the cargo compartment. The assembly was compact, but powerful—its main charge meant to turn the SUV itself into shrapnel.

Mounted beside the firing assembly was a pair of small, prepaid mobile phones—one a primary, the other a backup. The Cambodian SIM cards were already installed.

He checked the connections, making sure the detonator leads were seated properly. Blast damage would destroy the handsets, but in a design like this, fragments of the SIM would survive. Investigators would find exactly what his clients wanted them to find.

Next, he verified the initiator circuit, confirming that the incoming call would trigger the firing sequence. It was a simple, reliable system. Practically impossible to interrupt once armed.

Pressing the activation switch, he watched as a small green light blinked once and then settled into a steady pulse. The device was live.

Closing the panel, he shut the vehicle's hatch and retrieved his backpack from the front passenger seat.

He then walked away from the Fortuner without looking back.

CHAPTER 40

Morrell crouched beside the door and gently worked the tension wrench back and forth inside the lock. Harvath stood several feet away, watching both directions. The last thing they needed was for Koebler to show up and take them by surprise.

Upstairs, they had left the bombmaker's abode exactly as they had found it. The door had been relocked and the Coke can grenade trap had been reset. The cameras had been successfully spoofed and Koebler should have no idea that they'd been there.

Morrell gave his pick a final twist and the dead bolt lock fell into place with a solid *thunk*. "That should keep things interesting," he said as he straightened and brushed the dust from his hands.

Harvath took one last look at the building. He was already assembling a surveillance roster in his head. Ashby and Palmer would take first watch, followed by Staelin and Haney. "Let's get going."

They had only taken a few steps down the block when a massive, concussive *boom* rolled through the city.

Both men stopped dead in their tracks. It was heavy—like distant thunder. Seconds later, the unmistakable shock wave arrived.

All around them, corrugated metal rattled. Every single window in the neighborhood clattered against its frames. Countless car alarms began blaring.

"What the hell was that?" Morrell asked.

Harvath didn't answer. He knew what it was, just as well as Morrell did.

Suddenly, their radios crackled to life. "Did you guys hear that?" Mo asked.

"We did," Morrell replied, as they started walking toward the van. "What've you got?"

"Hold on."

Several moments passed as Mo scanned the police frequencies and ran them through a translation app on his laptop. Finally, his voice came back. "Large explosion reported. Central Bangkok."

Harvath felt his stomach tighten.

Morrell looked at him. "You thinking what I'm thinking?"

Harvath nodded. "Koebler."

KitKat's voice cut in over their earpieces. "Emergency channels are all lighting up. Multiple units responding."

Sirens began rising in the distance—first one, then another, then several more joining in.

"Royal Bangkok Sports Club," said Mo.

"Jesus," Morrell responded.

Harvath looked at him. "What?"

"It's Bangkok's swankiest country club. A real who's who. Politicians, military brass, business leaders. It'd be like hitting the Congressional Country Club in D.C."

Harvath didn't need the comparison. He already understood. If Koebler had just detonated a bomb there, the choice of target had been deliberate.

"What kind of a blast are we talking about?" he asked over the radio.

"Still sorting it out," Mo replied, the sound of his keyboard clacking in the background. "But initial reports are mentioning several vehicles on fire near the entrance."

Harvath and Morrell exchanged a look.

Morrell said it first, "Car bomb."

Harvath agreed. "Same playbook as Friday."

"Police are saying there are multiple casualties," KitKat added quietly.

More sirens could be heard now, screaming down the main road toward the city center. Harvath stared at the plume of black smoke rising above the skyline.

The Royal Bangkok Sports Club hadn't been chosen by accident. It was a message.

Harvath thought about the bolt-hole upstairs. The food. The supplies. The hair dye. It hadn't been stocked for comfort. It'd been stocked to allow him to stay off the radar.

Mo's voice came back over the radio. "Police are locking down the entire district around the Royal Bangkok Sports Club."

Harvath turned to Morrell. "You should call Davi back."

"You sure?"

Harvath nodded. "We may have already sat on Koebler's identity too long."

The CIA operative pulled out his phone and hit redial. Davi answered on the first ring.

"Not a good time," she said.

"Where are you?"

"En route," she replied over the sound of sirens. "Royal Bangkok Sports Club. There's been another bombing."

"I know," Morrell said. "We think we may have something."

There was a fraction of a beat. "Then say it."

"Not over the phone."

Another pause. "I'm coming up to Rama IV," she stated. "Where are you?"

"Khlong Toei. Near the port."

"They're locking the city back down. Get to the river. Catch the express boat to Sathorn Pier. I'll meet you there."

"And Richard," she added, "whatever you've got, it had better be good."

Morrell ended the call and slipped the phone back into his pocket. "We've got to move. We'll get to Davi by boat."

"Roger that," Harvath replied.

They reached the van and quickly filled KitKat and Mo in. The two techs would stay put and keep their eyes on the building. If

Koebler or anyone else showed up, they were to let Morrell know immediately.

Harvath told them he'd have Ashby and Palmer there as soon as possible to back them up.

Then he and Morrell headed for the pier.

CHAPTER 41

As Harvath and Morrell neared the river, the increased police presence was impossible to miss. Patrol cars and motorcycles clustered at intersections feeding the pier. Their lights flashed as officers waved some vehicles through, turned others back, and pulled still more over for inspection. The city was tightening by the minute.

They pushed through the crowd at the landing and boarded just as the express boat was taking on passengers. Once aboard, they moved up to the bow.

Morrell pulled out his phone and called the CIA station, pressing for anything they might have on the attack.

Harvath made his own call and Ashby picked up on the first ring.

"We found where Koebler has been hiding out," he said—no hello, no preamble. "Morrell has two tech officers there watching it. I want you and Palmer on-site ASAP, backing them up."

"We'll start gearing up right away," she replied. "What are our ROEs?"

Harvath looked out over the brackish, green-gray water. It was the right question. Establishing rules of engagement was important. "I want him alive," he said. "But if he gives you no other choice, kill him. Nobody on our team dies on this assignment. Is that clear?"

"Crystal."

They spent another minute on logistics. He passed her the cell numbers Morrell had given him for KitKat and Mo, told her where to find their van, and then ended the call.

Morrell was wrapping up his own and slipped his phone back into his pocket as the boat pulled away from the dock.

"What have you got?" Harvath asked.

"It'll take days to sort through the wreckage, but Thai police already have CCTV from the club. Definitely a vehicle-borne device. But there's a twist. The truck was made to look like it belonged to ISOC. It pulled up near the main entrance to the clubhouse, parked, and the driver walked away a couple minutes before the blast."

"Can they ID him?"

"Not with what they've got so far. He was wearing a helmet, face covering, and sunglasses."

Harvath shook his head. "Jesus. Davi is going to be pissed."

"You think?" Morrell replied. "Maybe we don't get off at Sathorn. We keep going. There's a great spot further upriver. Dollar beers and fifty-cent oysters. How's that sound?"

"If Davi's going to kill us, I'd rather not make her travel."

The express boat churned north, its engine hammering beneath their feet, as it nosed into the Chao Phraya current. Morning traffic on the river was already heavy. Commuter vessels moved in both directions. Boats known as longtails darted back and forth. Barges filled with cargo crawled through the shallow water closer to shore.

On the express, office workers in pressed shirts stood shoulder to shoulder with laborers, tourists, and women carrying vinyl bags. Nearly all of them had their phones out. Some were speaking in rapid, clipped Thai. Others were scrolling social media, craning to compare what they were seeing on their screens with the distant cloud of smoke hanging over the city.

Harvath kept coming back to Koebler's choice of target. The Royal Bangkok Sports Club was where wealth, influence, and senior leadership—civilian and military—intersected. A bomb there would do more than kill. It would trigger a ferocious response and put the Thai government under intense pressure to act fast, whether they had enough evidence or not. Whatever China's role in this was, it couldn't be good.

Fifteen minutes later, Sathorn Pier emerged through the haze—crowded, noisy, and choked with the usual morning crush—plus tons of additional cops. Morrell spotted her first.

Davi was standing just beyond the landing near a dark sedan, flanked by two Thai officers. She was scanning the arriving passengers with an expression that made it clear she was in no mood to wait.

By the time Harvath and Morrell stepped off the boat, she was already moving toward them.

"You owe me a corpse," she said, her right hand on her hip—just forward of her service weapon. "This had better be good."

Morrell reached into his pocket, took out his phone, and brought up the image. "The print you asked us to run came back," he said. "His name is Kevin Koebler."

Davi took the phone and looked at the photo. "Who is he?"

"American. Former Navy SEAL," Harvath replied. "Before that, he was an explosive ordnance technician. He's got a lot of experience with bombs. Big, nasty ones."

"Do you think he's in Bangkok?"

"I think there's a strong possibility," Harvath answered.

"Let's say he is," Davi replied. "What makes him our bomber?"

Morrell picked it up. "He was dishonorably discharged after multiple killings in Iraq were tied to explosives he had built. The Navy couldn't prove it cleanly, so they drummed him out on lesser charges. But if you're asking whether he's the kind of man who could do something like this, the answer is yes."

"That doesn't make him our bomber."

"No," Harvath replied. "But he's the first name we've got that fits the blast."

Davi handed the phone back. "What's the rest of it? What are you not telling me?"

Morrell took the phone. "We found a location in Khlong Toei. We believe he's been using it as a bolt-hole."

She stared at him for a beat. "And you didn't think to lead with that?"

Morrell met her gaze. "The minute any of this goes wide, we lose our shot."

"I'm the law here in Thailand," Davi responded. "I decide how and where information flows. You do not hold out on me. Give me the Khlong Toei address."

"Fine," Harvath said. "But if you flood that neighborhood with cops,

Koebler will smell it before the first car door opens. And once he does, he's gone."

"Is it under surveillance?"

"Yes."

"By whom?"

"Two of ours," Morrell answered. "More backup is on the way."

Davi turned to one of her officers and issued a quick order in Thai. He nodded once and stepped away, already reaching for his phone.

"No local units," she agreed, looking back at Harvath. "No marked vehicles. No sirens. But no one goes near that address unless I authorize it. Is that clear?"

"Agreed," Harvath replied. "And tell your people the upstairs entry door and the overhead light just beyond it are booby-trapped."

She made note of the warning and then delivered one of her own. Shifting her eyes to Morrell, she said, "One last thing. When this is over, you still owe me a body."

CHAPTER 42

The Royal Bangkok Sports Club had offered Koebler two advantages. One, it had been built in such a way that members and guests never had to see staff moving from structure to structure. And two, no one on the property had known that a bomb was about to go off.

Carrying his backpack, he had walked away from his vehicle, keeping his pace measured. At the rear of the clubhouse, he veered onto a paved service path that groundskeepers used to move between storage sheds, maintenance bays, and the far side of the property. Screened by mature trees and clipped hedges, it was the kind of route no one really saw, even when they were staring right at it.

Near the club's golf cart storage barn, he stepped behind an equipment pen and set down his backpack. Stripping off his tactical uniform, he changed into khakis, a button-down shirt, white tennis shoes, and a lightweight blazer. He placed his old clothes into the pack, then topped off his outfit with a new ball cap and a disposable surgical mask. The transformation had taken less than ninety seconds. By the time he stepped back out, the man in the ISOC uniform had ceased to exist.

A golf cart whined past at the far end of the path. He waited for it to disappear and then continued east.

The barbed wire–topped boundary wall that marked the perimeter of the RBSC was interspersed with sections of dense vegetation and chain-link fence. Along one stretch, a row of shrubbery had grown thick enough to screen it from the path. That was where Koebler would make his escape.

Ducking behind it, he set down his pack again, pulled out a pair of compact cutters, and got quickly to work. Once he had clipped enough of the links, he bent the mesh back until there was just enough room to slip through.

He emerged onto a service road that ran behind the King Chulalongkorn Memorial Hospital campus. The sounds of the city once again enveloped him—engines, horns, voices, the distant whine of an ambulance siren. He checked his watch. It was time.

Removing the small black Nokia phone from his pocket, he powered it up. There were only two numbers saved to it—both of which were attached to the bomb parked in front of the clubhouse. He highlighted the top number and activated the call.

Far behind him, muffled by buildings and trees, the enormous blast erupted. The concussion rolled across the golf course and ripped through the neighborhood a split second before the blast itself.

Car alarms began to wail. Birds lifted from the treetops in a frenzied burst. Across the medical campus, people began shouting.

Calmly, Koebler walked to the corner, merged with a stream of pedestrians, and kept moving.

Disassembling the phone, he dropped a piece in a public trash can outside a convenience store. Two blocks later, he fed a couple more pieces into a storm drain. The rest were tossed into the back of a garbage truck near an open-air market and quickly covered with damp cardboard and rotting produce.

At the subway, he bought a ticket with cash, kept his head down, and boarded with everyone else. He was just another commuter starting his week.

Everyone around him was getting text alerts that something had happened. They all had their phones out, trying to figure out where the bombing had taken place. The news was spreading in fragments, and fear gripped the train car.

Koebler stood by the door, watching his own reflection slide across the darkened window. Beneath his mask, he smiled. The assignment had been executed perfectly. If the money landed as planned, he was finished. No more clients. No more handlers. No more jobs with too many moving parts. All he had to do now was get out of Bangkok alive.

He got off two stops later, changed direction twice, and spent the next forty minutes putting distance between himself and the blast. He used reflective glass, mirrored elevator doors, parked cars, and the simple rhythm of foot traffic to make sure he wasn't being followed. There was no one tailing him.

Even so, when he approached the broader maze of streets feeding into Khlong Toei, he slowed and didn't go straight in. He *never* went straight in.

Instead, he made a loose box around several blocks, using storefront windows to see who might be behind him, and studying the pulse of traffic for anything that seemed off. The bomb at the club would have every cop in Bangkok scrambling.

When he came around the far end of his block, he saw the van. It was parked three doors down from his building, its nose pointed toward the main thoroughfare for a fast exit. White paint, no tinted glass. It was plain. Anonymous. There was nothing outwardly remarkable about it, except that it didn't belong. Not here. Not on this street. Not at this hour.

He had lived in the neighborhood long enough, and paid close enough attention, to notice when something was wrong.

Continuing to walk, he kept his eyes forward and gave it no more than a casual glance, like any passing pedestrian. Inside, though, all of his alarm bells were ringing.

The windshield had been cleaned recently, but not the rest of the vehicle. The tires were too good. Company vehicles in Thailand were rolling billboards, yet this one had no markings. There was nothing in the cab—no pens, no clipboards, no empty coffee cups or food wrappers. And while the cargo area was totally enclosed, the rear suspension sat just low enough to suggest there was weight in the back.

As he drew closer, he caught the faint shudder of the engine through the chassis and noticed the slightest tremble in the side mirror. The van was idling. In Bangkok heat, that wasn't unusual. What was unusual was a work van parked half a block from his building, running its air-conditioning, with no driver present and no apparent delivery or job in progress. He kept walking.

Thirty yards on, he crossed the street, using the opportunity to check the block behind him.

Other than the van, everything looked fine. No one was loitering near the entrance to his building. There were no unmarked units tucked around the corner. No rooftop silhouette where there shouldn't be one. That only bothered him more, not less.

The men who had shown up at the storage unit hadn't looked like police. Neither had the men who had ambushed his meeting at Teens. Whoever was trying to disrupt this operation knew how to stay out of sight until the last possible second.

He was certain that whoever owned that van was in the cargo area, watching through hidden optics or cameras. His building was under surveillance, which meant that the bolt-hole was burned. Everything left inside was gone to him now. Clothes, burner phones, IDs, cash, the remaining supplies—none of that mattered enough to risk walking into a trap.

All that mattered now was who was in that van, and how much they knew. Unzipping his pack, his hand went for his pistol.

If he walked away now, most likely he'd live. If he killed the surveillance team, he might buy himself a few answers via their phones, laptops, and cameras. He might even learn who had sent them.

He took a breath and tried to let his mind settle. He knew what the right choice was. The safe choice.

Walking away was cleaner, but it would leave too many questions unanswered—chief among them, how he had been discovered. That would haunt him. Questions like that got men killed. He couldn't let it go.

He tucked the pistol into his waistband, zipped his pack back up, and slipped down a covered side passage.

Laundry hung overhead on sagging lines. Plastic buckets and broken pallets were stacked against stained walls. The entire place stank. Koebler moved through it without a sound.

At the far end, he stepped out and, coming around the corner, carefully doubled back. He used a parked car for cover. From here, he had a partial view of the rear of the van and its double doors. The hunted had just become the hunter.

He studied his target for several minutes. He still had two grenades with him. The easiest course of action would have been to pull the pins and roll them underneath as he walked by. That, however, would draw entirely too much attention and likely destroy any useful items he hoped to gain from inside.

His only course of action was to assault the van head-on and hope that the element of surprise would provide enough of an edge.

Taking a deep breath, he counted to three and then stepped out from behind the parked car and began walking down the sidewalk.

If this was an actual surveillance vehicle, he would have to assume that they would see him coming. What he hoped was that they wouldn't be able to anticipate what he would do when he drew even with them.

He was still wearing his ball cap and surgical mask and kept his head down as he approached. The less they saw of his face, the better.

Drawing even with the back of the vehicle, he stepped behind it and, with his right hand wrapped around the butt of his pistol, reached out with his left and tested the latch. *Unlocked.*

Pulling out his gun, he went to yank the door open, but before he could, there was the metallic *click* of it being locked from the inside.

They had not only seen him—as expected—but had reacted. From inside the van, he could hear two men speaking. *In English.*

Raising his pistol, he began firing through the van's thin metal skin. The first three rounds punched through just above the door handles. One of the men inside cried out.

Shifting his aim beneath the handles, Koebler fired again, right where he believed center mass would be if anyone was crouching behind the doors.

This time, something heavy thudded against the interior. It was followed by a ragged choking sound. He could hear the frantic movement, like someone scrambling, maybe trying to get a weapon or maybe trying to get away from the back of the van entirely.

He shifted off the line of fire, tried the latch again, and this time it gave. Ripping the left-hand door open, he fired into the cold air spilling out.

Inside, the cargo area had been converted into a compact surveillance bay. A table sat cluttered with batteries, cables, and other electronic equipment, along with a laptop showing a live feed of his building's entrance.

One man was collapsed against the left wall. Blood was pumping through his fingers where he was clutching his neck. Another was down on one knee near the opposite wheel well, one hand reaching for a pistol hidden behind a Pelican case.

Koebler shot him in the face and the man dropped where he was.

They were both Caucasian. Mid-twenties. Thin builds. Civilian clothes. They were definitely not Thai military or police. And they didn't look anything like the men who had attacked him at Teens and at the storage unit. The first one was still alive.

His headset had been knocked to the right and blood flecked the microphone boom. He stared up with wide, wet eyes as he tried to drag air through his ruptured throat.

Koebler stepped into the van and kicked the pistol away from the other man's dead hand. He then looked down at the survivor.

"Who sent you?" he asked.

The man tried to speak, but all that came out was a bubbling hiss.

Koebler crouched beside him and grabbed a fistful of his shirt. "Is it just you? How many others are there?"

Once again came the hiss.

Koebler patted him down quickly. Phone. Wallet. Keys. He moved to the dead one next. Another phone. Another wallet. An encrypted radio handset.

Looking at a second laptop that must have slid off the table, he could see that somehow the men had been able to tap into his wireless camera feeds. That took significant technical know-how. The fact that they'd been able to do it without tripping any of the alarms built into the encrypted software was an incredible feat. Whoever these people were, they were very high-level.

Opening the first wallet, he had his answer. Inside was a United States Embassy Bangkok access badge. There was one in the second wallet as well. *Americans.*

For a moment, Koebler didn't move. So that was who had found him. Not the Cambodians. Not Thai police. Not ISOC.

How the hell had the Americans picked up his trail? And who specifically was hunting him?

Based on their technical prowess and the embassy affiliation, he had to assume it was the CIA. Then, all of a sudden, "how" they had found him became glaringly apparent. His Glock.

It all made perfect sense. Thailand had his pistol and were probably able to lift a fingerprint or two from it. When nothing turned up in any of their databases, they would have reached out to their international partners for help. Someone at the U.S. Embassy was able to locate the only official set of his fingerprints in the world—his U.S. Navy service file.

How they'd made the jump from ex-SEAL to rooms above a shuttered storefront in Khlong Toei was a discussion for another time. Right now, he needed to focus on disappearing.

Outrunning Thai authorities was one thing. Escaping the CIA was another thing entirely.

He had only worked with them a handful of times, but he learned very quickly that they were particularly relentless, especially their paramilitary units. In their world, there were no rules, and they were backed to the hilt with the full force of the United States government.

Behind him, the wounded man made another wet, choking attempt to breathe. Turning around, Koebler placed the muzzle of his weapon against the man's forehead and pressed the trigger, painting the back of the van with blood, bone, and pieces of brain.

Grabbing his backpack, he prepared to move. He had already lingered too long. Time was now his most precious commodity.

CHAPTER 43

WASHINGTON, D.C.

By the time Shawna Vaughn stepped through the Northwest Gate, the White House behind her had taken on that strange Sunday-night stillness Washington did so well. Not quiet, exactly, but muffled. Lights still burned in offices throughout the grounds. Nobody was easing off. The return from Camp David had not lessened the pressure. If anything, the long day had intensified it.

The focus remained the same. China. Taiwan. Troop and equipment movements. Satellite imagery. Naval dispositions. Timing. Intent. No one Vaughn had heard claimed to know anything for certain. But everyone knew enough to be worried.

And running quieter and uglier beneath all that talk was a second conversation. Erin Delaney hadn't come back to work.

That alone had been enough to get people talking. Erin was Type A with a capital T and a capital A. She was always the first one in to the office and the last one out. After a Camp David weekend built around the Taiwan crisis, nobody at her level simply vanished and failed to show up for work.

Then the rumors had started. A federal agent murdered at her house. Two other men shot and killed at her ex-fiancé Connor's apartment. Connor missing. Erin missing. He was a Marine with multiple combat tours. The PTSD had gotten him fired. Erin had broken off their engagement. Had Connor snapped? Had he taken Erin hostage?

Every version had a different twist. Every version had been wrong. Or at least partly wrong. That was how Vaughn knew the story was spreading fast and through all the wrong channels.

Crossing Pennsylvania Avenue, she cut through Lafayette Square and her eyes scanned everything—tree line, benches, the slow drift of headlights beyond the iron fence. October had brought with it a damp chill. A thin ground fog had gathered low over the grass, giving the park the look of an old photograph left too long in the dark.

Normally, she liked this part of D.C. at night—the history, the architecture, the quiet hum of democracy. Tonight, she didn't trust any of it.

At least three people were dead—one of them a Department of Homeland Security agent and another a Diplomatic Security Service agent Vaughn herself had worked with. That was something she couldn't shake.

Not that men with badges couldn't go bad. They could. Money, ideology, blackmail, grievance—every agency in Washington was vulnerable to the same old human weaknesses. One bad apple was absolutely tragic and disgraceful. Two bad apples—in separate, but adjacent barrels—-went from looking disgraceful to looking coordinated.

If the people behind the attacks had been able to reach into multiple agencies, there was no telling how long and how powerful their arms were.

By helping Erin and Connor, she had probably just vaulted herself from observer to participant. And at that point, the jump from participant to target wasn't much of a jump at all. She brushed her hand against the outside of her coat, confirming that her sidearm was still right where it should be. She was taking nothing for granted.

Moving quickly across H Street, she headed for the Hay-Adams hotel. The warm glow from its windows was bleeding softly into the mist. The sooner she got inside, the sooner she could begin unpacking what was going on.

She knew Jennifer Fields only slightly, but slightly had been enough. Several years earlier, Fields had interviewed her during an FBI counterintelligence investigation involving a possible access agent somewhere in the wider White House orbit.

An access agent wasn't a spy in the classic sense—someone photographing documents or carrying secrets out in a briefcase. An access agent was more dangerous in certain ways—someone positioned to open doors, someone who could help a hostile foreign intelligence service get close to the people and places that mattered.

Vaughn had not been a suspect. She had been one of several people quietly debriefed because her job put her close enough to notice things—faces, routines, behavior, and people who seemed comfortable where they shouldn't have been. The interview had lasted less than an hour, but it had made an impression.

Fields had been younger than Vaughn expected, sharper than a lot of the agents she had dealt with, and almost impossible to read. She had asked precise questions, listened more than she spoke, and given away nothing. Vaughn had left the interview with two impressions—first, that Jennifer Fields was smart as hell, and second, that lying to her would have been a very big mistake.

As she approached its semicircular drive, the Hay-Adams loomed out of the mist, elegant and watchful. Vaughn entered through the large front doors, thankful to be out of the cold. Crossing the elegant lobby, she made her way downstairs to the Off the Record bar.

The bar, as always, was dimly lit. With its low ceilings and dark wood paneling, it was a room built for secrets. At this hour on a Sunday, the crowd was thin. More political caricatures lined the walls than there were customers sitting at the bar.

Vaughn stepped in and took a table with a view of the entrance. When the waiter came over, she ordered a club soda. Fields arrived right on time five minutes later.

The FBI agent came in quietly, expert at not drawing attention to herself. Not an easy task for such an attractive woman.

She was of medium height, had her dark hair pulled back, and wore a black wool coat. Her eyes found Vaughn almost immediately. Crossing the room, she slid into the chair opposite her.

"A Secret Service request for an off-books meeting on a Sunday night," she said. "That's either very good for me or very bad for you."

"Bad for everyone," Vaughn replied.

The waiter returned with her club soda. Fields ordered a bourbon, neat.

Once he was gone, she looked at Vaughn and said, "You look like hell."

"It's been a long day."

"I figured. White House still running full tilt over Taiwan?"

Vaughn nodded

"That isn't why I'm here, though, is it?"

"No."

The bourbon arrived. Fields waited until the waiter was gone and then, taking a sip, asked, "What kind of problem are we here to discuss?"

Vaughn didn't answer right away. She conducted a slow scan of the room before settling back on Fields. "Three dead bodies. Maybe more before this is over."

Fields's expression remained unchanged. "Go on."

"Two men broke into an apartment in Adams Morgan last night to kill a former United States Marine. Suppressed weapons. No phones. No identification. He killed them first."

Fields said nothing.

"This morning, another man, also looking for the Marine, forced entry into a second location and threatened to kill the home's owner."

"And?"

"That assailant's dead too."

Fields's eyes stayed on hers. "Who was the homeowner?"

"She's a member of the National Security Council staff."

That got the smallest shift out of her. "Who killed the intruder? The Marine or the NSC staffer?"

"The Marine."

Fields wasn't surprised. "How'd the intruder know to look for the Marine at her house?"

"They were engaged."

"So they have a history together. Where are they now?"

"Some place safe."

Fields took another sip of bourbon. "You're being careful."

"I have to be."

"Why come to me? Sounds like this is a job for Metro PD."

"No," Vaughn replied. "This stopped being a job for Metro when federal ties started surfacing at both scenes."

That landed. "What kind of federal ties?" she asked, setting down her glass.

"Of the two dead men at the Marine's apartment, one of them I recognized as DSS. We worked a joint detail together a while back. The dead man at the NSC staffer's house was carrying DHS credentials."

For the first time since she had sat down, Jennifer Fields went completely still. "Those are extremely serious accusations."

"Now you know why I asked you for an off-books meeting on a Sunday night."

Fields leaned back slightly, her large brown eyes studying Vaughn. "These are the same two crime scenes that have been all over the news today?"

Vaughn nodded. "I'm not sure how the federal connection hasn't leaked yet. But it will. And when it does, that's going to be a shitstorm."

Fields agreed. "You said you recognized one of the men. Does that mean you've got photos?"

"Not just photos," said Vaughn as she reached into her coat and removed her phone. Placing it on the table between them, she then took out a folded ziplock bag and laid that beside it.

"You came prepared."

"Because I trust you."

Fields appreciated her confidence. Unfolding the bag, she saw the DHS ID belonging to a Special Agent Mark Scofield.

"Jesus," she said quietly. "If that credential isn't genuine, it's an exceptionally good counterfeit."

"That's what I thought," said Vaughn.

Fields placed the DHS credential back on the table and picked up Vaughn's phone. Swiping through the photos, she studied the dead men from Connor's apartment. "Which one is the DSS agent?"

"The one closest to the door."

"Do you remember his name?"

Vaughn shook her head.

Setting the phone down, Fields folded her hands around her bourbon glass. "Okay," she said. "Walk me through it again. Slowly."

"The Marine's name is Connor Jameson. The NSC staffer is Erin

Delaney. Last night two men hit Jameson's apartment in Adams Morgan. He shot and killed them both. This morning, a man identifying himself as Special Agent Mark Scofield from DHS forced his way into Erin Delaney's home. He claimed to be there looking for Jameson. When he pulled his weapon and threatened to kill Erin, Jameson shot and killed him."

"What set all of this in motion?" Fields asked. "Why were they looking for him?"

"That's the part I'm still trying to get my arms around. Jameson has been making lots of noise about Taiwan. He believes China wants the U.S. and its allies fixated there while it moves against a more important objective somewhere else."

"What else do you know about him?"

"Multiple combat tours and PTSD issues," said Vaughn. "He was working at a think tank, but got let go. Since then, he's been blogging and podcasting—specifically about China."

"Do you think he got close to something?"

"Close enough. Why else try to kill him? Who has the ability to compromise federal agents and run targeted violence at an American citizen?"

Fields was quiet for a moment. "That's the part that bothers me the most. Could a criminal network do pieces of this? Maybe. But using Feds? At that level, you're talking about a state actor."

"Which brings us right back to China," Vaughn stated.

"If this is Beijing," said Fields, "then we're not just looking at a murder plot. We're looking at an active penetration of the United States government."

CHAPTER 44

BANGKOK

By the time Harvath and Morrell returned to Khlong Toei, Koebler's block was actively being locked down. Thai police vehicles were blocking both ends of the street, their light bars washing the buildings in undulating pulses of red and blue. Uniformed officers had cordoned off the area with tape and were pushing back a knot of residents, shopkeepers, and passersby who had gathered to watch.

Harvath's pulse had already quickened. He saw the van before he saw anything else. It was riddled with bullet holes and its rear doors stood wide open. He felt something inside him drop. Morrell saw it a split second later and the color drained from his face.

They started for the cordon, but Ashby intercepted them before they got halfway there. Palmer was right behind her. One look at Ashby's expression told Harvath what he didn't want to know.

"We got here just before the first patrol units set their perimeter," she said quietly. "Several locals had already called it in."

Morrell's eyes never left the van. "KitKat and Mo?"

Ashby gave a single, grim nod. "Both in back."

For a moment, Morrell didn't move.

Harvath kept his voice low. "What did you see?"

"The shooter stood behind the van and put multiple rounds through the rear doors," Ashby replied. "Then he climbed inside, fired several more shots, and according to a witness who spoke English, spent a couple moments looking around at everything before fleeing the scene."

"They give a description?"

"Male. About six feet. Baseball cap and surgical mask. Carrying a black backpack."

Morrell stared past Ashby. His eyes still on the van. "It was him."

Nobody argued.

"If he climbed in to take a look around," said Palmer, "he wasn't doing it just to make sure they were dead. He wanted to figure out who they were."

That was all Harvath needed. Koebler had found the van, understood what it was, and had taken the time to figure out who had put it there. That meant they hadn't only lost KitKat and Mo, they had also lost the element of surprise.

Morrell forced himself back into the moment. "Did the witnesses say which way he went?"

Ashby pointed down the block. "He was on foot and disappeared into one of the side lanes."

"Any cameras?"

"This is a pretty low-rent area," Palmer replied, "but we spotted a few. Mostly shops. There may be some traffic cams further out. The problem is time."

"Then Davi needs to get on them now," said Morrell. Pulling out his phone, he stepped away to call her.

Harvath looked at Ashby and Palmer. "He's burned now. Very soon, if not already, every cop in Bangkok is going to have his photo. He's going to be radioactive. Unless he has another bolt-hole, nobody is going to want to help him."

"So what's his next move?" Palmer asked.

Harvath glanced down the block toward where the shooter had disappeared. "Exfil."

CHAPTER 45

As soon as Morrell had connected with Davi, they put their own wheels in motion. Ashby and Palmer were sent back to the safe house, where they were told to brief Haney and Staelin, gear up, and be ready to move on a moment's notice.

Harvath and Morrell walked back to Morrell's Land Cruiser and drove to his apartment.

The drive took longer than it should have. Police checkpoints had sprung up on major roads and had begun to bleed into the side streets. Sirens rose and fell in every direction. In storefronts and open-air restaurants, televisions all carried the same images—fire, smoke, shattered glass, and the kind of chaos and confusion that only made people more afraid.

Neither man said much. Morrell kept both hands on the wheel, his eyes moving between the traffic and his mirrors. Harvath couldn't imagine what he was feeling. KitKat and Mo hadn't just been part of the operation. They had worked with Morrell at the embassy. He had known them. Trusted them. And now they were dead.

Morrell pulled into the garage beneath his building and parked. Having taken the elevator up to the seventeenth floor, they walked into his apartment, a corner unit at the end of the hall. It was quite luxurious with marble floors, polished nickel fixtures, and modern furniture. On any other day, Harvath might have made a remark about Morrell being on the take, but not after what had just happened.

Locking the door behind them, Morrell told Harvath to make himself at home while he went to call his station chief. News about KitKat and Mo would eventually make it to the embassy, and the ambassador shouldn't hear any of it for the first time from Thai authorities.

Harvath walked across the living room and took in the view of the Bangkok skyline. It was gleaming skyscrapers and green treetops for as far as the eye could see, but over it all hung a pall of smoke from the RBSC bombing.

When Morrell came back out of his bedroom, he looked haggard. Motioning Harvath over to the open kitchen, he said, "My chief's handling the embassy side. Ambassador, DSS, whoever needs to be read in. He's leaving us alone, for now."

"That's good," Harvath replied.

Morrell reached for the coffee machine, but was interrupted by a knock at the door. "That should be Davi."

He crossed the room, checked the peephole, and opened the door.

Davi stepped inside carrying the bombing scene with her. There was soot on one of her sleeves, a faint streak of grime near her collar, and a look on her face that suggested whatever reserve she had started the day with had long since been burned away.

"How bad was Khlong Toei?" she asked.

"Bad," Morrell replied. "We lost two good operatives. And Koebler now knows who was watching him."

Removing her shoes, Davi pushed past him and headed for the fridge. "You're positive it was Koebler?" she asked, as she removed a bottle of water, took off the top, and sat down at the island.

"Positive enough," Harvath replied. "Male. Roughly six feet. Baseball cap. Surgical mask. Black backpack. According to a witness, he came up behind the van and fired through the rear doors. Then he climbed inside, fired a couple more rounds, and then spent time looking through the cargo area before leaving."

Davi drank from the bottle and set it down. "My people are already pulling any footage they can get from Khlong Toei. And from the area around the club. If there's a connection, we'll find it."

"It was him," said Harvath, echoing Morrell's words from earlier. "Both places. I guarantee it."

"There's something else," she added. "Overnight, there was an explosion and a fire at a small storage facility. Two unidentified men are dead."

"Any idea what caused it?" Harvath asked.

Davi shook her head. "No, but a Toyota Fortuner, the same make and model we believe may have been used in the RBSC bombing, was seen exiting the property."

"It's Koebler," Harvath asserted.

"It very much looks that way," she agreed. "Originally, it didn't match his attack pattern, so we kept it quiet in order to not create a panic. Now, however, we assume it's connected."

"It's all connected," said Morrell. "Which means the clock just sped up."

Davi looked at him. "Because of your two colleagues in the van?"

He nodded. "Before Thai police connect them to my embassy, I briefed my station chief. He's getting the ambassador on board and handling the fallout on that side."

"Good," she replied. "Because once they're identified, the press will move fast."

"The bigger problem," Harvath interjected, "is Koebler. He just lost his bolt-hole. He knows the police will be pushing his image everywhere. He's not going to wait around to see how tight the city gets."

"You think he'll attempt to leave."

"I know he will."

"The entire country has been locked down since Friday. Airports, train stations, ferry terminals, border crossings, ports, highways—everything. Now, every province, right down to their beat cops, will have his photo—on top of their orders to stop anyone and anything that looks wrong."

"Koebler will have planned for that. He'll have a contingency."

"And how do we figure out what that contingency is?" she asked.

Harvath thought about it for a moment. "The best way would be to look at what he's done before when a job went bad."

"You want to see what happens when his pattern is under pressure," replied Morrell, as he turned back to his coffee machine and hit the switch.

"Exactly," said Harvath. "Not his normal pattern. His worst-day pattern."

"Do you think Nicholas could pull that out of the data he's compiled?"

Harvath removed his phone from his pocket and dialed. "If it's doable, he's the guy."

When Nicholas answered, he got straight to it. "Koebler knows we're onto him. We think he's going to try to leave the country. His name and photograph will be everywhere. That means official ports of entry are off the table for him. In everything you pulled up on him, has he ever had a job go wrong and suddenly his exit gets ugly? We're trying to get a sense of what he does when forced to pivot."

"Give me a minute," Nicholas replied, already typing. "I've got his bombing and travel overlays. I just need to strip out the clean departures and isolate the outliers."

While Nicholas worked, Morrell poured coffee into two mugs and slid one toward Harvath. Davi, who he knew well enough to know wasn't a coffee person, took another drink of her water.

Finally, Nicholas came back on the line. "Okay," he said. "I've got one."

Harvath put him on speaker. "What do you have?"

"His standard rhythm is what we already knew. He stages locally, executes, and gets out fast. When the environment stays permissive, he prefers commercial air travel under the same identity he used to enter. With so much being computerized and countries keeping a closer eye on lengths of stays, that makes the most sense."

"But?" Morrell asked.

"But there appears to have been one operation where the heat came down too quickly for that."

"What happened?"

Nicholas paused, keys clicking in the background. "He vanished."

Harvath's brow furled. "Meaning?"

"Meaning no outbound flight. No documented land crossing. No recorded departure at all. Then, less than three weeks later, facial recognition picks him up in another country under a different alias."

"So, he didn't get out through normal channels," Morrell said.

"That's my read," Nicholas responded. "He used some sort of route that bypassed official scrutiny."

"Such as?"

"That's the part I am still trying to nail down."

Harvath took a sip of his coffee and said, "Whatever it was, I'm guessing he didn't improvise it from scratch after the attack."

"Probably not," Nicholas replied. "When the clean exits disappear, you don't suddenly invent a whole new pipeline, not under duress. You fall back on something preexisting. A route. A facilitator. A set of contacts. Maybe all three."

Davi said nothing, but Harvath could see her processing it.

"Then what's the common denominator?" Morrell asked.

"I'm still trying to unravel it," Nicholas answered. "But if I had to guess, it's not passenger movement. It's freight. Cargo. Something with enough volume that Koebler could hide in."

Harvath nodded. That tracked. "Can you narrow it any further than that?"

"Not yet. I can tell you this, though—if it worked before, there's a good chance Koebler will try it again. You don't forget a solid exit, especially one that came through in a pinch."

Nicholas kept typing. "One more thing."

"What is it?"

"In the outlier case, what forced the pivot was a fuel truck driving by at the last moment. It turned the attack into something bigger than he expected. It jammed up law enforcement systems and pushed every visible exit to maximum scrutiny."

"Just like what Thailand is experiencing now."

"Exactly," said Nicholas. "If he's forced to flee, he doesn't necessarily need to know the exact route yet. He just has to know what kind he needs."

"The kind that survives a countrywide lockdown," Harvath replied. "Freight. Food. Fuel. Coastal traffic. Any commercial transport no government wants to shut down unless they absolutely have to."

"Bingo."

"Keep on it. I want every single piece of data you can find."

"Working it now," Nicholas stated.

Ending the call, Harvath slid the phone back into his pocket.

For a moment, nobody spoke.

Then Davi set down her water bottle. "Thailand is already checking highways, borders, ports, ferries, rail. The question is where we can focus faster than everyone else."

"The criminal pipelines hiding inside legitimate traffic," Harvath said.

Both of them looked at him.

"When Nicholas and I were talking earlier about how the bomb components might have made their way into Thailand, he pointed out that contraband is sometimes concealed beneath seafood in refrigerated trucks. If this operation is tied to an existing smuggling network, Koebler may not need the quickest route out. He just needs one that already knows how to slip through the cracks."

"That's where we focus then," Davi said, as her phone buzzed. Pulling it out, she glanced at the screen and answered in Thai. Her expression hardened almost immediately. She listened, asked two rapid-fire questions, then ended the call and looked up.

"What is it?" Morrell asked.

"That was my tech team at RBSC," she said. "The FBI evidence recovery people have started sorting debris."

Harvath looked at her. "What did they find?"

"Unlike the devices from Friday, the white phosphorus component either didn't ignite properly or didn't burn all the way through," she said. "They've recovered a partial SIM card and identified a component signature. Both of which point back to Cambodia."

CHAPTER 46

Koebler didn't call his handler right away. First, he needed to put distance between himself and the two CIA operatives he had shot in the surveillance van. Distance bought time. And right now, time was survival.

He kept moving. Head down. Eyes alert. He was being hunted by the most aggressive predator on the planet—the United States government. Even a small mistake could get him killed.

The Americans had found his building, penetrated his cameras, and put a team on his doorstep. They had resources, reach, and patience. By now, they'd be working backward and outward at the same time; focused on every single detail. They'd leave no stone unturned.

He crossed another street, checked behind him without looking like he was checking, and kept walking. Still nothing.

Two questions kept circling. How long had the CIA had him in their sights? And what had they been waiting for?

He had to assume that Thai authorities now had both his real identity and the Dutch alias he'd used to enter the country. Soon, his face would be everywhere. He needed to be well on his way out of Thailand before that happened.

At a run-down clothing shop, he paid cash for a pair of cargo pants, a long-sleeved T-shirt, sunglasses, and a purple bucket hat. Two doors down, he bought a rust-colored backpack. In an alley a block later, he changed, transferred what he needed into the new pack, and tossed everything else into a dumpster. The only thing he kept was the surgical mask.

Then he headed for his last fallback—a luggage storage facility at the back of an auto shop off Kasem Rat Road. There, he had left a go-bag with the items he might need if everything went bad.

He stayed on foot for four blocks, then cut through a market lane and flagged down a motorbike taxi on the other side. He gave the driver a phony destination two neighborhoods away and climbed on. Halfway there, he tapped the man on the shoulder, paid him, and got off early.

He walked for a block, making sure he wasn't being followed, then crossed against the light, slipped between two delivery trucks, and came out on Kasem Rat Road.

The auto shop looked the same—two open bays, fluorescent lights, a pickup on a lift, tires stacked in crooked columns out front. Nothing special. Forgettable. That was why he had chosen it.

Behind the shop, in a fenced yard half-hidden by scrap and old oil drums, was the luggage storage facility. The sign next to the door was so faded it was barely legible.

His locker was in the back, third from the end. He went straight to it, took a knee, and plugged in his combination. When the lock released, he opened the door, removed his bag, and set it on the floor.

Cash. Passport. Meds. Clean phone. Charger. A change of clothes. A compact toiletry kit. Everything was exactly as he had packed it. Taking out the phone, he powered it up.

While it searched for a signal, he opened the passport and checked the photo, the laminate, and the stamps. Then he put it back.

Once the phone had connected, he opened its encrypted communications app, keyed in the number from memory, and lifted it to his ear.

Matías answered on the first ring. "Go ahead."

"We've got a problem. And before you ask, no I am not damaged."

"Did you achieve the objective?"

"Yes."

"Have you been compromised?"

"Yes."

"More Cambodians?"

"No," Koebler replied. "Americans. They had my place under surveillance. Even managed to tap into my cameras."

Silence.

"I checked their credentials," Koebler continued. "U.S. Embassy Bangkok. I'm confident they were Agency."

Matías was quiet for a half second longer. When he spoke again, his tone had gone flatter. More serious. "What's their status?"

"Both dead."

"Any idea how long they were on to you?"

"None," said Koebler. "But we should assume they have my photo and the Dutch alias."

"Agreed. Can you still move?"

"For the moment."

"Good," his handler replied. "You need to find some place to hole up."

"With Langley now on my tail? No way. What I *need* is an exit."

There was a pause on the line and Koebler read it in the silence. "You don't have one."

"Not one I can give you tonight," said Matías.

"That's not how this works. I did my job. Now you do yours."

His handler didn't rise to it. "Listen to me carefully. We knew Bangkok would lock down tight after the first bombings. It'll be even worse now. I don't have a clean route that I can instantly stand up."

Koebler's grip tightened on the phone. "How long?"

"One that we can trust? Now that the Americans are in the hunt? Forty-eight hours," Matías admitted. "Seventy-two on the outside."

"That's unacceptable."

"It's unfortunate, but that's our current reality."

"That may be our reality," said Koebler. "But I'm the one in the field carrying all the risk."

"Right now," said Matías, "the clock is your enemy. Not me. I need you off the board long enough for me to solve this. The moment I have something, I'll ping you."

Koebler looked down at the bag on the floor. Cash. Passport. The charger for his burner phone. None of it solved the real problem. Then it came to him.

"The client," he said.

Matías didn't respond, and Koebler could almost hear him sorting through the possibilities. He was trying to understand why, after everything that had happened, he'd want to drag the client back into the conversation.

"What about them?" his handler asked.

"They may be our best, and only, option."

There was one of the longest pauses yet on the line. Finally, Matías asked, "For what? Exfiltration?"

"Yes."

"You can't be serious."

"I am," Koebler replied.

"You're a liability. You've got both the Thais and the Americans after you. Why would they risk exfilling you?"

"Because of what I know. They provided the SIM cards and the Cambodian-signature munitions for the RBSC operation. They wanted that bombing to be linked to Friday's so all of it pointed across the border. If I end up in Thai custody—or in the hands of the CIA—and start talking, that narrative begins to fall apart."

"Why wouldn't they simply kill you?" Matías said.

"Because I documented everything."

"You did what?"

"Notes and photographs," said Koebler.

Matías was not happy. "That was not part of the arrangement. In fact, it was extremely reckless."

"It was insurance."

"It was a unilateral move that could have gotten us both killed. It still might."

"Only if you don't play it right," Koebler replied. "If they move against me, you release it. All of it. You blow their false flag right out of the water. Bangkok learns it wasn't the Cambodians who attacked them. It was the Chinese."

Matías wasn't fully convinced. "You're asking me to trust the people who were tied to two compromised locations."

"You don't have to trust them. You just need to convince them that they're better off with me alive and as far away from Thailand as possible."

Koebler looked down at the bag again. Cash. Passport. Charger. Enough to keep moving. Not enough to get out. "Can you do it?" he asked.

"Make the approach? Yes," said Matías. "Whether they accept our logic is another matter."

"They will."

"I want you to listen to me," his handler replied. "From this point forward, assume two things. First, if the client agrees to help, it's only because keeping you alive serves them for the moment. Second, that moment may not last."

"I understand," Koebler said. "What do you need from me?"

"Discipline. Stay off the grid. Don't use that phone again unless I tell you to. Find some place safe. Don't move unless you have to. And when instructions come from me, you follow them exactly."

"Understood."

"One more thing," said Matías. "Until your exfil is complete and you and I are standing at a bar somewhere, approach every person you meet as a threat. Because I guarantee you, more than one of them will want you dead."

CHAPTER 47

"Were you two ever going to tell me about the Chinese safe house?" Davi asked, her glossy black bob swinging as angrily as she was walking.

They had all exited Morrell's ritzy condo building on Lang Suan Road and were headed down the sidewalk south, toward Lumphini Park.

While everyone in Bangkok was talking about the RBSC bombing, no one around them would have guessed that they were also discussing Cambodia, a covert Chinese team, and a geopolitical situation that was growing more combustible by the hour.

"You assholes," Davi continued. "The Chinese safe house. The blister packs. The shootout at the periodontist's building. The dead embassy security agents. The missing corpse I stupidly lent you. Were any of those details ever going to make their way to me, or was I supposed to keep finding them out one surprise at a time?"

Morrell, who was well acquainted with Davi's salty language when angry, looked over at Harvath, who took his time responding.

"Yes," he finally said, "we were going to tell you."

Davi stopped so abruptly that both men had to check themselves. "You were going to tell me," she repeated. "After what? After Thailand blamed Cambodia and full-scale war broke out? After Koebler disappeared? After this entire thing slipped even further out of our hands?"

"We didn't want to give you fragments," said Morrell.

Davi cut him a look. "You were sitting on evidence tied to a string of mass-casualty bombings. I don't care if they were subatomic particles. Any and all evidence should have come to me."

"We were wrong," Harvath said. "We should have brought it to you sooner. That's on me."

They crossed the street in silence. When they reached the other side, Davi said, "Start with the safe house."

"We got the address from the surviving embassy security agent," he said. "He told us he'd driven the embassy physician there to treat a Chinese businessman with a gunshot wound. By the time we got there, the place had been abandoned—in a hurry."

Davi kept her eyes on him. "What did you find?"

"Signs of recent medical treatment," he replied. "Burned papers in one of the sinks. A bloodied jacket in the bedroom with what looked like a bullet hole. And in the kitchen trash, Rick found the two empty blister packs for Cambodian SIM cards."

Her expression hardened. "And the shootout at the periodontist's building?"

"We triggered the beacon on the watch we told you about," said Morrell, picking it up. "First a woman posing as a cleaning lady came, took a quick look around, and then bugged out. Then came the embassy security agents. When they started shooting, a Chinese tactical team showed up and also started shooting. During the firefight, we lost the corpse you loaned us."

It was obvious by her glare that she knew he wasn't being completely forthright. Nevertheless, they were getting close to their rendezvous in the park. "The embassy security agent," she asked. "The one you took captive. Where is he now?"

"He's being looked after."

"That's not what I asked, Richard."

"My guys have him in a safe house. He's fine."

Davi's eyes widened. "*Fine?* Nothing about this is fine. I've got dead Chinese and dead Cambodians all over the fucking place, not to mention dead and injured Thai citizens, Americans, Brits, Aussies, Japanese, Kiwis, and scores more. So stop telling me things are fine."

Even though Morrell hadn't technically told her "things" were fine, he knew better than to argue and, instead, kept his mouth shut. Better to let Harvath walk face-first into that buzz saw, which was exactly what he did.

"For what it's worth," said Harvath, "we honestly weren't trying to cut you out. We were trying to understand what we had before dumping it in your lap."

Davi stared at him for several steps. "You don't get to decide that for me."

They walked on without talking as the edge of Lumphini Park came into view. Parents with strollers, picture-taking tourists, and joggers moved along the paths ahead, none of them paying the trio any attention.

Finally, Davi spoke again. "If you're still leaving anything out, now's the time to tell me."

"You're fully up to speed now," said Harvath, as he noticed Ashby and Palmer at the rendezvous point.

She looked at him as if deciding whether or not to call bullshit. "Let's hope you're right."

Harvath's two teammates were approaching from the opposite direction. Palmer was carrying a plain canvas tote.

When he went to hand the bag to Morrell, Davi extended her hand. "Right here. Thank you."

Palmer looked to Morrell, who gave a small nod.

Davi took the tote and opened it. Inside were two clear plastic bags. Each contained an empty blister pack with Khmer script. She studied them for a moment and then looked up at Harvath.

"Who else knows about these?" she asked.

"Just us."

"Not the embassy? Not Langley?"

"Not yet," said Morrell. "Why?"

"Because whoever is behind these bombings," Davi replied, "they want Thailand focused squarely on Cambodia."

"When maybe they should be focused on China."

Davi nodded. "If Beijing is responsible, Thailand should be the one who learns it first. And Thailand should decide what action to take. All

I want is a fair crack at this before your CIA and State Department get involved."

"I think we owe you that much," said Morrell. "In the meantime, we need to find Koebler before he leaves the country. The minute he crosses the border, we may never see him again."

"And what he's done in Bangkok," Harvath added, "he may do on an even greater and more horrific scale somewhere else."

She didn't disagree. Closing the tote, she said, "If Koebler's trying to get out, he'll need help. Find him, and we may find the people behind him."

CHAPTER 48

Hang Shuo despised being dependent on other people. It was one thing to command them, or to measure and exploit their weaknesses. It was another thing entirely to be reliant upon them for something as simple as putting on a shirt.

He sat upright on the edge of the bed, his injured arm held away from his body, while one of his men helped guide the sleeve over it. The shoulder had been cleaned, irrigated, and stitched by the embassy physician who had been dispatched by the Chinese ambassador and knew better than to ask any questions. The bullet had passed through, but the wound was deep and ugly. He had lost a great deal of blood, and every movement sent a blade of pain through his upper back and across his chest.

Getting up to use the toilet, he had caught sight of his reflection. At forty-seven, Hang looked older than he had forty-eight hours earlier. The skin around his eyes had drawn tighter. His face, slim to begin with, had acquired a sharper, more hollow appearance. Even his mouth looked different—grayer at the edges, as if the blood he had lost had drained something from him.

He had been born in Shanghai, a city that valued refinement and appearances—two traits he had learned early to use to his benefit.

Though he was still lean and muscular, his carefully combed black hair was beginning to show the faintest thread of silver at the temples. Pain, however, had a way of rippling to the surface. In the mirror, he no longer looked like the polished commercial attaché or unassuming trade representative he could so easily impersonate. He looked like what he was—a man under strain, held together by discipline and force of will.

When the shirt was finally in place, he buttoned it one-handed and let the operative settle his arm into the sling the doctor had provided. He slipped his good arm into a dark suit jacket, which was draped carefully over his injured shoulder. Though his team would not have cared, Hang did. As commander of the unit, he insisted on looking like one.

Stepping out of the back bedroom, he walked down the short hallway to the main room of the safe house. The apartment occupied the second floor above a dingy print shop whose best days were long behind it. Dust filmed the front windows, behind which cardboard boxes had been stacked in the display space and left there long enough to have bleached unevenly in the sun. It was the kind of sad, forgettable property no one bothered to look at twice.

Upstairs in the apartment, the curtains had been drawn against the late-morning glare. A television mounted in the corner carried nonstop coverage of the explosion at the Royal Bangkok Sports Club. It didn't matter that the sound was off. Hang could read enough from the images alone—the smoldering clubhouse, the emergency vehicles, the sea of media—so far, the attack was right on track.

A second strike had always been part of his design. The first bombings were meant to terrify Bangkok; the next was meant to direct its anger. Once he had seen how the city had recoiled—and which symbol of the Thai establishment still lay within reach—he had chosen his target.

Around the dining table, which his team had converted into a temporary operations center, sat seven men. Three were intelligence officers from the Ministry of State Security, selected for experience, languages, and the ability to operate in the field for long stretches without supervision. They were lean and muscular like their boss. Their eyes sharp and alert. Their hair cut short and neat.

The other four belonged to a compartmented support element whose existence would have been denied by every layer of the Chinese state, including the senior leadership that had deployed them. These were the harder ones. Less polished in manner, they were not there to recruit sources or cultivate influence. They were there for the uglier tasks.

The remainder, Hang thought to himself as he crossed to the table. A city map of Bangkok had been spread out beside three laptops, a cluster of burner phones, and several handwritten pages covered in times, locations, and Thai names. One operative monitored police radio traffic. Another cycled through local news sites and social media feeds. A third refreshed his encrypted app, waiting for word from Hang's Thai law enforcement source who was close to the evidence recovery chain. At the moment, that was the only report that mattered. Even more than confirmation of the blast itself.

Hang looked up at the TV again. The bombing at the club had only achieved its mechanical purpose. By all accounts, it had killed, maimed, terrified, and even humiliated. It had struck precisely where it needed to strike—directly inside the protected world of Thailand's military, political, and business elite. The RBSC hadn't been chosen simply because it was prestigious. It had been chosen in order to shatter the illusion that the kingdom's ruling class was insulated from the horror and pain being felt by the rest of the country.

Now that illusion was gone, but the explosion itself did not make the operation a success. For the bombing to do real political work, the Cambodian evidence their American bombmaker had planted in the device had to be found. The SIM card fragments. The munitions signature. The clues placed carefully and subtly enough that Thai investigators would believe they had uncovered something authentic, rather than something left for them to find.

Once that happened—once that evidence was logged, briefed up the chain, and quietly circulated, then the leaks would begin. They would be repeated and amplified until anti-Cambodian outrage hardened into national certainty. Then and only then would the bombings begin doing what Hang had designed them to do.

Thai nationalists on television and online would demand retaliation. Senior military officers would begin raging in private that the civilian government had failed to protect their fallen brethren. Ministers would stammer in front of microphones while the army's confidence in them would curdle into contempt. The citizenry would be paralyzed by fear wondering when and where the next attack would come.

That was how it would unfold. The pressure would build in layers. First fear. Then anger. Then blame. And once blame took hold, the government would begin to buckle under the weight of its own weakness.

Hang turned his attention away from the television and looked down at the map of Bangkok. All of the bombing locations, including the latest, were circled in green. But that wasn't the color that most concerned him.

Circled in red was the damage the Cambodians had inflicted. Teens. Tommy Sombat's. The periodontist building.

It represented three shocks or, more accurately, three losses of control. And it meant that something much deeper was wrong.

At Teens, the assault on his meeting with the American bombmaker had been disciplined, direct, and thoroughly professional. They had entered fast, using the element of surprise to their advantage, and had killed without hesitation. According to one of his Thai intelligence sources, several of the dead discovered at the scene were believed to be Cambodian nationals. That alone had been enough to unsettle him.

Cambodia's sole role—whether they knew it or not—was to absorb blame. The idea that Phnom Penh and its inept intelligence community might ever catch wind of his plot, much less try to interfere with it, had never entered his mind.

The obvious explanation had been Tommy Sombat. Whether the Thai fixer had sold out the meeting, had been turned, or had simply been under surveillance, Hang needed an answer. And he had sent his three best interrogators to get it. Two of them had been killed at Sombat's, but the third had somehow managed to get away. Then his watch had signaled.

Hang had responded exactly as he was supposed to respond. A recovery team had been sent to the periodontist building, only for that to become another disaster.

Details remained maddeningly incomplete. He knew members of his team had died on-site. He knew the embassy security officers he had requested to go in had also died, with one remaining unaccounted for. Had the Cambodians tracked the surviving interrogator from Sombat's? Or had his people collided with some other unforeseen force? The only thing Hang hated more than the uncertainty was the pattern.

Three violent disruptions in rapid succession? The only explanation was that the Cambodians had penetrated his operation. He wasn't facing a tactical problem. It was structural.

A phone vibrated on the table and every head turned. The MSS officer monitoring the encrypted app picked it up and read the incoming message. "Our source says the evidence technicians at RBSC have identified the Cambodian signatures."

Hang held out his hand. "Let me see it."

Taking the phone, he read the message for himself. Recovery teams at the club had confirmed the SIM card fragments as Cambodian. The component signatures in the bomb had also been matched to matériel previously tied to Cambodian military stockpiles. Senior investigators were being briefed and word was beginning to move up the chain.

Hang read the message a second time. Slower this time. At last, the explosion had done its real work.

He handed the phone back. "Tell him we want a copy of that report right away."

The officer nodded and began texting a reply.

On the TV, as the country waited for someone authoritative to tell them who to hate, anchors were speculating—Islamic terrorists, domestic extremism, criminal networks, foreign sabotage. Everyone was filling airtime until they had an answer.

Knowing what the answer would be, Hang was already prepared and had his propagandists all lined up. There was the once-respected newscaster with a large, patriotic following, who had been forced into early retirement by scandal. There was a retired colonel turned "citizen journalist" with ties to the officer corps. Two online outlets popular with the nationalist movement willing to ask reckless questions, draped in patriotic language. None of them needed to be told what to do. All they needed was a nudge and a plausible line of attack. Once the report landed, Hang would be able to give them both.

One of his officers tilted forward to get a better look at his laptop, and Hang saw the man's expression change. "What is it?"

"There are reports that authorities in Pattani Province have interrupted a BRN cell in advance of a major terrorist attack."

Barisan Revolusi Nasional was Thailand's deadliest Islamist independence movement and leader of the separatist insurgency in the south. Spreading terror and uncertainty through well-trained secret militia units, they used assassinations, guerrilla warfare, and bombings in particular, to pursue their ultimate goal of making southern Thailand ungovernable.

The room went still.

"How?" Hang demanded.

"According to what I'm seeing, a courier was stopped and questioned. Officials became suspicious and searched his vehicle. Bomb-making materials were found. Due to heightened threat levels in the wake of the Bangkok bombings, local authorities moved quickly and with overwhelming force. They were able to identify and arrest the entire cell."

Hang asked to see the laptop so he could once again read the information for himself.

There it was on the screen—a stupid, ordinary explanation. A traffic stop combined with a weak courier and sloppy, local handling. It was the sort of petty incompetence by which entire operations had been lost before. It was also one of the reasons Hang hated outsourcing operations to insurgent groups. If only religious fervor came coupled with equivalent competence.

Making him even angrier, the timing was impossible to ignore. Teens. Tommy Sombat. The beacon trap. Now this.

Sliding the laptop back, he reached for the map that marked the southern districts.

The northern track had never been intended to stand alone. Attacks from Cambodia would inflame patriotic outrage and focus elite anger. Pressure from inside the kingdom, from the loud and often violent south, would widen the crisis, making the situation feel more dangerous and even more unstable.

Together, they would make Thailand look and feel like a country whose civilian government could no longer protect its people and no longer hold the nation together.

Suddenly, however, his entire plan was in jeopardy.

After taking a moment to think, he looked at his team and announced, "We're going dark. Shut down all nonessential channels. No one moves without direct authorization. I want every southern contact, every cache, every courier, and every safe house revalidated. Until proven differently, assume that the Cambodians have fully compromised this operation."

The men moved at once while Hang remained where he was, still studying the map and Thailand's southern districts. If this was really about his operation being penetrated, the entire network he had devoted himself to building might be no longer usable. And without the Islamist separatist component, the entire plan could fall apart.

If that happened, he might be left with no other option than to shoot himself—saving Beijing the trouble and his family the indignity of paying for the bullet.

An encrypted app on one of the phones began to ring, and the MSS officer nearest it checked the display. Looking up at his boss, he said, "The Mexican."

Hang took the phone and activated the call. "Something wrong with the payment?"

"No," Matías replied. "The payment was received. Thank you. I have a problem, however, and you may be the only man in Thailand who can fix it."

Hang said nothing.

"Your infrastructure is better than mine. How can I put this? It has gotten a bit warmer where you are than we expected. I am unable to help our mutual friend with his departure."

"Your contractor, your problem."

As a seasoned intelligence officer, Matías paused, weighing how much truth to spend.

"Ordinarily," he admitted, "I would agree. Job complete. Job paid for. However, if our mutual friend fails to depart in a timely manner, he may find himself subject to parties who could make your life quite difficult."

Hang's stance didn't move. "You overestimate our friend's value."

"Respectfully, I must disagree," Matías replied. "He knows a lot. He knows what the contract called for and he knows who supplied the ingredients. To a party willing to accommodate him, he could be quite useful."

While it was true of most Western cultures, Hang had found that the

Americans were exceedingly quick, especially when their backs were against the wall, to resort to blackmail. The Mexican's veiled threat didn't come as a surprise. And he had no desire to play the man's game.

Hang did, however, have a game of his own. To win it, he needed the handler to fully impale himself on the hook. So, he waited.

Hearing nothing, Matías pressed on. "The situation is deteriorating quickly. He cannot stay where he is. He requires movement, shelter, and a cleaner route out than I can provide on such short notice."

That, Hang thought, *was the most honest thing the Mexican had said*. And all of a sudden, the problem in front of him looked very different.

CHAPTER 49

By the time the trio left Lumphini Park, the day—with its overwhelming humidity and intense sunlight—had turned even more oppressive.

Davi went back to her office with the SIM card blister packs, Morrell returned to his condo, and Harvath walked south, alone, toward the safe house in Suan Phlu. The city traffic, with its tuk-tuks coughing blue smoke into the air, rolled past without him taking much notice. His mind was focused on Koebler.

Every minute the man remained on the loose, it increased the odds that he was putting distance between himself and Bangkok. Maybe he was holed up somewhere, waiting for night to fall so he could use the darkness to slip away. Or maybe he was already in the back of a refrigeration truck headed east. He could have been on his way to the coast. Maybe he'd already found a riverboat to aid in his escape. There were too many ways to disappear in a city like this and too many people willing to mind their own business for the right amount of cash. And they would take that cash not knowing that it meant more people somewhere in the world would die.

He crossed a small lane jammed with scooters, thinking of all the people Koebler had killed and the countless others who had been injured. Then he thought about KitKat and Mo. That one landed harder than he expected.

They hadn't been shooters or hardened men looking for a gunfight.

They were the kind of CIA officers who fought with laptops, cameras, and whatever miracle gadget the nerds at Langley had recently dreamed up. They had been support personnel—smart, useful. The kind of people who made successful missions possible and rarely got their names included in the stories that were told afterward. Koebler had killed them anyway.

It hadn't mattered who they were. Only that KitKat and Mo were in the way.

That told Harvath something important. Koebler wasn't just skilled. And he wasn't just disciplined. He was the kind of person who erased whoever stood between him and the next step in his operation. He made no distinctions. He did not hesitate. Which meant there would be more dead bodies if they didn't stop him soon.

Refocusing his attention, Harvath took a lengthy SDR (surveillance detection route) to make sure he wasn't being followed, before finally turning down the quiet street where the safe house sat. Its worn exterior and banged-up gate were doing exactly what made the home so attractive to the CIA—not standing out and definitely not being memorable.

He knocked the rhythmic knock only his teammates knew, unlocked the door, and then stepped into the relative cool of the interior.

Haney looked up first. Staelin was at the kitchen counter stripping down his M250, making sure it was clean and properly oiled.

"How'd the handoff go with Davi?" Haney asked.

"Good," Harvath replied. "Ashby and Palmer make it back?"

"They're on a lunch run," said Staelin. "I hope you like Thai food."

Harvath nodded.

"So now that Davi's got the blister packs," Haney continued, "what's our next move?"

"For right now, there is no next move," said Harvath. "We sit tight and wait."

Neither of his teammates looked happy about it, but they knew waiting was a part of the job.

Stripping off his sweat-soaked shirt, he headed for the shower. The water pressure was lousy and the temperature left a lot to be desired, but it was enough to wash the dirt and grime off of him.

When he stepped out, he shaved and then pulled on clean clothes, which resulted in him feeling marginally more human. While he wasn't rested, he was at least cleaner.

By the time he walked into the kitchen, Ashby and Palmer were back and they'd laid a feast on the counter. There were take-out containers of Tom Yum Goong, Moogata, Gai Yang, Khao Moo Daeng, and tons of fried rice. He grabbed a bottle of water from the fridge, loaded up a plate, and sat down at the dining table.

Ashby saw him reaching for the spicy Thai chili sauce called Nam phrik and gave him a friendly warning. "Careful with that. It'll burn the hair off your chest."

"Less to snag on my wet suit."

The team smiled and everyone tucked into their food.

For several moments, all that could be heard was the sound of lunch and the muted hum of the air conditioner laboring against the heat outside.

Finally, Haney said, "How long do you think Davi's going to need?"

Harvath swallowed a bite of food and, put off by how legitimately hot the Nam phrik was, chased it with two long slugs of water.

When the fire in his mouth had cooled, he replied, "Her people want Koebler just as bad as we do. It's going to take what it's going to take. When she has something, we'll hear from her."

Palmer looked up from his phone. "Why would she tip us off? If her people get a lead, wouldn't they jump on it themselves?"

"Because that was our deal," Harvath replied, getting up to get some yogurt sauce to de-escalate the Scoville scale of his lunch. "Morrell and I made the case that as former SEALs, we understand Koebler's training and how he thinks. Also, our smaller team has a better chance than a big Thai unit of getting close without him seeing us."

"And she bought that?"

"She bought that if we screw it up, it won't blow back on her. And if we get him, she takes the credit."

Palmer glanced back down at his phone. "Thai media's all over the place. Islamists. Organized crime. Domestic radicals. Everybody's got a theory."

"Any mention of Cambodia?" Harvath asked.

"Not yet. But it feels like they're circling it."

Harvath nodded, added some yogurt sauce, and went back to eating. Davi had been right. He could feel where this was headed. Chinese safe house. Cambodian SIM card packaging. Cambodian signatures at RBSC. None of it was accidental. Someone wanted Thailand blaming Cambodia, not China.

When he was done eating, he carried his plate to the sink and rinsed it off. Behind him, Haney said, "You want us rotating an exterior watch?"

Harvath turned around. "No. Stay inside and keep an eye on the cameras. Let's stage our gear. If Davi comes back with something, we move fast."

Carrying his water bottle, he returned to the room he had been using, pulled the blackout curtains a little tighter, and lay down on the bed.

If Koebler got out of Thailand, everything got exponentially harder. Catching him had always mattered, but now it mattered even more. Davi had been right—if they caught him, they might get the people behind him. But if they lost him, they didn't just lose the bomber. They lost the clearest path to who had hired him and what the ultimate endgame was.

Closing his eyes, he tried to quiet his mind, but it kept returning to all the ways Koebler could, at this moment, be executing his getaway.

Eventually, despite himself, his mind let go of all those thoughts and he was able to drift off. It wasn't deep and it wasn't near long enough, but it was sleep.

When his phone vibrated against the wooden nightstand, Harvath came awake rough, dragging himself up through the last heavy layers of sleep. It took him a second to remember where he was. Then the room snapped back into focus—the blackout curtains, the ceiling fan, the air conditioner rattling on the wall.

He reached for his phone before it buzzed again. It was Morrell.

Harvath sat up and answered immediately. "What's up?"

"Davi's got something," Morrell replied. "Not enough to nail him down, but enough to move."

The last of the sleep vanished. "How solid?"

"Solid enough that I'm on my way to you."

Harvath swung his legs off the bed. "Where's Davi?"

"We're meeting her there."

"What are we headed into?"

"She didn't want to discuss it over the phone," said Morrell. "All I know is that her tech people got a match from cameras around the Royal Bangkok Sports Club and Khlong Toei. Get your team ready. I'll be there in five."

The line went dead.

"Morrell's inbound," said Harvath as he stepped into the kitchen. "Davi's got something."

Chairs scraped back. Staelin killed the camera feeds he'd been watching and reached for his rifle. Haney was already moving the gear they had staged. Palmer and Ashby, who had been monitoring news feeds and social media, stood up.

"Something good?" Ashby asked.

"Good enough. We're wheels-up in five."

The team loaded their vehicle in record time. By the time Morrell rolled up to their front gate, they were ready to go.

Harvath hopped in the passenger seat and the rest of the team followed behind in the second Land Cruiser.

As they pulled away from the drive, Harvath asked, "What'd she tell you?"

"Not much," Morrell replied. "Based on the description you gave her from the shooting in Khlong Toei, her people were able to pick Koebler up exiting a hospital campus bordering RBSC moments after the bombing. From there, they tracked him back to his bolt-hole in Khlong Toei, then on to a clothes change and a bag swap before heading to a luggage storage place near Kasem Rat Road. Apparently he retrieved another bag, and after that, dropped into a dead zone."

"That's it?"

"They've only been working the cameras they control—traffic cams, public security feeds, city-owned systems. Davi didn't want uniforms out knocking on doors for private footage and spooking him if he's still in the area. Besides, it would take too long anyway."

Harvath nodded. "Smart. So what do they actually have?"

"A last known location and a figurative box around it."

"How good is the box?"

Morrell shook his head. "Not good enough to say X marks the spot. He dropped off a camera a couple of hours ago in a stretch near Kasem Rat where the coverage gets thin."

"Also smart. What's around there?"

"Warehouses, workshops, storage yards, river traffic, that sort of thing. But unless he climbed into the back of a vehicle completely off-camera, Davi's people have a high degree of confidence that he hasn't come back out."

Harvath let that sit for a moment. "So he's either still in there, or somebody moved him clean."

"Exactly."

The afternoon traffic was thickening. Behind them in the second Land Cruiser, Staelin held close on their bumper. To their right, the muddy Chao Phraya flashed between buildings and tangles of utility wire.

"How big an area are we talking about?"

"Big enough that we're not going door to door," Morrell said. "Small enough that Davi thinks it's worth a try."

"Any drones up?"

"Negative. No helicopters either. If he's inside their box, they didn't want to risk tipping him off."

"Good," Harvath replied. "We keep it that way unless he rabbits."

Morrell nodded. "That's her thinking too."

Fifteen minutes later, Morrell slowed down and eased the Land Cruiser to the side of the road behind a dark blue van lettered in Thai for a broadband internet provider. Along its side was a large faded decal advertising fiber installation and same-day service calls. Thirty yards beyond it, near the mouth of a side street lined with machine shops, two unmarked Thai sedans sat with their engines idling. They were the only vehicles Harvath could see, but he assumed there were plenty more plainclothes ISOC assets tucked into the surrounding blocks.

"She's in the van," the CIA man said.

Harvath checked his mirror and saw that Staelin had already brought the second Land Cruiser in behind them. Everyone inside looked alert and switched on.

Davi stepped out of the van before they had even put their SUV in park. She had a phone in one hand and a slim tablet in the other. She looked tightly wound and as if she was moving on adrenaline.

Harvath and Morrell got out as the rest of the team debussed from the second vehicle behind them.

Davi wasted no time. "Follow me."

She moved to the back of the van, where one of her men opened the rear door. The interior had been turned into a rolling command post—screens, keyboards, radios, and a wall of weapons that included TASERs, tear gas launchers, short-barreled shotguns, compact submachine guns, and a range of other tools of the law enforcement trade. Clipped in the corner was a small fan that did almost nothing to move the air.

Cueing the screens via her tablet, Davi brought up a sequence of stills.

"This is your man leaving the hospital campus bordering the RBSC," she said, increasing the size of the first image. "Baseball cap. Surgical mask. Black backpack."

She then transitioned to her next image. "This was taken two blocks from his building in Khlong Toei. By the way, our bomb squad was able to defuse the door and overhead light booby traps at Koebler's bolt-hole. There's no telling how many officers that might have killed. Thank you again for the tip."

"You're welcome," Harvath replied. "After the shooting, where does he go?"

"Several blocks over," she answered, pulling up a series of new stills. "We don't have constant coverage, and he disappears multiple times. But when we pick him up again, he's changed clothes. New pants, shirt, hat, even sunglasses. Still wearing the face covering though."

"And he has a new backpack," remarked Morrell.

"Yes, he does."

She continued to narrate as she cycled through more images. "He catches a motorbike taxi, rides for a while, and then is back on foot.

Eventually, we believe he ends up at a luggage storage business just beyond view of this camera. When we see him again, he has picked up a second bag. Not long after this, we lose him."

Harvath asked if he could have her tablet so he could cycle through the images himself. He took his time. Zooming in and out where needed. The one constant was that Koebler never looked flustered. Even when the images were blurry or he was half-turned away from the camera, he looked like a man operating on a plan.

When he handed the tablet back to her, Davi enlarged the final still and also brought up a map where a cluster of streets were lit up in red.

"This is where he falls off the board," she said. "After this, we're relying on our best guesses."

Harvath studied the map. "And what do your best guesses tell you?"

"He's not going to be anywhere that he needs to show ID. That means no hotels, no hostels, and no rooming houses. He knows he's blown and should expect that soon enough we'll be pushing photos of him to every lodging and accommodation in town."

"Agreed. He wants to avoid his face being seen. That means he'll be looking for a place without people. Anywhere he can stay out of sight for a few hours, keep an exit open, and move when it gets dark."

One of Davi's men pulled up a satellite image of the search area and slowly panned across it.

Harvath watched for several seconds until something caught his eye. "There," he said, pointing at a property pressed right up against the river.

It was a cluttered boat-repair yard that sat between what looked like a sheet-metal warehouse and a fenced storage lot. Ten or eleven vessels were scattered across it. The majority were dry-docked workboats up on blocks. There were also a couple of long-tail river craft under patchwork tarps, as well as a squat barge sitting half out of the water near a slip. A travel lift stood near the river, with scaffolding, stacks of timber, and open-sided sheds spread across the property. Leading down from the street, a service road bent through the yard before curling back toward the water.

Davi looked at the image, then back at him. "Why that one?"

"Because it's the perfect place to disappear," said Harvath. "Lots of clutter. Lots of places to bed down unseen. There's only one route in that he needs to watch. If things go bad, he can sneak out via the business on either side or, ultimately, the river. It's the spot I'd choose."

Morrell nodded. "I would too."

After radioing a series of orders, she turned back to Harvath and Morrell. "My people will keep the perimeter soft. We're pulling the uniforms back, redirecting through-traffic a block or two out, and our plainclothes teams are watching anything coming out."

"Good," Harvath replied. "The last thing we need is Koebler hearing sirens or seeing a wall of cops."

"If he goes for the river, we've got an unmarked interdiction boat holding nearby," she said. "They stay out of sight unless he runs."

"That works."

"You've got fifteen minutes," Davi replied. "After that, I start squeezing the box."

"Understood," said Harvath, who gave the signal to his team to mount up.

He looked back at the screen with the satellite imagery one last time. If he was right, Koebler was hiding less than two klicks away. If he was wrong, they were about to give him fifteen more minutes to disappear.

"Let's move."

CHAPTER 50

Davi's people had done exactly as she had promised. Two blocks out from the boatyard, there was no uniformed police or military presence to be seen. Traffic was being peeled away before it got close, diverted by men in plain clothes in unmarked vehicles whose flashing lights remained dark.

From out on the river, there were neither sirens nor visible patrol craft. In fact, there was no sign anywhere in the neighborhood that anything had changed at all. Harvath, however, knew that wasn't true.

They had parked their SUVs a block away and gone in on foot. When they got near the boatyard, Harvath took a moment to study the terrain ahead.

The yard sat behind a sagging chain-link fence, patched in places with mismatched wire and sheet metal. He allowed his eyes to move across the property the way Koebler's would have and saw the broken sight lines, elevated perches, and multiple choke points.

There were shadowed pockets where a man could disappear five feet from a search team and never be seen. There were multiple routes to the water. Every rusting piece of machinery, every battered hull, every shed wall offered concealment or cover. So many obstacles meant that any pursuit was guaranteed to turn into a series of blind corners.

"Still like it?" Haney asked.

Harvath shook his head. "No. Which is why he probably does."

Haney followed his gaze. "Lot of places to hide."

"And to kill from."

A few yards away, Staelin adjusted his suppressed SBR. Ashby and Palmer were already widening the team's shape, fanning out in opposite directions. Morrell stayed with Harvath and Haney, while Staelin trailed a step back, his eyes working the fence line and the sheds.

In the brutal heat of midafternoon, the humid air hung hard over the yard. Perspiration was already running down Harvath's back as he tried to formulate a plan.

He intended to use the clutter to his advantage. The dry-docked hulls and low sheds, not to mention the old fuel drums and other randomly strewn pieces of junk, broke the yard into usable pieces and provided the team enough cover to work their way forward without undue exposure. But it all came with a cost.

Any hidden pocket that they could exploit, so could Koebler. There was no telling where one of his wireless cameras or a trip wire might be hiding.

He indicated the path they would take and added a warning over the radio. "Use the cover, but don't trust it. Check for cameras and expect traps."

With that, they slipped through a section of fence that had been bent down and flattened, possibly by a truck backing out too fast.

As soon as they crossed the property line, it began to smell like diesel, bilgewater, and rot. Beneath it all was the thick, muddy scent of the river. Harvath paused beside a peeling fishing boat and listened. No voices. No clang of tools. No radio coming from one of the sheds. Whatever this place had been earlier in the day, it wasn't that now. Activity here had wound down and stopped.

He raised his hand and gestured. Ashby peeled left toward a stack of drums and an aging work bay. Palmer drifted right, using a trawler up on blocks as cover.

The team moved in short bounds, covering each other when they had to cross more exposed ground. Harvath kept checking the obvious places Koebler might have hidden cameras, but so far, he hadn't seen any. Then, at the far end of the nearest work bay, something caught his eye—a workbench covered with a tarp.

Immediately, it felt wrong. Nothing else in the yard had been protected like that. Then he spotted the corner—taped up to form a small triangular opening. It was at just the right height for a man lying beneath the tarp to watch the approach without being seen.

Harvath froze. It was a blind.

He dropped low and motioned Morrell and Haney down with him. Across from them, Ashby stopped behind the drums. Palmer disappeared behind the trawler's hull. Staelin sank in beside a rusting winch and brought his rifle up to bear.

Harvath seated his own weapon against his shoulder. It was exactly the sort of position Koebler would have chosen—concealed, shaded, and with a clean view across the approach.

He was preparing to angle Haney and Morrell around one side, while Staelin covered the opening, when he noticed something else—something that made even less sense.

The opening in the tarp wasn't aimed at the route Harvath's team had taken in. It was trained on the service road as it cut through the property and hooked back toward the water. Whoever had built the blind wasn't concerned with intruders coming through the damaged perimeter fence. He was lying in wait for a vehicle.

That thought had barely formed in Harvath's head when the tarp moved. Not much. Just enough for Harvath to catch the dark circle of a rifle optic nestled in the tarp's opening.

A second later, the barrel beneath it shifted a fraction and settled again. Not toward Harvath and his team, but even more toward the service road.

Morrell saw it too. "What the hell?" he breathed.

Harvath didn't answer. Using his own optic, he was already scanning, looking past the blind, searching deeper into the work bay for anything he might have missed the first time. And then he found it.

Half-buried in shadow, behind an engine block stand near the back wall, was another armed figure, crouched low and motionless, except for the faintest turn of his head.

He had no idea who these two were, but he had a pretty good feeling he wasn't looking at Koebler, and he definitely wasn't looking at private security hired by a boatyard that couldn't be bothered to repair its fence. Something was going on.

Barely above a whisper, Harvath said into his radio, "Two concealed shooters in the bay, eleven o'clock. They're oriented on the service road, not us. Hold."

One by one, the team members clicked their acknowledgment of Harvath's message over their radios, as they solidified their positions.

Across the yard, Ashby sank lower behind the drums. Palmer faded even deeper into the shadow beneath the trawler. Haney scanned for perimeter threats, while Morrell made sure no one was creeping up on their six. Staelin, who had never taken his eyes off the target, held his rifle steady on the tarp.

"I'll take the sniper under the tarp," Staelin whispered to Harvath over the radio. "You take the other guy in the bay. We'll fire simultaneously. Just say the word."

"Right now the word is *hold*," Harvath quietly replied. "We have no idea who these guys are. Everybody stay frosty. Keep your eyes peeled for Koebler."

No sooner had Harvath issued his order than the figure under the tarp made another minute adjustment. At almost the same moment, the second figure, behind the engine block, shifted as well, his head moving again, this time toward the far end of the property.

Seconds later, Harvath heard it. An engine. Faint at first. Then closer.

Morrell looked at him and mouthed, *Vehicle*.

Harvath gave the slightest nod. Over the radio, still barely above a whisper, he said, "Inbound vehicle. Everybody hold. Let it come."

It was moving slowly, cautiously, its tires crunching over gravel and patches of old shell. The sound drifted ahead of it, down the crooked service road as it drove toward the river.

Harvath kept his eyes fixed on the bay. Whoever was under the tarp was now as still as a corpse. At the back of the bay, the second hidden figure had tucked himself tighter into the shadows and was bringing his weapon up.

Then the SUV appeared.

Dark and dusty, with deeply tinted windows, it emerged between two dry-docked hulls and moved at a crawl, following the service road down to the water. There, it made a tight, deliberate turn, until the vehicle was pointed back toward the street.

The hidden shooter under the tarp didn't move. Neither did the second man in the bay.

The SUV began moving again. Twenty meters later, it rolled to a stop.

For a moment nothing happened. Its engine kept on running. Then all four doors opened almost at once.

Heavily armed Chinese operatives, all carrying PP-2000s, came out fast and in sequence. One man moved immediately to the front corner of the SUV, another to the rear, while the other two pivoted outward and scanned the yard with the eyes of men who had already lost too many teammates and were guarding against losing any more.

For several long seconds, it was nothing but Chinese heads on swivels; their eyes scanning this way and that. Once they were in place, none of them moved.

The SUV idled where it had come to a stop, its engine emitting a low, steady growl beneath the ticking of hot metal and the distant slap of the river water against pilings.

One of the Chinese, at the front corner, said something quietly in Mandarin. Another answered from beside the rear passenger door. Then the man at the front called something out.

It wasn't particularly loud, just loud enough to carry. Nevertheless, he got nothing back.

Harvath didn't need to know exactly who these new arrivals were to understand what he was looking at. Koebler had been working for the Chinese. Koebler got burned. And now a heavily armed Chinese team, all carrying the telltale PP-2000 personal defense weapons, had shown up at a remote site to help get him out. This was his extraction.

There was only one problem. Nothing happened. Koebler didn't materialize.

The Chinese operative called out for him again. They waited. But still, nothing happened.

Morrell leaned in. "He's not coming out."

"No," Harvath replied. "He probably thinks it's a trap."

That was when the tarp flexed and the second concealed figure brought his weapon up another inch.

As the Chinese operative took a step forward, Harvath instinctively applied pressure to his trigger. That was when Koebler made his move.

CHAPTER 51

From his hiding place, Koebler's shot cracked across the boatyard, punching through the triangular opening and jerking the hidden shooter backward.

At the back of the bay, the second gunman opened fire on the Chinese, hitting the operative at the front of the SUV. He spun violently as bullets tore through his chest and shoulder, slamming him into the fender.

Under the tarp, the wounded shooter thrashed and tried to roll clear. He never made it. Koebler's next volley finished him.

Then the entire boatyard erupted in gunfire.

Snapping their weapons up and returning fire, the Chinese raced for cover. Glass burst from one of the shed windows, as the side mirror on their SUV exploded and round after round tore through their vehicle.

"Contact left!" Haney yelled.

Harvath was already moving. "We've got Chinese plus a second team, probably the Cambodians," he shouted into his radio. "Stay clear of that fight. Don't let Koebler escape."

Morrell moved with him. Across the property, Ashby and Palmer shifted their fire, not trying to win the fight, but to keep the Chinese and the second team locked onto each other. Staelin leaned into his rifle, picking his shots carefully and making sure neither side could cleanly break contact. Haney pushed left, working for a better look at where Koebler had last appeared.

Harvath had already disengaged from the firefight. There was no question in his mind that Koebler would use the chaos as a distraction and was already on the run. He was also certain that the bomber had already chosen his escape route out of the boatyard and had identified the gaps, blind corners, and pieces of cover he intended to use.

To his left, Harvath caught movement. Carrying a carbine, Koebler was staying low and using the canted hull of a half-disassembled ferry to mask his escape and cut deeper across the yard. At some point, he had shaved his beard and dyed his hair, but Harvath still recognized him.

"There!" he exclaimed. "Nine o'clock. Moving."

Rounds cracked overhead and punched into fiberglass somewhere off to his right. Together, he and Morrell sprinted toward the rusting ferryboat Koebler had just used for cover, and dropped behind a crate of engine parts. Behind them, they could hear the gunfight intensifying—short, hard bursts, the splintering of wood, and ricochets screaming off metal.

Harvath risked a look around the side of the crate and caught sight of Koebler again. He was less than twenty feet ahead, rounding the far side of the ferry. He was staying low and moving fast, using every piece of cover available. It made it impossible to get a clean shot at him.

He had just pivoted toward the service road, when Harvath saw him pull something out of the left pocket of his cargo pants.

"Grenade!" he yelled.

Morrell saw it at the same instant. "Move!"

Koebler pulled the pin and blindly threw it in a high, tumbling arc over his shoulder.

Harvath grabbed Morrell and drove both of them down as the blast tore through the yard with a concussive crack, showering them with debris.

By the time Harvath got his head back up, Koebler had bought himself even more distance. Leaping to his feet, Harvath chased after him, with Morrell close behind.

Harvath ran with his rifle up, searching for the one clean shot Koebler refused to give him. For a split second, he caught him crossing open ground and started to press his trigger, only to have him disappear behind another hull, forcing Harvath to abandon the shot.

"Damn it," he cursed, pushing himself harder.

Ahead, Koebler continued to use the obstacles and stacks of junk, exactly the way Harvath had feared he would. The man moved rapidly from cover to cover, never staying exposed long enough to engage. All Harvath saw was flashes of shoulder, elbow, or the dark blur of his rifle.

Over the radio, he gave instructions to the team, "Ashby and Palmer—collapse on the service road. Haney, cut left and get ahead of him. Staelin, move your location and watch for a breakout toward the street."

Near a pile of timber cribbing, Harvath caught sight of him again and prepared to shoot. Koebler, however, charged into a corrugated shed behind the pile and disappeared from view.

Harvath reached the opening seconds later and buttonhooked inside, ready to fire, but it was empty. Koebler had slipped through a gap in the side.

Back at the service bay, the rhythm of gunfire had changed. The Cambodians were still hammering the Chinese, but the fire was no longer fixed in place. It was spreading, pushing up the service road, as if the Chinese were trying to break contact and get out.

Harvath lunged out the side opening of the shed and kept going. Forty yards ahead, the SUV sat in the middle of the service road, its nose pointed toward the boatyard's entrance and the street beyond. The windshield was starred in multiple places, and its passenger-side windows were crazed white, but still holding.

Armored, Harvath realized.

One Chinese operative was crouched behind the SUV's engine block, firing in short, disciplined bursts into the bay. Another stood half-exposed behind the open rear door, shouting for Koebler.

Seconds later, the bombmaker answered, tossing out two smoke grenades. The canisters skittered across the service road and began vomiting thick, white smoke.

Harvath and Morrell brought their weapons to bear, but the Chinese operative behind the engine block opened up on them first, driving both men back behind cover.

By the time Harvath risked another look, Koebler, who had his head down and was running hard, had hit the edge of the fast-thickening sheet of smoke.

The Cambodians doubled down on their blistering attack.

Rounds hammered the SUV. Sparks jumped from the hood and the front door panel. A spiderweb of fresh white bloomed across the windshield, but it still didn't collapse.

Knowing that he was running out of time, Harvath leaned out, ready to take the shot, but all he got was a final glimpse of Koebler's silhouette as he was shoved inside. Then the other operatives jumped in, the doors slammed shut, and the driver hammered the accelerator.

As the SUV went speeding up the service road, Harvath and Morrell sprinted after it, firing as many rounds as they could. They stitched the rear hatch and succeeded in blowing what was left of the back window into the cargo area.

The gunfight, however, was over. The Chinese were breaking contact.

Harvath still had one ace up his sleeve.

He slowed only long enough to radio and quickly fill Davi in. "Koebler's with the Chinese. Five men in total. All heavily armed. They're in a dark Nissan Patrol SUV. It's armor-plated with ballistic glass. Lots of damage. They'll ditch the vehicle fast. I can't see the street, so we don't know which way they're headed."

She confirmed his transmission and immediately switched to an ISOC channel. Then off to his right, movement caught Harvath's eye.

Under cover of the smoke, one of the shooters from the second team had advanced farther up the service road than Harvath had realized. The Cambodian-looking man was trying to close the distance with the fleeing SUV, when his legs gave out. The man dropped to one knee and then collapsed hard near the fence line.

Harvath got to him first and kicked the man's rifle away. Morrell stopped a few feet away and covered the yard behind them.

The man had been shot, maybe more than once, and a dark, widening pool of blood was spreading beneath him.

His weapon—a compact carbine—lay where Harvath had kicked it. He had spare magazines, good boots, an earpiece, and a comms wire that disappeared beneath his shirt. Civilian clothes, professional gear.

Harvath's eyes flicked once in the direction of where the SUV had disappeared and then back to the wounded man. The man and his team hadn't fired a single round toward Harvath and his people. That mattered.

"Radio Davi," Harvath told Morrell as he set his rifle aside. "Tell her we need medics on the service road. One patient. Assume multiple gunshot wounds."

Morrell nodded as Harvath removed his blowout kit and kneeled down next to the man. "You're going to be okay," he said. "Stay with me."

Pulling on a pair of nitrile gloves, he grabbed his trauma shears.

"Medics are on the way," Morrell reported.

Harvath cut away the man's shirt to access the worst of the bleeding. As he did, a braided prayer cord slipped free.

Morrell saw it too. "Cambodian?"

"It looks like it."

The wound was ugly. Side shot. Maybe more than one. It was hard to tell with all the blood. Harvath packed the hole he could find with gauze, driving it in with two fingers until the man's body tightened and his jaw flexed against the pain. Then he stacked more on top and pressed down hard with the heel of his hand, putting his weight into it.

With his other hand, he did a quick frisk. No wallet. No phone. Just a folding knife and, attached to his belt beneath his shirt, an old, beaten-up multiband inter/intra team radio, or MBITR for short. Removing it, Harvath slipped it into one of his own pouches.

The wounded man's breathing was shallow and wet. He shifted as though trying to speak. Blood appeared at the corner of his mouth. But whatever he was trying to say never came. His eyelids fluttered.

Harvath pushed down harder on the dressing. Sirens could be heard entering the boatyard.

Soon thereafter, the first ISOC agents appeared, weapons up, followed by a tactical medical team carrying trauma bags and a folding stretcher.

One of the medics dropped to a knee opposite Harvath and took over. Harvath gathered his gear and stood back next to Morrell.

Since Friday's bombings, Thai personnel had grown used to foreign law enforcement and support teams showing up all over Bangkok. But a shattered boatyard, a man on the ground with gunshot wounds, and a team of armed Americans already on scene were something else entirely. Still, this was Davika Rattanprasert's operation, and the orders coming over the radio had been clear—comply and cooperate.

Behind them, more ISOC men and Thai police were flooding into the yard, fanning out between the hulls and stacks of marine equipment.

At the water, a figure flickered briefly between the sheds as if weighing coming back for the fallen man. Then, with the property filling with armed Thai security forces, he disappeared.

Harvath and Morrell had both seen him.

"Those guys are gone," said Morrell.

Harvath nodded. Whoever was left of the second team had made the only call they could.

The Chinese had won. They had lost. And Koebler was gone.

CHAPTER 52

Washington, D.C.

It was already after midnight when Jennifer Fields had badge-swiped into FBI headquarters and taken the elevator to her office.

Had the story come from anyone other than a U.S. Secret Service agent and had it not been supported by photographs, and what Fields had seen in the press, she doubted she would have believed it. Certainly not over drinks at the Hay-Adams.

Which had been hours ago, and she had barely moved from her chair except to refill her coffee and make one trip to the ladies' room.

A legal pad next to her keyboard was filled with names, dates, arrows, and questions written in a hand that had grown progressively sharper as the night wore on. What Shawna Vaughn had told her couldn't wait until morning.

Three federal agents. Two dead in Connor Jameson's apartment. One dead at Erin Delaney's house. And if Vaughn was correct, all had been there to kill.

Fields rubbed one of her temples and looked back at her screen. She had started with Scofield because he'd been the easiest to verify. His credentials had looked good, and within minutes she had confirmed that they were. He was legitimate DHS. The confirmation sent a chill through her.

From there, she had moved to the DSS agent Vaughn had identified from Jameson's. That trail had taken time, but had eventually locked. The man's name was Craig Hollis. His partner, also DSS, was Ryan Kessler.

Kessler had been the easiest. Once she had Hollis, his partner had surfaced quickly enough.

They had similar protection backgrounds and almost identical training profiles. They had the kind of résumés that made them useful in dangerous places and, under ordinary circumstances, trustworthy. Which was exactly what bothered her.

Connor Jameson had killed all three of them. Fields knew that. That wasn't the mystery.

The mystery was why three federal agents had been sent after him in the first place. And once Erin Delaney had entered the picture, why she needed to die too.

That hadn't happened by accident. Somebody had selected these men. Someone had given them a target and had set them loose.

Fields grouped Hollis and Kessler with Scofield and set her link analysis program to work.

The system wasn't perfect. It was clunky and took time. Most of what came back was noise—false positives and the bureaucratic exhaust of three men who had spent their careers moving through overlapping federal ecosystems. Sometime after four o'clock, however, a pattern began to emerge.

Scofield had attended a protective intelligence seminar in Baltimore. Hollis had logged reimbursable travel to the same event. Kessler hadn't appeared on the attendee roster, but he had surfaced in the vendor-support records tied to it through a Northern Virginia contractor Fields had never heard of. She clicked on the company name—Strategis Solutions—and opened its profile.

The website was generic almost to the point of parody: protective consulting, event security, executive support, site coordination, logistical planning, just to name a few. It was the kind of firm that handled the invisible work around important people and expensive events, making itself useful to government clients, private sponsors, and anyone else willing to pay for discretion and order.

Fields ran the company again, this time against Hollis and Scofield. Hollis had crossed paths with Strategis Solutions more than once. Not as an employee, but as outside support on two separate protective assignments—once tied to advance work for a visiting foreign delegation and once at the Baltimore seminar.

Scofield had never been assigned directly to the company either, but he had attended the same seminar and a separate surveillance detection block where Strategis had provided instructors, site support, and logistics.

Fields sat back in her chair.

One hit might have meant nothing. Two were harder to explain. At least five hits, across three different men, from two different agencies, was a pattern. Which meant Strategis Solutions wasn't just some forgettable Beltway contractor. It was beginning to look like a point of convergence.

She dug into the company's officer listings, archived event rosters, and subcontractor support records. She was looking less for the loud names than the quiet ones—the facilitators, sponsors, and advisors who often turned up near a company's machinery without ever directly standing in front of it.

One name surfaced in a buried conference program. Fields clicked on it and got almost nothing back, just a thin metadata stub where a fuller record should have been.

She tried again through a different route but received the same result. Fields frowned and tried a third route in, this time through archived event-support records instead of the conference file itself.

Same result.

At four thirty in the morning, there was no clerk sitting at a desk somewhere, deciding what Jennifer Fields could and couldn't see. If the record had been walled off, it had been walled off long before she ever came looking.

She copied the name to her legal pad, circled it once, and then went wider with her search rather than deeper.

This time, she went for things like corporate filings, shell entities, and prior names—anything that could possibly tie Strategis Solutions to Hollis, Kessler, and Scofield without relying on a single protected file.

It didn't take long.

The same name surfaced again in connection with a closed-door protective intelligence forum in Northern Virginia. It appeared again on an archived sponsorship page for an international security and logistics conference in Singapore, where Strategis had handled event support and coordination. The buried name had been listed as a liaison.

She pulled up the Singapore conference and began working through the sponsor list. Most of it was what she expected: security firms, risk management outfits, logistics companies, and a host of infrastructure and government-adjacent consultants. Then she spotted one corporate name she recognized from a counterintelligence brief the Bureau had circulated the year before. It was a Beijing-linked front.

Not openly. Not on paper. But close enough that someone in her line of work would be able to catch a whiff and tell that something was off.

Vaughn had been right to be suspicious. This wasn't random. Someone had found a way to spot the three federal agents, assess them, and steer them. And that someone had taken pains to make sure the path back was deliberately difficult to follow.

Fields looked at the clock in the corner of her monitor: 4:36 a.m. She reached for her phone and dialed.

Vaughn answered on the second ring. "Tell me you've got something."

"I do," said Fields. "I identified the DSS agent you recognized from Jameson's apartment. His name was Craig Hollis."

A beat passed.

"His partner was Ryan Kessler," Fields continued. "Also DSS."

"Jesus," Vaughn said.

"And Scofield was legit. Actual DHS. That's why his creds were spot-on."

The line went quiet again.

"So," Vaughn said at last, "all three were real."

"Yes," Fields replied. "Which means they weren't pretending to be federal agents. They were federal agents. The question is who sent them after Jameson?"

"And?"

"I started looking for overlap. Hollis and Kessler made sense together. Scofield didn't. The first place I've found where his history overlaps theirs is a Northern Virginia contractor called Strategis Solutions."

"Never heard of them," said Vaughn, rubbing the sleep from her eyes. "What do they do?"

"According to their website, protective consulting, event support, and logistics."

"That's vague."

"Very," Fields agreed. "Typical contractor soup."

"So what are you really telling me?"

"I want to be clear. I'm not saying that Strategis sent them. But it may be where someone found them."

"Found them how?" Vaughn asked.

Fields swiveled in her chair and looked at the name she had circled on her legal pad. "I'm still working on that part. But Strategis operates in exactly the kind of space where men like Hollis, Kessler, and Scofield could be identified, evaluated, and approached without setting off alarms."

"Approached by who?"

"I don't know yet," said Fields. "But Strategis turns up in records for a security conference in Singapore. One of the sponsors had Beijing ties."

"Do you think the company's dirty?"

"I think somebody in or around it may be. Could be someone inside. Or someone adjacent. But every time I push on one associated node, I hit a wall."

"What kind of wall?"

"Protected records. Thin search returns. Partial metadata where a full file ought to be," Fields replied. "Somebody took pains to make part of this hard to trace."

"How bad do you think this is?" Vaughn asked.

Fields looked at her monitor. "I don't know. Men like Hollis, Kessler, and Scofield don't all wind up in something like this by accident."

"You think they were compromised?"

"I think somebody got to them," said Fields. "How and why is the part I don't know yet."

"What do you want me to do?" Vaughn asked.

"Do what you do best. Keep Erin and Connor safe. And keep them hidden. Don't trust anyone you don't have to."

"You think they'll come again?"

"Yes," Fields replied. "Somebody with this kind of reach doesn't leave unfinished business."

"Understood," said Vaughn. "What about you?"

Fields looked again at the circled name on her legal pad. "I'm going to keep pulling on Strategis."

"Do it carefully."

Fields ended the call and returned to the blocked name on her computer. "Who are you, Tom Olson? And why does somebody want you hidden?"

CHAPTER 53

Bangkok

Davi stood next to her mobile command van and looked from Harvath to Morrell as if trying to decide which one of them she wanted to shoot first.

Inside the vehicle, live feeds from five drones, as well as multiple perimeter teams, filled the screens. ISOC operators talking on radios, marking locations, and pushing fresh information came and went.

The boatyard's service road was clogged with Thai police vehicles, unmarked SUVs, and a handful of military trucks. Sirens still sounded in the distance. Somewhere closer, a helicopter chopped the air as it conducted a grid search.

"The Chinese are gone," Davi stated. "Koebler is gone. And after everything that has happened in this city since Friday, I'm standing in another blood-soaked crime scene with nothing I can put my hands on except shell casings, bodies, and a pair of Americans who always seem to show up half a second before everything goes to hell."

Morrell started to say something, but she cut him off with a look. "No. You've both had enough chances to explain yourselves."

Holding Harvath's gaze, she then said, "Everywhere the two of you go, the body count rises, the scenes get uglier, and the fallout lands on me. I'm running out of room to protect you from the consequences of how you operate."

An ISOC operative approached and spoke quietly in Thai. Davi listened, asked two questions, and sent him to speak to one of the techs in the van.

"I signed off on what happened here," she continued, her voice lower, but no less hard. "Which means this failure belongs to me too. The difference is that by nightfall, I'll be the one answering for it."

Morrell began to speak. "Davi—"

"No," she said, cutting him off again. "This operation is over. From this moment on, my people run things. No more improvising. No more unilateral moves. If you get something, you bring it to me. Immediately. You do not act on it. You're done."

One of the techs stepped out of the van and handed Davi her tablet. She scanned it, shook her head, and handed it back.

"Still no confirmed sighting of the SUV beyond the outer perimeter," she said. "We're checking garages, warehouses, and likely transfer points, but if that vehicle was as banged up as you described, the smart move would have been to dump it as soon as possible."

"They were prepared for exactly this type of contingency," Harvath replied.

Davi nodded. "My people will keep monitoring cameras and working our sources. If they made a switch, we'll find them eventually."

"In the meantime," said Morrell.

"In the meantime," she broke in, cutting him off yet again. "I want both of you away from my crime scene and on the other side of my perimeter."

Without waiting for a response, she turned and climbed back into the van.

Morrell watched the door slide shut behind her. "She seems upset."

"You think?" Harvath replied, as they started walking up the street toward Morrell's Land Cruiser.

The rest of the team had already returned to their vehicle. Harvath had wanted them out of earshot and out of Davi's line of sight.

But before her people had flooded the yard, he had sent Staelin and Haney to check for any dead or wounded. The Cambodians had lost two men. The bodies had no IDs, no phones, and no usable comms. If they had been carrying radios, Staelin and Haney reported, their teammates had stripped them as they pulled out. The only intact handset then was the one now in Harvath's possession.

Once he and Morrell were clear of Davi's van and there were no officers in sight, he said, "I borrowed something from our wounded Cambodian buddy."

Morrell stopped. "What?"

Harvath opened his pouch just enough for him to see the radio.

"It's like you didn't hear a word she said."

"I made an executive decision," Harvath replied.

"And it won you a great paperweight. I hope it fits in your suitcase, because that's all it's good for. Whoever those Cambodians are, they're professional enough to have already moved to a new frequency. You're not going to get any operational intel from that."

"What if it's not about what I can get from them," said Harvath, "but what they can get from me?"

Morrell looked back toward the command van. "You think the Cambodians will talk to you?"

"Maybe."

"Because?"

"Because they're operating covertly in Thailand. Because they never fired at us. And because whoever runs that team might want to know what happened to their man who didn't make it back with them."

Morrell considered that. "And if he's changed frequencies?"

"He probably has. But he may still monitor the old channel for a while."

"Out of concern for his missing operator."

"Or curiosity," Harvath replied.

"Same thing," said Morrell as they arrived at his vehicle and he opened the doors. "But if it gets him to respond, that's all that matters. You going to try him from here?"

Harvath shook his head. "Not with Davi's people blanketing the area. And not if anyone on the other end is smart enough to figure out we're transmitting from inside an ISOC perimeter."

"So we move."

"To somewhere public. Crowded enough where a couple of *farangs* can disappear. Easy to leave if we have to. And not tied to Davi, ISOC, or the embassy."

Morrell thought for a moment. Then he said, "Pak Khlong Talat."

Harvath looked at him.

"It's Bangkok's twenty-four-hour flower market. Busy, noisy, and completely anonymous."

Pulling out his phone to text the rest of the team, Harvath said, "That works."

They rode in silence, letting the boatyard and the gunfight fall away behind them. The afternoon rush hour traffic was beginning to build. At more than one intersection, uniformed police were visible directing traffic around checkpoints that hadn't been there before the RBSC bombing that morning.

Bangkok was still moving, but the city felt even further strained, like a cable taking more weight than it had been designed to hold.

Morrell drove with one hand on the wheel, the other dangerously flicking through text messages on his phone. "You want to tell me what happens if someone answers you back on that radio?"

Harvath took the MBITR from his pouch and turned it over in his hands. "If they speak English, I'll try to build rapport and get some information out of them."

"Like what?"

"Like who they're working for and how we might be able to help them nail the Chinese."

Morrell looked over at him. "So now we're going to work with the Cambodians?"

"The enemy of your enemy could turn out to be your new best friend," said Harvath, putting the radio away. "They also could end up being our only lead to Koebler."

They continued driving, using side streets whenever the main roads jammed. People everywhere were still gathered around television sets, reliving the horror, together, as if it might somehow relieve some of the emotional and psychological pain of the attacks.

By the time they reached Pak Khlong Talat, the district was alive with the churn of late-day business. Pickups and delivery trucks crowded the curbs. Men in aprons moved carts stacked with colorful flowers, while women seated on low stools stripped leaves and threaded intricate garlands. Along the gutters, ribbons of water swept petals, dirt, and cigarette butts toward clogged drains. The market had its own distinct atmosphere—humid, fragrant, and in constant motion.

Morrell turned down a side street lined with wholesale stalls and found the one remaining place to park near the back of the block.

"Busy enough?" he asked.

In front of them, men were loading orchids into a truck, while throngs of foot traffic passed without giving them a second look.

"It'll do," said Harvath.

Morrell kept the engine running so the air-conditioning could continue to blow. Easing his seat back, he remarked, "If this works, I owe you a dozen roses."

Harvath checked his watch. It was a little before 5 p.m. He switched the radio on and listened.

There was nothing. No voice traffic. No burst he could make sense of. Just the encrypted hiss of an otherwise dead channel.

Morrell settled back in his seat. "I hear it helps if you say 'Come in Berlin' and play with the knobs at the same time."

"It's a wonder nobody ever liked working with you."

The CIA man grinned. "Like I told you, I'm an acquired taste."

Harvath shook his head and continued to listen, but there was only the hiss. After another few seconds, he keyed the mic and said, "Boatyard. Your man is alive. I repeat. Boatyard. Your man is alive."

He released the button. The hiss returned. He waited several moments. There was no answer.

Keying the mic again, he said, "Boatyard. This channel. Thirty minutes."

Releasing the button, he listened. Nothing. He turned the radio off.

"You remember that movie with Will Smith?" Morrell asked, his eyes half-closed.

"*Bad Boys*? Where he's saddled with a dipshit partner? Funny you should bring that up."

Morrell smiled again. "Great film, but no. I'm thinking of *I Am Legend*. He keeps putting out the same radio call every day saying he'll be at the South Street Seaport when the sun is highest in the sky. Talks about all the stuff he can do for anyone who's listening."

Harvath remembered the film. "You think I should offer the Cambodians food, shelter, and security?"

"I think you should offer them the Chinese."

"I don't have anything on the Chinese."

"They don't know that," the CIA man said. "All they know is that we were in the same place, at the same time, shooting at the same people. We're practically family."

"Family may be stretching it," said Harvath as he looked through the windshield.

"All I know is that if you and your new friend really do have a shared enemy, there's nothing he'd love more than hearing how you can crush him together."

Harvath tapped the MBITR against his thigh thinking about what Morrell had said. The man did have a point.

A proof-of-life message might be enough to keep the Cambodians listening, but if it didn't spur a response, it was a waste of time. Dangling something about the Chinese might make the difference.

Two minutes before the next communications window opened, Harvath cracked the car window and checked his watch.

Outside, the market continued to swirl around them. Somewhere nearby, as if they were in some sleepy corner of Paris, a radio was playing French jazz music.

At the appointed time, Harvath switched the radio back on and slipped its antenna out the window.

But once again, all he heard was the encrypted hiss.

"Boatyard. Your man is alive," he said. "I repeat. Boatyard. Your man is alive."

"Screw roses," Morrell commented. "I should have said you owe me two cases of Jack."

Harvath ignored him. After a pause, he radioed, "Boatyard. If you're listening, we're after the same people. The men in the SUV. Maybe we can help each other."

He took his finger off the button and the hiss rushed back.

Morrell rolled onto his side, hoping to grab a nap. "Better."

Harvath waited, but nothing came back over the radio.

He was about to switch it off when a male voice, speaking in accented English, cut through the static. "Who am I talking to?"

Morrell sat up in his seat and he and Harvath looked at each other.

"I'm the person who gave your operator medical assistance," replied Harvath.

There was a pause. "Is he alive?"

"He lost a lot of blood and was taken to a hospital, but yes, he's alive."

A moment passed. "What do you want?" the man asked.

"A meeting."

"For what?"

"To discuss what happened at the boatyard," said Harvath. "We know why the men in the SUV were there."

"Tell me then."

"Not over an open channel."

There was another pause, as if the man was considering Harvath's request. "Why should I believe you?" the man asked.

"Because I know the man they picked up," replied Harvath. "And I also know how they plan to blame your country for everything that has happened."

There was no response. Just more silence. Outside, a large truck lumbered by.

Finally, the voice returned. "Come alone. No surveillance. No police."

Harvath pulled out his phone and opened a blank note. "Where?"

The man gave him an address, told him to be there in an hour, and then once again the channel went dead.

CHAPTER 54

By 6:30 p.m., the sun was gone. What remained over the nineteenth-century Buddhist temple known as Wat Prayun was the last of the blue sky slipping into black. There was a thin wash of cobalt above the temple's white, bell-shaped *chedi*. The pond surrounding the compound's miniature rock mountain dotted with shrines, known as the Khao Mo, reflected back what little light the day had left.

Beyond the temple walls, traffic trundled across the Memorial Bridge as the river slipped like black glass beneath it.

From where Harvath stood, just inside the grounds, he watched as the temple complex—its prayer halls, low walls, and trees shifting in the humid air—began to darken. A bell sounded once and then was still.

There was a serenity to it, which Harvath supposed was the point. Had he come looking for peace, this might have been the type of place he could find it. Harvath, however, hadn't come looking for peace.

He checked his phone screen again. No new messages. Morrell and the rest of the team were in place. They were spread well beyond visual range and under strict instructions to stay that way unless things went bad. The man had said to come alone. Harvath had no intention of honoring that.

The complex had another hour before closing and there were still people about. Across from him, a pair of ochre-robed monks moved along a walkway, heads bowed, speaking too softly to be heard. Near the entrance, an old woman knelt before a shrine, incense smoke threading around her like the tail of a dragon. A young couple passed near the pond, the man pretending not to notice how often she was looking at her phone. Not everyone, not even here, could disconnect from the outside.

Harvath kept his hands visible and his posture loose. He didn't reach down to reassure himself that his pistol was still there; chambered and ready to go. He knew it was.

His eyes took in the various sight lines, bottlenecks, and distances to cover. There were too many places for a backup team to hide and more than one route they could use to approach without being seen until the very last minute. Which was probably why the Cambodian had chosen it.

Or maybe it was because temples were neutral ground. Harvath had no idea if the man he was meeting believed in neutral ground.

A vibration buzzed in his pocket and he activated the call via his earpiece. "Status," he said quietly.

"Nothing moving from the west entrance," said Haney. "A couple of tourists. One groundskeeper. So far, no obvious surveillance."

"North side clear," Ashby said.

"South wall's quiet," Palmer added. "One guy smoking by the street. Hasn't moved in six minutes."

"All clear here," said Morrell.

"Ditto," Staelin replied.

"Everybody continue to keep your eyes open," Harvath said, before disconnecting the call.

As he did, he heard a footstep on the gravel behind him. Removing his earpiece, he slid it into his pocket and turned.

The man approaching wore dark trousers and a pale open-collar shirt. He was medium height, compactly built, and moved with the kind of economy Harvath associated with men who had spent a long time around violence.

His face was composed, but there was strain in it too. It wasn't fear. It was fatigue—the kind that came when operations went bad and problems, along with bodies, continued to mount.

By all appearances, the man had come alone. But Harvath had been at this game long enough to know that appearances were almost always deceiving.

He let his eyes sweep past the man once. There was no one in the distance; no shadow lurking in the trees.

The Cambodian stopped ten feet away, and for a moment each man stood assessing the other. Neither spoke.

Harvath was almost certain this was the same man he had seen at the boatyard—the figure who had lingered at the water's edge as if weighing whether to go back for his fallen comrade, until the rush of Thai security forces had made the decision for him.

"As you asked for this meeting," the Cambodian said, breaking the silence, "perhaps you should go first."

His English was excellent. His tone strictly business.

"Your operator is still in surgery, but I've been told he is tough, and they expect him to pull through," said Harvath, relaying the update Morrell had gotten from Davi.

"What hospital?"

Harvath shook his head. "I can't give you that."

"Why?"

"I guarantee you, the Thais will have cops watching his room. If I give you the hospital and you send men there, they're going to get spotted," Harvath replied. "Then I've burned you, your operator, and any chance we have of a relationship."

"You assume there's a relationship to have."

"I assume you wouldn't be standing here if there wasn't."

A faint grin touched the man's mouth and disappeared. "And what would the nature of this relationship be?"

"Temporary," Harvath answered. "Transactional. And probably over the second either one of us gets what we need."

That seemed to satisfy the man. At least enough to move on. "Why were the Chinese at the boatyard?" he asked. "Who was the man they extracted?"

"He's a bombmaker. He's also American."

"Two facts we already knew," said the man. "What else can you tell me?"

"His name is Kevin Koebler," Harvath replied. "He's an ex–Navy

SEAL. Before that, he was an explosive ordnance disposal technician. He's got a lot of experience with explosives and he now rents that experience to the highest bidder."

"Like the Chinese," said the man.

Harvath nodded. "Your turn. Why would the Chinese want to detonate bombs across Bangkok?"

The Cambodian was quiet for a moment, as if deciding how much to say. "Because bombings do more than kill people," he eventually replied. "They unnerve survivors. Entire populations. They can be a way to erode confidence; to make governments look weak and incapable of protecting their citizens."

Harvath was good at not filling silences. He said nothing and waited for the man to begin speaking again.

"Bangkok is the center of gravity for this country," the man continued. "Strike it hard enough and you do more than create fear. You create pressure. On the police. On the cabinet. On the prime minister. Even the military."

"To what end?" Harvath asked.

"Instability," the Cambodian stated. "You create public anger. And a belief that civilian leaders can't maintain order."

Harvath studied him. "And Cambodia?"

"Is a useful villain. The enemy next door; a monster under the bed. We're an easy sell to frightened people by ambitious men."

"Maybe I can help make that sale a little more difficult," said Harvath.

The Cambodian looked at him. "How?"

"At this morning's bombing at the Royal Bangkok Sports Club, the Thais recovered evidence that points to Cambodian involvement."

"What kind of evidence?"

"Fragments of a Cambodian SIM card and munitions signatures tied to Cambodian military stockpiles. Not enough to close the case, but enough to start shaping assumptions."

The man's expression hardened. "Go on."

"At a recently abandoned Chinese safe house, we found empty blister packs for two Cambodian SIM cards."

"So they're building a trail and making sure it leads right to us."

Harvath nodded.

The man nodded too, as if something had just been confirmed for him. "The team you're dealing with is not ordinary Chinese intelligence," he said. "They're an elite unit from the Ministry of State Security. External operators, who are highly compartmented and very disciplined."

"If they're so disciplined, how have you been able to track them?"

"We have a source close to the inside. That's all I am prepared to say."

"Who's *we*?" Harvath asked, familiar with some of Cambodia's intelligence operations. "Military intelligence?"

The man shook his head. "Our Military Intelligence Department is filled with way too many Chinese spies. My unit is from the Ministry of National Defense. Off-book. I assume you are CIA?"

"Off-book as well," Harvath stated, withholding the full picture. Thailand was an ally. Cambodia was not. What's more, it was better that the man thought he was working with a CIA unit. It was an organization that foreign intel services recognized and respected. It also tended to make them a lot more cooperative.

"How reliable is your source?" Harvath asked, steering the conversation back to the Chinese.

"It has been intermittent," the Cambodian replied.

"Meaning?"

"Meaning I don't know all the members of their cell, I don't know all of their safe houses, and I don't know where they took Koebler after the boatyard. Not yet."

"Any idea what they plan to do with him?"

"None," the man replied. "But they didn't pull him out under that kind of fire to let him sit idle."

Harvath agreed. Considering what the Chinese had risked to extract Koebler, more bombs were probably in the offing. He let that sit for a moment.

Finally, he said, "So you think Beijing wants to push Thailand toward a coup?"

The Cambodian chose his words carefully. "I think they want Thailand unstable enough that stronger hands begin to look attractive."

"*Stronger hands.* As in the military?"

The man nodded.

"To what end?"

"That," he replied, "I don't know yet."

For a moment, once again, neither of them spoke. The traffic continued over Memorial Bridge and another bell could be heard.

"When either of us gets more information, how do we contact the other?" Harvath asked.

"The radio," the Cambodian said, removing a slip of paper with a new frequency written on it. "We'll monitor that channel seventeen minutes past and seventeen minutes before each hour."

Harvath took the paper. "I just have one more thing."

"Which is?"

"What should I call you? Now that we've met, Boatyard doesn't fit you anymore."

The man was quiet for a beat. Then he said, "Tevy."

Harvath extended his hand. "Scot."

As the men shook hands, the Cambodian said, "You asked for this meeting because you want Koebler. Understand that I want him too. At Teens, I lost men. At the boatyard, more. Before the Royal Bangkok Sports Club bombing, two of my operators hit a storage unit tied to this operation. It exploded before they could secure it."

"We heard about the explosion. I'm sorry. I didn't know those were your men."

"Koebler is the center of all of this," Tevy replied. "Which means he's not just your problem. He's mine too."

"Find the Chinese and we'll find Koebler. After that, we can begin eliminating our problems."

The Cambodian nodded, then disappeared back the way he had come.

Harvath watched him go, slipped the paper into his pocket, and headed for the gate.

Somewhere out there, Koebler was still one step ahead of all of them.

CHAPTER 55

Koebler's clients—who had become his protectors and now his exfiltrators—had once again thought of everything.

The armored Nissan Patrol had been intended to take him all the way back to the safe house. Had it not been shot up in the boatyard, it would have. With no other choice, the Chinese had shifted to their contingency.

They drove only far enough to reach a prearranged property—a garage hidden among repair shops and small warehouses where a damaged SUV could vanish behind a corrugated steel door in broad daylight.

The place belonged to a Chinese national. Like so many in the diaspora, he had learned that when Beijing made a request, refusing it could have consequences for family members half a world away. There, in less than three minutes, the switch happened.

Koebler was hustled out of the vehicle while a dead Chinese operative was dragged from the front seat, and a wounded one was helped out of the back seat of the vehicle. Weapons, radios, and shell casings were placed in a large duffel. Then the diplomatic plates went back on. By the time Thai authorities found the Nissan, the Chinese embassy would have already been alerted and instructed to report it stolen.

Two Chinese operatives stayed behind to finish sterilizing the vehicle and to dispose of their dead colleague. The rest, including Koebler, pulled on full-face helmets, mounted waiting motorbikes, and vanished into the neighborhood.

They cut through alleys and market lanes too cramped for checkpoints. Once, they slowed for a pair of Thai police officers standing next to a pickup, but the officers never so much as gave them a second look. They had no idea the most wanted man in Bangkok was looking right at them from behind the tinted glass of his helmet.

When they finally arrived at the safe house, they rolled in through the rear entrance of the narrow commercial building. Koebler climbed off his bike and followed the other men upstairs. Inside, the rooms were cooler than outside, but only just.

The air smelled faintly of bleach, sweat, and day-old rice. The curtains at the front were drawn and the TV in the corner was muted. The dining table was covered with maps, papers, and laptops. On a sideboard, radios sat in chargers and what Koebler assumed were burner phones stood in a tight row, each marked with a sticky note and what looked like Chinese characters.

A man handed him a bottle of water and pointed him toward a chair. Koebler sat, unscrewed the cap, and took a long swig. He was dehydrated and still trying to slow his pulse.

After swallowing, he closed his eyes for a moment to let the room stop moving. When he opened them again, his client was standing in the room.

Koebler hadn't seen him since Teens. At the time, he hadn't known whether the man had survived. Now he could see the sling, the careful way he carried himself, and the fact that, despite the pain in his face, he was still very much alive.

The client's eyes went first to Koebler and then to the men who had brought him back. There was a brief exchange in either Mandarin or Cantonese. One of the men answered. Another gave a single, almost imperceptible shake of his head.

Koebler didn't need to understand the language to understand the meaning. One dead. One wounded. The rest accounted for.

He set his water bottle down. "You took losses."

"But you're still alive," the client said, his expression implacable.

It wasn't reassurance. It was more of an accounting. Koebler heard it loud and clear. You still have value. But if that changes, so does your situation.

Matías had warned him that the Chinese would help, but only if he helped them first. What worried him was whether they would uphold their end once the work was done.

"Bangkok is closing," the man continued. "The police and military are everywhere. Vehicles are being searched. We hear that one minute it's based on size, the next it's based on color. There's no rationale, and checkpoints are multiplying by the hour."

"Believe me," said Koebler, "I'd rather already be on a plane."

"Yes. Unfortunately, your photos are everywhere and that is no longer an option for you."

Koebler had assumed as much. Everything was much more dangerous now. Dangerous, but not impossible.

"When do we move?" he asked.

The client didn't answer right away. Instead he glanced down at the table and a map one of his men was studying.

"The roads south are already ugly," the man said. "They'll be worse after dark and worse still by morning."

"So we stay put."

"For the moment."

Picking up the bottle, Koebler took another drink of water. "What about avoiding roads altogether? Alternate routes?"

"We're examining multiple strategies," the client replied.

They'd better be, Koebler thought. Whether by boat, rail, or some form of diplomatic cover, the next move had to be airtight. He was a foreign operative being smuggled toward the next phase of a mass-casualty attack. One screwup and all of them would be apprehended. Or worse.

CHAPTER 56

McLean, Virginia

By 8 a.m., Connor had already checked the trail cameras three times. There was nothing on them. No vehicles creeping up the road, no hikers on the trail. Just the gravel drive, the gate, and the break in the trees where the property ran down to the creek. It was the same still frames, the same dead quiet.

It should have reassured him, but it didn't. Instead, it made him feel penned in. Jumpy.

After pouring himself a third cup of coffee, he stood at the kitchen window and looked out over the back. As safe houses went, this one ticked all the boxes. It sat far enough off the main road, and far enough from the nearest neighbor, to feel like it had been dropped in the woods by mistake. The sight lines were good, it had limited access, and it was difficult to approach without being seen. It was harder still to approach by accident. It was a good place to disappear and Connor was already starting to hate it.

Erin watched him from the table. Since getting up, he had checked the trail cams multiple times, practically worn a groove in the floor pacing the kitchen, and had spent more time staring out the windows than seeing what was beyond them. She couldn't tell whether it was instinct, or something darker and more unsettling pushing at him from beneath the surface.

She remembered those stares and the strain of a man fighting to stay in the present while some part of him insisted on scanning for the next threat. She doubted he had gotten much sleep last night, if any at all. Fatigue had always made things worse.

He turned from the window and caught her looking at him. "What?"

"Nothing," Erin replied.

Taking a sip of coffee, he grimaced. It had been bad with the first cup. By the third, it tasted like Vaughn had found it in the very back of one of the cabinets and decided it was still technically legal to serve.

Erin noticed. "That bad?"

"Worse," he replied, setting the mug down on the counter.

It got the smallest flicker of a smile out of her, but only for a second. Then she looked back at the notepad in front of her.

Before dawn, Vaughn had managed to get through on their burner phone. The call had lasted long enough for her to relay the names Fields had uncovered. It was a terrible connection and Vaughn had been forced to repeat herself more than once. Erin had written everything down while Connor listened, all three of them expecting the call to drop at any second.

Craig Hollis, DSS
Ryan Kessler, DSS
Mark Scofield, DHS
Strategis Solutions
Tom Olson

Five names and no context worth a damn. At least no context beyond the first three being federal agents who show up at people's homes looking to kill them.

"What are you doing?" Connor asked.

"Trying to make these names make some sort of sense."

"And?"

"And Tom Olson is about as useful as Tom Smith without more to go on," she replied.

Connor came over and looked down at the page. "Vaughn's FBI contact will keep digging. She'll get more."

"What if she doesn't?" Erin asked. "What if Olson is a dead end?"

"He might be, but I think Fields may be onto something."

"Based on what?"

He pulled out the chair opposite her and sat. "Based on the fact that Scofield, Hollis, and Kessler were all real. Whoever came after us, they didn't just grab three random trigger pullers off the street. They wanted men who could not only do the job, but who could also—ostensibly—get away with it."

"Hence Feds."

Connor nodded. "Badges, especially federal ones, open a lot of doors."

"It opened mine," Erin replied, a shudder passing through her as she momentarily flashed back to what had happened just early yesterday morning at her house.

He tapped Olson's name with his finger. "Men like that don't simply drift into the same black operation by accident. Somebody had to know where to look for them."

"And you think that somebody is Olson."

"I think he's close to it. Maybe he's the broker or a cutout of some sort. What I will say is that Fields didn't hit a wall because she stumbled onto an event planner from Northern Virginia who ticked a box on the FTC's website to get his name removed from mailing lists. If Fields says she thinks it's fishy, it's fishy."

Erin looked at him. "That's a lot to build off one name."

"Maybe," Connor admitted. "But it's more than we had yesterday."

The sudden crunch of tires on gravel pulled both their heads toward the front window.

Before Erin could speak, Connor had drawn his pistol and was already moving. Vaughn had said she'd be out sometime this morning, but with the burner only working when it felt like it, any more advance notice than that was hit-or-miss.

At the window, he parted the curtain a fraction of an inch and saw a familiar SUV roll into view.

"It's her," he said, returning the pistol to his waistband and covering it with his shirt. "I hope she brought fresh coffee."

Vaughn got out of her vehicle in jeans, boots, and a leather jacket. A pair of sunglasses were pushed up on her head. In one hand she carried a tray with three coffees. In the other was a paper to-go bag. Under her arm was a manila envelope. She used her hip to close the SUV's door.

"I stopped at Madison Deli," she said, holding up the bag.

Connor had already opened the door and stepped out onto the porch. "You brought real coffee. God bless you."

"Breakfast sandwiches too. Where's Erin?"

"Inside," he said, standing back so she could pass.

They walked back to the kitchen, where Vaughn said good morning to Erin and started putting the food on plates.

"You guys able to get any news on your burner?"

Erin shook her head. "We were lucky just to get your call this morning. Why?"

"There was another bombing in Bangkok. Targeted a country club popular with a lot of politicians and Thai military brass."

"That's dangerous terrain," Connor replied. "If Bangkok doesn't get a handle on things, the Thai military has a history of solving problems its own way."

"Eat while it's warm," Vaughn said, handing him a plate.

He took it, along with one of the coffees, and sat down. "You didn't have to bring all this. Though we're glad you did. Thank you."

She pulled out one of the chairs and joined him. Erin sat too.

"I figured it was easier than repeating myself a thousand times over the phone. Fields has continued to pull on the Olson thread and there's a few things I want you to see. Just in case they spark anything."

Taking a bite of her breakfast sandwich, Vaughn opened the manila envelope and pulled out several printouts, which she laid on the table. Both Connor and Erin leaned in.

The first page was a conference program. Not the glossy public version. It was something more internal, nuts-and-bolts information acknowledging sponsors and hosts, as well as staff, facilitators, and support personnel.

Connor scanned it. "Singapore," he said.

Vaughn nodded. "It's from one of the events Fields was able to tie Olson to."

Erin looked at it. "And?"

"Keep going."

Halfway down, Olson's name appeared under Event Facilitation and Strategic Support. But there was another name, an event sponsor, that Vaughn had highlighted in yellow, Wei Lijun—Haiyuan Logistics Group.

Connor read it as well. "Who is he?"

"Officially? Founder of a Hong Kong logistics advisory firm," Vaughn replied.

"How about unofficially?" Erin asked.

Vaughn took a sip of coffee. "Unofficially, a guy interesting enough to have popped up in a couple of U.S. counterintelligence reports. According to Fields, he's not designated as a foreign spy, but he's a businessman with ties close enough to the upper echelons of the Chinese Communist Party that he raises eyebrows."

Connor picked up the second printout. It was a trade journal photograph from the same conference. A commemorative photo had been taken at the close of the event. Special guests were in the front row, sponsors stood behind them, and staff and facilitators were at the edges. Wei stood with the sponsors. Olson was six or seven feet away at the edge of the staff cluster.

Connor set it down and looked at the next one. It was a different year and a different event. Washington, D.C., this time. Another closing night shot, with Wei and Olson again. They were never side by side; never in a way that could prove anything, but they were always there.

"He keeps turning up," Erin remarked.

"That's exactly what Fields said," Vaughn replied. "They kept showing up at enough conferences and trade symposiums together that she stopped calling it incidental."

Connor examined the last page. It was a boring write-up from some international shipping journal, but once again, Vaughn had highlighted the most important part—Wei was a principal sponsor of an industry networking event, and Olson, via Strategis Solutions, was credited for "coordination support."

"It's so boring, it makes you want to gouge your eyes out with a spoon."

Vaughn smiled. "Welcome to the wonderful world of espionage.

Everybody wants to be James Bond. Nobody ever gives a second look to the trade rep."

Erin looked at them both. "So Wei's running Olson?"

"Not in a traditional sense," said Vaughn. "Fields thinks Wei is the conduit and instructions flow through him. She believes the shot caller is back in Beijing. But there's a lot more work that's got to get done on this."

Connor was still staring at Wei's name. "What if we don't have the time?"

"What do you mean?" Erin asked.

"Two DSS federal agents at my place. One at yours. Who else are they trying to kill? And how long until they find us again? What are we supposed to do? Just sit here?"

"It may feel like you're just sitting here, but you're staying out of Fields's way so she can do her job," said Vaughn.

"I don't want to sound ungrateful, but she's one person, doing you a favor by pulling on threads from behind a desk. We've got two solid local leads now—Olson and Strategis. We should act on those. Today."

Erin's expression tensed. "What are you suggesting?"

"That we put eyes on Strategis," said Connor. "Nothing more. See who comes and goes. See if Olson shows."

"And if he does?"

"We just watch. No contact. No improvisation. Listen, if nothing shakes loose, fine. We come back here and Fields keeps working. But if something does shake loose, we're ahead of it for once instead of behind it."

"I'm worried you're too on edge for this," Erin replied.

The room went quiet.

"It doesn't make him wrong," said Vaughn, who wondered if maybe Connor had a point. Fields could only do so much from her computer and she'd been at it all night. "If we keep a low profile and don't do anything stupid, we might actually learn something."

Erin shook her head. "You're seriously considering this?"

"If Connor agrees to the rules."

"What rules?" he asked.

"I can think of a few," Erin said immediately. "No heroics. No getting cute. No accosting Olson in the parking lot just because you get a bad feeling and decide the moment is right."

"Give me a break, Erin."

"I think those are good rules," Vaughn replied. "We stay outside. We watch. And that's all. Nobody even gets out of the car."

Erin exhaled through her nose. "Fine. But the first sign this thing is going sideways, we leave."

Connor didn't like the rules, but he knew if he pushed back, the whole thing died right there.

He looked at Vaughn and said, "When do we leave?"

CHAPTER 57

BANGKOK

Harvath was on the roof of the CIA safe house when the encrypted handset chirped once and went silent. Beside him, Morrell had been adjusting the small directional antenna they'd lashed to a vent pipe with a length of paracord. It was precisely seventeen minutes before the hour.

"That's him," said Morrell.

Harvath keyed the radio. "Go."

For a moment, all he heard was the wash of static. Then Tevy's voice came through. "They're moving the cargo south. Tonight."

"What time?"

"Soon."

"From where?"

Tevy gave him the location—a canal-side transfer point in an industrial quarter of the city. Harvath looked at Morrell, who nodded.

"Are you there now?"

"En route."

"What else can you tell me about the location?"

"It's a handoff point. Nothing more. Move."

With that, the channel went dead.

As Morrell took down the antenna, Harvath texted the team that it was time to roll. By the time they were downstairs, Ashby already had the drone case slung over one shoulder and Palmer was checking magazines. It took less than three minutes to load both Land Cruisers.

Morrell's was parked beneath the overhang, still covered with the dust and grime of the last twenty-four hours. Harvath took the front passenger seat and Morrell got behind the wheel. Before they were even through the gate, Harvath had the handoff location up on his phone.

"How's it look?" Morrell asked as he turned onto the street.

"Bad," Harvath replied. "About a thousand ways in and out, and too many places to position shooters."

"Well, let's hope they don't do that," Morrell quipped.

Harvath widened the map and traced the waterways leading away from the area. "This city has more canals than Venice."

"That's where the word Khlong comes from. Khlong Toei is actually named for a plant that used to grow along the southern bank of the canal in that area."

Harvath glanced up at him. "Read a couple books while recovering from that heart attack, huh?"

Morrell shook his head. "I learned it from Davi. Bangkok used to be called the Venice of the East. Something like sixteen hundred canals stretching more than twenty-six hundred kilometers. It's crazy."

"What else did you learn from Davi, beyond that eating Viagra out of a Pez dispenser isn't good for you?"

Turning left, Morrell raised his right hand, gave Harvath the finger, and said, "Keep making jokes, asshole."

Harvath grinned and went back to studying the map. Ball-busting and graveyard humor were necessary to maintain one's sanity in their line of work. With as much as they gazed into the abyss, as Nietzsche would say, it was what prevented the abyss from gazing back into them.

When they got to the canal Tevy had identified, they saw that the area was nothing but warehouses and scrapyards. The neighborhood's biggest industry seemed to be stacks of rusting pipes lying in weed-choked lots.

Morrell killed the headlights a block and a half out and eased the Land Cruiser into the shadow of a vacant fabrication shop. Behind them, the second Land Cruiser pulled in along a sagging wall plastered with old product posters. It wasn't perfect, but it was off the street and far enough from the transfer point that the vehicles wouldn't be seen and the engine noise wouldn't carry.

After using the MBITR to quietly announce their arrival, they donned their tactical gear, powered up their night vision goggles, and went to link up with the Cambodians.

They found Tevy on the roof of an old garment factory two buildings over. He was down to three men. One watched the canal through a pair of aging night vision binoculars, while another covered the road with a carbine. The third man was at the other side of the roof, keeping an eye on the alley below.

Harvath dispatched Haney with his Heckler & Koch HK241 battle rifle to relieve the Cambodian covering the road, and sent Staelin and his SIG Sauer M250 light machine gun to help watch the alley. As Ashby unpacked the drone, Palmer took up position at the far corner of the roof.

Tevy watched the Americans fan out and then, looking Morrell up and down, with his HK MP5 MLI submachine gun and all the thirty-round magazines he carried in his vest and the drop holster strapped to his thigh, said, "You came prepared."

"Always better to have it and not need it," Morrell replied.

Harvath looked at the three men the Cambodian had left. His fight against the Chinese had cost him dearly. "Your operator made it through surgery. He's resting now."

Tevy appreciated the update. "Thank you," he said.

Harvath removed his handheld thermal device, activated the power button, and flipped up his night vision goggles. "Which building is the handoff supposed to happen at?"

The Cambodian pointed to an old warehouse along the canal. The roll-up door to the left was shut, but the one to the right was cracked just enough to throw a weak strip of light onto the loading apron. In the water, tied to one of the pilings, was a workboat with a steel canopy over the rear half of the deck. Off to the side was a refrigerated truck and a smaller delivery van.

"Any activity?" Harvath asked.

"Three men so far," Tevy replied. "One on the road. One by the warehouse door. And one on the boat. All carrying small arms."

Harvath gave the property a slower scan, taking his time until he had picked out each man. "Any sign of Koebler?"

"Not yet."

"You said they are moving him south. Why?"

"The Chinese had a bombmaking cell in Pattani Province, but it has been compromised."

"How?"

"We don't know. All we know is that Koebler is being moved in to replace it."

"Was it part of an Islamist separatist network?"

Tevy nodded. "Barisan Revolusi Nasional. Koebler's job is to build bombs that will look like they came from the BRN."

"Another false flag," said Morrell.

Harvath agreed. "Which will create new waves of chaos and fear, not to mention stress the Thai government even further."

A few feet away, Ashby had unpacked the drone, checked the props, and made sure it had a fully charged battery.

Looking at Harvath, she said, "Skippy's ready to launch."

"Keep it high," he replied. "If they hear a drone, this whole thing falls apart."

Ashby flashed him the thumbs-up and activated the small quadcopter, which climbed above the rooftops and traveled out over the water to take a position well above the canal.

Working off the tablet feed, Ashby began tracking the approaches. For several minutes, nothing moved. Then, headlights appeared at the far end of the canal road.

The vehicle crept in, its suspension bouncing over the bad pavement, as it navigated around potholes big enough to take out one of its wheels.

A moment later a box truck could be seen entering the yard. It made a three-point turn and backed toward the loading bay and the partially cracked warehouse door.

At almost the same time, a long-tail boat came gliding out from under a bridge farther down and crossed toward the pilings.

"Smugglers?" Harvath wondered aloud.

"If any of this was legitimate," said Tevy, "they wouldn't have been hiding under a bridge. They'd already be at the pier."

It was a good point and Harvath nodded in reply.

The warehouse door rolled up halfway, and a man carrying a rifle ducked out from beneath and walked down to the pier to meet the long-tail.

Two more armed men appeared from inside. The first took up a position facing the road. The other stopped where he could watch both the loading dock and the canal.

The truck jostled as something, or someone, moved inside.

Suddenly, there was a flash of movement as a figure dropped to the apron and rushed beneath the half-raised door, disappearing inside.

Tevy looked at Harvath. "Was that him?"

"Yes," Harvath replied. "It was him."

Haney, who'd had eyes on the truck the entire time, radioed, "No clean shot."

It was decision time.

Koebler was inside the building. Two boats were waiting. And Harvath was running out of time.

CHAPTER 58

Koebler quickly disappeared into the warehouse, forcing Harvath to make up his mind. They couldn't afford to wait.

Keeping Haney on the roof, with Ashby working the drone feed, he sent Tevy and his men to the canal side. They had one job—to lock down the pier and prevent anything from leaving by water. Harvath, Staelin, Palmer, and Morrell would hit the warehouse.

He had given Haney one last order before leaving. "If he comes back out and you have the shot, take it."

"Roger that," Haney had replied.

Then, Harvath gave the signal and the teams headed for the stairwell and descended from the roof.

On the ground floor, before exiting the building, he radioed for a sitrep.

"Still no movement," Haney replied. "Trucks, long-tail, and workboat all where they were."

"Nothing new from Skippy," replied Ashby. "No additional vehicles. No additional watercraft."

Harvath gave Tevy the thumbs-up, letting him know that he and his team were good to go.

As they exited the front of the building and peeled off toward the canal side, Harvath and his team went out through the back with Morrell on point.

The alley smelled like stagnant water and old chemical residue. Broken pallets and rusted barrels lined the factory wall. They moved quickly, their weapons up and at the ready, constantly scanning for threats.

Emerging onto a service road that ran parallel to the canal, they cut left, using the shadows cast by the buildings to mask their approach.

The only thing that mattered now was timing. If the handoff started before they were in position, it was game over. The moment Koebler got on one of those boats, he was as good as gone. They couldn't let that happen.

Ahead, Morrell slowed and raised a fist. The entire team stopped. Across the canal road, they had their first on-the-ground view of the transfer point. The truck was still backed tightly into the loading bay, the long-tail remained tied off at the pier, and the workboat hadn't moved. But there was more activity now.

Two men came out of the warehouse and headed for the pier. Another took up a position halfway between the pier and the warehouse.

"They're getting ready for something," Morrell said quietly.

Harvath nodded and keyed his Cambodian radio. "Are you seeing this?"

"We have them," Tevy replied. "We're almost in place."

Harvath looked at Morrell and then Staelin. "We'll cover you. Move."

The men raced across the road, using the truck and an old shipping container for cover. To their right, Harvath could see Tevy and his men getting into place near the canal.

Suddenly, Haney's voice came over their radio. "Movement. Two o'clock."

Harvath and Palmer froze as Staelin and Morrell dropped to one knee. The warehouse door began rolling the rest of the way up as the lights inside were extinguished.

Killing the lights only made the three men who stepped out more difficult to see with the naked eye. But via their night vision goggles with overlaid thermal imaging, Harvath and his team could see the trio almost as clear as day.

The man who stepped out first had his weapon up and his eyes were working the road and the pier. Giving a command, he then began moving rapidly forward. Right behind him came Koebler, followed by another armed man, half a step back. They were driving Koebler straight for the pier.

Radioing Haney, Harvath said, "Three men exiting the warehouse. Koebler's the one in the middle. Do you have him?"

"Fifty-fifty," Haney replied. "They're moving too fast."

"Stay on him," said Harvath.

Seconds later, Koebler was almost at the pier. Harvath had to make a call. "Take him," he ordered.

Haney's shot cracked across the canal road and the man just in front of Koebler went down hard. That was when all hell broke loose.

One of the men on the pier spun toward the shot, only to be cut down by Staelin before he could get his weapon fully up.

Before the man's rifle had clattered onto the dock, Harvath and the rest of the team sprang from cover.

Morrell and Palmer broke left for the warehouse door while Harvath and Staelin drove straight for the water. As they did, Tevy and his team began shooting.

Rounds snapped off the concrete of the loading bay and sparked off the truck's rear bumper.

The men from the warehouse answered right back, firing in controlled bursts, trying to hold Harvath's team off long enough for Koebler to get clear.

At the pier, the bomber didn't hesitate. He knew better than to stay out in the open. The dock was a kill zone. So he did the only thing he could.

Lunging for the edge, he dove into the canal.

"He's in the water!" Harvath shouted.

The men from the warehouse opened up even harder. They raked the banks and the loading bay with vicious covering fire.

Staelin took aim and let the M250 roar. The heavy rounds tore through the loading bay, cutting one of the shooters in half. Palmer took out the man who had been stationed midway between the dock and the warehouse, while Morrell slammed a volley of rounds into the man who had been bringing up the rear behind Koebler.

Tevy's men focused on the long-tail, pinning its crew where they were. As they did, Harvath sprinted for the canal, determined to not let his quarry escape.

Ahead, the workboat engine coughed once, caught, and then settled into a rough but steady rumble.

Harvath hit the pier just as a hand appeared on the far side of the workboat's gunwale.

Koebler.

The man had gone into the water on one side and come up on the other, where the hull masked him from being seen.

Water streamed off his clothes as he hauled himself aboard. One of the crewmen grabbed his arm and dragged him fully onto the deck.

Harvath fired.

From this angle, all he had was the crewman and snatches of Koebler as both men scrambled behind the engine housing.

Harvath's first round punched into a canopy support, while the second blew out glass in the wheelhouse. The third shot went through the engine housing and struck the crewman, knocking him backward, just as the helmsman shoved the throttle forward.

The workboat lurched and, having already been untied, began to pull away from the pilings.

Over the radio, Harvath ordered Staelin to take it out. Once again, the ex–Delta Force operative brought the big gun to bear.

Maneuvering the M250, Staelin hammered the waterline, the stern—anything he could hit without risking Harvath.

Tevy's men added their fire from shore, but Koebler stayed out of sight and the boat kept moving.

Harvath, however, didn't give up. He drilled round after round into the rear of the boat, hell-bent on killing Koebler or, at the very least, rendering the boat itself dead in the water to prevent his escape.

He was halfway through swapping in a fresh magazine, when Ashby's voice snapped across his radio. "Second boat. Fast. Coming out from under the bridge."

Looking up, he saw a smaller boat racing toward them. Whether it was to pick up Koebler or cover his escape, it didn't matter. There had been a contingency. *Fuck.*

Slamming the new mag home, Harvath continued firing at the

workboat, until someone in the bow of the smaller boat scored the entire canal bank with heavy automatic weapons fire.

Harvath had no choice but to break off the pier and race to cover before he was ripped to pieces.

By the time he looked back, the workboat had vanished beneath the bridge.

CHAPTER 59

Tysons Corner, Virginia

Connor was already regretting it when Vaughn turned into the lot across from Strategis. Not because he had changed his mind about Olson, he hadn't, but because the office park looked like every other unsightly office park in Northern Virginia. It was full of low buildings, too much glass, and far too many parking spaces. There was not a damn thing to separate one private firm from the next. And that went double for their employees. All the buttoned-up worker bees looked the same.

"This is it?" Erin asked from the back seat.

Connor kept his gaze on the lobby. "This is it."

Vaughn killed the engine. "How long do you want to sit?"

His eyes flicked to the side lot and then he mentally inventoried the vehicles parked along the curb. "Depends on what we see."

They all knew what that meant. This could very easily turn into one big wild goose chase.

"At least there's a Panera across the street," said Erin, looking over her shoulder, trying to add a little levity. "And we're in luck. I brought my MyPanera card with me and I think I've got a free bagel coming."

No one laughed. No one even smiled. It was shaping up to be a long, uneventful day.

The first hour came and went. Then the second. Then the third. People entered the building and left the building. Delivery vans of all sorts pulled up, dropped off packages, and departed. The most interesting thing they saw all morning wasn't that interesting at all. A postal worker showed up wearing a winter hat, coat, and gloves, which considering how mild the day was, seemed a bit odd. Other than that, everything had been normal. Too normal in fact.

Connor was getting ready to suggest they pull the plug when a black Range Rover turned into the lot and slowed in front of the building.

The former Marine sat up straighter.

"What?" Vaughn asked.

"I think that's Olson," he said, feeling his pulse quicken.

When the Range Rover pulled into one of the reserved spots and the driver got out, they all recognized him. He looked exactly like he had in the photos, just older in the face and harder around the eyes. Mid-forties, fit, controlled. He also wasn't alone.

A second man climbed out of the passenger side and walked with him toward the lobby's glass doors. He was late fifties to early sixties, trim, graying at the temples. Connor was normally good with faces. Sometimes, however, he could have trouble placing them.

"You know him?" Vaughn asked.

He didn't answer right away, but kept watching the man walking beside Olson.

Then Erin leaned forward between the seats. "Oh my God," she said.

Connor looked at her. "What?"

"Your old think tank's Christmas party," she replied. "He spent half the night talking my ear off."

He looked back at the man. "About what?"

"My job."

"At the NSC?"

Erin nodded. "At the time, I thought he was just another self-important Beltway asshole trying to sound plugged in. But he kept asking questions. What I worked on. Who I worked for. Who at the NSC had access to what. I remember because he wouldn't let it go."

"You never told me that."

"At the time, I didn't think it mattered. D.C. parties always have a handful of people like that."

Vaughn looked at him. "Who is he?"

Connor shook his head. "He was one of the senior research guys. Asia policy, if I remember correctly. What the hell is he doing with Olson?"

Erin sat back as the two men disappeared into the building. "You think he had something to do with you getting pushed out of your job?" she asked.

Connor didn't answer. His mind had already been entertaining the same thought. Maybe they hadn't fired him because he was damaged. Maybe they had fired him because he was getting too close to something that somebody wanted buried.

They sat staring at the entrance for ten more minutes to see if Olson or the man whose name no one could remember came back out again. Neither man did.

"Maybe we should go," said Erin.

Connor kept watching, focused like a hawk on the lobby. "Not yet. A few more minutes."

After several had passed, Vaughn finally said, "We've been here long enough."

He knew she was right. Looking at the doors for another beat, he then nodded. "Okay, let's go."

Vaughn started the SUV, and as they pulled away, Connor checked the building one last time. No sight of them. The feeling, however, stayed with him.

While Vaughn drove, Erin sat quiet in the back.

As he watched Strategis fade from view in the side mirror, Connor said, "I wasn't crazy."

Neither woman said anything. They didn't have to.

Above the lobby, behind a wall of reflective glass on the building's top floor, Olson stood at the window and watched the SUV turn onto the road.

As it drove out of sight, he smiled. Their attention had been so consumed with watching the lobby, that they had never noticed the thumb-sized black disc that had been affixed beneath their vehicle.

CHAPTER 60

Pattani City
Southern Thailand
Tuesday

The smugglers had pushed the small boat as hard as they dared. With its engine whining, they had run dark through the last of Bangkok's canals and out into the Gulf of Thailand. The spray coming over the bow had kept Koebler soaked to the skin the entire way.

The transfer to the larger vessel had been done with a rope ladder and without a lot of conversation. The crew didn't speak much English and weren't looking to make new friends. That was fine by Koebler.

He was shown to a cramped cabin, given a change of clothes and an expected ETA. He locked the door, then stripped out of his wet clothes and hung them to dry.

Next, he peeled the money belt from around his waist. Inside was the cash, passport, and phone he had retrieved from his fallback bag at the luggage storage facility on Kasem Rat Road. As a SEAL, he knew the best time to waterproof things was before ever getting near the water, so when he learned from the client the means by which he was being moved south, he had wrapped each item in the Thai version of a ziplock bag.

As was their shitty custom, the client's men had once again disarmed him. And once again, they had missed his polymer knife, which he placed under the pillow on his bunk.

The weather-beaten ship stank of old diesel and even older fish. It had gotten underway as soon as he was on board and was now rolling on mild swells. He had been told tea was available in the galley, but there'd be no food until morning. Food was the farthest thing from his mind at the moment.

He sat on the bunk listening to the hull groan as the vessel worked its way south. Beyond the bulkhead a deckhand called out to one of his shipmates and the sound was swallowed by the engine. Koebler ignored it and forced his mind to think several moves ahead.

The Americans at the canal were his most immediate problem—and two things were obvious. One, they were working with the Cambodians. And two, they were steps ahead of, and apparently not working with, Thai authorities. That meant this was a black operation and they were playing by their own rules. Neither of which was good for him. He had to assume they would keep coming.

His next most pressing problem was his client. While he and his network had ultimately proven resourceful in developing an exfiltration plan from Bangkok, what they had not been was transparent about what came after the Pattani City operation. That troubled him.

In his experience, men that meticulous, who suddenly wanted you to be patient and to trust them, were normally some of the most untrustworthy people there were. They didn't suddenly become vague by accident.

Which meant from this point forward, he needed to think beyond this next operation itself. He needed to study the target package, understand the terrain, and quietly begin preparing for the very possible moment that the client decided his work was complete and he had become more dangerous alive than dead.

He spent another hour running every detail and every scenario he could come up with through his head. Then he quieted his mind, closed his eyes, and got some sleep.

Hours later, he was awakened by a change in the engine's pitch. The vessel was slowing down.

His first concern was that they might have been stopped by the Royal Thai Navy, but the voices and activity on the deck overhead suggested otherwise.

They were followed by a sharp knock at the cabin door and a voice in broken English, which said, "Ten minutes."

The ship had carried him far enough south through the night to clear any dragnet that might have been established in the aftermath of the canal warehouse firefight.

He repacked his money belt, got dressed, and prepared to move. They had reached the next handoff.

Up on deck, two crewmembers lowered a launch into the water and ferried him ashore to an empty stretch of coast in Prachuap Khiri Khan Province.

From beyond the tree line, he was met by two smugglers and a dented truck, which took him deep into the interior. By dawn, they had delivered him to a grass strip so narrow and uneven that it looked abandoned.

The airplane was a decrepit, single-engine utility craft held together, it seemed, by fading paint and patched aluminum. It lifted off in a long, shuddering climb and flew south at low altitude, skirting military airfields and radar coverage.

After landing on another rough strip outside Songkhla, Koebler was handed off again, this time to a single driver from a local network who moved him in a poultry truck.

Despite being secreted in a hidden compartment fed by air-conditioning from the vehicle's cab, both the smell and the noise were terrible. But be that as it may, the truck got him past the police checkpoints and the military presence without any secondary inspections.

By the time they finally drove into Pattani City and turned through the gates of the safe house, he was overheated, filthy, and hungry. He needed a shower and food.

The house was set behind a high wall topped with broken beer bottles and shaded by two overgrown mango trees—neither of which did much to blunt the heat. The driver helped him out of the compartment and then led him inside.

The place smelled faintly of curry and stale cigarette smoke. The furnishings were sparse. There were a few cane chairs, a sagging sofa, and a table with an oscillating fan that clicked at the end of every sweep. In short, the place was a dump, but Koebler tried to concentrate on the positive. He was out of Bangkok, which meant he was one step closer to being on his way out of Thailand.

He took a ten-minute shower in a bathroom with rust-stained tile and weak water pressure. When he came out, the driver was long gone.

In the kitchen, he found food in the fridge and helped himself, washing it all down with a tall bottle of water.

He had just finished eating when he heard the gate open and a car come crunching up the drive. Looking out the window, he saw a gray SUV with a handful of switched-on-looking Chinese. The client had arrived.

Two of the security goons came in first and patted him down—though where he would have found a weapon on his trip south was beyond him. They then swept the safe house and gave the all clear.

The client entered in fresh clean clothes, soft leather loafers, and his arm still in the sling. He took a seat at the dining table, laid a thin folder atop it, and invited Koebler to join him.

Koebler sat down and paused, holding the man's gaze longer than necessary. He was tempted to ask whether they had served steak or salmon on his flight, but decided against it. There was no sense in antagonizing him and making the situation worse. Nobody had forced him to come. He had agreed to be here. All that mattered was completing the job and making sure the client held up his end of the bargain.

"Are those the details?" he asked, looking at the folder.

The client nodded. "Everything's there. Reconnaissance. Components. Placement windows. Detonation."

"What's the time frame?"

"We want it done by tonight."

Koebler chuckled. "You want speed, attribution, and clean execution in a city I've never worked in, without even telling me what I have to work with?"

"You'll have everything you need."

"That timetable is a bit reckless, don't you think?"

"We hired you for your expertise," said the client, "not your opinion."

Reaching for the folder, Koebler reminded himself to stay calm. Opening it, he studied the contents. There were photographs, maps, radius projections, and handwritten notes in English.

Closing the folder, he said, "And after?"

The client folded his hands. "Once the job is done, we get you out."

"How?"

"When the time comes, you'll be told."

Koebler smiled. "I'd like to be told now."

"What happens," said the client, leaning forward just enough for the movement to register as deliberate, "is that you do the work you were brought here to do. You do it well. And then you leave Thailand alive. That is the arrangement."

The bombmaker heard the words, but not a single one of them rang true. With each passing moment, he was becoming increasingly convinced that the client was going to try to kill him.

CHAPTER 61

WASHINGTON, D.C.

Checking the clock on her dash, Vaughn pressed her accelerator a little harder. She hated being rushed.

She hated even more arriving at a secure post with the feeling that her mind was still somewhere else. Nevertheless, part of it was still back at the teahouse with Erin and Connor. They were no closer to understanding why someone wanted them dead.

Nearing the White House complex, she removed her credentials and presented them at the outer checkpoint. The officer scanned her in and signaled her forward.

She guided her SUV into the vehicle screening lane and stopped where indicated. Another officer stepped into view and motioned for her to hold. She put the SUV in park.

A mirror rig was brought around, followed by another piece of equipment. Vaughn had seen the process hundreds of times. Usually it was a simple routine. Tonight, however, something was different. She could see the shift in the screeners' body language the second it happened.

In her rearview, one of them had raised a hand while the other crouched lower. Then both men stepped back at once. As they did, Vaughn's pulse kicked up.

"Ma'am," said the first officer as he came to her window, "please turn off the vehicle and step out. Slowly."

It was the tone that got to her.

He wasn't expressing suspicion or caution. It was alarm.

Killing the engine, she opened the door and stepped out. The second officer directed her to step back from the SUV while a third moved in and manually checked beneath her chassis.

"What'd you guys find?" she asked, bending down and looking for herself.

And then she saw it—a small black disc the size of a heavy coat button. No one needed to tell her what it was. She knew the moment she saw it. It was a tracker.

Instantly, her mind went to Erin, Connor, and having dropped them off at the teahouse.

Son of a bitch. Olson, or one of his people, must have spotted them in the Strategis parking lot.

In a flash she had her phone in her hand and was already dialing Erin and Connor's burner.

The call tried to connect, hung for two beats, and failed. She immediately tried again. She got the same result. The call didn't even go to voicemail.

Damn it.

The teahouse had no Wi-Fi and the cell service out there was garbage. She knew that and had warned them about it herself. Now their comms were being cut off right when she needed them most.

She found Fields in her contacts and hit "call."

The FBI agent picked up on the second ring. "You okay?"

"Olson knows where Erin and Connor are. I need your help. Right now."

CHAPTER 62

McLean, Virginia

With no TV and no internet, they had tried to take their minds off the situation with whatever distractions the house offered. Erin had discovered two ancient board games—one called Sorry! and another called Masterpiece—both of which Connor had eventually lost patience with and quit.

In the same closet, there had also been a handful of old paperbacks and she decided to occupy herself by reading. Pulling one out called *Memories of Midnight* by Sidney Sheldon, she made herself comfortable near the fire and tried to tune everything else out.

The little house had never been meant to hold people under strain. During the day, the light filtering through the trees and the charm of the mid-century architecture had made the place feel almost like a retreat. But at night, with the woods pressing in from all sides and the black glass of the windows giving back only their own reflections, it felt more like a trap.

Connor stood at the front window. He had been there for the better part of twenty minutes. It wasn't because he had seen anything. He just couldn't shake the feeling that something outside in the dark had shifted. Finally, he moved to check the kitchen window.

Erin looked up from her book as he passed. "You're doing it again."

"Doing what?"

"Wearing a path in the floor."

"Sorry," he said, as he stopped at the sink and stared into the darkness.

"No, you're not."

That was true. He wasn't. Like it or not, this was how he was wired.

He bent closer to the window. There was barely enough ambient light from the sliver of a moon to make out the nearest trees. Beyond them, the woods fused into layers of black. Every now and then a branch shifted in the breeze. Beneath the window, a tangle of leaves skittered past, scraping over one another. The sounds were perfectly normal. The problem was that his nerves no longer trusted normal.

Stepping away from the window, he picked up the tablet. Its battery was down to 42 percent and he made a mental note to charge it overnight.

One of the camera thumbnails was black, another showed a fixed view of the gravel drive, and a third was frozen on a patch of woods dense enough to hide an army.

There was a sharp crack from the suspended fireplace and both of them flinched. Connor's hand shot to the back of his waistband before he saw the shower of sparks collapse behind the mesh screen. One of the burning logs had split.

Erin let out a breath. "Jesus."

Connor didn't answer. He was busy tapping the screen, trying to refresh the feeds.

The driveway camera came back first, washing the strip of gravel in chalky-pale infrared. There were no headlights. No movement.

The frozen image of the woods resolved next, then steadied. Again nothing.

Connor waited, watching.

"Anything?" Erin asked, seeing the tablet in his hand.

"Hang on."

The third camera hesitated, its icon spinning. Finally, it resolved into a grainy image of the south side of the property. The picture flickered once and then held.

He brought the tablet closer.

At first, all he saw were tree trunks and undergrowth, washed flat by the cheap infrared. Then something moved at the edge of the frame. It was just a blur and was gone as soon as it appeared.

Connor held perfectly still.

"What?" asked Erin, setting her book aside.

He held his finger to his lips and kept watching.

The feed stuttered, and when it came back, a figure crossed between two trees and disappeared again. *Not a deer.*

Erin was on her feet now, coming toward him. "Connor?"

He enlarged the image, which only made the resolution worse, but there was still enough to see what mattered. A second man slid into view, offset from the first by several yards. He moved with the same practiced precision.

The picture faded, but came back again. This time, farther back and on a parallel line, two more shapes appeared and vanished through the trees.

Two pairs, spaced apart, moving with purpose. Connor felt his blood go cold.

Erin looked from the screen to him. "Who are they?"

Setting down the tablet, he drew his pistol. "Get away from the windows."

"Connor—"

"Now."

She backed away without another word.

Connor looked once more at the screen. Four men divided into two teams. Moving through the dark and closing in on the house like they had done this many times before.

He didn't know who they were, but he knew exactly why they were there.

They had come to kill them.

CHAPTER 63

Connor crossed the room and killed the lights. The only illumination left, the fire in the suspended hearth, threw its dull orange glow across the floor and up the walls.

"Move," he said, pointing into the kitchen. "And stay low."

Erin did exactly as he told her, keeping her head down as she slipped past. Connor followed, all his senses on high alert.

Glancing at the tablet, he could see the feed was still holding. The four men had closed the distance. One pair was angling toward the front of the house. The other had drifted wider and was circling to cut off the rear.

Connor looked at the faded runner on the floor and the bump beneath. *The crawl space.*

Tight, dark, and with no guarantee of a second way out, it wasn't a fabulous option. But if the men outside breached fast, it might buy Erin a few extra seconds, maybe more. That in and of itself was worth it.

"Listen to me," he said.

She was watching his face now—not the gun, not the tablet. His face.

"I want you to get in there and no matter what happens, no matter what you hear, I don't want you to make a sound. Do you understand me?"

She nodded. "Understood."

Kneeling, he shoved the runner aside, found the iron ring, and pulled. The hatch came up with a quiet screech of warped wood against warped wood. The scent of dirt and cold air rose from below.

Erin peered into the darkness. "How deep is it?"

"A couple feet at most. You got this."

She lowered herself into the opening as Connor kept one hand on the hatch and the other on his pistol. The crawl space was shallow; barely enough room for her to crouch.

"You okay?" he asked.

"Yes," she replied.

"Good. Stay down and stay quiet."

He eased the hatch back into place and covered it with the runner. Straightening up, he grabbed the tablet and checked the cameras again.

One of the feeds had gone dead.

He stared at the black square for half a second. Was it a transmission failure? Or had someone taken the camera down? Either way, the result was the same.

Moving to the sink, he stayed far enough back from the window not to silhouette himself.

At first he didn't see anything. Then, off to his left, something passed between the house and the trees. *They were here.*

Backing away, he moved into the main room and took up a position that gave him a view of both the front door and the short hall leading to the bathroom, while keeping him away from the windows. It wasn't much. The teahouse had practically no real cover. A determined man with a rifle could shoot halfway through the structure without much trouble.

Squatting down behind a wooden sideboard, he slowed his breathing and listened.

For a moment, he heard nothing. Then came the faintest creak from somewhere outside.

It wasn't from the woods. It was from the house. Someone was testing the porch.

Connor stayed pressed against the sideboard, head on a swivel. Then he heard it again—the board on the front porch.

But a second later, he heard something else—a faint metallic test of the back door latch.

Front and rear. Probing. Coming to a decision.

Or maybe they were testing him; trying to split his attention.

He tightened his grip on his pistol, took a breath, and stayed where he was. The worst he could do was to start shooting too soon. He didn't need them firing from the outside. He needed them inside. With him.

The front door gave an almost imperceptible shudder in its frame.

Another probe.

Connor shifted his aim toward the kitchen and was greeted by the soft scrape of metal, followed by pressure against the back door. Not enough to force it, just enough to feel whether it would give.

It didn't.

For half a heartbeat, everything went still. Then the back door exploded inward.

CHAPTER 64

The back door crashing open might have been meant to shock and awe, but as a combat-tested Marine, Connor Jameson knew how to hold his fire.

A dark shape filled the rear doorway and paused, only long enough to scan the room.

As he swept his muzzle across the kitchen, Connor held.

The attacker took two more steps inside, and as he did, a second silhouette appeared behind him in the doorway.

Connor continued to wait.

Then, when both men had committed, he opened fire.

The easiest shot would have been to take out the man already deeper in the kitchen. Connor, however, didn't want to risk losing the second attacker in the doorway and so he shot him first.

His 1911 roared like thunder. Two rounds tore into the man at the door. Before either attacker could react, Connor shifted and followed up with another two rounds directed at the man already standing in the kitchen.

The man in the doorway slammed back against the frame and spun into the dark outside. The guy in the kitchen, bleeding from two shots to his chest, attempted to raise his suppressed weapon to fire back. Connor shot him again, this time right in the face, and he went down, dead.

Then the whole house erupted.

Bullets tore through the wall above the sink, showering the air with splinters and drywall dust. Apparently, the attacker who had tumbled backward outside was still alive.

As Connor swapped out his magazine and prepared to return fire, a boot hit the front door—heavy and loud. A second strike, louder and harder, followed immediately after and the lock assembly ripped loose, followed by the door flying inward.

The kicker came through with his carbine up, no stranger to making entries under hostile fire. Connor, however, shot first.

His 1911 bucked in his hands and the hallway flashed white. The round caught the man high in the shoulder, turning him just enough so that his teammate, stacked close behind him, had to pivot to the side.

Connor fired twice more, but both rounds went wide. Then it was their turn and the two attackers opened up.

As their suppressed weapons erupted, the teahouse came apart. Rounds ripped through the sideboard and crashed through the Sheetrock behind him. Knowing better than to stay in place, Connor dropped low and moved as fast as he could. A fraction of a second later, rounds chewed up the spot he had just vacated.

He came up near the far end of the room and, taking aim at the man he had winged coming in the front door, fired again.

The attacker tried to drive deeper into the house anyway, but Connor's second shot slammed right into his sternum, rupturing his heart and dropping him dead, half-in and half-out of the front door.

His partner stepped over his body and kept coming.

At the same time, fresh movement came from the kitchen. The wounded attacker who had been shooting through the back of the house had returned to the doorway.

Now, from the front entry and the rear, they had Connor bracketed. It wouldn't take long to dial in their kill shot.

Connor dropped flat as both men opened up.

Rounds tore through the room from two directions. More wood splintered. More glass shattered. And the suspended fireplace rang incessantly as rounds ricocheted off its metal hood and flue.

The bullets were getting closer. Connor needed to disrupt their triangulation or he was done for.

Leaning his pistol out, he fired in the general direction of the front door, causing the attacker to retreat behind cover.

It was the only break Connor was going to get and he scrambled for the dining table. Now the wounded attacker at the back door would have to either hold his fire or risk hitting his partner.

What Connor hadn't counted on, however, was that both men would press their luck—and that they would do it at precisely the same moment.

In unison, they came rushing into the room, training their fire on the dining room table. Connor had nowhere else to go.

The last thing that would go through his mind was his fear of what would happen to Erin and his guilt over having let her down.

Forever a Marine, he wasn't about to surrender this fight. If he was going down, he was taking at least one more of these guys with him. As he was already angled toward the kitchen, the easiest would be the wounded attacker at the back door. Bringing up his pistol as fast as he could, he pressed his trigger and fired.

At the same moment, he heard gunshots right behind him.

As the man at the back door fell dead, Connor spun, amazed that none of the bullets fired from the front door had struck him. He looked up just in time to see the other attacker jerk violently and collapse inside the threshold.

Standing over the body was a woman in tactical body armor emblazoned with three gold letters: FBI. She now had her weapon pointed at Connor.

"Special Agent Jennifer Fields!" she yelled. "Drop your weapon!"

Connor set the 1911 on the floor and raised his hands. "Don't shoot," he said.

"Any other hostiles in the house?"

"I counted four," he said. "Two at the front. Two at the rear."

Without lowering her weapon, Fields stepped past the body and began clearing the room.

All four attackers were dead. There were no signs of any others.

Holstering her weapon, she helped Connor up. "Shawna Vaughn sent me. Where's Erin?"

Connor picked up his pistol and pointed toward the runner in the kitchen. "In the crawl space."

Only then did he see the tablet. It lay shattered, its screen blown out. The camera feeds were gone.

As the steel was too hot to tuck the weapon back in his waistband, Connor set the 1911 on the counter. Then, dropping to one knee, he pulled the runner back, found the iron ring, and lifted the hatch.

"Erin," he called down. "It's me. You can come out."

"Don't."

It was a man's voice and had come from the edge of the kitchen.

With one hand holding up the hatch and the other extended into the darkness below, Connor froze. Fields spun so fast her jacket flared. But with her weapon holstered, she was half a second too late.

Olson stood in the doorway with his pistol leveled. His expression was flat and unreadable.

Shifting his muzzle toward Fields's hip, he said, "Take it out slowly and put it on the floor."

Fields held his gaze, then reached down, drew her weapon with two fingers, and lowered it carefully to the boards.

Olson flicked his eyes to the counter. "And the 1911."

Connor straightened only enough to reach it and then set it on the floor next to Fields's weapon.

"Kick them to me."

Fields did what he asked.

"Now," Olson said, gesturing to the crawl space, "get her out."

Connor looked down into the darkness. "Erin, take my hand."

She emerged dirty and shaken.

The moment she was clear of the opening, Olson motioned with his pistol toward the living area. "All of you," he said. "Move."

They did.

Like the kitchen, this room also looked like a tornado had raged through it. Shards of glass were everywhere. The front door hung open. The air was thick with smoke, drywall dust, and the smell of blood. Olson walked them backward until they were in front of the suspended fireplace.

"Kneel," Olson ordered.

Connor felt Erin hesitate beside him. Then they all knelt.

Looking up at him, Connor said, "You should have sent more men."

"I sent enough," Olson replied. "Then Agent Fields arrived and complicated things."

Fields kept her eyes on him. "Who do you work for?"

Olson ignored her. He was staring at Connor now. "Losing your job should have been enough. With your reputation damaged, you should have learned your lesson. But you kept digging."

"At the think tank?" Connor asked.

Olson nodded. "You saw activity you weren't meant to see. Just enough for you to become a problem."

"And Erin?"

Olson's expression never changed. "You brought her too close to things she was never supposed to see."

"What about you?" Fields asked. "What's your role?"

This time, Olson looked at her. "Finding talented people with debilitating weaknesses. Debt and ego. Resentment, fear, or ambition. We all have our pressure points. My strength lay in finding the ones who were the most useful."

He shifted the pistol, settling it first on Connor and then on Fields.

"Unfortunately," he said, "none of you are useful anymore. In fact, you've been quite a liability."

Suddenly, three mysterious shots cracked from the entryway. The first two hit him in the head. The third tore through his throat, just below his Adam's apple.

He was dead before he'd even hit the floor.

All eyes were drawn to Vaughn, who stood just inside the front door, her pistol gripped in her hands. She moved quickly, making sure the rooms were clear. "Is anyone else in the house?"

"Negative," said Fields, who was already on her feet.

Rushing to Olson, the FBI agent kicked his pistol away and checked for a pulse, just to make sure. *Nothing.* "He's dead," she said, walking over to retrieve her own weapon.

Connor rose next and helped Erin to her feet. "Are you hurt?" he asked, checking her over.

She shook her head. "I'm okay."

When Vaughn returned to the living room, her gaze went from Olson's body to the four dead gunmen and then back to Connor. "I leave you alone for five minutes . . ."

Connor couldn't help a small grin. "It was a little longer than five."

Fields wasn't smiling. Until she got them all back to the FBI building, she wouldn't feel truly safe. "We need to move," she said. "Right now. I don't want to wait around for any more surprises."

Connor picked up his 1911, inserted a fresh magazine, and, with the steel having cooled, tucked the weapon into his waistband. Killing Olson had solved only one problem. Until someone got to the bottom of why he had been targeted, neither he nor Erin would ever be safe.

CHAPTER 65

PATTANI CITY
THAILAND

By the time the Carlton Group jet touched down at Pattani's small regional airport, the sky to the east had begun to lighten.

Harvath had slept for about twenty minutes on the flight south. As badly as he needed the sleep, it hadn't helped.

The minute they were wheels-down, he was already gaming out scenarios. How many places in and around Pattani City could serve as safe houses? How many routes in and out? How many local networks still existed after the bombing cell was rolled up by Thai authorities? How many of those could the Chinese possibly leverage?

It was simply impossible to know. The short answer was: too many. Even attempting to get his arms around it was giving him a headache.

The lead that had brought them here had come from one of the smugglers who had survived the canal warehouse gunfight. Under pressure the man had given up only one useful piece of information—that Koebler was being smuggled south to Pattani City. No names. No routes. Just a destination. It was pretty thin, but it was all they had.

He and Morrell had decided not to share it with Davi. There were less than forty-five thousand people in the city and she would have parachuted in the entire Thai army.

Tevy and his team had remained behind, working their source inside the Chinese intelligence unit, trying to develop something more useful than a city on a map. If they didn't, Harvath was going to have to work the rest out on his own.

As soon as the forward door opened, the morning air came in hot, heavy, and humid. The one saving grace was that Pattani was a coastal city and its breezes blew in off the ocean. It smelled a lot better than Bangkok.

Waiting for them at the edge of the tarmac was a convoy that had been put together by one of Morrell's CIA colleagues. It was comprised of two dusty Toyota pickups and a black SUV that looked like it had seen enough rough mileage to qualify for combat pay.

They offloaded their gear quickly, keeping their heads down. Pattani was a place where outsiders drew outsized attention, even when they were trying to blend in.

At the SUV, a middle-aged Thai man named Jira greeted them. Opening the rear hatch, he filled the cargo area with the team's larger bags and equipment.

He wore a faded polo shirt, cheap loafers, and had a sidearm tucked in the back of his jeans. Morrell hadn't offered an explanation for who the locals were and Harvath didn't ask. The CIA had lots of interesting bedfellows.

Harvath and Morrell rode in the SUV with Jira, Ashby and Palmer took the pickup behind them, and Staelin and Haney rode in the one behind that. All of them were carrying their own sidearms and plenty of spare ammo just in case.

The convoy rolled out of the airport, and the Muslim influence was evident immediately. Arabesque architecture, mosques, and women in hijabs were everywhere. But for the difference in facial features, they could have been driving through a town somewhere on the water in North Africa. It was both exotic and alien, and no surprise that Pattani was referred to as the center of Thailand's Muslim south.

Unlike the sprawl of Bangkok, nothing here felt expansive. The place pressed inward. The streets were narrower, the buildings were lower, and the walls were closer together. Military and police presence was everywhere, as was the sense that violence could explode at any moment. You could feel it in the checkpoints. In the sandbags. And in all the hard glances.

Whoever had chosen Pattani for this operation had chosen well. If a bomb went off here, and it even remotely looked like the work of separatists, the powers that be in Bangkok would waste no time assigning blame.

"Jira, where are we headed?" Harvath asked their driver.

"Temporary base," the man replied, his accent heavy.

"That sounds pretty official."

"Nothing about your visit here," Jira replied, "is official."

Morrell smiled. "I think I like this guy."

Five minutes later, they turned off the main road and entered a walled compound. Inside was a one-story concrete building with barred windows, an old VW on blocks, and a brown canvas awning beneath which three men sat smoking and cleaning rifles.

Jira introduced the men, and then Harvath, Morrell, and the rest of the team gathered up their gear from the convoy vehicles and carried everything inside.

It was cooler than outside, but not by much. Two ceiling fans did nothing more than push the humid air around the main room. In addition to some old furniture, there were several paper maps of the city of Pattani and Pattani Province taped to one of the walls, along with a corkboard pinned with photographs. Adjacent was a whiteboard covered in Thai script.

In the kitchen, next to a medical box, was bottled water, canned food, and a case of instant noodles.

"You should have enough for now," Jira said. "If your team needs anything else, tell me and I will get it for you."

Haney was going through the cabinets in the open kitchen. "I see tea. What about coffee?"

"I can get coffee."

"And maybe some prime rib?" Staelin added, looking into the empty fridge.

"Make the man a list," Harvath said. "In the meantime, I want somebody from our team awake at all times and with eyes on the gate. Palmer and Ashby will take first watch. Haney and Staelin, get the comms up and running. Morrell, you're with me."

As the rest of the team broke away, Jira crossed to the corkboard and removed three photographs. He brought them to the table, but didn't put them down right away.

"You wanted to know what the original Pattani plot looked like," he said.

Harvath stepped closer. "What have authorities been able to figure out?"

"Unfortunately, only bits and pieces of the operation," Jira replied. "They haven't gotten things like timing or final placement of the devices. They don't even have all the names involved yet. But they do have enough to understand the targets and part of the delivery method."

He set the photos on the table.

Each image showed the same essential elements in different combinations—white concrete buildings, Thai flags, Ministry of Education signage, drop-off areas, faculty parking.

Morrell looked from one photo to the next. "Schools?"

"State schools," said Jira. "Boys and girls. Ages six through twelve."

Harvath examined the pictures in silence for a moment. "Why?"

"Because it will outrage Thai citizens and humiliate the Thai government."

From a folder on the table, he extracted another set of photos and laid them out. They were close shots this time—backpacks, school bags. Some had cartoon characters. Others were bright colors.

"The devices," Jira continued, "were to be concealed in what looked like students' bags. They would then be left around the school grounds where they wouldn't immediately attract attention—near entrances, drop-off points, playground areas. That sort of thing."

"Jesus," said Morrell. "And then what?"

"Then once the first blasts hit and police, military, and medics all arrive, a follow-on attack takes place targeting them."

There was a pit in Harvath's stomach. Shaking his head, he asked, "And what steps have been taken since the cell was rolled up?"

Jira spread a map across the table and marked the schools one by one. "Security has been increased at all of them," he said. "Heightened police and military presence. More patrols at arrival and dismissal. Bags checked. Random vehicle inspections. Even some plainclothes officers as well."

He tapped the largest school on the map. "This was the easiest to harden once they knew what to look for. It has a big perimeter with clear approaches."

He moved to the second. "This one sits in a busier civilian area. It has more vehicles, more parents, and more vendors. That makes it harder to control without controlling half the neighborhood."

Then the third. "This one caused the most concern. While it's a smaller campus, it's crammed with a bunch of shops and houses. The foot traffic alone is a nightmare. Not to mention how many places there are to hide before an attack and simply blend in and disappear after."

Harvath studied the school on the map. Jira was right. It was a tangled mess of side streets, alleyways, passageways, and courtyards. Next to impossible to control, and even harder to protect.

Looking back at the school photos, he said, "I want to see them with my own eyes."

"The schools?" Jira asked. "Why?"

"To understand why they made sense," Harvath replied. "And now that they're harder to hit, I want to see what else in Pattani might make an attractive target."

Morrell nodded. "They're not going to reinvent the wheel. They'll keep what works and change what doesn't."

Harvath looked at Jira. "Let's take a ride."

CHAPTER 66

They drove into Pattani along a wide stretch of white sand beach. With the windows down, so as not to overtax the old SUV's air-conditioning, they enjoyed the wind blowing in from the Gulf of Thailand.

Jira explained that everyone was getting ready for next month when the high season would begin. Temperatures would go down and prices would go up.

In a city that was 90 percent Muslim and in which alcohol sales were practically nonexistent, Harvath figured they weren't drawing much, if any, of the *farang* tourists flocking to Phuket or Bangkok.

As far as natural beauty was concerned, the area had a lot going for it. Culturally, however, Harvath had never cared for the tenets of Islam. He doubted he'd be booking a sun-drenched holiday in Pattani anytime soon.

Jira took them to the largest of the three schools first, and even before they reached it, Harvath could see why the original plot made sense. The school wasn't built like a stronghold.

A low wall marked the perimeter, but the front of the school was wide open, allowing parents to pull up and children to be dropped off or picked up. There was room for cars, scooters, foot traffic, and all the ordinary chaos that came with getting kids through a school day. What had changed was the security.

Two Thai soldiers stood near the main entrance armed with automatic rifles. A police pickup was parked beneath a tree across the street, and two local beat cops were working their way through passing scooters and delivery vehicles, stopping some, but waving the majority through.

The second school sat in a busier part of town and was also publicly facing. It had not been built with a serious setback from the street. Just a school absorbed by the life around it.

There was a row of food carts not far from the entrance, and at one point, parents and older siblings would have probably mixed there with teachers and other residents from the area. Now, however, things were markedly different. Four Thai soldiers stood out front, a military truck sat half on the curb, and local police worked the edge of the drop-off zone, checking bags at random and asking drivers to open their trunks.

To access the third school, they had to park a block out and head in by foot. Just as the map had revealed, the neighborhood was crisscrossed with side lanes, cut-throughs, and covered walkways. There were people everywhere. It was exactly the kind of environment where the movement of ordinary life could hide something dangerous until it was too late. And now, even here, local authorities were making their presence known.

There were uniformed cops and Thai soldiers, but what really stuck out were the plainclothes cops. Even in jeans and T-shirts, they still had a very obvious look to them.

Harvath took it all in. "This was the school that worried them the most?"

Jira nodded.

Morrell scanned their labyrinthine surroundings. "Simply securing the entrance doesn't solve the problem."

"Because the whole neighborhood layout is part of the problem," Harvath replied, glad that they had taken the time to visit all three schools.

Whatever Koebler and the Chinese had hoped to achieve, these targets appeared hardened enough to make them look elsewhere.

If local authorities were smart, and Harvath had no reason to believe they weren't, they'd be beefing up security at all the other schools as well.

Terrorists were a lot like sharks. They swam in wide circles, gradually shrinking them, as they gathered information. If you could convince them you weren't worth the risk, they'd go off in search of an easier meal.

And while Harvath was against the loss of any innocent life, at the top of his list were the lives of children. If Koebler and the Chinese had been forced to choose different targets, ones that didn't involve kids, that was a win, albeit minor, in his book.

Looking farther down the street, Harvath saw a host of brightly colored awnings and umbrellas surrounding an outdoor marketplace. Rows of parked scooters lined the curb and people moved in and out through the breaks between the stalls, carts, and tables. Even from here, the place looked packed.

Jira followed his gaze. "That's where we're getting supplies."

Harvath reached into his pocket and pulled out the list Haney had given him before leaving the safe house.

"What do we need?" Jira asked.

He read off the list and then added Ashby's caveat written at the very bottom, "And anything edible that's *not* noodles."

Morrell laughed. "Kids these days. They have no idea what safe houses used to be like."

"I make them listen to all my stories," Harvath assured him. "Believe me, they know."

Jira nodded toward the market. "Come."

The closer they got, the bigger the market became. What had appeared from a distance like a cluster of awnings and umbrellas turned out to be an entire world unto itself stretching for blocks.

There were rows of stalls and tables, produce stacked in crates and baskets, fish laid out on metal trays packed with melting ice, garments hung from cords stretched overhead, plastic tubs, cheap toys, and cookware.

The first thing that hit Harvath was the smell. It was a pungent mix of fish, spice, hot oil, and fruit beginning to turn in the heat. The second was the sound.

Vendors were calling out prices, metal was clanging against metal, and generators were thrumming from somewhere deeper inside. It was a place where everyone was occupied with something.

They passed a woman haggling over limes, a halal butcher working through a side of lamb, and an old man fanning smoke away from a charcoal brazier. At several points, people had to turn sideways to squeeze past each other.

It reminded Harvath of all the busy souks he had seen across the Middle East, and Jira moved through it like a pro. He knew which stalls had the best products and even produced two reusable shopping bags from his back pocket.

As Jira negotiated for oranges, Harvath let his eyes wander. He noted how the aisles fed one another, where the crowd bunched up and where it thinned.

"I don't like this place," Morrell remarked.

"Too classy?" Harvath asked.

Morrell subtly rubbed his eye with his middle finger and then got serious again. "It's a death trap. We're only a few rows in and if a stampede started in here, we'd be lucky to make it out alive. The bodies would pile up all over the place."

A woman with a toddler brushed past them and they stepped aside to let her pass. After she did, Harvath scanned the market again. Morrell wasn't wrong. It was definitely crowded. And to be honest, he wasn't thrilled by that either. They were both glad when Jira held up his two bags, announced that he had purchased everything on the list, and they were able to leave the market and head back to his SUV.

Before returning to the safe house, Harvath wanted to see the rest of Pattani and game out other possible targets. As Jira pointed out other locations that could be attractive—a bus depot, several government buildings, and a crowded commercial strip, Harvath took notes. Each made sense in its own way and each came with its own set of problems. What was clear, however, was that Pattani was still full of places where Koebler could do an incredible amount of damage.

By the time they turned back toward the safe house, Harvath still didn't know where or when the man would strike.

CHAPTER 67

Back at the safe house, after putting away the supplies, Harvath studied the maps with Morrell and Jira. If the schools were no longer targets, the question became what in Pattani could still deliver the same effect of shock, humiliation, and panic?

Jira was pointing with the tip of a wax pencil. "The provincial offices are here," he said. "District administration here. Police and military buildings. And these commercial blocks."

He then highlighted waterfront roads, adding, "If your bomber wants to get out quickly, he has multiple ways to move. The fastest would be via a prearranged boat in one of the local fishing villages. With that said, in three hours he could be at the Thai/Malay overland border, or he could cut across to the west coast and catch a ferry to Langkawi on the Malaysian archipelago."

"But he'd have to pass through Thai border control and customs before entering Malaysian territory," said Morrell. "Correct?"

Jira nodded. "That is correct. Not to mention any number of checkpoints along the way."

"What if he didn't leave Thailand and simply headed back north?" Harvath asked.

"If he didn't want to stand out, you're talking a big city like Phuket, which is eight hours by car, or all the way back to Bangkok, which takes fourteen. But again, there are the checkpoints to worry about."

Morrell studied the Pattani City map. "What about via train? Does Pattani have a train station?"

"Yes, but it is technically not in Pattani. It is in Khok Pho, about thirty kilometers away. And once he's on a train, assuming he can sneak past authorities at the station, he can't hide. Not completely. If the Thai military decide to stop and search it, he runs a great risk of being caught."

"Which is why airports are also probably off the table."

"I think we should assume that if the Chinese have found a way to smuggle him down here, they'll have a way to smuggle him out," said Harvath. "The key is to get to him before he can carry out his next attack."

Over the next several hours, they went through the map of Pattani block by block. And with each block, Harvath only grew to better understand why the Chinese had chosen it. There was simply no end of places in which they could cause damage.

Some felt important locally, but not nationally. Others made sense tactically, but not symbolically. And some seemed guaranteed to light up Bangkok the instant they were hit.

The problem with every single target was that they were looking at them hypothetically. Without some sort of an idea of what Koebler was planning, he would continue to be one step ahead and they would continue chasing their tails.

Harvath stepped away from the maps, walked over to the window, and looked out into the compound.

The old VW up on blocks tugged at something from his childhood—Southern California beach towns, faded paint, and aging, sunburned hippies. The memory gave way to the stranger truth that more than a few SEALs he knew had loved refurbishing and driving them around simply for the joke of it.

Nostalgia, however, wasn't going to help him find Koebler.

Pulling his attention back, he returned to the business at hand.

By late afternoon, the heat had turned the safe house into even more of an oven. One of Jira's men rolled a portable fan into the room and plugged it in near the maps, but it did little to bring the temperature down.

No one was doing much talking at this point. They had spent the better part of the day pulling Pattani apart on paper and putting it back together again, only to wind up where they had started—with too many possibilities and not enough certainty.

Then, the encrypted communications app on Harvath's phone rang. It was Tevy.

Harvath activated the call and put him on speaker. "What do you have?"

"My source heard enough to pass something, but it's not much," the Cambodian warned.

"Give it to me."

"He said bags are still the delivery mechanism."

Harvath felt the room sharpen around him. "Anything else?"

"Yes," Tevy replied. "He said responders will be dealt with in the parking lot."

Morrell was already moving toward the maps.

"What parking lot?" Harvath asked. "What's the target?"

"He doesn't know. All he could tell me was that the attack was imminent."

"How *imminent*?"

"Before nightfall," Tevy replied.

Harvath checked his watch. They didn't have much time. "Stay on your source. It's critical. We need anything he can give us."

When he disconnected the call and looked up, everyone in the room was watching him. Taking Jira's wax pencil, he joined Morrell at the detailed map of Pattani City. "Bags still in play," he said. "And a parking lot of some sort. Big enough for first responders to assemble in. What are we looking at?"

"Let's assume schools are out," said Morrell.

"Agreed."

"If they're using bags and want responders converging in a parking lot," said Haney, "it's got to be a transport hub of some sort."

Harvath nodded and circled three locations on the map. They weren't perfect, but they were all plausible, especially considering that the first-choice targets had been taken off the board.

"Ashby and Palmer," he said, "I want you at the Pattani railway station. Haney and Staelin, the airport. Morrell and I will take the bus station.

Keep your heads on swivels and report anything unusual. I don't care if someone sets a bag down and only walks two feet away—call it in. And remember, if cornered, these guys may decide to detonate rather than be taken alive, so keep your distance. Is that understood?"

Once everyone confirmed, they began gearing up. Outside, Jira and his men fired up the vehicles.

As soon as they had their gear, they hurried outside and climbed into the same vehicles they had ridden in from the airport.

Hopping into Jira's SUV, Harvath and Morrell double-checked their weapons and told him to hit it.

All they had to do now was get there first.

CHAPTER 68

When Jira pulled into the Pattani Provincial Transport Station, it was busier than Harvath had expected.

He hadn't been aware of how many people commuted into the city daily for work. Now they were all on their way home.

As coaches and minibuses idled under the outdoor canopy, travelers stood in line at the ticket windows, while others grabbed shade wherever they could find it. Vendors worked the crowd, selling snacks and bottled drinks. There were bags everywhere. If someone wanted a place where a bag wouldn't draw attention and responders could be pulled into a parking area after a mass casualty attack, this was definitely it.

Jira pulled into a spot where they could see both the station entrance and the main lot. Harvath counted two uniformed police officers. That was it.

While Jira remained with the SUV, Harvath and Morrell got out to take a closer look.

They moved like a pair of predators, searching for anything and anyone that didn't belong.

The lot was broken into sections for private vehicles, taxis, and the buses themselves. There were plenty of places for a bag to be left behind by accident and plenty more for one to be left on purpose.

So far, however, they hadn't seen anything that looked like obvious trouble.

Walking down the concrete median that divided the bus bays, they noticed how many bags had already been placed in open cargo holds and left unattended. If one of those bags had a bomb, the shape of the hold would only help send the force of the bomb outward and make it more devastating. In Harvath's mind, this was a nightmare waiting to happen.

As he got to the end of the median, his phone rang. Checking the caller ID, he saw it was Haney. "What's your situation?"

"Airport's crowded with uniforms. Cops, military, and airport security. They're everywhere. Even in the parking lot. If this is the play, they'd need balls the size of church bells."

"Stay on it," Harvath advised. "Call me back if you see anything." Then he disconnected the call.

"Haney?" Morrell correctly assumed. It was going to take Ashby and Palmer a while longer to get out to the train station in Khok Pho.

He nodded. "Sounds like the airport is locked down pretty tight. He doesn't think it's the target."

"Then the odds just went up for us and for Palmer and Ashby."

Two students in white shirts and black trousers sat on a concrete divider looking at a phone together. Near the curb, an unattended duffel sat beside a support column for three long seconds before a sweaty man in sandals hurried back to reclaim it.

Harvath clocked it all.

"Any reason this place would matter more than the others?" he asked.

Morrell continued to look it over. "Maybe not like dead schoolchildren, but it would send a message that southern Thailand can't be controlled. That'd definitely erode confidence in the government."

As they neared the front of the station, a distorted announcement crackled over the speakers of the PA system. Groups of people started making their way toward the buses.

That was when the first explosion detonated.

The sound landed like a giant fist punching through concrete. A second followed almost immediately, then a third, and a fourth—each one rolling over the rooftops in the same direction, close enough together that no one with any experience could mistake them as random.

For a split second, people in the bus station froze. Then heads turned and people began shouting all at once. A driver near the bus bays yelled something in Thai and started running toward the street.

Jira had already put the SUV in gear and was driving toward them.

As he raced up, he pointed east and said, "It came from the market!"

Just then, a fifth blast rolled in.

The shock wave rolled across Pattani and set off even more panic at the bus station.

As he and Morrell jumped into the SUV, Harvath took out his phone and called Ashby. "There were just five detonations," he said when she answered. "Sounds like the market. Break off and head back to Pattani fast."

Disconnecting, he immediately called Haney.

"We heard them too," the former Marine said before Harvath could speak. "Definitely not the airport."

"Get back into the city," Harvath ordered. "Coordinate with Ashby and Palmer. Head for the market district."

"What about you?"

Looking at Jira, Harvath asked, "Where's the nearest parking lot to the market?"

The man shook his head. "It's in the old part of the city. There is no parking lot."

Harvath's mind raced back through Tevy's fragment of intel. Bags were the delivery mechanism. Responders would be dealt with in the parking lot. But if there was no parking lot near the market . . .

Suddenly it all came into focus.

The follow-on attack wasn't meant to happen at the site of the primary attack. It was meant to be its own standalone attack at a completely different location.

"Pattani Hospital," Harvath shouted. "Move!"

CHAPTER 69

Cutting through side streets and racing down service roads, the drive to Pattani Hospital took less than ten minutes, but it felt like twenty.

Like Bangkok before it, the city had been turned completely upside down. Scooters drove against traffic. People stood on sidewalks with their phones out, filming the plume of black smoke rising above the market district. Sirens could be heard everywhere. Police and military came from all directions and in ever-increasing numbers.

Once again, Harvath replayed Tevy's intel—bags as the delivery mechanism, responders being dealt with in the parking lot. He'd understood it wrong. The bus terminal, the train station, the airport—none of that was germane. The intel had never been about where the first strike would happen. It was about where the city would send its wounded once the first strike had taken place.

"You think he's going to be somewhere in the lot?" Morrell asked, conducting a press check on his pistol to reassure himself, yet again, that a round was indeed chambered.

"No," Harvath replied. "That'd be too close and way too risky."

"But somewhere within line of sight. An overwatch position."

Harvath nodded. "That's what I'd do."

Jira glanced at him in the mirror. "The hospital is just ahead."

They shot through an intersection as an ambulance came screaming past them from the opposite direction, lights flashing and klaxon blaring.

Another ambulance followed. Then a police pickup. All racing to the market district.

"He'll wait until the lot is full," said Harvath, watching them zoom past. "He's going to aim for the biggest body count that he can get."

Jira turned onto the road in front of the hospital and the place was already coming apart. People were abandoning cars along the curb and on the shoulders, many of them having brought the wounded in themselves because it was faster than waiting for medics. Pickups, taxis, private cars, and even tuk-tuks were disgorging bloodied victims into the hands of hospital staff.

Uniformed police were trying to establish a perimeter, but it was piecemeal and incomplete. Civilians crowded the sidewalks, carrying the hurt wherever they could, yelling for medical attention.

A man on a motorcycle nearly clipped the SUV's front bumper as he tried to squeeze through with a badly injured woman.

Jira hit the brakes. "This is the closest I can get."

Harvath and Morrell leapt out before the man had thrown the SUV into park.

Neither of them looked at the chaos unfolding outside the hospital. As far as their job was concerned, that was a distraction. If Koebler had proven anything, it was that he was both disciplined and careful. He would be watching the lot and the flow of vehicles.

For the follow-on attack to carry real weight, Harvath knew it couldn't be more bombs hidden in bags. Not against a hospital parking lot filling with ambulances, police, private vehicles, and civilians unloading the wounded themselves.

It had to be something bigger. It had to be a car bomb.

The thought pulled Harvath back to the RBSC bombing. Koebler had already hidden behind a fake official vehicle once. If he had done it there, he could do it here.

As they neared the lot that fed the emergency room entrance, Harvath's eyes swept the area. What would Koebler use for camouflage? In the aftermath of such a horrific attack, what would people not even think twice about?

A pair of ambulances screamed through the gate, one right after the other, as doctors and orderlies rushed to meet them. Random cars were everywhere, some with doors still hanging open, others still with their back seats slick with blood.

That was what legitimate vehicles looked like. Motion. Panic. Unattended for a reason.

Then, Harvath saw it.

One row back sat another ambulance. No lights. No crew. No movement whatsoever. Harvath stopped.

"What is it?" Morrell asked.

"That," he replied, nodding toward the vehicle. "Every working ambulance in a scene like this should be coming, going, or unloading."

Harvath kept his eyes on the ambulance. There was zero activity around it. In the middle of everything that was happening, it sat there untouched. As if it were waiting.

Shifting his gaze, Harvath scanned the buildings across the road. Koebler would want the best view possible, but also enough distance to survive the blast.

To the south, beyond a pharmacy and a row of retail storefronts, stood an unfinished concrete shell wrapped in green construction mesh. The upper floor was open to the air. With the sun beginning to dip toward the horizon, there were plenty of shadows and plenty of spots where a man with a cell phone detonator and a pair of binoculars could hide himself.

Harvath turned his back to it. "See that building over my left shoulder?" he asked Morrell. "The one under construction? If I were him, that's where I'd be."

The CIA man noticed at once. "Good sight line."

"And a clean view of the lot."

As if on cue, another ambulance, with its lights strobing and its klaxon screaming, hurtled through the gate and was waved toward the entrance, where two orderlies sprinted to meet it. Right behind it were more civilian vehicles.

The lot was filling fast. Too fast.

Harvath turned to look back at the unfinished building. There was no movement, no obvious shape in the shadows he could pick out at this distance.

Then the lowering sun caught something along the top floor and flashed. Just once. *Glass.*

But not a window. Not at that angle. *Optics.*

Harvath felt the hair on the back of his neck stand up. Looking back at Morrell, he asked, "Did you see that?"

The CIA man nodded, adjusted the pistol beneath his shirt, and prepared to cross the street. "That's going to be the last mistake that asshole ever makes."

CHAPTER 70

The binoculars Koebler had been provided with were garbage. The barrels were out of alignment, giving him a double image and an instant headache from the eye strain. With all the trouble the Chinese had gone to on this operation, the fact that no one had even checked the optics before handing them over told him everything he needed to know.

Use him. Pay him if they had to. Trust him with absolutely nothing they didn't have to. The optics were only his latest reminder.

The client had given him a burner phone for comms, but no gun—despite his having asked for one, as operations could go sideways in ways no one predicted. The client had listened, but then calmly told him that there was no need. His people would be close by. Watching. If anything went wrong, they would take care of it. That still bothered him.

It had been offered as reassurance, but Koebler had heard it for what it really was—a reminder that he wasn't a member of their team. He was the hired help. Paid to do a job. Nothing more.

Shifting his weight, he changed his angle and pulled back a little from the opening. The green construction mesh hung limp along this side of the building, snapping now and then when a breeze came through. Around him it smelled like hot concrete dust and old rainwater. Massaging his eyes once more, he brought the binoculars back up.

The lot outside Pattani Hospital's emergency entrance was changing by the minute. Ambulances were racing in, civilians with bloodied family members were rushing the doors, and waves of police and soldiers continued to show up in hopes of maintaining order.

Death. Destruction. And chaos. The market team had placed the bags where they had been told and done their job. That alone was almost surprising.

The client had managed to scrape together a working Plan B from the wreckage of his original Pattani operation. Under better circumstances, Koebler would have had more time, better people, and the ability to rebuild the operation from the ground up. Instead, he'd gotten whatever had survived the arrests—both the materials and a handful of separatists with just enough intelligence to follow instructions.

Coupled with Chinese handlers who wanted speed more than elegance, it made for an ugly situation. But ugly could still kill. And ugly made for compelling images.

He still had no idea what their endgame was. All he knew was that the client wanted the bombings in Bangkok to ultimately look like Cambodia was behind them and for the bombings in Pattani to be blamed on separatists. It was some sort of a destabilization campaign. What China got out of it, however, was anyone's guess. He didn't care.

Sweeping the lot, he found the ambulance again. It sat one row from the entrance to the ER, exactly where the local cutout had been told to park it—an object so contextually correct that it disappeared into the broader panic.

So far, no one had given it a second look.

Another ambulance came in fast, followed by a pickup that jumped the curb and came to a stop just shy of the doors. A woman jumped out, clutching a blood-soaked towel to a boy's face, screaming for help.

Koebler continued to surveil the lot. Knowing when to detonate was just as much art as it was science. Every vehicle that arrived meant more metal, more bodies, more confusion. He was almost ready.

Then he felt a vibration in his pocket. Pulling out the burner, he looked at the screen.

Armed men coming up.

Koebler swung his head toward the dark stairwell as the first man came out of it already firing.

But by then, Koebler was already moving, diving through the mesh onto the bamboo scaffolding.

CHAPTER 71

They had come up the last flight, slow and silent, hugging the unfinished wall until the stairwell opened onto the top floor. Then, Harvath had come out firing.

Koebler launched himself right through the green mesh at the edge of the unfinished floor and the bamboo outside cracked as his weight hit the scaffolding.

The binoculars lay where he had abandoned them, along with a phone. But as Koebler hit the construction netting, Harvath caught a glimpse of a second phone in his hand and fired again.

The round hit a crosspiece near Koebler's face and the phone slipped from his grasp, vanishing over the side.

As it did, he snatched at the empty air and almost went with it. Whatever had just fallen mattered. A lot.

Gunfire suddenly erupted from the other end of the unfinished floor, showering him with concrete chips. Harvath spun to engage the threat and instantly recognized one of the Chinese operatives from the boatyard. Pressing his trigger, he sent multiple rounds flying in the man's direction.

Then all of a sudden there was another muzzle flash near a stack of cinder blocks halfway across the floor. An additional Chinese gunman was in the fight and trying to help cover Koebler's escape.

Without breaking stride, Morrell scooped up the abandoned phone and fired back.

"Take the stairs!" Harvath shouted. "Cut him off below."

Without waiting for a response, he blasted through the torn mesh and hit the bamboo at full speed as he chased after Koebler.

The scaffolding shuddered beneath him, but Harvath ignored it and kept going. Koebler was already thirty feet ahead and moving fast through a maze of poles, hanging mesh, and uneven planks.

Harvath pushed after him, searching for any chance to get off a clean shot. Then, as he was about to make a ninety-degree turn around the edge of the building, Koebler glanced back. That gave Harvath the window he needed and he didn't hesitate.

Pressing his trigger, he fired.

Koebler grunted and slammed sideways into the mesh, twisting as the scaffolding lurched under both of them. But before Harvath could follow up with a second shot, the man disappeared over the side.

Harvath raced to the spot and looked out through the mesh, trying to figure out what happened. From inside the building, he could hear Morrell exchanging gunfire with the Chinese.

There was blood on the netting, but no body on the sidewalk.

Then, leaning farther over, he figured it out. Koebler had flipped over the edge and dropped down to the next level of scaffolding. The trail of blood was the only evidence Harvath needed. Swinging one leg over the side, he found purchase on a lower crosspiece and dropped down after him.

From up above, Morrell yelled an update, "One dead. One down. Go!"

At the first window opening, Koebler had ducked back inside the building. Following the blood, Harvath went right after him.

The space was littered with buckets, tile, wire, and stacks of cement board panels. Catching sight of Koebler, Harvath brought his pistol up and fired, just as the man ducked into the far stairwell and vanished again.

Dodging the debris, Harvath charged down the stairs after him.

By the time he hit the ground floor, the hospital perimeter was a cacophony of sirens, horns, and people screaming for doctors.

Koebler burst through a wide opening where glass storefront windows would eventually go and spilled out into the chaos beyond.

The gunfire from the unfinished building had already rippled through the crowd. People were ducking behind vehicles, pointing, and shouting.

A Thai soldier had turned toward the structure with his rifle up, trying to see where the shots had come from, while two policemen started pushing that way through the crush outside the ER.

Shoving through a knot of people near a double-parked pickup, Koebler headed for the hospital.

Harvath checked himself before bursting out after him. He couldn't go charging into the open waving a pistol around—not with half the Thai security presence outside the ER trying to figure out where the shots had come from.

Returning his pistol to the holster inside his waistband, he covered it with his shirt and ran after Koebler before the crowd could swallow him up.

Harvath had hit him somewhere near where his left shoulder met the base of his neck. Not good enough to drop him, but good enough that Koebler was losing a lot of blood. What it hadn't done, however, was slow him down.

Up ahead, a woman screamed as Koebler slammed into her and kept going. Suddenly, Harvath felt his blood go cold. Koebler wasn't headed away from the hospital, he was headed right for it.

Now everything clicked. The phone Koebler had lost over the side of the scaffolding had likely been his remote detonator. But if there was a manual trigger, or some sort of timer on the bomb he could activate, the phone didn't matter anymore. He just needed to get back to the ambulance. And if he did, scores of people were going to die.

Harvath pushed harder through the crowd, shoving terrified civilians out of the way as best he could without knocking them down or injuring them. It made the crowd angry. People started shouting at him and some even began pushing back. As they did, it clogged his path even more and Koebler got farther ahead.

Then, to his right, Harvath saw Morrell. The CIA man came out from between a military truck and a police cruiser, moving in fast at an angle to help cut Koebler off.

Koebler saw him too. And for the first time since the scaffolding, he hesitated. But only for an instant.

Two feet away, a woman was trying to help an elderly victim out of her car. Koebler grabbed a fistful of her hair and yanked her backward against him.

From underneath his blood-soaked shirt, he produced some sort of all-black knife and held it to the woman's throat.

She screamed and the sound cut through everything. Harvath stopped short and so did half the people around them.

Koebler's face had gone chalky from blood loss. He dragged the woman with him as he backed into the ER lot, the blade pressed so hard against her skin that a bright red line appeared beneath it.

"Don't," he warned.

Harvath kept coming anyway. Not fast. Not slow. Just one step at a time. "Let her go, Kevin."

Koebler gave a grim smile. "Not yet."

Closer, Harvath could now see the ambulance.

Koebler kept backing up. "Another step," he rasped, "and she dies."

Harvath stopped. Even if he could draw his pistol quick enough to fire, he didn't have the shot.

The woman was sobbing, her eyes pleading for someone to help her. Harvath looked for Morrell, but all of a sudden, he was gone.

The crowd was peeling away in every direction. People were dragging each other backward, ducking behind cars, getting as far away from this fresh horror as they could.

Harvath returned his eyes to Koebler, who still had his knife pressed against the woman's throat.

Raising his gaze to the ambulance, Harvath edged a step to his left.

"Stop," Koebler warned, pivoting with the hostage to keep her between them.

Harvath did as the man commanded. He stopped and held completely still, meeting Koebler's gaze.

That was the moment Morrell came back into view, just off Koebler's flank.

With his pistol already drawn, he took aim and pressed his trigger once. The round tore through the side of the bomber's head, dropping him straight to the pavement. His knife skipped across the asphalt as the woman ripped free, screaming.

Looking down at Kevin Koebler's dead body, Morrell said, "That was for KitKat and Mo, asshole."

For half a second, the lot seemed to seize. Then it exploded in panic. Civilians scattered.

Morrell dropped to his knees and tossed his weapon on the ground in front of him. Raising his hands in the air as Thai police and soldiers rushed in, he looked straight ahead at Koebler's delivery vehicle and yelled, "Bomb! There's a bomb in the ambulance!"

And in the chaos Morrell had just unleashed, Harvath found his opening to escape.

CHAPTER 72

WEDNESDAY

The black sedan moved through the last gray minutes before dawn, its tires thrumming over damp pavement as the road unwound between rubber plantations and low pockets of morning mist. To the east, the sky over the Gulf had begun to pale and the warming horizon was turning the color of old brass.

Inside the car, nobody spoke. The diplomatic plates had been attached before first light. The bright red-and-gold diplomatic passports in the glove box were clean and official. Their weapons were gone, broken down and discarded kilometers behind them. By the time the sun cleared the hills, they would be in Malaysia.

On the other side of the border, a senior official from the Chinese embassy in Kuala Lumpur would be in place, waiting to smooth their passage and move them quickly beyond the reach of Thai authorities.

Hang Shuo had disposed of his sling so as not to stand out. Sitting in the back seat, he used the armrest to support his injured shoulder and watched the last bits of Thailand slide past.

The road curved along a rise, offering a brief glimpse of the ocean below. For a few seconds, the early light made everything look cleaner than it was—as if the country itself refused to acknowledge what Hang had set in motion.

Then a shadow raced across the road and over the hood of the sedan. It was accompanied by the thunder of rotors as the first helicopter came in low over the trees.

The driver jerked his eyes upward just as the AH-1 Cobra of the Royal Thai Army swept across their path.

Fifty meters ahead, it flared, dropped onto the pavement sideways, and aimed its 20-millimeter, nose-mounted cannon right at them.

The sedan braked hard. But before it came to a full and complete stop, it was overtaken by another shadow from above.

An eleven-ton Airbus H225 from the Royal Thai Air Force descended behind them with brutal precision. Its downwash tore leaves from the roadside trees and blasted dust, grit, and sand in all directions. The large helicopter settled onto the road, boxing the car in between two walls of metal. Hang and his remaining three operatives had nowhere to go.

As the Cobra sat in front of them, its rotors still spinning and the early morning sun glinting off the glass of its canopy, behind them, the H225's side door slid open.

A four-man team jumped out. They moved hard and fast, their weapons up and at the ready. But they weren't Thai soldiers. They were Cambodians. And Tevy was in the lead.

Surrounding the sedan, they kept their rifles trained on the occupants—only one of whom really mattered. That was the deal Tevy had made.

Dragging Hang out of the car, he bent him over the trunk, patted him down for weapons and then, slinging his rifle, painfully flex-cuffed him.

As he marched him back to the H225, his men didn't linger. The remaining three Cambodians opened up on the remaining three Chinese. They fired in quick, controlled bursts and didn't stop until they were certain the men were dead.

They stripped the MSS operatives of their phones, located and secured the diplomatic passports, and then, sweeping the immediate area one final time with their eyes, helped Tevy load Hang onto the Thai transport helicopter.

The Cobra lifted first and banked out over the water. The H225 came up after it and followed the same path.

By the time the first civilian vehicle reached the bend in the road, both helicopters were gone.

CHAPTER 73

WASHINGTON, D.C.
FRIDAY

By the time Erin Delaney stepped out of the White House, the day had settled into one of those crisp fall afternoons that she loved Washington for. The sky hung low over Lafayette Square, the leaves of its trees a symphony of oranges, reds, and bright golds.

Shawna Vaughn had come out with her and momentarily turned her face to the sun. "That was some briefing," the Secret Service agent said.

Erin let out a breath that might have been a laugh if there had been anything funny about it. "You're telling me."

Vaughn looked back toward the White House. "Can't say I ever expected to get read in on something like that."

"Pretty intense."

They walked a few more steps in silence before Vaughn slowed. Across the square, near the iron fence, Connor Jameson stood waiting with his collar turned up against the chill.

Vaughn looked at Erin. "You want me to stay?"

Erin shook her head. "I'm okay."

"You sure?"

"Yes."

Vaughn studied her for a moment, then nodded. "Fields really cracked it."

"She did," Erin replied. "And you kept Connor and me alive long enough for her to do it. Thank you, Shawna."

"You're welcome. Thank you for trusting me," said the Secret Service agent, who gave her a quick squeeze on the arm before heading back across Pennsylvania Avenue.

As she did, she gave Connor a friendly wave and he waved back. They had all been through a lot together.

Connor walked up to Erin and they hugged. It didn't feel weird or uncomfortable, as it might have just a week ago. It felt good. And good was a nice place to be.

"How'd it go?" he asked.

Erin glanced toward the White House, then back at him. "Let's take a walk."

They headed north, toward H Street, and Connor waited for her to speak. He had always been bad with hiding his impatience, but today he managed it.

"The FBI has effectively taken everything over from Metro Police," she said. "As far as anyone is concerned, you acted in self-defense. Given what Fields uncovered, nobody sees you as the problem."

He absorbed what she had said and the tension visibly lifted from his shoulders. "No gun charge either?"

"No gun charge."

They walked another several yards before Erin continued. "Fields was right to keep pulling at Olson. Turns out he was working for the Chinese."

Connor's expression changed, but only slightly. Not in surprise. More like disgust. "What about Wei?"

"They're all but certain he's tied to Chinese intelligence. He's back in Beijing and out of reach for now."

"And that stooge from my old think tank?" he asked.

"In custody. Quietly cooperating."

Connor shook his head. "That figures."

They got to the edge of the park, waited for the light to change, and then headed up 16th Street.

"You were right about China," she said, as they passed the Hay-Adams. "Not about every detail, but about the shape of it. Taiwan was being used as a distraction."

"From what?"

"Thailand."

He stopped walking and stared at her.

"All the recent bombings over there," Erin stated, "were meant to create enough panic and instability to help foment a military coup."

His brow furrowed. "Why?"

"Because the civilian government in Bangkok had already said no to Beijing's offer to construct a canal across Thailand's southern Kra Isthmus."

"Jesus," Connor said, more to himself than to her, as they started walking again. "This is all about the Strait of Malacca."

Erin nodded.

"A huge portion of China's imported oil and shipping has to pass through it. That's the choke point. Beijing hates depending on a narrow passage it can't control, especially one the U.S. Navy can shut down at will."

"Yes," Erin replied. "And their fears only increased after the Iran war started and they saw the impact of the Strait of Hormuz."

"And a canal across Thailand would change all that. It would give them a massive strategic advantage. The Chinese would be able to transit from the Pacific all the way to the Indian Ocean."

Erin nodded again. "Beijing didn't need to stage the coup. It just needed to help create the conditions where a coup started to look like the inevitable Thai solution."

"And a junta," Connor said, "would be easier to work with. It's centralized. No parliament. No public debate."

"Exactly. China would be first in line to recognize the junta—giving it instant international legitimacy. There'd also be economic and intelligence assistance, allowing Thailand's generals to stabilize the country and shield it from sanctions."

As evil as it was, Connor marveled at the plan. "So the bombings break the country politically and the military takes over. Beijing recognizes the new government, offers help, and then resurfaces the canal project. Talk about audacious."

"You saw the Chinese better than the rest of us," she admitted.

He looked away and gave a small nod, as though accepting something he had needed for a long time.

They passed a couple walking their dog and then moved to a stretch of sidewalk with no one close enough to overhear.

"How much of this is going to become public?" he asked.

"Almost none of it."

He gave a quiet laugh. "Of course."

They walked on in silence for several moments. Finally, Connor asked, "What happens now?"

Erin knew that meant more than one thing. "For the country?" she said.

"The country, for now, will be fine. I meant for us."

That was the one question she had known was coming. Folding her arms against the cold, she took her time.

So much had been broken between them before any of this had started. Some of it because of Connor's PTSD. Some of it because he had pushed too hard, too often, and too unfairly. Some of it because she had stopped believing there was any version of him that could find its way back to himself. Now here they were.

"I don't know," she admitted. "I don't think we can decide all of that today."

He accepted that with a small nod.

"But," she continued, "I also don't think today ends with us where we were."

Connor slid his hands deeper into his coat pockets. "So what are you saying?"

"I guess I'm saying the door's not shut. That's all I know for certain right now."

"I can live with that," he replied, a smile forming on his face.

They kept walking, side by side, with neither of them who they had been, and neither in a hurry to turn back.

CHAPTER 74

BANGKOK

Harvath reached the restaurant just as the sun was beginning to set. Morrell had picked a great spot.

Dollar beers and fifty-cent oysters, the view west over the river, and the classic country music playing from speakers on the outside deck were terrific. Even better was the company. Morrell and Davi were already there.

They had taken a table near the railing. Two bottles of beer were sweating on the wood between them, along with a dented bucket full of oysters on ice. Davi, in heels and a sleeveless dress, looked much different than her ISOC persona. Morrell, in jeans and a linen shirt, was still Morrell.

"You're late," Davi said, waving Harvath over.

"I had to make sure my team got off okay."

"To Phuket, right?" Morrell asked.

Harvath pulled out an empty chair. "I promised them some R&R in Manila, but then dragged them straight to Bangkok. I'm a man of my word. This was overdue."

Davi gave a slight nod. "At least one man at this table keeps his promises."

Morrell shook his head. "We just got here and you're already taking swings?"

"I'm just warming up," she replied, smiling.

Harvath sat down and a waiter appeared, dropping a cold beer in front of him before disappearing again without a word.

They all needed this. No bombs. No bullets. No bullshit.

A George Jones song started playing. Harvath reached for his beer and the trio toasted. Sitting back in his chair, he took a long swallow.

For a few moments, nobody spoke. The river moved below them, green and slow. Across the water, the opposite bank took on a soft blur.

Eventually, Harvath had to ask, "How bad is it?"

"Bad," Davi replied, taking a sip of her beer and setting it back on the table. "The official line is that Thai authorities uncovered a coordinated campaign of bombings in Bangkok and the south, directed by foreign extremists and carried out with help from local militant facilitators. The operation's chief architect was killed in Pattani City before he could unleash a second wave of attacks on first responders. The broader network is being dismantled. Additional arrests are expected. Investigations are ongoing."

Harvath reached for one of the oysters. "What's being said privately?"

"Privately, people are scared shitless that the plot made it this far. Imagine if we'd decided to go to war with Cambodia? That said, no one is in a hurry to accuse Beijing. They want it airtight, watertight, and spin-tight before they go public. They want the evidence so obvious and so damning that the Chinese can't lie their way out of it claiming Hang was some sort of a rogue operator."

"Speaking of which, is he continuing to cooperate?"

Davi paused. "He understands that he's standing in front of several doors. Only one has anything halfway decent on the other side. Whether he walks through that door depends on how useful he remains."

"What about Tevy?"

"He, along with his team—including his wounded man in the hospital—have all been quietly repatriated to Cambodia. Just as we agreed."

"He's a good man," said Harvath.

"Who was running black ops in Thailand," Davi clarified.

Harvath took that in. "I guess if Mexican intelligence was inserting itself into my affairs, I wouldn't like it either."

Raising his beer to take a sip, Morrell said, "We'd all be up in arms."

Harvath nodded and kept pressing Davi for more information. "In

Pattani, Hang had two men nearby, protecting Koebler. One was KIA. What happened to the other?"

"He died before local police could get anything useful out of him."

Harvath looked at Morrell. "What about our Chinese Embassy friend from the periodontist's building?"

"The security agent?" Morrell asked, grabbing the last oyster from the bucket and signaling the waiter to bring more. "Beyond what he gave us about the embassy physician, he was pretty useless. My guys wrung out of him what they could. After that, they took a photo of him in front of Bangkok's golden Buddha with him holding up a sign that said 'I talk too much,' and then put him on a flight to Beijing. An hour before the flight landed, they sent the photo to every known email address in the Chinese diplomatic corps."

"That's not going to do much for his career advancement."

"I take my pleasures in this job where I can find them," Morrell replied.

"By the way," said Harvath, "I never got around to asking—how was the Pattani prison system?"

"Blessedly brief."

"Thanks to me," Davi said.

"Whatever you had to trade for him, it wasn't worth it."

Taking the first oyster from the new bucket that had just arrived, Davi replied, "Thai authorities got to claim credit for foiling the attack and Richard was released into my custody."

"For the record," Morrell replied, "I thought the handcuffs were completely unnecessary and entirely too tight."

"You used to like that," she said, looking up from under her lashes.

"I still do," he smiled.

"I'm out," Harvath declared, laying a thousand-baht note on the table and standing up. "It's wonderful to see you both reconnecting, but I miss my wife and have no desire to be anywhere near the blast radius if this turns ugly."

Davi laughed. "Sit down."

"Yeah, moneybags," Morrell added. "You're paying."

"Me?" Harvath asked, before turning to Davi. "Doesn't he still owe you a body? Isn't that worth something?"

"Actually," she replied, "I did release that corpse to *both* of you."

Morrell rolled his eyes. "You can't believe a single thing this guy says."

"Nevertheless, we're here and I'm in the mood for the tomahawk. You two can figure out who's paying."

Harvath laughed. Morrell laughed.

For the moment, they could relax.

Then both of their phones went off at the same time.

ACKNOWLEDGMENTS

Twenty-five Scot Harvath novels. That's an amazing thing to be able to say. When I began this journey with *The Lions of Lucerne*, I had no way of knowing that Harvath's story would continue across twenty-five books, or that I would feel as much excitement, pride, and gratitude as I do today. Reaching this milestone with *Choke Point* is deeply meaningful to me, and I am enormously proud of all that this series has become.

Now comes the part where I get to thank the many people whose talent, hard work, generosity, and unwavering support helped bring this novel to life (and there are a lot of them, so buckle up!).

Above all, I want to thank you, my wonderful **readers**. Your loyalty and enthusiasm have propelled these novels from the very beginning. You have embraced Scot Harvath and ridden shotgun with him on every mission. You have allowed me the extraordinary privilege of continuing to tell these stories. There would be no twenty-fifth novel without your support, and I am profoundly grateful for it.

While writing may seem a solitary endeavor, getting the book out of an author's head and into your hands (or ears) is anything but. I have been fortunate, once again, to be backed by a first-rate group of people.

To all the outstanding **booksellers**, thank you. You are one of the most important and indispensable forces in the literary world. Your passion and tireless support do far more than put books on shelves—you connect readers with stories and keep us writers alive.

I'm fortunate to have two incredibly helpful friends like **Sean Fontaine** and **Paul Craig**. It also doesn't hurt that they have seen and done some amazing things in service to the United States. Thank you, once again, for your service and all the insight you provided me.

Though the exceptional **Jon Karp** has stepped back from his role as president and CEO of Simon & Schuster, I—as well as everyone else at the company—continue to owe him an enormous debt. Jon took the reins at a pivotal moment in the organization's history, and we are so fortunate that he did. Thank you, Jon, for all you have done for me. I wish you the best as you return to the part of the business you love so deeply.

My writing career was launched because of one thing my phenomenal publisher and editor, **Emily Bestler**, said: "Yes." Together, we have published twenty-seven books (including *The Athena Project* and *Cold Zero*). Emily, your instincts, judgment, and fantastic sense of humor make every book better. I am deeply grateful for our many years together and for all the care you bring to my work.

The visionary **team at Emily Bestler Books**, particularly **Lara Jones**, **Hydia Scott-Riley**, and **Wren Watkins**, have done an outstanding job guiding this novel through every stage. Your professionalism and precision are invaluable, and I appreciate you more than I can say.

My superb publisher, **Libby McGuire**, and fabulous associate publisher, **Dana Trocker**, continue to set the bar. Your energy, focus, and commitment to getting these books to readers far and wide are nothing short of remarkable. Thank you for everything you do and for continuing to be such a major part of my career.

To the best director of publicity and marketing in the universe, **David Brown**—you work tirelessly and always figure out how to position my books for maximum impact. You're not only amazing, but you're also a dear friend. I'd never want to go into battle without you. Thank you for everything.

It is my honor to be a member of the Simon & Schuster family. They are the best people to work with, particularly **Kim Shannon**, senior VP of sales, and her unparalleled sales team. There are no "sales" without the sales team. Your efforts behind the scenes are vital, and I deeply appreciate everything you do to support my books.

Simply put, **Jen Long** and her **team at Pocket Books** are nothing short of awesome. Thank you for continuing to give my books such a strong life in paperback. It's always gratifying to see these books reach new readers, and that happens because of the work you do. I'm very grateful.

A big thank you to the incomparable **Jason Chappell**, **Paige Lytle**, **Rick Willett**, and the **Atria/Emily Bestler Books production departments**. Your commitment to excellence shows on every page. Thank you for your craftsmanship and attention to detail.

I also want to extend my thanks to the astounding **Suzanne Donahue** and **Karlyn Hixson**. Your hard work and support make it easy for me to stay focused where I need to be focused, and I appreciate each and everything you do.

To the out of this world **Atria/Emily Bestler Books** and **Pocket Books sales teams**, thank you. You put in the work every day, territory by territory and account by account. Your persistence and drive show. I appreciate you all.

The genius **Atria/Emily Bestler Books** and **Pocket Books art departments**, led by the brilliant **Jimmy Iacobelli**, have once again done an amazing job. Books are judged by their covers and each year you deliver. Thank you for your creativity and your skill.

Thank you to the sensational **Simon & Schuster audio team**—**Chris Lynch**, **Tom Spain**, **Sarah Lieberman**, **Desiree Vecchio**, and my longtime narrator, **Armand Schultz**. I am incredibly proud of the audio editions of my books—and that's because of the level of talent and care you bring to them. Thank you for another superb production.

My career as an author would not be what it is without my spectacular agent, **Heide Lange** of Sanford J. Greenburger Associates. Heide, you continue to be one of the great blessings of my personal and professional life. Your wisdom, loyalty, and more than two decades of support continue to mean everything to me. Thank you for always being in my corner.

In addition to my entire wonderful **SJGA family**, I also want to thank the all-star trio of **Iwalani Kim**, **Madeline Wallace**, and **Charles Loffredo**. Your professionalism and commitment to getting it right make all this possible. You are the best.

Words fail to express my gratitude for the masterful **Yvonne Ralsky**, who once again helped make my life more manageable and my work more possible. YBR—you will never know how much I appreciate all that you do for me. From small things to big things, they all make such a huge difference. Thank you.

To my dear friend and the world's best entertainment attorney, **Scottie Schwimer**, what a year it has been! Thank you for all your sage counsel, all the laughs, and for your incredible negotiating skill. You are the one shark I truly enjoy swimming with.

Twenty-five Scot Harvath novels wouldn't have been possible without **my beautiful family**, especially my incredibly gifted wife (and first editor), **Trish**. You have lived every deadline, every book tour, and every adventure with me. Day after day, what you have given me has made this life and this work possible in more ways than I can count. Thank you for every second of it.